Cranford

Cranford

ELIZABETH GASKELL

Edited with an Introduction and Notes by
PATRICIA INGHAM

PENGUIN CLASSICS
an imprint of
PENGUIN BOOKS

PENGUIN CLASSICS

Published by the Penguin Group
Penguin Books Ltd, 80 Strand, London WC2R ORL, England
Penguin Group (USA) Inc., 375 Hudson Street, New York, New York 10014, USA
Penguin Group (Canada), 90 Eglinton Avenue East, Suite 700, Toronto, Ontario, Canada M4P 2Y3
(a division of Pearson Penguin Canada Inc.)
Penguin Ireland, 25 St Stephen's Green, Dublin 2, Ireland (a division of Penguin Books Ltd)
Penguin Group (Australia), 250 Camberwell Road, Camberwell,
Victoria 3124, Australia (a division of Pearson Australia Group Pty Ltd)
Penguin Books India Pvt Ltd, 11 Community Centre,
Panchsheel Park, New Delhi – 110 017, India
Penguin Group (NZ), 67 Apollo Drive, Rosedale, North Shore 0632, New Zealand
(a division of Pearson New Zealand Ltd)
Penguin Books (South Africa) (Pty) Ltd, 24 Sturdee Avenue, Rosebank, Johannesburg 2196, South Africa

Penguin Books Ltd, Registered Offices: 80 Strand, London WC2R ORL, England

www.penguin.com

First published 1853
Published in Penguin Classics 2005
This edition published 2008
4

Editorial material copyright © Patricia Ingham, 2005

The moral right of the editor has been asserted

Cover design and illustration Coralie Bickford-Smith

Typeset by Rowland Phototypesetting Ltd, Bury St Edmunds, Suffolk
Printed in Great Britain by Clays Ltd, St Ives plc

A CIP catalogue record for this book is available from the British Library

978-0-141-44254-9

www.greenpenguin.co.uk

Penguin Books is committed to a sustainable future
for our business, our readers and our planet.
The book in your hands is made from paper
certified by the Forest Stewardship Council.

Contents

Acknowledgements

I should like to thank Jenny Harrington and Emma Plaskitt for their help in preparing this edition and Laura Barber for her helpful advice. I am also grateful to the staff of St Anne's College Library and to the News International Research Fund.

My work on this edition is dedicated to Andrew, Trish, Hannah and Rosie.

Chronology

1810 *29 September*: Elizabeth Cleghorn Stevenson born to William and Elizabeth Stevenson in Chelsea

1811 *October*: Mother, Elizabeth Stevenson, dies; Elizabeth moves to Knutsford, Cheshire, to live with her mother's sister Hannah Lumb

1814 William Stevenson marries Catherine Thomson

1821–6 Elizabeth attends Byerley sisters' boarding school (school near Warwick, but moves to Avonbank, Stratford-upon-Avon in 1824)

1822 Brother, John Stevenson (b. 1799), joins Merchant Navy

1828 John Stevenson disappears on a voyage to India; no definitive information about his fate

1829 *March*: William Stevenson dies
Elizabeth stays with uncle in Park Lane, London and visits relations, the Turners, at Newcastle upon Tyne

1831 Visits Edinburgh with Ann Turner; has bust sculpted by David Dunbar, and her miniature painted by step-mother's brother, William John Thomson; visits Ann Turner's sister and brother-in-law, Unitarian minister John Robberds, in Manchester, where she meets Revd William Gaskell (1805–84)

1832 *30 August*: Elizabeth and William marry at St John's Parish Church, Knutsford; they honeymoon in North Wales, and move to 14 Dover Street, Manchester

1833 *10 July*: Gives birth to stillborn daughter

1834 *12 September*: Gives birth to Marianne

1835 Starts *My Diary* for Marianne

1837 *January*: 'Sketches Among the Poor', No. 1, written with William, in *Blackwood's Magazine*

7 February: Gives birth to Margaret Emily (Meta)

1 May: Hannah Lumb dies

1840 'Clopton Hall' in William Howitt's *Visits to Remarkable Places*

1841 *July*: Gaskells visit Heidelberg

1842 *7 October*: Gives birth to Florence Elizabeth

Family moves to 121 Upper Rumford Road, Manchester

1844 *23 October*: Gives birth to William

1845 *10 August*: William (son) dies of scarlet fever at Porthmadog, Wales, during family holiday

1846 *3 September*: Gives birth to Julia Bradford

1848 *October*: *Mary Barton* published anonymously; Elizabeth is paid £100 for the copyright by Chapman and Hall

1849 *April–May*: Visits London, meets Charles Dickens and Thomas Carlyle

June–August: Visits the Lake District, meets William Wordsworth

1850 *June*: Family moves to 42 (later 84) Plymouth Grove, Manchester

19 August: Meets Charlotte Brontë in Windermere

1851 *June*: 'Disappearances' in *Household Words*; visited by Charlotte Brontë

July: Visits London and the Great Exhibition

October: Visits Knutsford

December–May 1853: *Cranford* in nine instalments in *Household Words*

1852 *December*: 'The Old Nurse's Story' in the Extra Christmas Number of *Household Words*

1853 *January*: *Ruth* published

April: Charlotte Brontë visits Manchester

May: Visits Paris

June: *Cranford* published

September: Visits Charlotte Brontë at Haworth

December: 'The Squire's Story' in the Extra Christmas Number of *Household Words*

1854 *January*: Visits Paris with Marianne, meets Madame Mohl
September–January 1855: *North and South* in *Household Words*

1855 *February–March*: Visits Madame Mohl in Paris with Meta
June: Asked to write a biography of Charlotte Brontë by Patrick Brontë; *North and South* published
September: *Lizzie Leigh and Other Tales* published

1856 *1 January*: Signs petition to amend the law on married women's property
May: Visits Brussels to conduct research on biography of Brontë
December: 'The Poor Clare' in *Household Words*

1857 *February–May*: Visits Rome, where she meets Charles Norton
March: *The Life of Charlotte Brontë* published, the first book to carry Elizabeth Gaskell's name on the title-page; it was soon followed by a heavily altered third edition.

1858 *January*: 'The Doom of the Griffiths' in *Harper's New Monthly Magazine*
September–December: Visits Heidelberg with Meta and Florence, and visits the Mohls in Paris

1859 *March*: *Round the Sofa and Other Tales* published
Summer: Visits Scotland
October: 'Lois the Witch' in *All the Year Round*
November: Visits Whitby, which provides the setting for *Sylvia's Lovers*
December: 'The Crooked Branch' published in the Extra Christmas Number of *All the Year Round*, as 'The Ghost in the Garden Room'

1860 *February*: 'Curious, if True' in *Cornhill Magazine*
May: *Right at Last and Other Tales* published
July–August: Visits Heidelberg

1861 *January*: 'The Grey Woman' in *All the Year Round*

1862 Visits Paris, Brittany and Normandy to conduct research for articles on French life

1863 *February*: *Sylvia's Lovers* published; Elizabeth is paid
£1,000 by Smith, Elder
March–August: Visits France and Italy
1864 *Cousin Phillis* published
August: Visits Switzerland
August–January 1866: *Wives and Daughters* in *Cornhill
Magazine*
1865 *March–April*: Visits Paris
June: Buys The Lawns, Holybourne, near Alton, Hampshire,
as a surprise for William
October: Visits Dieppe; *The Grey Woman and Other Tales*
published
12 November: Dies at Holybourne
16 November: Buried at Brook Street Chapel, Knutsford
Cousin Phillis, and Other Tales published
1866 *February*: *Wives and Daughters*: *An Every-day Story*
published (Elizabeth died without quite completing it)

Introduction

*(New readers are advised that the Introduction makes
details of the plot explicit.)*

Cranford is based on the Cheshire town of Knutsford, the home
of Elizabeth Gaskell's childhood, to which she was taken in
1811 at the age of thirteen months to be brought up after the
death of her mother by her maternal aunt, Hannah Lumb. Her
father remarried and settled in London where he died in 1829.
In 1832 she married the Unitarian minister, William Gaskell,
and settled down in Manchester or Cottonopolis. Much of the
raw material for her novel, which was published in 1853, can
be found in an account of her life at Knutsford, seen with the
nostalgia often associated with recollections of childhood; it is
called 'The Last Generation in England'[1] and was published in
an American periodical in 1849. As Jenny Uglow points out, at
the time of the composition of *Cranford*, Gaskell had been
reading autobiographical works such as Wordsworth's *Prelude*,
Dickens's *David Copperfield* and Robert Southey's *Life* when
she wrote her own similar piece.[2]

So it is evidently Gaskell's own past as well as that of a rapidly
disappearing section of English society which is interwoven in
Cranford, a narrative which deploys an inconsistent and shifting chronology. The first chapter when Deborah Jenkyns is still
alive is set in the 1830s; the rest of the work apparently in the
1840s and early 1850s; but the narrator, Mary Smith, continues
to be treated as a young protégée. The dominant impression is
of a relatively recent past into which memories of early times
infiltrate. It is with the effect of memories breaking through
into the present time that the novel operates. The details of the
courtship of the Reverend Jenkyns and his wife in the late
eighteenth century are triggered by their letters which Miss

Matty reads before destroying them. Similarly, a letter from their son Peter Jenkyns evokes her tearful account of the violent and hitherto unknown events which led to a disruption of the family and his exile in some distant and unknown place. Miss Matty also has early memories of youthful dances in the Assembly Rooms which evoke folk memories of the time before she was born when aristocrats danced there. The past is not only another country but works with a time frame which shifts to take in large parts of two centuries.

This contradictory chronology is unique to *Cranford* and is not found in 'The Last Generation', the title of which sets it firmly in the past and ambiguously refers to either the preceding generation or the last generation of its kind. The story merely records everyday events and attitudes in an unnamed town, treating them with the mild amusement which informs their selection: the relish for card games; the strict rules for time and length of social visits; the treasuring of fine lace even to the extent of causing a cat to vomit up a piece it had swallowed; the calculatedly meagre provision of party food; the concealment of such food under a sofa; a cow dressed in warm flannel; the frugal use of sedan-chairs; the adulation of remote higher classes; the taste for horror stories. All these things recur in *Cranford* itself which led contemporary reviewers to regard it as an innocently nostalgic work. When it first appeared as a single volume in 1853, after appearing as a series of articles in *Household Words*, reviewers focused on its 'charm' and the '"soul of goodness" living and breathing and working in an orbit so limited'. It was said to reveal 'Touches of love and kindness, of simple self-sacrifice and of true womanly tenderness . . . naturally and truthfully just as they are found in the current of real life.'[3] The 'limited' orbit would seem to imply not only the limitation to women of a certain age and class in a town isolated from its neighbours but an escapist retreat from real life and its darker sides. Gaskell herself goes along with this reading when in 1865 she responded to John Ruskin's approval of the work: 'whenever I am ailing or ill, I take "Cranford" and – I was going to say *enjoy* it! (but that would not be pretty!) laugh over it afresh!'[4]

But her work is about much more than the cow with flannel drawers that she goes on to allude to. It relates in various ways to the concerns of the day which later critics have unpacked: gender, class, the economy and empire. The most obvious of these is gender and it is this aspect of the novel which has most frequently been interpreted by earlier critics as a kind of utopian vision of a female society which comically resists the intrusion of men. The evidence for this begins with the opening sentence which asserts that 'In the first place, Cranford is in possession of the Amazons'; and thereby identifies a group of middle-aged or elderly women as warriors. This is underlined when the reader is informed that 'If a married couple come to settle in the town, somehow the gentleman disappears ... whatever does become of the gentlemen, they are not at Cranford.' The question is then raised 'What could they do if they were there?'; and the answer given for the moment is that they are superfluous: ' "A man ... is *so* in the way in the house!" ' (Chapter I).

But by her treatment of Cranford society, Gaskell is engaging with the contemporary debate which raged in the mid nineteenth century concerning, among other matters, that of the ability of women without men to form friendships with their own sex or to thrive in an all-female community. An insistence that women could do neither of these things followed from a belief in the doctrine of separate spheres: domestic and nurturing for women (born for marriage and motherhood); and active and competitive in the outside world for men. Since this meant that women and men were seen as complementary to each other, those women who were without men were thus seen as lacking what was necessary to existence. There was much discussion for and against the view that women were capable of creating friendships and living harmoniously with other women.

On the other hand, proponents of the idea of women as unable to live together happily were reinforced by an increase in their numbers by those who detested the idea of communities of women. They shuddered at the idea of women living in convents, which seemed to them to reek of Roman Catholic intrigues and manipulation. Eliza Lynn Linton, novelist and journalist, for example, insisted that women were given to jealousy, spite and vindictiveness, and one of them wrote: 'I doubt if any woman's friendship ever existed free from jealousy. If we are not jealous about men we are about other women, and guard our rights against division with the vigilance of a house dog guarding his domain. No man can understand the unresting pettiness of jealousy that exists between women-friends: no man knows it for his own part, and no man would submit to it from his friend.'[5] Articles were written to argue that women were instinctively hostile to each other. Gaskell's own life suggests that she was a supporter of a different view since she formed strong ties with many women including Charlotte Brontë, Harriet Martineau, Florence Nightingale, her daughters, and many other relatives. In addition she extended her friendship to her servants such as her nurse, Hearn, who shares the surname of the sweetheart of Miss Matty's servant Martha. Hearn showed signs of depression at times and Gaskell expressed real and practical concern for her, writing in a letter: 'Hearn is not well at all just now, as much depression of spirits as anything, I think. – She wants some change of thought and scene, & we have a variety of plans for giving her it, as she has no home to go to, now-a-days. She is a dear good valuable *friend*. We want some very retired, *yet* very near a doctor, – place to go.'[6]

Gaskell's *Cranford* is a direct riposte to such views, presenting a case for the loyalty of women to their friends and for their ability to create a harmonious society among themselves. Cranford is a place built on relationships and friendships between women without men, central to which is that between Miss Matty Jenkyns and her intimidating elder sister Deborah. Despite the older woman's autocratic control over Miss Matty's life, which is used to prevent her youthful marriage to Holbrook as socially unsuitable, it persists even after Deborah's death when Miss Matty remains constant to her sister's standards. A similar relationship between sisters is seen in Captain Brown's family where the terminally ill older woman is nursed uncomplainingly by her sister Jessie, on whom she vents her ill-temper. Friendships are also forged across class barriers as the affluent but not quite genteel widow Mrs Fitz-Adam is accepted by the middle-class ladies Miss Matty, Miss Pole and the widowed Mrs Forrester. They are also stirred to compassion by the impoverished and weary wife of the travelling conjurer Signor Brunoni (alias Samuel Brown), who is nursing him after he has suffered a bad injury, when all rally to her help and even the sceptical Miss Pole becomes a kind friend.

In the light of what Gaskell says about Ann Hearn in her letter and Gaskell's efforts on behalf of a servant who became pregnant while unmarried, it is less surprising that Miss Matty is moved after the death of her ex-suitor Holbrook to disregard Deborah's rule of abstaining from marriage and of 'no followers' for Martha. She sees that by insisting on the rule she may condemn the girl to a lonely life like her own and she submits to 'Fate and Love' by allowing her to see the infatuated Jem Hearn (Chapter IV). Martha reciprocates Miss Matty's friendship later with a vehement refusal to leave her bankrupt mistress: her sympathy is transformed into the triumphant serving of a pudding, paid for and cooked by the maid herself, shaped like a 'lion *couchant*' with currant eyes.

The bonds of friendship between women in the community show themselves most strongly when one of them is in distress, and they are prepared not merely to give time and money but even to sacrifice their cherished prejudices to help and support the current broken reed. Captain Brown with his bluntness, his indifference to social snubs and his preference for Charles Dickens over Samuel Johnson is no favourite with Deborah Jenkyns, nor is his ill-tempered daughter or the too prettily dimpled younger daughter, Jessie. But when Captain Brown and his older daughter die, even the severe Deborah (or *Miss* Jenkyns as an eldest daughter was properly called) does not hesitate to go to Jessie's help. She suppresses her deep sense that it would be improper for Jessie to go to her father's funeral at a time when women were not supposed to attend; and accompanies her out of a feeling of 'propriety and humanity' as a chaperone and support (Chapter II). She then sacrifices her vaunted abhorrence of marriage to reunite Jessie with her former lover Major Gordon in an action paralleling Miss

Matty's later treatment of Martha. The pivotal event in the narrative is the failure of Miss Matty's bank, which leaves her penniless. At this point the spinsters and widows of Cranford meet secretly and plan not only to subsidize her with money from their own, mainly frugal, resources but also to conceal from her what they have done in order to save her pride.

Clearly it is women who manage, at least, the emotional economy of Cranford so that it works for the welfare of all. Reinforcing this is the fact that such men as do intermittently appear seem to trample unwittingly on the feelings of others. Mr Holbrook, who once proposed to Miss Matty, meeting her after many years, can only focus on her changed and ageing appearance by repeatedly telling her 'I should not have known you . . . I should not have known you!' In this unthinking fashion he destroys any illusion of 'sentimental romance' she might have cherished, depriving her of even that consolation (Chapter III). Miss Matty's brother Peter, when reunited with her after a long absence, also opens the old wound caused by her enforced refusal of Holbrook. Peter has brought from India presents of a muslin gown and a pearl necklace suitable for the pretty young sister he remembers. Momentarily Miss Matty too imagines herself youthful and dwells 'complacently on the idea of herself thus attired; and instinctively she put her hand up to her throat – that little delicate throat which . . . had been one of her youthful charms'. The touch disenchants her while Peter smiles, indicating that he is 'amused at the idea of the incongruity of his presents with the appearance of his sister' (Chapter XV). He later even harps on her unmarried state: 'If anybody had told me that you would have lived and died an old maid then, I should have laughed in their faces.' Jokingly he tells her 'You must have played your cards badly, my little Matty . . . wanted your brother to be a good go-between, eh! little one?' (Chapter XVI). Yet this is the man who in his youth carried out a hoax so ill-judged in relation to the feelings of others that it led to the destruction of his family life and the death of his grieving mother.

What Gaskell demonstrates beyond doubt by all this is that women are more skilled at managing the relationships that hold society together and sustain the individuals within it. This does not amount to an argument that men are superfluous; but, on the contrary, a comic subtext is created which undermines the idea that an all-female society is best in every respect. This is effected by a device which Gaskell shares with William Makepeace Thackeray's *Vanity Fair* (1848): the presence of a narrator with a double identity. Mary Smith has 'vibrated' between Cranford and Drumble – as Gaskell in her married life did between Knutsford and Manchester, though Drumble is never represented in the narrative. She is thus a spectator viewing Cranford from outside, but since in every chapter she is involved in events there and uses the inclusive 'we' when describing them, she becomes a participant and also part of the object of her own irony. When listing the individual economies practised by the Cranford ladies, she confesses to her own pointless habit of undoing and saving bits of string even as she resents Miss Matty's limitations on the use of candles. She tells how, for instance, when paying social calls, '*We* kept ourselves to short sentences of small talk' (Chapter I, emphasis added). She shares the naive enjoyment of Signor Brunoni's magic tricks and the worry that there may be something heathenish and not quite respectable about them; the ludicrous nightly safety routines of the Panic; the excitement over the arrival of the earl's widow, Lady Glenmire; and the horror at the latter's marriage to the surgeon Hoggins. In this disingenuous way she identifies herself as one of the Cranford ladies. Unlike Thackeray's narrator (who is there merely as an onlooker), Mary Smith even intervenes in events by summoning her father to sort out Miss Matty's dire money problems and effecting the return of her absent brother Peter by seeking him out in India and telling him of his sister's plight.

The presence of such a narrator holding a dual passport is the major difference between the 1849 'The Last Generation' and *Cranford*, enabling Gaskell to transform a whimsical narrative into a form of pre-emptive satire. Contemporary reviewers may not have recognized it as such but Charlotte Brontë did when she wrote to Gaskell after reading it while it was still appearing in *Household Words* in 1852: 'Satirical you are . . .

I believe a little more so than you think.' She even believes that in this line Gaskell has something to teach the novelist that Brontë most admired. Thackeray, she asserts, could learn from *Cranford* by taking the current chapter to his chamber where he should 'put himself to bed, and lie there – till he had learnt by diligent study how to be satirical without being exquisitely bitter'.[7]

Perhaps Brontë had recognized the narrator's double role as commentator and communal autobiographer whose first step is to explain from within the absence of men, which leaves 'the Amazons' in possession: if a man arrives with his wife: 'he is either fairly frightened to death by being the only man in the Cranford evening parties, or he is accounted for by being with his regiment, his ship, or closely engaged in business all the week in the great neighbouring commercial town of Drumble.' She expresses for herself and others the pleasure taken in this phenomenon of disappearance: 'We had congratulated ourselves upon the snugness of the evenings; and, in our love for gentility, . . . we had almost persuaded ourselves that to be a man was to be "vulgar".' As she points out, 'vulgar' is 'a tremendous word' in Cranford, the ultimate condemnation (Chapter I).

But it is 'prim little Mary', as Peter Jenkyns calls her on his return from India, who comments as a spectator would on the fact that 'if gentlemen were scarce, and almost unheard of in the "genteel society" of Cranford, they or their counterparts – handsome young men – abounded in the lower classes' (Chapter III). In practice, these young men are the answer to the question in the novel's opening 'What could [men] do if they were there?' Even there it was admitted that a surgeon, though male, was necessary, though he verges on the invisible, like the other men, because his profession is not gentlemanly. He is a surgeon not a physician and therefore belongs to a profession that had not long separated itself from the Barbers and Surgeons Company of London whose logo was a blood-stained bandage because they performed the cruder medical butchery of treating wounds, drawing teeth, setting or amputating limbs. However, his social status is ambiguous since the reference to him at this point in the first chapter means that he has claims to be a gentleman. But for the ladies he is unacceptable socially and has been 'tabooed' by the arbitress of social matters, the Honourable Mrs Jamieson, as 'vulgar' and 'inadmissible to Cranford society; not merely on account of his name, but because of his voice, his complexion, his boots, smelling of the stable, and himself, smelling of drugs' (Chapter XII). It is even rumoured that he 'sups on bread-and-cheese and beer every night', a charge brought also against the surgeon, Dr Gibson, in Gaskell's *Wives and Daughters* (1866) until his genteel second wife, Mrs Kirkpatrick, forbids it. Aside from the surgeon, what these other men could do is act as 'the joiner ... the butcher ... the gardener', draper (Johnson), postman (Thomas), or (anonymously) carry the ladies in the sedan-chair to their evening parties. Martha's husband-to-be, Jem Hearn, can even in an emergency put a roof over Miss Matty's head. In addition to these men of 'the lower orders' there is Mary Smith's father who intervenes effectively at his daughter's request. So prim little Mary quietly indicates that, though women run the emotional economy with great skill, they are in practical terms supported by men.

Mary Smith also draws attention to the way that the dislike of men is extended by the town of Cranford to the idea of marriage with them, which is described as though it were a contagious disease. Miss Pole, stung by the views of the widowed Lady Glenmire on the alleged robberies at Cranford, claims to believe that marriage 'always made people credulous to the last degree; indeed, she thought it argued great natural credulity in a woman if she could not keep herself from being married' (Chapter XI). She urges her companions including Miss Matty and Mary Smith to congratulate themselves on having 'so far ... escaped marriage'. Mary obligingly does so, telling the reader: 'We were thankful, as Miss Pole desired us to be, that we had never been married.' When Lady Glenmire shows yet greater natural credulity by becoming engaged to the surgeon Hoggins and risking a subsequent second marriage, Miss Matty fears an epidemic: 'Marry! . . . Well! I never thought of it. Two people that we know going to be married. It's coming very near! . . . One does not know whose turn may come next. Here, in Cranford, poor Lady Glenmire might have thought herself safe' (Chapter XII).

These disavowals of any inclination to marry, however, are undermined by Mary Smith's revelation of her own and Miss Matty's private views on matrimony. Miss Matty, who had quietly adopted a widow's cap after Holbrook's death, now confesses that, though she sees marriage as a risk, she also remembers the time 'when she had looked forward to being married as much as anyone'. Mary herself also admits to a more realistic view of the risks of marrying than one dictated by fear of becoming credulous. She has seen the poverty and misery of Signora Brunoni / Mrs Brown, six of whose children have died in India where she had followed her soldier husband: 'If I had been inclined to be daunted from matrimony, it would not have been Miss Pole to do it; it would have been the lot of poor Signor Brunoni and his wife' (Chapter XI).

Lady Glenmire's marriage to Hoggins turns out – like that of Jessie Brown and Major Gordon; the Jenkyns's parents, Major Jenkyns and his wife; and Martha and Jem Hearn's – to lead to a happily contented life. The possibility is also left, since she is evidently not 'inclined to be daunted' by Miss Pole, that Mary Smith will follow the same course, though neither she nor the other ladies sanction the marriage of Hoggins and Lady Glenmire by congratulating either party. Their real response to the news of Lady Glenmire's engagement is evident in behaviour that Mary Smith has previously noticed elsewhere and now sees in Cranford. She observes that 'the unmarried ladies in that set flutter out in an unusual gaiety and newness of dress, as much as to say, in a tacit and unconscious manner, "We also are spinsters"' (Chapter XII). The clear indication of this comment is that they too are available to be turned into wives.

Here, the ironically comic façade that Mary Smith creates is revealed for what it is, a defensive strategy, when reality breaks through. Similarly the loss of Miss Matty's savings as her bank fails is the point at which the text engages more seriously with the state of unmarried middle-class women at the time: the economic problem presented by such women at a mature age.

They are defined as 'superfluous' or 'redundant' as the result of two factors: demographic and ideological. The census of 1851 showed that the population consisted of half a million more females than males. Given also the doctrine of separate spheres, the absence of husbands for these women left them in excess of demand. One remedy frequently recommended was their emigration to the colonies where wives of British stock were in short supply. Education and training for middle-class women was scanty. There were far more schools for boys, including those run by Dissenters or Anglicans as well as an increasing number of large and expensive public schools. Until the 1850s, when the North London Collegiate School (1850) and Cheltenham Ladies' College (1854) were founded, there were only charity schools like Lowood in Brontë's *Jane Eyre* (1847), a few small private schools like the one at Roe Head that the Brontë sisters attended for a time, or establishments like the Ladies' Seminary in Cranford where 'accomplishments' are taught. These were the decorative activities thought suitable for those entering the middle-class marriage market: music in the form of piano-playing, drawing, painting, and maybe a little French.

This is the education undergone by Miss Matty while the only son of the family naturally goes to a boys' public school at Shrewsbury, with Cambridge University in prospect. Though Peter's education is cut short when he runs away, it is thorough enough to enable him to set himself up in India and return with a comfortable fortune. For Miss Matty her defective education proves disastrous when the outside economy impinges on her life. She is suddenly bankrupted at a time when the law had not caught up with changes in banking practices. Before this, banks were usually made up of a small number of partners who not only invested their own money in the business but ran it. Consequently they were, as a matter of course, individually liable if the bank failed. By the mid nineteenth century Joint Stock banks had, in addition to those who set up the bank, numerous smaller investors who had neither knowledge nor control of the bank's financial activities. With the law unchanged, these small investors like Miss Matty bore equal financial responsibility for losses and debts as those who managed the bank.[8]

So Miss Matty is liable to lose all her earthly possessions and accepts this as a moral responsibility by replacing a creditor's useless banknote. Fortunately Mary Smith, brought up in an industrial city, secretly takes control of Miss Matty's finances, helped by her commercially active father who is able to secure a small capital for Miss Matty. Mary still needs to find work for her friend by which she may secure the necessary income 'without materially losing caste': she has to assess Miss Matty's potential for paid work and does not find the outlook promising. Mary Taylor, Charlotte Brontë's friend, a vigorous and unconventional woman who emigrated to New Zealand and set up a shop, wrote in a letter of 1849: 'There are no means for a woman to live in England but by teaching, sewing or washing. The last is the best. The best paid[,] the least unhealthy & the most free ... Moreover it is impossible for any one not born to this position to take it up afterwards. I don't know why but it is.'[9] Taylor is referring to a working-class occupation of the kind that Miss Matty could not accept, even if equipped for it, without losing social status. For Miss Matty, Mary Smith first considers 'teaching', virtually the only work available to middle-class women, since governesses, though ill-paid, might still be half-considered as 'ladies'. Looking first for ability to teach music, Mary finds that the 'faint shadow of musical acquirement had died out years before'. Miss Matty had once learnt to trace patterns to be used in muslin embroidery but 'that was her nearest approach to the accomplishment of drawing'. She has little talent for needlework and her eyesight is now failing. Even a primitive knowledge of geography is beyond her and she is unclear as to the distinction between astronomy and astrology. The only accomplishments of which she feels proud are the making of spills or candle-lighters and the knitting of delicate garters (Chapter XIV).

Coming to the more basic skills of reading, writing and arithmetic, Mary finds that Miss Matty can read reasonably well and has pleasant handwriting but no grasp of spelling. Arithmetic does not get a mention here and we later learn that

Miss Matty is nervously slow to calculate the change due when selling tea. This survey of Miss Matty's potential for earning creates a generic picture of the middle-class spinster left to fend for herself. Such women were the object of attention for those who at this time were increasingly arguing for educational and work opportunities for women. They urged the case more discursively but it is the same case that Gaskell is making here.

This does not mean that she went so far as activists such as her friend Florence Nightingale who saw domestic life as a cruel impediment to women's progress. Nightingale shook off the domestic and all that went with it in her own life and, unlike the Cranford ladies, refused real offers of marriage. In 1852, at the time when Gaskell was producing the Cranford serial, Nightingale wrote a vivid and passionate attack on what she saw as the entombing prison of women's domestic life in her religious work 'Cassandra': 'Women often strive to live by intellect . . . But a woman cannot live in the light of intellect. Society forbids it. These conventional frivolities, which are called her "duties" forbid it. "Her domestic duties", high-sounding words, which, for the most part are but bad habits.'[10] In *Cranford* Gaskell describes the detail of the women's daily activities with pleasure: the frugal parties, the sedate card games, the polite visits. Nightingale does the opposite, satirizing the pointless visits made for the sake of form, the conversation restricted to trivia so as not to prolong the visit beyond the prescribed limit, the useless needlework, the letters, the meals conducted according to elaborate rules.

She had in mind gifted women like herself and Gaskell, who at about this time seized the chance to stay in Nightingale's home at Lea Hurst and push on with the composition of *North and South*. She writes gleefully from there of a life free of domestic cares: 'It is getting dark. I am to have my tea, up in my turret – at 6. – And after that I shall lock my outer door & write. I am stocked with coals, and have candles up here; for I am a quarter of a mile of staircase . . . away from every one else in the house.'[11]

Though Gaskell and Nightingale had this much in common, Gaskell regards domestic life and women's part in it as having social value, even for women like herself who had a profession. Her letters show her torn between her writing and her house-hold: 'I am sure it is healthy for [women] to have the refuge of the hidden world of Art to shelter themselves in when too much pressed upon by daily small Lilliputian arrows of ped-dling cares.' She is convinced that 'assuredly a blending of the two is desirable. (Home duties and the development of the Individual, I mean).'[12]

Mary Smith's evaluation of an impoverished middle-class spinster throws a new light on the Cranford community of spinsters and widows educated like Miss Matty, or rather not educated at all. It is seen to be basically unviable, not least because its central characters are shown to belong to a society that survives by pretending that the rest of the world does not exist and looks only to the past, though its physical survival depends on what they call 'the lower classes'. The women cling to the clothes and mores of a supposedly golden past when Queen Charlotte, wife of George III (1760–1820), and Queen Adelaide, wife of William IV (1830–1837), set the fashions in dress. Such clothes are merely a sign of the assumption that the ladies imagine themselves to belong to the static hierarchy of a ranked society which had been largely superseded in the early decades of the century by a society of large groups or classes of workers, entrepreneurs and landowners. In the ranked society of a largely agrarian society, deference from below was allegedly matched by benign care from 'superiors'. Such a concept made sense in a society where the individual worker knew his employer and was born into a certain position/ rank where God had placed him but not in the industrialized society of the 1840s. The Cranford ladies look up deferentially to the upper classes and are anxious to behave according to what they assume to be a traditional protocol that involves a reverential attitude to their 'superiors', particularly if they are titled. Hence the excited discussion as they attempt to discover the correct form of address for Lady Glenmire, the widow of a Scottish earl; and hence their disappointment at finding that she does not wear a coronet. Her sister-in-law, the widow of a younger brother of the earl, the dozy Honourable Mrs

Jamieson, is naturally appointed guardian of the rules of social etiquette. Mrs Forrester, another widow, occupies the rank below her, as someone born 'a Tyrrell' and allied to 'the Bigges, of Bigelow Hall'. At the bottom of the scale are Betty Barker, well-to-do but an ex-milliner, and the affluent but lower-class Mrs Fitz-Adam who achieves acceptance by the skin of her teeth on the general grounds that 'No one, who had not some good blood in their veins, would dare to be called Fitz.' This belief is reached through the erroneous assumption that the name Fitz-Clarence was that of 'the children of dear good King William the Fourth' (Chapter VII) whereas Fitz-something was the patronymic given to such offspring when they were illegitimate.

This perception of society and history suggests that, like the novel, the ladies too mentally shift from one time-frame to another. The community does not seem to notice that aristo-crats are ghosts that haunt the town rather than populate it. The Earl of Glenmire and his younger brother are represented in Cranford only by their relics. The phantom of one of the beautiful Gunning sisters, Maria, who married an earl, or Eliza-beth, who married two dukes, survives only in the memories of those who danced in the Cranford Assembly Rooms many years before. Her spirit is evoked along with the ghost of Lady Williams who married a faithless artist whom she met among the dancers. Mrs Forrester's Tyrrell blood, ironically, derives from two long-dead infamous ancestors, Sir Walter Tyrrell who killed 'King Rufus' in the twelfth century, and Sir James Tyrrell who 'murdered the little Princes in the Tower' in the sixteenth century – as Mary Smith points out. All of these ghosts haunt the imagination of the Cranford ladies and so does the Lady Jane, daughter of an earl, who once long ago lived in the house now inhabited by Mrs Fitz-Adam. Her presence there is thought to confer 'a patent of gentility upon its tenant', especially as her sister, Lady Anne, married the long-dead General Burgoyne, a hero of the American War of Independence (Chapter VII).

Such fantasies are comically absurd and apparently harmless, given the harmony that exists in the community, but they are too fragile to survive in an alien world. Strikingly, Miss Pole, a ringleader in the fantasy-world game, momentarily recognizes this in considering standards of social acceptability for the group: 'As most of the ladies of good family in Cranford were elderly spinsters, or widows without children, if we did not relax a little, and become less exclusive, by-and-by we should have no society at all' (Chapter VII). The absence of 'gentlemen' and the age of the ladies exclude the possibility of another genteel generation and the only infants who impinge on the ladies' lives are the fake baby that figures in Peter Jenkyns's disastrous hoax and Miss Matty's dream-child (Chapter XI). Miss Matty's recurrent dream is of the daughter she longs for, who is a representation of what Cranford mores have caused her to lose by preventing her from marrying 'below her rank'.

In this way Gaskell draws attention to the limited nature of even this harmonious society which cannot change or grow and ignores the threat to its way of life represented by the outside world that the unseen and unvisited Drumble represents. When Miss Matty says of Lady Glenmire's marriage that she might have thought she was safe in Cranford but 'It's coming very near', she might well be referring to the larger threat. The world of industry and its repercussions is physically approaching in the shape of the 'obnoxious railroad' which brings its employee Captain Brown to the town. Now that the railway mania of the 1840s has apparently taken hold, its spread is irreversible, despite the fact that it has been 'vehemently petitioned against' by the Cranfordians. When the chivalrous Captain Brown is symbolically killed by an oncoming train, its power to devastate the life even of Cranford is made clear. This symbolic intrusion of the real world that exists geographically beyond the boundaries of the town matches that brought about by the bank failure which shatters Miss Matty's life. There is no hope for the town unless it comes to terms with the larger society, for it needs the skills of the great neighbouring town of Drumble in the shape of Mr Smith to deal with Miss Matty's predicament. Not that the inhabitants of Drumble can avoid all disaster, since Mary Smith's father also loses money, but an accommodation has to be made.

The outside world also creeps in as the form of the more distant empire which to the Cranford ladies appears a romantic

and glamorous place, not the commercial and militaristic enterprise it really represents. They interpret it in terms of luxurious
commodities and people that reach them from a place so exotic
that a hint of its very presence thrills them: they view Major
Jenkyns's 'Hindoo body servant' as an amazing curiosity which
greatly 'excited' Cranford; they expect Peter Jenkyns, returned
from India as a 'wonderful traveller', will tell them true stories
'as good as an Arabian night'. They find the fascinating 'magic'
of Signor Brunoni typical of what they expect from the East,
with possibly heathenish practices that can defy the laws of
nature at its source. When Peter returns, they like him 'the
better, indeed, for being what they called "so very Oriental" '.
Before his arrival their contact with India has taken the form
of rich gifts sent back by male relatives serving there in the
military or the administration. There is the opulent white shawl
sent by Peter to his mother which serves only to act as her
shroud since, unknown to him, she is already dead (Chapter
VI). It is useless – like the India muslin gown and pearl necklace which significantly, like the shawl, come too late, as well
as the 'rare and delicate Indian ornaments' that are to grace
'the drawing-rooms of Mrs Jamieson and Mrs Fitz-Adam'
(Chapter XV). There were repressive colonial battles in and
around India, such as the Second Burmese War of 1852 started
by Lord Dalhousie, Governor-General 1847–56. It was insti-
gated by British merchants who were having disagreements
with the King of Burma; and ended with, as usual, an extension
of British territory. Such wars are mentioned in the novel only
from the perspective of heroic Peter who served in the victorious
siege of Rangoon. Again, as with the intrusion of a new and
commercially-minded society at home, the true nature of the
British occupation of India breaks through into lives at Cranford. Significantly it comes from the lips of 'the honest, worn,
bronze face' of the poverty-stricken wife of Samuel Brown (aka
Signor Brunoni) as she describes the life of the majority of the
British in India, the lower ranks of the army. This explains how
Brown was reduced, on leaving the army, to the life of an
itinerant conjuror. Mrs Brown gives an elaborately pathetic
account of the death of six children and the extreme poverty

which led to her arduous journey on foot to secure the survival of her last child by reaching a port from which she could sail for home. She succeeded because of the equally impoverished Indian women. This sudden glimpse of life in India for those who could not afford to send luxurious presents home evokes one source of the new industrial world's wealth. Miss Matty is only restored to her former position because Peter has been able to extract from *his* Indian enterprises enough money to live 'very genteelly' with his sister. By the end of the novel the old order has been restored – but only apparently so, for by this time Gaskell has made clear that the outside world and its problems are closing in on Cranford.

NOTES

1. This appeared as by 'THE AUTHOR OF "MARY BARTON"' in *Sartain's Union Magazine* (July 1849). It is reprinted in Appendix I.
2. Jenny Uglow, *Elizabeth Gaskell: A Habit of Stories* (London: Faber and Faber, 1993), p. 279.
3. Angus Easson (ed.), *Elizabeth Gaskell: The Critical Heritage* (London and New York: Routledge, 1991), p. 194.
4. Ibid., p. 199.
5. Pauline Nestor, *Female Friendships and Communities* (Oxford: Clarendon Press, 1985), p. 66.
6. J. A. V. Chapple and Arthur Pollard (eds.), *The Letters of Mrs Gaskell* (Manchester: Manchester University Press, 1966), p. 760.
7. Easson, *Elizabeth Gaskell: The Critical Heritage*, p. 193.
8. Andrew H. Miller, 'Subjectivity Ltd.: The Discourse of Liability in the Joint Stock Companies Act of 1856 and Gaskell's *Cranford*', *English Literary History* 61: 4 (1994), pp. 139–57.
9. Margaret Smith (ed.), *The Letters of Charlotte Brontë* (Oxford: Clarendon Press, 2000), II, 179.
10. Mary Poovey (ed.), *Florence Nightingale, Cassandra and Other Selections from Suggestions for Thought* (New York: New York University Press, 1993), pp. 215–16.
11. Chapple and Pollard, *The Letters of Mrs Gaskell*, p. 308.
12. Ibid., p. 106.

Further Reading

BIOGRAPHICAL

J. A. V. Chapple and A. Pollard (eds.), *The Letters of Mrs Gaskell* (Manchester: Manchester University Press, 1966)

John Chapple and A. Shelston (eds.), *Further Letters of Mrs Gaskell* (Manchester: Manchester University Press, 2000)

Shirley Foster, *Elizabeth Gaskell: A Literary Life* (Basingstoke: Palgrave Macmillan, 2002)

Jenny Uglow, *Elizabeth Gaskell: A Habit of Stories* (London: Faber and Faber, 1993)

BIBLIOGRAPHICAL

W. E. Smith (ed.), *Elizabeth C. Gaskell: A Bibliographical Catalogue of First and Early Editions, 1848–66* (Los Angeles: Heritage Bookshop, 1998)

Jeffrey Welch, *Elizabeth Gaskell: An Annotated Bibliography 1929–1975* (London and New York: Garland Publishing, 1977)

CRITICISM

Wendy K. Carse, 'A Penchant for Narrative: "Mary Smith" in Gaskell's *Cranford*', *Narrative Technique* 20 (1990), pp. 318–30

Jeffrey Cass, 'The Scraps, Patches and Rags of Daily Life: Gaskell's Oriental Other and the Conservation of *Cranford*', *Papers on Language and Literature* 35 (1999), pp. 417–39

Dorothy W. Collin, 'The Composition and Publication of Gaskell's *Cranford*', *Bulletin of the John Rylands University Library of Manchester* 69 (1986), pp. 59–95

—, 'Strategies of Retrospection and Narrative Silence in *Cranford* and *Cousin Phillis*', *Gaskell Society Journal* 11 (1997), pp. 25–42

Tess Cosslett, *Woman to Woman: Female Friendship in Victorian Fiction* (Brighton: Harvester, 1988)

Wendy A. Craik, *Elizabeth Gaskell and the English Provincial Novel* (London: Methuen, 1975)

Martin Dodsworth, 'Women without Men at Cranford', *Essays in Criticism* 13 (1963), pp. 132–45

Tim Dolin, '*Cranford* and the Victorian Collection', *Victorian Studies* 36 (1993), pp. 179–206

Angus Easson, *Elizabeth Gaskell* (London: Routledge and Kegan Paul, 1979)

— (ed.), *Elizabeth Gaskell: The Critical Heritage* (London and New York: Routledge, 1991)

J. M. Fenwick, 'Mothers of Empire in Gaskell's *Cranford*', *English Studies in Canada* 23 (1987), pp. 409–26

Maria A. Fitzwilliam, 'The Needle not the Pen: Fabric (Auto) Biography in *Cranford*, *Ruth* and *Wives and Daughters*', *Gaskell Society Journal* 14 (2000), pp. 1–13

Rowena Fowler, '*Cranford*: Cow in Grey Flannel or Lion Couchant?', *Studies in English Literature* 24 (1984), pp. 717–29

Adrienne E. Gavin, 'Language among the Amazons: Conjuring the Creativity in *Cranford*', *Dickens Studies Annual* 23 (1994), pp. 205–25

Eileen Gillooly, 'Humour as a Daughterly Defence in *Cranford*', *English Literary History* 59 (1992), pp. 883–910

Lorna Huett, 'Commodity and Collectivity in the *Cranford* Context of *Household Words*', *Gaskell Society Journal* 17 (2003), pp. 34–49

Joseph Kestner, *Protest and Reform: The British Social*

Narrative by Women 1827–1867 (Madison: University of Wisconsin Press, 1985)

Borislav Knezevic, 'An Ethnography of the Provincial: The Social Ethnography of Gentility in Elizabeth Gaskell's *Cranford*', *Victorian Studies* 41 (1998), pp. 405–26

Andrew H. Miller, 'The Fragments and Small Opportunities of *Cranford*', *Forms of Discourse and Culture* 25 (1992), pp. 91–111

—, 'Subjectivity Ltd.: The Discourse of Liability in the Joint Stock Companies Act of 1856 and Gaskell's *Cranford*', *English Literary History* 61:1 (1994), pp. 139–57

James Mulvihill, 'Economics of Living: Gaskell's *Cranford*', *Nineteenth Century Literature* 50 (1995), pp. 337–58

Pauline Nestor, *Female Friendships and Communities: Charlotte Brontë, George Eliot, and Elizabeth Gaskell* (Oxford: Clarendon Press, 1985)

M. Reeves, 'Textual, Contextual and Ideological Contradictions in Elizabeth Gaskell's *Cranford*', *English Studies in Canada* 23 (1997), pp. 389–407

Hilary M. Schor, 'Affairs of the Alphabet: Writing and Narrative in *Cranford*', *Novel* 22 (1989), pp. 288–304

—, *Scheherazade and the Marketplace: Elizabeth Gaskell and the Victorian Novel* (Oxford: Oxford University Press, 1992)

J. G. Sharps, *Mrs Gaskell's Observation and Invention: A Study of Her Non-Biographic Works* (London: Open Gate Press, 1970)

Patsy Stoneman, *Elizabeth Gaskell* (Brighton: Harvester, 1987)

Patricia A. Wolfe, 'Structure and Movement in *Cranford*', *Nineteenth Century Fiction* 23 (1968), pp. 161–76

Note on the Text

Elizabeth Gaskell's *Cranford* was not originally written as a novel. It had its genesis in a series of eight episodes about the imaginary village of Cranford, based on Knutsworth where Gaskell was brought up. The stories appeared at irregular intervals in Dickens's periodical *Household Words* between December 1851 and May 1853. They had been solicited by Dickens in 1850 when, after the success of her first novel *Mary Barton* (1848), he wrote asking her for 'a *short* tale, or any number of tales'.[1] The popularity of the first Cranford essays led to his willingness to print as many more as she cared to write, and he chided her for the sometimes long gaps between them. He and Gaskell did not see eye to eye over alterations to her texts nor over money, and he was eventually glad to wash his hands of her – but not before serializing *North and South* (1854) in *Household Words*.

It was apparently while completing *Ruth* (1853), with the subsequent uproar over its subject matter, a 'fallen' woman, that Gaskell decided to turn the Cranford episodes into a one-volume novel. With the help of John Forster, associate and future biographer of Dickens, Gaskell arranged for its publication by Chapman and Hall in June 1853, shortly after the appearance of the final instalment in *Household Words*. *Cranford* was immediately taken up and advertised by one of the largest circulating libraries, C. E. Mudie's, despite the fact that such libraries preferred three-volume novels which could be rented out piecemeal to two or three readers at a time.

The novel was published shortly in America by Harper Brothers, and again in 1855, along with some of Gaskell's other tales, by Chapman and Hall. Controversy arose later over the Gaskells' resale of what they took to be Chapman and Hall's expired right to Smith Elder (Charlotte Brontë's publisher). But in 1864 the new firm published an illustrated edition of *Cranford*.

The present edition uses the first volume edition of 1853, collated with the *Household Words* versions. The changes between the two texts show organizational alterations, not extensive revisions. It is clear from the collation that the last three episodes which were to make up the five final chapters of the novel were written as a coherent closing sequence. The following table shows how the texts were reorganized with the original titles (changed to delete the unnecessary repetition of 'Cranford' in the novel):

Episode titles in *Household Words* (followed by novel chapter numbers)
  Our Society at Cranford (1–2)
  A Love Affair at Cranford (3–4)
  Memory at Cranford (5–6)
  Visiting at Cranford (7–8)
  The Great Cranford Panic (9–11)
  Stopped Payment at Cranford (12–13)
  Friends in Need, at Cranford (14)
  A Happy Return to Cranford (15–16)

Some divisions into shorter paragraphs were made for the volume version as well as minor grammatical changes; but significant textual alteration is confined to the earlier chapters. The most striking of these is the reappearance in the volume of frequent favourable references to Dickens's *Pickwick Papers*. They mostly occur when the Cranford ladies and the Captain discuss the relative merits of Dickens's vivid writing which he prefers to the ornate and long-winded style of Dr Johnson which suits their taste better. The changes by Dickens (as editor of the periodical) were a cause of anger to Gaskell when they were proposed. But he sent the revised text to press and *then* wrote in December 1851 to Gaskell telling her that her

objection came '*too late* to recall your tale'. This statement
seems to be untrue but he added: 'I am truly concerned for this,
but I hope you will not blame me for what I have done in perfect
good faith. Any recollection of me from your pen, cannot . . .
be otherwise than truly gratifying to me; but with my name on
every page of Household Words there would be – or at least I
should feel – an impropriety in so mentioning myself.' He said
that he has been careful at 'the most important place – I mean
where the Captain is killed' to alter the reference to 'Hood's
Poems'.[2] Thomas Hood was a poet who wrote many satirical
pieces and was perhaps chosen to make a strong contrast with
Johnson.

Other changes – presumably Gaskell's own – are the
occasional switching of dialogue between Miss Pole and Miss
Matty and some alterations to the names of characters. Betty
Barker was 'Betsy' in the first episode in *Household Words*, and
Gaskell failed to correct to 'Betty' in 1853. Miss Matey in
Household Words becomes Miss Matty (see Chapter II, note
3), and Major Campbell becomes Major Gordon throughout
the volume. The reason for such changes is not clear, but
the revision from Dr Colburn to Mr Hoggins for the surgeon
is presumably to stress his plebeian status which horrifies the
ladies of Cranford when Lady Glenmire chooses to agree to
marry him. Some of the more interesting readings of the *Household Words* version are given in the Notes.

No further editions were published in Gaskell's lifetime after
that of 1864.[3]

Housestyling for this Penguin edition includes: spelling, e.g.
everyone, anyone (for 1853's every one, any one, respectively);
tonight, tomorrow, upstairs (to-night, to-morrow, up-stairs);
Phoebe, Encyclopaedia (Phœbe, Encyclopædia); the occasional
'grey' (for 'gray); but spelling acceptable in Gaskell's time is
not altered, e.g. sate (sat), secresy, Shakspeare, chace. Punctuation is standardized, e.g. no full stop after chapter numbers
and titles; single quotation marks (for 1853's doubles) and
doubles inside singles; end punctuation outside closing quotation marks (as now accepted) and round brackets, e.g. pp. 6:21,
18:23; no full stop after personal titles (Dr, Mr, Mrs) and 'St';

spaced en-dashes and em-dashes (for em-dashes and 2em-
dashes); errant apostrophes, its, don't, Rowlands' (it's, dont,
Rowland's); capitalization and hyphenation regularized, e.g.
ma'am, Rector, dining-parlour, Fitz-Adam (for the occasional
Ma'am, rector, dining parlour, Fitz Adam); and quotation
marks for all occurrences of 'St James's Chronicle' as other
periodicals in the text are presented.

Significant substantial emendations are listed below, with
their sources:

HW   *Household Words* (1851–3)
Ed.   Editor

Penguin edition		*1853 first volume edition*
20:9	the miss *Ed.*	miss
42:33	things *HW*	these
49:8	dim *HW*	grim
50:15	curtsey *Ed.*	courtesy
50:26	Jem *Ed.*	Jim (+ *HW*)
60:37	badly-sealed *HW*	baldly-sealed
69:23	Dor *HW*	Don
78:13	War *Ed.*	war (+ *HW*)
82:20	looked *HW*	looking
108:18	War *Ed.*	war (+ *HW*)
111:35	storey *Ed.*	story (+ *HW*)
162:1	them all *HW*	the mall
166:14	sell *HW*	see
170:32	to take *Ed.*	take
183:1	had *Ed.*	has
183:15	Hearn *HW*	Hearne
184:16	is *Ed.*	as

In Appendix I, the only housestyling is single quotation marks
for doubles. The spelling of 'brobdingnagian' in 'The Last Generation in England' is corrected (from 'brobdignagian'). In
Appendix II, the extracts from *Beeton's Book of Household
Management* are housestyled as for *Cranford*, but in the letters

only em-dashes are changed to en-dashes (as some appear in
their sources).

NOTES

1.   Graham Storey, Kathleen Tillotson and Nina Burgis (eds.), *The
     Letters of Charles Dickens* (Oxford: Clarendon Press, 1988),
     VI, 21.
2.   Ibid., pp. 548–9.
3.   I am indebted for this reference and in this account generally
     to Dorothy W. Collin's 'The Composition and Publication of
     Elizabeth Gaskell's *Cranford*', *Bulletin of the John Rylands
     University Library of Manchester*, 69 (1986), pp. 59–95.

Quasi-facsimilie of the title-page of the first edition.

CRANFORD.

BY THE AUTHOR OF

"MARY BARTON," "RUTH," &c.

LONDON:
CHAPMAN & HALL, 193, PICCADILLY.
1853.

Contents

CHAPTER I

OUR SOCIETY

In the first place, Cranford is in possession of the Amazons; all the holders of houses, above a certain rent, are women.[1] If a married couple come to settle in the town, somehow the gentleman disappears; he is either fairly frightened to death by being the only man in the Cranford evening parties, or he is accounted for by being with his regiment, his ship, or closely engaged in business all the week in the great neighbouring commercial town of Drumble,[2] distant only twenty miles on a railroad. In short, whatever does become of the gentlemen, they are not at Cranford. What could they do if they were there? The surgeon has his round of thirty miles, and sleeps at Cranford; but every man cannot be a surgeon. For keeping the trim gardens full of choice flowers without a weed to speck them; for frightening away little boys who look wistfully at the said flowers through the railings; for rushing out at the geese that occasionally venture into the gardens if the gates are left open; for deciding all questions of literature and politics without troubling themselves with unnecessary reasons or arguments; for obtaining clear and correct knowledge of everybody's affairs in the parish; for keeping their neat maid-servants in admirable order; for kindness (somewhat dictatorial) to the poor, and real tender good offices to each other whenever they are in distress, the ladies of Cranford are quite sufficient. 'A man,' as one of them observed to me once, 'is *so* in the way in the house!' Although the ladies of Cranford know all each other's proceedings, they are exceedingly indifferent to each other's opinions. Indeed, as each has her own individuality, not to say eccentricity, pretty strongly developed, nothing is so easy as verbal retaliation;

but somehow good-will reigns among them to a considerable degree.

The Cranford ladies have only an occasional little quarrel, spirted out in a few peppery words and angry jerks of the head; just enough to prevent the even tenor of their lives from becoming too flat. Their dress is very independent of fashion; as they observe, 'What does it signify how we dress here at Cranford, where everybody knows us?' And if they go from home, their reason is equally cogent: 'What does it signify how we dress here, where nobody knows us?' The materials of their clothes are, in general, good and plain, and most of them are nearly as scrupulous as Miss Tyler, of cleanly memory; but I will answer for it, the last gigot, the last tight and scanty petti-coat[3] in wear in England, was seen in Cranford – and seen without a smile.

I can testify to a magnificent family red silk umbrella, under which a gentle little spinster, left alone of many brothers and sisters, used to patter to church on rainy days. Have you any red silk umbrellas in London? We had a tradition of the first that had ever been seen in Cranford; and the little boys mobbed it, and called it 'a stick in petticoats'.[4] It might have been the very red silk one I have described, held by a strong father over a troop of little ones; the poor little lady – the survivor of all – could scarcely carry it.

Then there were rules and regulations for visiting and calls; and they were announced to any young people, who might be staying in the town, with all the solemnity with which the old Manx laws were read once a year on the Tinwald Mount.[5]

'Our friends have sent to inquire how you are after your journey tonight, my dear, (fifteen miles, in a gentleman's car-riage); they will give you some rest tomorrow, but the next day, I have no doubt, they will call; so be at liberty after twelve; – from twelve to three are our calling-hours.'

Then, after they had called,

'It is the third day;[6] I dare say your mamma has told you, my dear, never to let more than three days elapse between receiving a call and returning it; and also, that you are never to stay longer than a quarter of an hour.'

'But am I to look at my watch? How am I to find out when a quarter of an hour has passed?'

'You must keep thinking about the time, my dear, and not allow yourself to forget it in conversation.'

As everybody had this rule in their minds, whether they received or paid a call, of course no absorbing subject was ever spoken about. We kept ourselves to short sentences of small talk, and were punctual to our time.

I imagine that a few of the gentlefolks of Cranford were poor, and had some difficulty in making both ends meet; but they were like the Spartans, and concealed their smart under a smiling face. We none of us spoke of money, because that subject savoured of commerce and trade, and though some might be poor, we were all aristocratic. The Cranfordians had that kindly *esprit de corps* which made them overlook all deficiencies in success when some among them tried to conceal their poverty. When Mrs Forrester, for instance, gave a party in her baby-house of a dwelling, and the little maiden disturbed the ladies on the sofa by a request that she might get the tea-tray out from underneath, everyone took this novel proceeding as the most natural thing in the world; and talked on about household forms and ceremonies, as if we all believed that our hostess had a regular servants' hall, second table, with housekeeper and steward; instead of the one little charity-school maiden, whose short ruddy arms could never have been strong enough to carry the tray upstairs, if she had not been assisted in private by her mistress, who now sate in state, pretending not to know what cakes were sent up; though she knew, and we knew, and she knew that we knew, and we knew that she knew that we knew, she had been busy all the morning making tea-bread and sponge-cakes.

There were one or two consequences arising from this general but unacknowledged poverty, and this very much acknowledged gentility, which were not amiss, and which might be introduced into many circles of society to their great improvement. For instance, the inhabitants of Cranford kept early hours, and clattered home in their pattens, under the guidance of a lantern-bearer, about nine o'clock at night; and the whole town was abed and asleep by half-past ten. Moreover, it was considered 'vulgar' (a tremendous word in Cranford) to give anything expensive, in the way of eatable or drinkable, at the evening entertainments. Wafer bread-and-butter and sponge-biscuits were all that the Honourable Mrs Jamieson gave; and she was sister-in-law to the late Earl of Glenmire, although she did practise such 'elegant economy'.[7]

'Elegant economy'! How naturally one falls back into the phraseology of Cranford! There, economy was always 'elegant', and money-spending always 'vulgar and ostentatious'; a sort of sour-grapeism, which made us very peaceful and satisfied. I never shall forget the dismay felt when a certain Captain Brown came to live at Cranford, and openly spoke about his being poor – not in a whisper to an intimate friend, the doors and windows being previously closed; but, in the public street! in a loud military voice! alleging his poverty as a reason for not taking a particular house. The ladies of Cranford were already rather moaning over the invasion of their territories by a man and a gentleman. He was a half-pay Captain, and had obtained some situation on a neighbouring railroad,[8] which had been vehemently petitioned against by the little town; and if, in addition to his masculine gender, and his connexion with the obnoxious railroad, he was so brazen as to talk of being poor – why! then, indeed, he must be sent to Coventry. Death was as true and as common as poverty; yet people never spoke about that, loud out in the streets. It was a word not to be mentioned to ears polite.[9] We had tacitly agreed to ignore that any with whom we associated on terms of visiting equality could ever be prevented by poverty from doing anything that they wished. If we walked to or from a party, it was because the night was *so* fine, or the air *so* refreshing; not because sedan-chairs were expensive. If we wore prints, instead of summer silks, it was because we preferred a washing material; and so on, till we blinded ourselves to the vulgar fact, that we were, all of us, people of very moderate means. Of course, then, we did not know what to make of a man who could speak of poverty as if it was not a disgrace. Yet, somehow Captain Brown made himself respected in Cranford, and was called upon, in spite of all resolutions to the contrary. I was surprised to hear his opinions quoted as authority, at a visit which I paid to Cranford, about a year after he had settled in the town. My own friends had been among the bitterest opponents of any proposal to visit the Captain and his daughters, only twelve months before; and now he was even admitted in the tabooed hours before twelve. True, it was to discover the cause of a smoking chimney, before the fire was lighted; but still Captain Brown walked upstairs, nothing daunted, spoke in a voice too large for the room, and joked quite in the way of a tame man, about the house. He had been blind to all the small slights and omissions of trivial ceremonies with which he had been received. He had been friendly, though the Cranford ladies had been cool; he had answered small sarcastic compliments in good faith; and with his manly frankness had overpowered all the shrinking which met him as a man who was not ashamed to be poor. And, at last, his excellent masculine common sense, and his facility in devising expedients to overcome domestic dilemmas, had gained him an extraordinary place as authority among the Cranford ladies. He, himself, went on in his course, as unaware of his popularity, as he had been of the reverse; and I am sure he was startled one day, when he found his advice so highly esteemed, as to make some counsel which he had given in jest, be taken in sober, serious earnest.

It was on this subject; – an old lady had an Alderney cow,[10] which she looked upon as a daughter. You could not pay the short quarter-of-an-hour call, without being told of the wonderful milk or wonderful intelligence of this animal. The whole town knew and kindly regarded Miss Betty Barker's Alderney; therefore great was the sympathy and regret when, in an unguarded moment, the poor cow tumbled into a lime-pit. She moaned so loudly that she was soon heard, and rescued; but meanwhile the poor beast had lost most of her hair, and came out looking naked, cold, and miserable, in a bare skin. Everybody pitied the animal, though a few could not restrain their smiles at her droll appearance. Miss Betty Barker absolutely cried with sorrow and dismay; and it was said she thought of trying a bath of oil. This remedy, perhaps, was recommended

by someone of the number whose advice she asked; but the
proposal, if ever it was made, was knocked on the head by
Captain Brown's decided 'Get her a flannel waistcoat and
flannel drawers, ma'am, if you wish to keep her alive. But my
advice is, kill the poor creature at once.'

Miss Betty Barker dried her eyes, and thanked the Captain
heartily; she set to work, and by-and-by all the town turned
out to see the Alderney meekly going to her pasture, clad in
dark grey flannel. I have watched her myself many a time. Do
you ever see cows dressed in grey flannel in London?

Captain Brown had taken a small house on the outskirts of
the town, where he lived with his two daughters. He must have
been upwards of sixty at the time of the first visit I paid to
Cranford, after I had left it as a residence. But he had a wiry,
well-trained, elastic figure; a stiff military throw-back of his
head, and a springing step, which made him appear much
younger than he was. His eldest daughter looked almost as old
as himself, and betrayed the fact that his real, was more than
his apparent, age. Miss Brown must have been forty; she had a
sickly, pained, careworn expression on her face, and looked as
if the gaiety of youth had long faded out of sight. Even when
young she must have been plain and hard-featured. Miss Jessie
Brown was ten years younger than her sister, and twenty shades
prettier. Her face was round and dimpled. Miss Jenkyns once
said, in a passion against Captain Brown (the cause of which I
will tell you presently), 'that she thought it was time for Miss
Jessie to leave off her dimples, and not always to be trying to
look like a child'. It was true there was something child-like in
her face; and there will be, I think, till she dies, though she
should live to a hundred. Her eyes were large blue wondering
eyes, looking straight at you; her nose was unformed and snub,
and her lips were red and dewy; she wore her hair, too, in little
rows of curls, which heightened this appearance. I do not know
if she was pretty or not; but I liked her face, and so did everybody, and I do not think she could help her dimples. She had
something of her father's jauntiness of gait and manner; and
any female observer might detect a slight difference in the attire
of the two sisters – that of Miss Jessie being about two pounds

per annum more expensive than Miss Brown's. Two pounds was a large sum[11] in Captain Brown's annual disbursements.

Such was the impression made upon me by the Brown family, when I first saw them altogether in Cranford church. The Captain I had met before – on the occasion of the smoky chimney, which he had cured by some simple alteration in the flue. In church, he held his double eye-glass to his eyes during the Morning Hymn,[12] and then lifted up his head erect, and sang out loud and joyfully. He made the responses louder than the clerk – an old man with a piping feeble voice, who, I think, felt aggrieved at the Captain's sonorous bass, and quavered higher and higher in consequence.

On coming out of church, the brisk Captain paid the most gallant attention to his two daughters. He nodded and smiled to his acquaintances; but he shook hands with none until he had helped Miss Brown to unfurl her umbrella, had relieved her of her prayer-book,[13] and had waited patiently till she, with trembling nervous hands, had taken up her gown to walk through the wet roads.

I wondered what the Cranford ladies did with Captain Brown at their parties. We had often rejoiced, in former days, that there was no gentleman to be attended to, and to find conversation for, at the card-parties. We had congratulated ourselves upon the snugness of the evenings; and, in our love for gentility, and distaste of mankind, we had almost persuaded ourselves that to be a man was to be 'vulgar'; so that when I found my friend and hostess, Miss Jenkyns, was going to have a party in my honour, and that Captain and the Miss Browns were invited, I wondered much what would be the course of the evening. Card-tables, with green-baize tops, were set out by day-light, just as usual; it was the third week in November, so the evenings closed in about four. Candles, and clean packs of cards were arranged on each table. The fire was made up, the neat maid-servant had received her last directions; and, there we stood dressed in our best, each with a candle-lighter in our hands, ready to dart at the candles as soon as the first knock came. Parties in Cranford were solemn festivities, making the ladies feel gravely elated, as they sat together in their best dresses. As soon as three had arrived, we sat down to 'Preference', I being the unlucky fourth.[14] The next four comers were put down immediately to another table; and presently the tea-trays, which I had seen set out in the store-room as I passed in the morning, were placed each on the middle of a card-table. The china was delicate egg-shell; the old-fashioned silver glittered with polishing; but the eatables were of the slightest description. While the trays were yet on the tables, Captain and the Miss Browns came in; and I could see, that somehow or other the Captain was a favourite with all the ladies present. Ruffled brows were smoothed, sharp voices lowered at his approach. Miss Brown looked ill, and depressed almost to gloom. Miss Jessie smiled as usual, and seemed nearly as popular as her father. He immediately and quietly assumed the man's place in the room; attended to everyone's wants, lessened the pretty maid-servant's labour by waiting on empty cups, and bread-and-butterless ladies; and yet did it all in so easy and dignified a manner, and so much as if it were a matter of course for the strong to attend to the weak, that he was a true man throughout. He played for three-penny points with as grave an interest as if they had been pounds; and yet, in all his attention to strangers he had an eye on his suffering daughter; for suffering I was sure she was, though to many eyes she might only appear to be irritable. Miss Jessie could not play cards; but she talked to the sitters-out, who, before her coming, had been rather in-clined to be cross. She sang, too, to an old cracked piano, which I think had been a spinet in its youth. Miss Jessie sang 'Jock of Hazeldean'[15] a little out of tune; but we were none of us musical, though Miss Jenkyns beat time, out of time, by way of appearing to be so.

It was very good of Miss Jenkyns to do this; for I had seen that, a little before, she had been a good deal annoyed by Miss Jessie Brown's unguarded admission (à propos of Shet-land wool) that she had an uncle, her mother's brother, who was a shopkeeper[16] in Edinburgh. Miss Jenkyns tried to drown this confession by a terrible cough – for the Honourable Mrs Jamieson was sitting at the card-table nearest Miss Jessie, and what would she say or think, if she found out she was in the

same room with a shopkeeper's niece! But Miss Jessie Brown
(who had no tact, as we all agreed, the next morning) *would*
repeat the information, and assure Miss Pole she could easily
get her the identical Shetland wool required, 'through my uncle,
who has the best assortment of Shetland goods of anyone in
Edinbro''. It was to take the taste of this out of our mouths,
and the sound of this out of our ears, that Miss Jenkyns proposed music; so I say again, it was very good of her to beat time
to the song.

When the trays re-appeared with biscuits and wine, punctu-
ally at a quarter to nine, there was conversation; comparing of
cards, and talking over tricks; but, by-and-by, Captain Brown
sported a bit of literature.

'Have you seen any numbers of "The Pickwick Papers?"'[17]
said he. (They were then publishing in parts.) 'Capital thing!'

Now, Miss Jenkyns was daughter of a deceased rector of
Cranford; and, on the strength of a number of manuscript
sermons, and a pretty good library of divinity, considered herself literary, and looked upon any conversation about books as
a challenge to her. So she answered and said, 'Yes, she had seen
them; indeed, she might say she had read them.'

'And what do you think of them?' exclaimed Captain Brown.
'Aren't they famously good?'

So urged, Miss Jenkyns could not but speak.

'I must say I don't think they are by any means equal to Dr
Johnson. Still, perhaps, the author is young. Let him persevere,
and who knows what he may become if he will take the great
Doctor for his model.' This was evidently too much for Captain
Brown to take placidly; and I saw the words on the tip of his
tongue before Miss Jenkyns had finished her sentence.

'It is quite a different sort of thing, my dear madam,' he
began.

'I am quite aware of that,' returned she. 'And I make allow-
ances, Captain Brown.'

'Just allow me to read you a scene out of this month's
number,' pleaded he. 'I had it only this morning, and I don't
think the company can have read it yet.'

'As you please,' said she, settling herself with an air of

resignation. He read the account of the 'swarry' which Sam Weller gave at Bath.[18] Some of us laughed heartily. *I* did not dare, because I was staying in the house. Miss Jenkyns sat in patient gravity. When it was ended, she turned to me, and said with mild dignity,

'Fetch me "Rasselas",[19] my dear, out of the book-room.'

When I brought it to her, she turned to Captain Brown:

'Now allow *me* to read you a scene, and then the present company can judge between your favourite, Mr Boz[20] and Dr Johnson.'

She read one of the conversations between Rasselas and Imlac, in a high-pitched majestic voice; and when she had ended, she said, 'I imagine I am now justified in my preference of Dr Johnson, as a writer of fiction.' The Captain screwed his lips up, and drummed on the table, but he did not speak. She thought she would give a finishing blow or two.

'I consider it vulgar, and below the dignity of literature, to publish in numbers.'[21]

'How was the "Rambler" published, ma'am?' asked Captain Brown, in a low voice; which I think Miss Jenkyns could not have heard.

'Dr Johnson's style is a model for young beginners. My father recommended it to me when I began to write letters. – I have formed my own style upon it; I recommend it to your favourite.'

'I should be very sorry for him to exchange his style for any such pompous writing,' said Captain Brown.

Miss Jenkyns felt this as a personal affront, in a way of which the Captain had not dreamed. Epistolary writing, she and her friends considered as her *forte*. Many a copy of many a letter have I seen written and corrected on the slate, before she 'seized the half-hour just previous to post-time to assure' her friends of this or of that; and Dr Johnson was, as she said, her model in these compositions. She drew herself up with dignity, and only replied to Captain Brown's last remark by saying with marked emphasis on every syllable, 'I prefer Dr Johnson to Mr Boz.'

It is said – I won't vouch for the fact – that Captain Brown was heard to say, *sotto voce*, 'D–n Dr Johnson!' If he did, he was penitent afterwards, as he showed by going to stand near Miss Jenkyns's arm-chair, and endeavouring to beguile her into conversation on some more pleasing subject. But she was inexorable. The next day, she made the remark I have mentioned, about Miss Jessie's dimples.

CHAPTER II

THE CAPTAIN

It was impossible to live a month at Cranford, and not know the daily habits of each resident; and long before my visit was ended, I knew much concerning the whole Brown trio. There was nothing new to be discovered respecting their poverty; for they had spoken simply and openly about that from the very first. They made no mystery of the necessity for their being economical. All that remained to be discovered was the Captain's infinite kindness of heart, and the various modes in which, unconsciously to himself, he manifested it. Some little anecdotes were talked about for some time after they occurred. As we did not read much, and as all the ladies were pretty well suited with servants, there was a dearth of subjects for conversation. We therefore discussed the circumstance of the Captain taking a poor old woman's dinner out of her hands, one very slippery Sunday. He had met her returning from the bakehouse[1] as he came from church, and noticed her precarious footing; and, with the grave dignity with which he did everything, he relieved her of her burden, and steered along the street by her side, carrying her baked mutton and potatoes safely home. This was thought very eccentric; and it was rather expected that he would pay a round of calls, on the Monday morning, to explain and apologise to the Cranford sense of propriety: but he did no such thing; and then it was decided that he was ashamed, and was keeping out of sight. In a kindly pity for him, we began to say – 'After all, the Sunday morning's occurrence showed great goodness of heart'; and it was resolved that he should be comforted on his next appearance amongst us; but, lo! he came down upon us, untouched by any sense of shame, speaking loud and bass as ever, his head thrown back, his wig as jaunty and well-curled as usual, and we were obliged to conclude he had forgotten all about Sunday.

Miss Pole and Miss Jessie Brown had set up a kind of intimacy, on the strength of the Shetland wool and the new knitting stitches; so it happened that when I went to visit Miss Pole, I saw more of the Browns than I had done while staying with Miss Jenkyns; who had never got over what she called Captain Brown's disparaging remarks upon Dr Johnson, as a writer of light and agreeable fiction. I found that Miss Brown was seriously ill of some lingering, incurable complaint, the pain occasioned by which gave the uneasy expression to her face that I had taken for unmitigated crossness. Cross, too, she was at times, when the nervous irritability occasioned by her disease became past endurance. Miss Jessie bore with her at these times even more patiently than she did with the bitter self-upbraidings by which they were invariably succeeded. Miss Brown used to accuse herself, not merely of hasty and irritable temper; but also of being the cause why her father and sister were obliged to pinch, in order to allow her the small luxuries which were necessaries in her condition. She would so fain have made sacrifices for them and have lightened their cares, that the original generosity of her disposition added acerbity to her temper. All this was borne by Miss Jessie and her father with more than placidity – with absolute tenderness. I forgave Miss Jessie her singing out of tune, and her juvenility of dress, when I saw her at home. I came to perceive that Captain Brown's dark Brutus wig and padded coat (alas! too often threadbare) were remnants of the military smartness of his youth, which he now wore unconsciously. He was a man of infinite resources, gained in his barrack experience. As he confessed, no one could black his boots to please him, except himself; but, indeed, he was not above saving the little maid-servant's labours in every way, – knowing, most likely, that his daughter's illness made the place a hard one.

He endeavoured to make peace with Miss Jenkyns soon after the memorable dispute I have named, by a present of a wooden fire-shovel (his own making), having heard her say how much

the grating of an iron one annoyed her. She received the present
with cool gratitude, and thanked him formally. When he was
gone, she bade me put it away in the lumber-room; feeling,
probably, that no present from a man who preferred Mr Boz
to Dr Johnson could be less jarring than an iron fire-shovel.

Such was the state of things when I left Cranford and went
to Drumble. I had, however, several correspondents who kept
me *au fait* to the proceedings of the dear little town. There
was Miss Pole, who was becoming as much absorbed in crochet
as she had been once in knitting; and the burden of whose letter
was something like, 'But don't you forget the white worsted at
Flint's', of the old song;[2] for, at the end of every sentence of
news, came a fresh direction as to some crochet commission
which I was to execute for her. Miss Matilda Jenkyns (who did
not mind being called Miss Matty,[3] when Miss Jenkyns was
not by) wrote nice, kind, rambling letters; now and then ven-
turing into an opinion of her own; but suddenly pulling herself up, and either begging me not to name what she had
said, as Deborah thought differently, and *she* knew; or else,
putting in a postscript to the effect that, since writing the
above, she had been talking over the subject with Deborah, and
was quite convinced that, &c.; – (here, probably, followed a
recantation of every opinion she had given in the letter). Then
came Miss Jenkyns – Debōrah, as she liked Miss Matty to call
her; her father having once said that the Hebrew name ought
to be so pronounced. I secretly think she took the Hebrew
prophetess[4] for a model in character; and, indeed, she was not
unlike the stern prophetess in some ways; making allowance,
of course, for modern customs and difference in dress. Miss
Jenkyns wore a cravat, and a little bonnet like a jockey-cap,
and altogether had the appearance of a strong-minded woman;
although she would have despised the modern idea of women
being equal to men.[5] Equal, indeed! she knew they were
superior. – But to return to her letters. Everything in them was
stately and grand, like herself. I have been looking them over
(dear Miss Jenkyns, how I honoured her!) and I will give an
extract, more especially because it relates to our friend Captain
Brown: –

'The Honourable Mrs Jamieson has only just quitted me; and, in the course of conversation, she communicated to me the intelligence, that she had yesterday received a call from her revered husband's quondam friend, Lord Mauleverer. You will not easily conjecture what brought his lordship within the precincts of our little town. It was to see Captain Brown, with whom, it appears, his lordship was acquainted in the "plumed wars",[6] and who had the privilege of averting destruction from his lordship's head, when some great peril was impending over it, off the misnomered Cape of Good Hope. You know our friend the Honourable Mrs Jamieson's deficiency in the spirit of innocent curiosity; and you will therefore not be so much surprised when I tell you she was quite unable to disclose to me the exact nature of the peril in question. I was anxious, I confess, to ascertain in what manner Captain Brown, with his limited establishment, could receive so distinguished a guest; and I discovered that his lordship retired to rest, and, let us hope, to refreshing slumbers, at the Angel Hotel; but shared the Brunonian[7] meals during the two days that he honoured Cranford with his august presence. Mrs Johnson, our civil butcher's wife, informs me that Miss Jessie purchased a leg of lamb; but, besides this, I can hear of no preparation whatever to give a suitable reception to so distinguished a visitor. Perhaps they entertained him with "the feast of reason and the flow of soul";[8] and to us, who are acquainted with Captain Brown's sad want of relish for "the pure wells of English undefiled",[9] it may be matter for congratulation, that he has had the opportunity of improving his taste by holding converse with an elegant and refined member of the British aristocracy. But from some mundane feelings who is free?'

Miss Pole and Miss Matty wrote to me by the same post. Such a piece of news as Lord Mauleverer's visit was not to be lost on the Cranford letter-writers: they made the most of it. Miss Matty humbly apologised for writing at the same time as her sister, who was so much more capable than she to describe the honour done to Cranford; but, in spite of a little bad spelling, Miss Matty's account gave me the best idea of the commotion occasioned by his lordship's visit, after it had occurred;

for, except the people at the Angel, the Browns, Mrs Jamieson, and a little lad his lordship had sworn at for driving a dirty hoop against the aristocratic legs, I could not hear of anyone with whom his lordship had held conversation.

My next visit to Cranford was in the summer. There had been neither births, deaths, nor marriages since I was there last. Everybody lived in the same house, and wore pretty nearly the same well-preserved, old-fashioned clothes. The greatest event was, that the Miss Jenkynses had purchased a new carpet for the drawing-room. Oh the busy work Miss Matty and I had in chasing the sunbeams, as they fell in an afternoon right down on this carpet through the blindless window! We spread newspapers over the places, and sat down to our book or our work; and, lo! in quarter of an hour the sun had moved, and was blazing away on a fresh spot; and down again we went on our knees to alter the position of the newspapers. We were very busy, too, one whole morning before Miss Jenkyns gave her party, in following her directions, and in cutting out and stitching together pieces of newspaper, so as to form little paths to every chair, set for the expected visitors, lest their shoes might dirty or defile the purity of the carpet. Do you make paper paths for every guest to walk upon in London?

Captain Brown and Miss Jenkyns were not very cordial to each other. The literary dispute, of which I had seen the beginning, was a 'raw', the slightest touch on which made them wince. It was the only difference of opinion they had ever had; but that difference was enough. Miss Jenkyns could not refrain from talking *at* Captain Brown; and though he did not reply, he drummed with his fingers; which action she felt and resented as very disparaging to Dr Johnson. He was rather ostentatious in his preference of the writings of Mr Boz; would walk through the street so absorbed in them, that he all but ran against Miss Jenkyns; and though his apologies were earnest and sincere, and though he did not, in fact, do more than startle her and himself, she owned to me she had rather he had knocked her down, if he had only been reading a higher style of literature. The poor, brave Captain! he looked older, and more worn, and his clothes were very threadbare. But he seemed as bright and cheerful as ever, unless he was asked about his daughter's health.

'She suffers a great deal, and she must suffer more; we do what we can to alleviate her pain – God's will be done!' He took off his hat at these last words. I found, from Miss Matty, that everything had been done, in fact. A medical man, of high repute in that country neighbourhood, had been sent for, and every injunction he had given was attended to, regardless of expense. Miss Matty was sure they denied themselves many things in order to make the invalid comfortable; but they never spoke about it; and as for Miss Jessie! 'I really think she's an angel,' said poor Miss Matty, quite overcome. 'To see her way of bearing with Miss Brown's crossness, and the bright face she puts on after she's been sitting up a whole night and scolded above half of it, is quite beautiful. Yet she looks as neat and as ready to welcome the Captain at breakfast-time, as if she had been asleep in the Queen's bed all night. My dear! you could never laugh at her prim little curls or her pink bows again, if you saw her as I have done.' I could only feel very penitent, and greet Miss Jessie with double respect when I met her next. She looked faded and pinched; and her lips began to quiver, as if she was very weak, when she spoke of her sister. But she brightened, and sent back the tears that were glittering in her pretty eyes, as she said:–

'But, to be sure, what a town Cranford is for kindness! I don't suppose anyone has a better dinner than usual cooked, but the best part of all comes in a little covered basin for my sister. The poor people will leave their earliest vegetables at our door for her. They speak short and gruff, as if they were ashamed of it; but I am sure it often goes to my heart to see their thoughtfulness.' The tears now came back and overflowed; but after a minute or two, she began to scold herself, and ended by going away, the same cheerful Miss Jessie as ever.

'But why does not this Lord Mauleverer do something for the man who saved his life?' said I.

'Why, you see, unless Captain Brown has some reason for it, he never speaks about being poor; and he walked along by his lordship, looking as happy and cheerful as a prince; and as they

never called attention to their dinner by apologies, and as Miss
Brown was better that day, and all seemed bright, I dare say
his lordship never knew how much care there was in the back-
ground. He did send game in the winter pretty often, but now
he is gone abroad.'

I had often occasion to notice the use that was made of
fragments and small opportunities in Cranford; the rose-leaves
that were gathered ere they fell, to make into a pot-pourri for
some one who had no garden; the little bundles of lavender-
flowers sent to strew the drawers of some town-dweller, or to
burn in the chamber of some invalid. Things that many would
despise, and actions which it seemed scarcely worthwhile to
perform, were all attended to in Cranford. Miss Jenkyns stuck
an apple full of cloves, to be heated and smell pleasantly in
Miss Brown's room; and as she put in each clove, she uttered
a Johnsonian sentence. Indeed, she never could think of the
Browns without talking Johnson; and, as they were seldom
absent from her thoughts just then, I heard many a rolling
three-piled sentence.[10]

Captain Brown called one day to thank Miss Jenkyns for
many little kindnesses, which I did not know until then that she
had rendered. He had suddenly become like an old man; his
deep bass voice had a quavering in it; his eyes looked dim, and
the lines on his face were deep. He did not – could not – speak
cheerfully of his daughter's state, but he talked with manly
pious resignation, and not much. Twice over he said, 'What
Jessie has been to us, God only knows!' and after the second
time, he got up hastily, shook hands all round without speaking,
and left the room.

That afternoon we perceived little groups in the street, all
listening with faces aghast to some tale or other. Miss Jenkyns
wondered what could be the matter, for some time before she
took the undignified step of sending Jenny out to inquire.

Jenny came back with a white face of terror. 'Oh, ma'am!
oh, Miss Jenkyns, ma'am! Captain Brown is killed by them
nasty cruel railroads!'[11] and she burst into tears. She, along with
many others, had experienced the poor Captain's kindness.

'How? – where – where? Good God! Jenny, don't waste

time in crying, but tell us something.' Miss Matty rushed out
into the street at once, and collared the man who was telling
the tale.

'Come in – come to my sister at once, – Miss Jenkyns, the
Rector's daughter. Oh, man, man! say it is not true,' – she cried,
as she brought the affrighted carter, sleeking down his hair,
into the drawing-room, where he stood with his wet boots on
the new carpet, and no one regarded it.

'Please mum, it is true. I seed it myself,' and he shuddered at
the recollection. 'The Captain was a-reading some new book as
he was deep in, a-waiting for the down train; and there was a
little lass as wanted to come to its mammy, and gave its sister
the slip, and came toddling across the line. And he looked up
sudden at the sound of the train coming, and seed the child,
and he darted on the line and cotched it up, and his foot slipped,
and the train came over him in no time. Oh Lord, Lord! Mum,
it's quite true – and they've come over to tell his daughters. The
child's safe, though, with only a bang on its shoulder, as he
threw it to its mammy. Poor Captain would be glad of that,
mum, would not he? God bless him!' The great rough carter
puckered up his manly face, and turned away to hide his tears.
I turned to Miss Jenkyns. She looked very ill, as if she were
going to faint, and signed to me to open the window.

'Matilda, bring me my bonnet. I must go to those girls.
God pardon me if ever I have spoken contemptuously to the
Captain!'

Miss Jenkyns arrayed herself to go out, telling Miss Matilda
to give the man a glass of wine. While she was away, Miss
Matty and I huddled over the fire, talking in a low and awe-
struck voice. I know we cried quietly all the time.

Miss Jenkyns came home in a silent mood, and we durst not
ask her many questions. She told us that Miss Jessie had fainted,
and that she and Miss Pole had had some difficulty in bringing
her round: but that, as soon as she recovered, she begged one
of them to go and sit with her sister.

'Mr Hoggins says she cannot live many days, and she shall
be spared this shock,' said Miss Jessie, shivering with feelings
to which she dared not give way.

'But how can you manage, my dear?' asked Miss Jenkyns; 'you cannot bear up, she must see your tears.'

'God will help me – I will not give way – she was asleep when the news came; she may be asleep yet. She would be so utterly miserable, not merely at my father's death, but to think of what would become of me; she is so good to me.' She looked up earnestly in their faces with her soft true eyes, and Miss Pole told Miss Jenkyns afterwards she could hardly bear it, knowing, as she did, how Miss Brown treated her sister.

However, it was settled according to Miss Jessie's wish. Miss Brown was to be told her father had been summoned to take a short journey on railway business. They had managed it in some way – Miss Jenkyns could not exactly say how. Miss Pole was to stop with Miss Jessie. Mrs Jamieson had sent to inquire. And this was all we heard that night; and a sorrowful night it was. The next day a full account of the fatal accident was in the country paper, which Miss Jenkyns took in. Her eyes were very weak, she said, and she asked me to read it. When I came to the 'gallant gentleman was deeply engaged in the perusal of a number of "Pickwick", which he had just received', Miss Jenkyns shook her head long and solemnly, and then sighed out, 'Poor, dear, infatuated man!'

The corpse was to be taken from the station to the parish church, there to be interred. Miss Jessie had set her heart on following it[12] to the grave; and no dissuasives could alter her resolve. Her restraint upon herself made her almost obstinate; she resisted all Miss Pole's entreaties, and Miss Jenkyns's advice. At last Miss Jenkyns gave up the point; and after a silence, which I feared portended some deep displeasure against Miss Jessie, Miss Jenkyns said she should accompany the latter to the funeral.

'It is not fit for you to go alone. It would be against both propriety and humanity were I to allow it.'

Miss Jessie seemed as if she did not half like this arrangement; but her obstinacy, if she had any, had been exhausted in her determination to go to the interment. She longed, poor thing! I have no doubt, to cry alone over the grave of the dear father to whom she had been all in all; and to give way, for one little half-hour, uninterrupted by sympathy, and unobserved by friendship. But it was not to be. That afternoon Miss Jenkyns sent out for a yard of black crape, and employed herself busily in trimming the little black silk bonnet I have spoken about. When it was finished she put it on, and looked at us for appro-bation – admiration she despised. I was full of sorrow, but, by one of those whimsical thoughts which come unbidden into our heads, in times of deepest grief, I no sooner saw the bonnet than I was reminded of a helmet; and in that hybrid bonnet, half-helmet, half-jockey cap,[13] did Miss Jenkyns attend Captain Brown's funeral; and I believe supported Miss Jessie with a tender indulgent firmness which was invaluable, allowing her to weep her passionate fill before they left.

Miss Pole, Miss Matty, and I, meanwhile, attended to Miss Brown: and hard work we found it to relieve her querulous and never-ending complaints. But if we were so weary and dispirited, what must Miss Jessie have been! Yet she came back almost calm, as if she had gained a new strength. She put off her mourning dress, and came in, looking pale and gentle; thanking us each with a soft long pressure of the hand. She could even smile – a faint, sweet, wintry smile, as if to reassure us of her power to endure; but her look made our eyes fill suddenly with tears, more than if she had cried outright.

It was settled that Miss Pole was to remain with her all the watching live-long night; and that Miss Matty and I were to return in the morning to relieve them, and give Miss Jessie the opportunity for a few hours of sleep. But when the morn-ing came, Miss Jenkyns appeared at the breakfast table, equipped in her helmet bonnet, and ordered Miss Matty to stay at home, as she meant to go and help to nurse. She was evidently in a state of great friendly excitement, which she showed by eating her breakfast standing, and scolding the household all round.

No nursing – no energetic strong-minded woman could help Miss Brown now. There was that in the room as we entered, which was stronger than us all, and made us shrink into solemn awestruck helplessness. Miss Brown was dying. We hardly knew her voice, it was so devoid of the complaining tone we had always associated with it. Miss Jessie told me afterwards that it, and her face too, were just what they had been formerly, when her mother's death left her the young anxious head of the family, of whom only Miss Jessie survived.

She was conscious of her sister's presence, though not, I think, of ours. We stood a little behind the curtain: Miss Jessie knelt with her face near her sister's, in order to catch the last soft awful whispers.

'Oh, Jessie! Jessie! How selfish I have been! God forgive me for letting you sacrifice yourself for me as you did. I have so loved you – and yet I have thought only of myself. God forgive me!'

'Hush, love! hush!' said Miss Jessie, sobbing.

'And my father! my dear, dear father! I will not complain now, if God will give me strength to be patient. But, oh, Jessie! tell my father how I longed and yearned to see him at last, and to ask his forgiveness. He can never know now how I loved him – oh! if I might but tell him, before I die; what a life of sorrow his has been, and I have done so little to cheer him!'

A light came into Miss Jessie's face. 'Would it comfort you, dearest, to think that he does know – would it comfort you, love, to know that his cares, his sorrows –' Her voice quivered, but she steadied it into calmness, – 'Mary! he has gone before you to the place where the weary are at rest.[14] He knows now how you loved him.'

A strange look, which was not distress, came over Miss Brown's face. She did not speak for some time, but then we saw her lips form the words, rather than heard the sound – 'Father, mother, Harry, Archy!' – then, as if it was a new idea throwing a filmy shadow over her darkening mind – 'But you will be alone – Jessie!'

Miss Jessie had been feeling this all during the silence, I think; for the tears rolled down her cheeks like rain, at these words; and she could not answer at first. Then she put her hands together tight, and lifted them up, and said, – but not to us –

'Though He slay me, yet will I trust in Him.'[15]

In a few moments more, Miss Brown lay calm and still; never to sorrow or murmur more.

After this second funeral, Miss Jenkyns insisted that Miss Jessie should come to stay with her, rather than go back to the desolate house; which, in fact, we learned from Miss Jessie, must now be given up, as she had not wherewithal to maintain it. She had something about twenty pounds a-year,[16] besides the interest of the money for which the furniture would sell; but she could not live upon that: and so we talked over her qualifications for earning money.

'I can sew neatly,' said she, 'and I like nursing.[17] I think, too, I could manage a house, if anyone would try me as housekeeper; or I would go into a shop, as saleswoman, if they would have patience with me at first.'

Miss Jenkyns declared, in an angry voice, that she should do no such thing; and talked to herself about 'some people having no idea of their rank as a Captain's daughter', nearly an hour afterwards, when she brought Miss Jessie up a basin of delicately-made arrow-root, and stood over her like a dragoon until the last spoonful was finished: then she disappeared. Miss Jessie began to tell me some more of the plans which had suggested themselves to her, and insensibly fell into talking of the days that were past and gone, and interested me so much, I neither knew nor heeded how time passed. We were both startled when Miss Jenkyns reappeared, and caught us crying. I was afraid lest she would be displeased, as she often said that crying hindered digestion, and I knew she wanted Miss Jessie to get strong; but, instead, she looked queer and excited, and fidgetted round us without saying anything. At last she spoke. 'I have been so much startled – no, I've not been at all startled – don't mind me, my dear Miss Jessie – I've been very much surprised – in fact, I've had a caller, whom you knew once, my dear Miss Jessie —'

Miss Jessie went very white, then flushed scarlet, and looked eagerly at Miss Jenkyns –

'A gentleman, my dear, who wants to know if you would see him.'

'Is it? – it is not —' stammered out Miss Jessie – and got no farther.

'This is his card,' said Miss Jenkyns, giving it to Miss Jessie;

and while her head was bent over it, Miss Jenkyns went through a series of winks and odd faces to me, and formed her lips into a long sentence, of which, of course, I could not understand a word.

'May he come up?' asked Miss Jenkyns at last.

'Oh, yes! certainly!' said Miss Jessie, as much as to say, this is your house, you may show any visitor where you like. She took up some knitting of Miss Matty's and began to be very busy, though I could see how she trembled all over.

Miss Jenkyns rang the bell, and told the servant who answered it to show Major Gordon upstairs; and, presently, in walked a tall, fine, frank-looking man of forty, or upwards. He shook hands with Miss Jessie; but he could not see her eyes, she kept them so fixed on the ground. Miss Jenkyns asked me if I would come and help her to tie up the preserves in the store-room; and, though Miss Jessie plucked at my gown, and even looked up at me with begging eye, I durst not refuse to go where Miss Jenkyns asked. Instead of tying up preserves in the store-room, however, we went to talk in the dining-room; and there Miss Jenkyns told me what Major Gordon had told her; – how he had served in the same regiment with Captain Brown, and had become acquainted with Miss Jessie, then a sweet-looking, blooming girl of eighteen; how the acquaintance had grown into love, on his part, though it had been some years before he had spoken; how, on becoming possessed, through the will of an uncle, of a good estate in Scotland, he had offered,[18] and been refused, though with so much agitation, and evident distress, that he was sure she was not indifferent to him; and how he had discovered that the obstacle was the fell disease which was, even then, too surely threatening her sister. She had mentioned that the surgeons foretold intense suffering; and there was no one but herself to nurse her poor Mary, or cheer and comfort her father during the time of illness. They had had long discussions; and, on her refusal to pledge herself to him as his wife, when all should be over, he had grown angry, and broken off entirely, and gone abroad, believing that she was a cold-hearted person, whom he would do well to forget. He had been travelling in the East, and was on his return home when, at Rome, he saw the account of Captain Brown's death in 'Galignani'.[19]

Just then Miss Matty, who had been out all the morning, and had only lately returned to the house, burst in with a face of dismay and outraged propriety: –

'Oh, goodness me!' she said. 'Deborah, there's a gentleman sitting in the drawing-room, with his arm round Miss Jessie's waist!' Miss Matty's eyes looked large with terror.

Miss Jenkyns snubbed her down in an instant: –

'The most proper place in the world for his arm to be in. Go away, Matilda, and mind your own business.' This from her sister, who had hitherto been a model of feminine decorum, was a blow for poor Miss Matty, and with a double shock she left the room.

The last time I ever saw poor Miss Jenkyns was many years after this. Mrs Gordon had kept up a warm and affectionate intercourse with all at Cranford. Miss Jenkyns, Miss Matty, and Miss Pole had all been to visit her, and returned with wonderful accounts of her house, her husband, her dress, and her looks. For, with happiness, something of her early bloom returned; she had been a year or two younger than we had taken her for. Her eyes were always lovely, and, as Mrs Gordon, her dimples were not out of place. At the time to which I have referred, when I last saw Miss Jenkyns, that lady was old and feeble, and had lost something of her strong mind. Little Flora Gordon was staying with the Misses Jenkyns, and when I came in she was reading aloud to Miss Jenkyns, who lay feeble and changed on the sofa. Flora put down the 'Rambler' when I came in.

'Ah!' said Miss Jenkyns, 'you find me changed, my dear. I can't see as I used to do. If Flora were not here to read to me, I hardly know how I should get through the day. Did you ever read the "Rambler"? It's a wonderful book – wonderful! and the most improving reading for Flora' – (which I dare say it would have been, if she could have read half the words without spelling, and could have understood the meaning of a third) – 'better than that strange old book, with the queer name, poor Captain Brown was killed for reading – that book by Mr Boz, you know – "Old Poz";[20] when I was a girl, but that's a long time ago, – I acted Lucy in "Old Poz" ' – she babbled on long enough for Flora to get a good long spell at the 'Christmas Carol', which Miss Matty had left on the table.[21]

CHAPTER III

A LOVE AFFAIR OF LONG AGO

I thought[1] that probably my connection with Cranford would cease after Miss Jenkyns's death; at least, that it would have to be kept up by correspondence, which bears much the same relation to personal intercourse that the books of dried plants I sometimes see ('Hortus Siccus', I think they call the things), do to the living and fresh flowers in the lanes and meadows. I was pleasantly surprised, therefore, by receiving a letter from Miss Pole (who had always come in for a supplementary week after my annual visit to Miss Jenkyns) proposing that I should go and stay with her; and then, in a couple of days after my acceptance, came a note from Miss Matty, in which, in a rather circuitous and very humble manner, she told me how much pleasure I should confer, if I could spend a week or two with her, either before or after I had been at Miss Pole's; 'for,' she said, 'since my dear sister's death, I am well aware I have no attractions to offer; it is only to the kindness of my friends that I can owe their company.'

Of course, I promised to come to dear Miss Matty, as soon as I had ended my visit to Miss Pole; and the day after my arrival at Cranford, I went to see her, much wondering what the house would be like without Miss Jenkyns, and rather dreading the changed aspect of things. Miss Matty began to cry as soon as she saw me. She was evidently nervous from having anticipated my call. I comforted her as well as I could; and I found the best consolation I could give was the honest praise that came from my heart as I spoke of the deceased. Miss Matty slowly shook her head over each virtue as it was named and attributed to her sister; at last she could not restrain the tears which had long been silently flowing, but hid her face behind her handkerchief, and sobbed aloud.

'Dear Miss Matty!' said I, taking her hand – for indeed I did not know in what way to tell her how sorry I was for her, left deserted in the world. She put down her handkerchief, and said –

'My dear, I'd rather you did not call me Matty. *She* did not like it; but I did many a thing she did not like, I'm afraid – and now she's gone! If you please, my love, will you call me Matilda?'

I promised faithfully, and began to practise the new name with Miss Pole that very day; and, by degrees, Miss Matilda's feeling on the subject was known through Cranford, and we all tried to drop the more familiar name, but with so little success that by and by we gave up the attempt.[2]

My visit to Miss Pole was very quiet. Miss Jenkyns had so long taken the lead in Cranford, that, now she was gone, they hardly knew how to give a party. The Honourable Mrs Jamieson, to whom Miss Jenkyns herself had always yielded the post of honour, was fat and inert, and very much at the mercy of her old servants. If they chose that she should give a party, they reminded her of the necessity for so doing; if not, she let it alone. There was all the more time for me to hear old-world stories from Miss Pole, while she sat knitting, and I making my father's shirts. I always took a quantity of plain sewing to Cranford; for, as we did not read much, or walk much, I found it a capital time to get through my work. One of Miss Pole's stories related to a shadow of a love affair that was dimly perceived or suspected long years before.[3]

Presently, the time arrived when I was to remove to Miss Matilda's house. I found her timid and anxious about the arrangements for my comfort. Many a time, while I was unpacking, did she come backwards and forwards to stir the fire, which burned all the worse for being so frequently poked.

'Have you drawers enough, dear?' asked she. 'I don't know exactly how my sister used to arrange them. She had capital methods. I am sure she would have trained a servant in a week to make a better fire than this, and Fanny has been with me four months.'

This subject of servants was a standing grievance,[4] and I could not wonder much at it; for if gentlemen were scarce, and almost unheard of in the 'genteel society' of Cranford, they or their counterparts – handsome young men – abounded in the lower classes. The pretty neat servant-maids had their choice of desirable 'followers'; and their mistresses, without having the sort of mysterious dread of men and matrimony that Miss Matilda had, might well feel a little anxious, lest the heads of their comely maids should be turned by the joiner, or the butcher, or the gardener; who were obliged, by their callings, to come to the house; and who, as ill-luck would have it, were generally handsome and unmarried. Fanny's lovers, if she had any – and Miss Matilda suspected her of so many flirtations, that, if she had not been very pretty, I should have doubted her having one – were a constant anxiety to her mistress. She was forbidden, by the articles of her engagement,[5] to have 'followers'; and though she had answered innocently enough, doubling up the hem of her apron as she spoke, 'Please, ma'am, I never had more than one at a time,' Miss Matty prohibited that one. But a vision of a man seemed to haunt the kitchen. Fanny assured me that it was all fancy; or else I should have said myself that I had seen a man's coat-tails whisk into the scullery once, when I went on an errand into the store-room at night; and another evening, when, our watches having stopped, I went to look at the clock, there was a very odd appearance, singularly like a young man squeezed up between the clock and the back of the open kitchen-door: and I thought Fanny snatched up the candle very hastily, so as to throw the shadow on the clock-face, while she very positively told me the time half-an-hour too early, as we found out afterwards by the church-clock. But I did not add to Miss Matty's anxieties by naming my suspicions, especially as Fanny said to me, the next day, that it was such a queer kitchen for having odd shadows about it, she really was almost afraid to stay; 'for you know Miss,' she added, 'I don't see a creature from six o'clock tea, till Missus rings the bell for prayers at ten.'[6]

However, it so fell out that Fanny had to leave; and Miss Matilda begged me to stay and 'settle her' with the new maid;

to which I consented, after I had heard from my father that he did not want me at home. The new servant was a rough, honest-looking country-girl, who had only lived in a farm place before; but I liked her looks when she came to be hired; and I promised Miss Matilda to put her in the ways of the house. The said ways were religiously such as Miss Matilda thought her sister would approve. Many a domestic rule and regulation had been a subject of plaintive whispered murmur to me, during Miss Jenkyns's life; but now that she was gone, I do not think that even I, who was a favourite, durst have suggested an alteration. To give an instance: we constantly adhered to the forms which were observed, at meal times, in 'my father, the Rector's house'. Accordingly, we had always wine and dessert;[7] but the decanters were only filled when there was a party; and what remained was seldom touched, though we had two wine glasses apiece every day after dinner, until the next festive occasion arrived; when the state of the remainder wine was examined into, in a family council. The dregs were often given to the poor; but occasionally, when a good deal had been left at the last party (five months ago, it might be), it was added to some of a fresh bottle, brought up from the cellar. I fancy poor Captain Brown did not much like wine; for I noticed he never finished his first glass, and most military men take several. Then, as to our dessert, Miss Jenkyns used to gather currants and gooseberries for it herself, which I sometimes thought would have tasted better fresh from the trees; but then, as Miss Jenkyns observed, there would have been nothing for dessert in summer-time. As it was, we felt very genteel with our two glasses apiece, and a dish of gooseberries at the top, of currants and biscuits at the sides, and two decanters at the bottom. When oranges came in, a curious proceeding was gone through. Miss Jenkyns did not like to cut the fruit; for, as she observed, the juice all ran out nobody knew where; sucking (only I think she used some more recondite word) was in fact the only way of enjoying oranges; but then there was the unpleasant association with a ceremony frequently gone through by little babies; and so, after dessert, in orange season, Miss Jenkyns and Miss Matty used to rise up, possess themselves each of an orange in silence, and withdraw to the privacy of their own rooms, to indulge in sucking oranges.

I had once or twice tried, on such occasions, to prevail on Miss Matty to stay; and had succeeded in her sister's life-time. I held up a screen, and did not look, and, as she said, she tried not to make the noise very offensive; but now that she was left alone, she seemed quite horrified when I begged her to remain with me in the warm dining-parlour, and enjoy her orange as she liked best. And so it was in everything. Miss Jenkyns's rules were made more stringent than ever, because the framer of them was gone where there could be no appeal. In all things else Miss Matilda was meek and undecided to a fault. I have heard Fanny turn her round twenty times in a morning about dinner, just as the little hussy chose; and I sometimes fancied she worked on Miss Matilda's weakness in order to bewilder her, and to make her feel more in the power of her clever servant. I determined that I would not leave her till I had seen what sort of a person Martha was; and, if I found her trustworthy, I would tell her not to trouble her mistress with every little decision.

Martha was blunt and plain-spoken to a fault; otherwise she was a brisk, well-meaning, but very ignorant girl. She had not been with us a week before Miss Matilda and I were astounded one morning by the receipt of a letter from a cousin of hers, who had been twenty or thirty years in India, and who had lately, as we had seen by the 'Army List',[8] returned to England, bringing with him an invalid wife, who had never been introduced to her English relations. Major Jenkyns wrote to propose that he and his wife should spend a night at Cranford, on his way to Scotland – at the inn, if it did not suit Miss Matilda to receive them into her house; in which case they should hope to be with her as much as possible during the day. Of course, it *must* suit her, as she said; for all Cranford knew that she had her sister's bed-room at liberty; but I am sure she wished the Major had stopped in India and forgotten his cousins out and out.

'Oh! how must I manage?' asked she, helplessly. 'If Deborah had been alive, she would have known what to do with a

gentleman-visitor. Must I put razors in his dressing-room?
Dear! dear! and I've got none. Deborah would have had them.
And slippers, and coat-brushes?' I suggested that probably he
would bring all these things with him. 'And after dinner, how
am I to know when to get up, and leave him to his wine?
Deborah would have done it so well; she would have been quite
in her element. Will he want coffee, do you think?' I undertook
the management of the coffee, and told her I would instruct
Martha in the art of waiting, in which it must be owned she
was terribly deficient; and that I had no doubt Major and Mrs
Jenkyns would understand the quiet mode in which a lady lived
by herself in a country town. But she was sadly fluttered. I made
her empty her decanters, and bring up two fresh bottles of wine.
I wished I could have prevented her from being present at my
instructions to Martha; for she frequently cut in with some
fresh direction, muddling the poor girl's mind, as she stood
open-mouthed, listening to us both.

'Hand the vegetables round,' said I (foolishly, I see now – for
it was aiming at more than we could accomplish with quiet-
ness and simplicity): and then, seeing her look bewildered, I
added, 'Take the vegetables round to people, and let them help
themselves.'

'And mind you go first to the ladies,' put in Miss Matilda.
'Always go to the ladies before gentlemen, when you are
waiting.'

'I'll do it as you tell me, ma'am,' said Martha; 'but I like
lads best.'

We felt very uncomfortable and shocked at this speech of
Martha's; yet I don't think she meant any harm; and, on
the whole, she attended very well to our directions, except
that she 'nudged' the Major, when he did not help himself as
soon as she expected, to the potatoes, while she was handing
them round.

The Major and his wife were quiet, unpretending people
enough when they did come; languid, as all East Indians are, I
suppose. We were rather dismayed at their bringing two servants with them, a Hindoo body-servant for the Major, and
a steady elderly maid for his wife; but they slept at the inn,

and took off a good deal of the responsibility by attending carefully to their master's and mistress's comfort. Martha, to be sure, had never ended her staring at the East Indian's white turban, and brown complexion, and I saw that Miss Matilda shrunk away from him a little as he waited at dinner. Indeed, she asked me, when they were gone, if he did not remind me of Blue Beard?[9] On the whole, the visit was most satisfactory, and is a subject of conversation even now with Miss Matilda; at the time, it greatly excited Cranford, and even stirred up the apathetic and Honourable Mrs Jamieson to some expression of interest, when I went to call and thank her for the kind answers she had vouchsafed to Miss Matilda's inquiries as to the arrangement of a gentleman's dressing-room – answers which I must confess she had given in the wearied manner of the Scandinavian prophetess,–

'Leave me, leave me to repose.'[10]

And *now* I come to the love affair.

It seems that Miss Pole had a cousin, once or twice removed, who had offered to Miss Matty long ago. Now, this cousin lived four or five miles from Cranford on his own estate; but his property was not large enough to entitle him to rank higher than a yeoman; or rather, with something of the 'pride which apes humility',[11] he had refused to push himself on, as so many of his class had done, into the ranks of the squires. He would not allow himself to be called Thomas Holbrook, *Esq.*; he even sent back letters with this address, telling the postmistress at Cranford that his name was *Mr* Thomas Holbrook, yeoman.[12] He rejected all domestic innovations; he would have the house door stand open in summer, and shut in winter, without knocker or bell to summon a servant. The closed fist or the knob of the stick did this office for him, if he found the door locked. He despised every refinement which had not its root deep down in humanity. If people were not ill, he saw no necessity for moderating his voice. He spoke the dialect of the country[13] in perfection, and constantly used it in conversation; although Miss Pole (who gave me these particulars) added, that he read aloud more beautifully and with more feeling than anyone she had ever heard, except the late Rector.

'And how came Miss Matilda not to marry him?' asked I.

'Oh, I don't know. She was willing enough, I think; but you know Cousin Thomas would not have been enough of a gentleman for the Rector, and Miss Jenkyns.'

'Well! but they were not to marry him,' said I, impatiently.

'No; but they did not like Miss Matty to marry below her rank. You know she was the Rector's daughter, and somehow they are related to Sir Peter Arley: Miss Jenkyns thought a deal of that.'

'Poor Miss Matty!' said I.

'Nay, now, I don't know anything more than that he offered and was refused. Miss Matty might not like him – and Miss Jenkyns might never have said a word – it is only a guess of mine.'

'Has she never seen him since?' I inquired.

'No, I think not. You see, Woodley, Cousin Thomas's house, lies half-way between Cranford and Misselton; and I know he made Misselton his market-town very soon after he had offered to Miss Matty; and I don't think he has been into Cranford above once or twice since – once, when I was walking with Miss Matty, in High Street; and suddenly she darted from me, and went up Shire Lane. A few minutes after, I was startled by meeting Cousin Thomas.'

'How old is he?' I asked, after a pause of castle-building.

'He must be about seventy, I think, my dear,' said Miss Pole, blowing up my castle, as if by gunpowder, into small fragments.[14]

Very soon after – at least during my long visit to Miss Matilda – I had the opportunity of seeing Mr Holbrook; seeing, too, his first encounter with his former love, after thirty or forty years' separation. I was helping to decide whether any of the new assortment of coloured silks which they had just received at the shop, would do to match a grey and black mousseline-de-laine that wanted a new breadth, when a tall, thin, Don Quixote-looking old man[15] came into the shop for some woollen gloves. I had never seen the person, (who was rather striking) before, and I watched him rather attentively, while Miss Matty listened to the shopman. The stranger wore a blue coat with brass buttons, drab breeches, and gaiters, and drummed with his fingers on the counter until he was attended to. When he answered the shopboy's question, 'What can I have the pleasure of showing you today, Sir?' I saw Miss Matilda start, and then suddenly sit down; and instantly I guessed who it was. She had made some inquiry which had to be carried round to the other shopman.

'Miss Jenkyns wants the black sarsenet two-and-twopence the yard'; and Mr Holbrook had caught the name, and was across the shop in two strides.

'Matty – Miss Matilda – Miss Jenkyns! God bless my soul! I should not have known you. How are you? how are you?' He kept shaking her hand in a way which proved the warmth of his friendship; but he repeated so often, as if to himself, 'I should not have known you!' that any sentimental romance which I might be inclined to build, was quite done away with by his manner.

However, he kept talking to us all the time we were in the shop; and then waving the shopman with the unpurchased gloves on one side, with 'Another time, sir! another time!' he walked home with us. I am happy to say my client, Miss Matilda, also left the shop in an equally bewildered state, not having purchased either green or red silk. Mr Holbrook was evidently full with honest, loud-spoken joy at meeting his old love again; he touched on the changes that had taken place; he even spoke of Miss Jenkyns as 'Your poor sister! Well, well! we have all our faults'; and bade us good-bye with many a hope that he should soon see Miss Matty again. She went straight to her room; and never came back till our early tea-time, when I thought she looked as if she had been crying.

CHAPTER IV

A VISIT TO AN OLD BACHELOR

A few days after, a note came from Mr Holbrook, asking us – impartially asking both of us – in a formal, old-fashioned style, to spend a day at his house – a long June day – for it was June now. He named that he had also invited his cousin, Miss Pole; so that we might join in a fly, which could be put up at his house.

I expected Miss Matty to jump at this invitation; but, no! Miss Pole and I had the greatest difficulty in persuading her to go. She thought it was improper; and was even half annoyed when we utterly ignored the idea of any impropriety in her going with two other ladies to see her old lover. Then came a more serious difficulty. She did not think Deborah would have liked her to go. This took us half a day's good hard talking to get over; but, at the first sentence of relenting, I seized the opportunity, and wrote and despatched an acceptance in her name – fixing day and hour, that all might be decided and done with.

The next morning she asked me if I would go down to the shop with her; and there, after much hesitation, we chose out three caps to be sent home and tried on, that the most becoming might be selected to take with us on Thursday.

She was in a state of silent agitation all the way to Woodley. She had evidently never been there before; and, although she little dreamt I knew anything of her early story, I could perceive she was in a tremor at the thought of seeing the place which might have been her home, and round which it is probable that many of her innocent girlish imaginations had clustered. It was a long drive there, through paved jolting lanes. Miss Matilda sate bolt upright, and looked wistfully out of the windows, as we drew near the end of our journey. The aspect of the country was quiet and pastoral. Woodley stood among fields; and there was an old-fashioned garden, where roses and currant-bushes touched each other, and where the feathery asparagus formed a pretty back-ground to the pinks and gilly-flowers; there was no drive up to the door: we got out at a little gate, and walked up a straight box-edged path.

'My cousin might make a drive, I think,' said Miss Pole, who was afraid of ear-ache, and had only her cap on.

'I think it is very pretty,' said Miss Matty, with a soft plaintiveness in her voice, and almost in a whisper; for just then Mr Holbrook appeared at the door, rubbing his hands in very effervescence of hospitality. He looked more like my idea of Don Quixote than ever, and yet the likeness was only external. His respectable housekeeper stood modestly at the door to bid us welcome; and, while she led the elder ladies upstairs to a bed-room, I begged to look about the garden. My request evidently pleased the old gentleman; who took me all round the place, and showed me his six-and-twenty cows, named after the different letters of the alphabet. As we went along, he surprised me occasionally by repeating apt and beautiful quotations from the poets, ranging easily from Shakspeare and George Herbert to those of our own day. He did this as naturally as if he were thinking aloud, that their true and beautiful words were the best expression he could find for what he was thinking or feeling. To be sure, he called Byron 'my lord Bўrron', and pronounced the name of Goethe strictly in accordance with the English sound of the letters – 'As Goëthe says, "Ye ever-verdant palaces",'[1] &c. Altogether, I never met with a man, before or since, who had spent so long a life in a secluded and not impressive country, with ever-increasing delight in the daily and yearly change of season and beauty.

When he and I went in, we found that dinner was nearly ready in the kitchen, – for so I suppose the room ought to be called, as there were oak dressers and cupboards all round, all over by the side of the fire-place, and only a small Turkey carpet in the middle of the flag-floor. The room might have been easily made into a handsome dark-oak dining-parlour, by removing the oven, and a few other appurtenances of a kitchen, which were evidently never used; the real cooking place being at some distance. The room in which we were expected to sit was a stiffly furnished, ugly apartment; but that in which we did sit was what Mr Holbrook called the counting-house, when he paid his labourers their weekly wages, at a great desk near the door. The rest of the pretty sitting-room – looking into the orchard, and all covered over with dancing tree-shadows – was filled with books. They lay on the ground, they covered the walls, they strewed the table. He was evidently half ashamed and half proud of his extravagance in this respect. They were of all kinds, – poetry, and wild weird tales prevailing. He evidently chose his books in accordance with his own tastes, not because such and such were classical, or established favourites.

'Ah!' he said, 'we farmers ought not to have much time for reading; yet somehow one can't help it.'

'What a pretty room!' said Miss Matty, *sotto voce.*

'What a pleasant place!' said I, aloud, almost simultaneously.

'Nay! if you like it,' – replied he; 'but can you sit on these great black leather three-cornered chairs? I like it better than the best parlour; but I thought ladies would take that for the smarter place.'

It was the smarter place; but, like most smart things, not at all pretty, or pleasant, or home-like; so, while we were at dinner, the servant-girl dusted and scrubbed the counting-house chairs, and we sate there all the rest of the day.

We had pudding before meat; and I thought Mr Holbrook was going to make some apology for his old-fashioned ways, for he began, –

'I don't know whether you like new-fangled ways.'[2]

'Oh! not at all!' said Miss Matty.

'No more do I,' said he. 'My housekeeper *will* have things in her new fashion; or else I tell her, that when I was a young man, we used to keep strictly to my father's rule, "No broth, no ball; no ball, no beef";[3] and always began dinner with broth. Then we had suet puddings, boiled in the broth with the beef; and then the meat itself. If we did not sup our broth, we had no ball, which we liked a deal better; and the beef came last of all, and only those had it who had done justice to the broth and the ball. Now folks begin with sweet things, and turn their dinners topsy-turvy.'

When the ducks and green peas came, we looked at each other in dismay; we had only two-pronged, black-handled forks.[4] It is true, the steel was as bright as silver; but what were we to do? Miss Matty picked up her peas, one by one, on the point of the prongs, much as Aminé ate her grains of rice after her previous feast with the Ghoul.[5] Miss Pole sighed over her delicate young peas as she left them on one side of her plate untasted; for they *would* drop between the prongs. I looked at my host: the peas were going wholesale into his capacious mouth, shovelled up by his large round-ended knife. I saw, I imitated, I survived![6] My friends, in spite of my precedent, could not muster up courage enough to do an ungenteel thing; and, if Mr Holbrook had not been so heartily hungry, he would probably have seen that the good peas went away almost untouched.

After dinner, a clay pipe was brought in, and a spittoon; and, asking us to retire to another room, where he would soon join us if we disliked tobacco-smoke, he presented his pipe to Miss Matty, and requested her to fill the bowl. This was a compliment to a lady in his youth; but it was rather inappropriate to propose it as an honour to Miss Matty, who had been trained by her sister to hold smoking of every kind in utter abhorrence. But if it was a shock to her refinement, it was also a gratification to her feelings to be thus selected; so she daintily stuffed the strong tobacco into the pipe; and then we withdrew.

'It is very pleasant dining with a bachelor,' said Miss Matty, softly, as we settled ourselves in the counting-house. 'I only hope it is not improper; so many pleasant things are!'

'What a number of books he has!' said Miss Pole, looking round the room. 'And how dusty they are!'

'I think it must be like one of the great Dr Johnson's rooms,' said Miss Matty. 'What a superior man your cousin must be!'

'Yes!' said Miss Pole; 'he's a great reader; but I am afraid he has got into very uncouth habits with living alone.'

'Oh! uncouth is too hard a word. I should call him eccentric; very clever people always are!' replied Miss Matty.

When Mr Holbrook returned, he proposed a walk in the fields; but the two elder ladies were afraid of damp, and dirt; and had only very unbecoming calashes to put on over their caps; so they declined; and I was again his companion in a turn which he said he was obliged to take, to see after his men. He strode along, either wholly forgetting my existence, or soothed into silence by his pipe – and yet it was not silence exactly. He walked before me, with a stooping gait, his hands clasped behind him; and, as some tree or cloud, or glimpse of distant upland pastures, struck him, he quoted poetry to himself; saying it out loud in a grand sonorous voice, with just the emphasis that true feeling and appreciation give. We came upon an old cedar-tree, which stood at one end of the house;

'The cedar spreads his dark-green layers of shade.'[7]

'Capital term – "layers"! Wonderful man!' I did not know whether he was speaking to me or not; but I put in an assenting 'wonderful', although I knew nothing about it; just because I was tired of being forgotten, and of being consequently silent.

He turned sharp round. 'Aye! you may say "wonderful". Why, when I saw the review of his poems in "Blackwood"[8] I set off within an hour, and walked seven miles to Misselton (for the horses were not in the way) and ordered them. Now, what colour are ash-buds in March?'

Is the man going mad? thought I. He is very like Don Quixote.

'What colour are they, I say?' repeated he vehemently.

'I am sure I don't know, sir,' said I, with the meekness of ignorance.

'I knew you didn't. No more did I – an old fool that I am! till this young man comes and tells me. Black as ash-buds in March. And I've lived all my life in the country; more shame for me not to know. Black: they are jet-black, madam.' And he went off again, swinging along to the music of some rhyme he had got hold of.

When we came back, nothing would serve him but he must

read us the poems he had been speaking of; and Miss Pole
encouraged him in his proposal, I thought, because she wished
me to hear his beautiful reading, of which she had boasted; but
she afterwards said it was because she had got to a difficult part
of her crochet, and wanted to count her stitches without having to talk. Whatever he had proposed would have been right
to Miss Matty; although she did fall sound asleep within five
minutes after he had begun a long poem, called 'Locksley Hall',[9]
and had a comfortable nap, unobserved, till he ended; when
the cessation of his voice wakened her up, and she said, feeling
that something was expected, and that Miss Pole was counting:–

'What a pretty book!'

'Pretty! madam! it's beautiful! Pretty, indeed!'

'Oh yes! I meant beautiful!' said she, fluttered at his dis-
approval of her word. 'It is so like that beautiful poem of Dr
Johnson's my sister used to read – I forget the name of it, what
was it, my dear?' turning to me.

'Which do you mean, ma'am? What was it about?'

'I don't remember what it was about, and I've quite forgotten
what the name of it was; but it was written by Dr Johnson, and
was very beautiful, and very like what Mr Holbrook has just
been reading.'

'I don't remember it,' said he, reflectively. 'But I don't know
Dr Johnson's poems well. I must read them.'

As we were getting into the fly to return, I heard Mr Holbrook
say he should call on the ladies soon,[10] and inquire how
they got home; and this evidently pleased and fluttered Miss
Matty at the time he said it; but after we had lost sight of
the old house among the trees, her sentiments towards the
master of it were gradually absorbed into a distressing wonder
as to whether Martha had broken her word, and seized on
the opportunity of her mistress's absence to have a 'follower'.
Martha looked good, and steady, and composed enough, as she
came to help us out; she was always careful of Miss Matty, and
tonight she made use of this unlucky speech:–

'Eh! dear ma'am, to think of your going out in an evening
in such a thin shawl! It is no better than muslin. At your age,
ma'am, you should be careful.'

'My age!' said Miss Matty, almost speaking crossly, for her; for she was usually gentle. 'My age! Why, how old do you think I am, that you talk about my age?'

'Well, ma'am! I should say you were not far short of sixty; but folks' looks is often against them – and I'm sure I meant no harm.'

'Martha, I'm not yet fifty-two!' said Miss Matty, with grave emphasis; for probably the remembrance of her youth had come very vividly before her this day, and she was annoyed at finding that golden time so far away in the past.

But she never spoke of any former and more intimate acquaintance with Mr Holbrook. She had probably met with so little sympathy in her early love, that she had shut it up close in her heart; and it was only by a sort of watching, which I could hardly avoid, since Miss Pole's confidence, that I saw how faithful her poor heart had been in its sorrow and its silence.

She gave me some good reason for wearing her best cap every day, and sate near the window, in spite of her rheumatism, in order to see, without being seen, down into the street.

He came. He put his open palms upon his knees, which were far apart, as he sate with his head bent down, whistling, after we had replied to his inquiries about our safe return. Suddenly, he jumped up.

'Well, madam! have you any commands for Paris? I am going there in a week or two.'

'To Paris!' we both exclaimed.

'Yes, madam! I've never been there, and always had a wish to go; and I think if I don't go soon, I mayn't go at all; so as soon as the hay is got in I shall go, before harvest-time.'

We were so much astonished, that we had no commissions.

Just as he was going out of the room, he turned back, with his favourite exclamation:

'God bless my soul, madam! but I nearly forgot half my errand. Here are the poems for you, you admired so much the other evening at my house.' He tugged away at a parcel in his coat-pocket. 'Good-bye, miss,' said he; 'good-bye, Matty! take care of yourself.' And he was gone. But he had given her a book, and he had called her Matty, just as he used to do thirty years ago.

'I wish he would not go to Paris,' said Miss Matilda, anxiously. 'I don't believe frogs will agree with him; he used to have to be very careful what he ate, which was curious in so strong-looking a young man.'

Soon after this I took my leave, giving many an injunction to Martha to look after her mistress, and to let me know if she thought that Miss Matilda was not so well; in which case I would volunteer a visit to my old friend, without noticing Martha's intelligence to her.

Accordingly I received a line or two from Martha every now and then; and, about November, I had a note to say her mistress was 'very low and sadly off her food'; and the account made me so uneasy, that, although Martha did not decidedly summon me, I packed up my things and went.

I received a warm welcome, in spite of the little flurry produced by my impromptu visit, for I had only been able to give a day's notice. Miss Matilda looked miserably ill; and I prepared to comfort and cosset her.

I went down to have a private talk with Martha.

'How long has your mistress been so poorly?' I asked, as I stood by the kitchen fire.

'Well! I think it's better than a fortnight; it is, I know: it was one Tuesday, after Miss Pole had been, that she went into this moping way. I thought she was tired, and it would go off with a night's rest; but, no! she has gone on and on ever since, till I thought it my duty to write to you, ma'am.'

'You did quite right, Martha. It is a comfort to think she has so faithful a servant about her. And I hope you find your place comfortable?'

'Well, ma'am, missus is very kind, and there's plenty to eat and drink, and no more work but what I can do easily, – but' – Martha hesitated.

'But what, Martha?'

'Why, it seems so hard of missus not to let me have any followers; there's such lots of young fellows in the town; and many a one has as much as offered to keep company with me;

and I may never be in such a likely place again, and it's like wasting an opportunity. Many a girl as I know would have 'em unbeknownst to missus; but I've given my word, and I'll stick to it; or else this is just the house for missus never to be the wiser if they did come: and it's such a capable kitchen – there's such good dark corners in it – I'd be bound to hide anyone. I counted up last Sunday night – for I'll not deny I was crying because I had to shut the door in Jem Hearn's face; and he's a steady young man, fit for any girl; only I had given missus my word.' Martha was all but crying again; and I had little comfort to give her, for I knew, from old experience, of the horror with which both the Miss Jenkynses looked upon 'followers'; and in Miss Matty's present nervous state this dread was not likely to be lessened.

I went to see Miss Pole the next day, and took her completely by surprise; for she had not been to see Miss Matilda for two days.

'And now I must go back with you, my dear, for I promised to let her know how Thomas Holbrook went on; and I'm sorry to say his housekeeper has sent me word today that he hasn't long to live. Poor Thomas! That journey to Paris was quite too much for him. His housekeeper says he has hardly ever been round his fields since; but just sits with his hands on his knees in the counting-house, not reading or anything, but only saying, what a wonderful city Paris was! Paris has much to answer for, if it's killed my cousin Thomas, for a better man never lived.'

'Does Miss Matilda know of his illness?' asked I; – a new light as to the cause of her indisposition dawning upon me.

'Dear! to be sure, yes! Has not she told you? I let her know a fortnight ago, or more, when first I heard of it. How odd, she shouldn't have told you!'

Not at all, I thought; but I did not say anything. I felt almost guilty of having spied too curiously into that tender heart, and I was not going to speak of its secrets, – hidden, Miss Matty believed, from all the world. I ushered Miss Pole into Miss Matilda's little drawing-room; and then left them alone. But I was not surprised when Martha came to my bed-room door, to ask me to go down to dinner alone, for that missus had one of her bad headaches. She came into the drawing-room at tea-time; but it was evidently an effort to her; and, as if to make up for some reproachful feeling against her late sister, Miss Jenkyns, which had been troubling her all the afternoon, and for which she now felt penitent, she kept telling me how good and how clever Deborah was in her youth; how she used to settle what gowns they were to wear at all the parties (faint, ghostly ideas of dim parties far away in the distance, when Miss Matty and Miss Pole were young!); and how Deborah and her mother had started the benefit society for the poor, and taught girls cooking and plain sewing; and how Deborah had once danced with a lord; and how she used to visit at Sir Peter Arley's, and try to remodel the quiet rectory establishment on the plans of Arley Hall, where they kept thirty servants; and how she had nursed Miss Matty through a long, long illness, of which I had never heard before, but which I now dated in my own mind as following the dismissal of the suit of Mr Holbrook. So we talked softly and quietly of old times, through the long November evening.

The next day Miss Pole brought us word that Mr Holbrook was dead. Miss Matty heard the news in silence; in fact, from the account of the previous day, it was only what we had to expect. Miss Pole kept calling upon us for some expression of regret, by asking if it was not sad that he was gone: and saying,

'To think of that pleasant day last June, when he seemed so well! And he might have lived this dozen years if he had not gone to that wicked Paris,[11] where they are always having Revolutions.'

She paused for some demonstration on our part. I saw Miss Matty could not speak, she was trembling so nervously; so I said what I really felt: and after a call of some duration – all the time of which I have no doubt Miss Pole thought Miss Matty received the news very calmly – our visitor took her leave. But the effort at self-control Miss Matty had made to conceal her feelings – a concealment she practised even with me, for she has never alluded to Mr Holbrook again, although the book he gave her lies with her Bible on the little table by her bedside; she did not think I heard her when she asked the little milliner of Cranford to make her caps something like the Honourable Mrs Jamieson's, or that I noticed the reply –

'But she wears widows' caps, ma'am?'

'Oh! I only meant something in that style; not widows', of course, but rather like Mrs Jamieson's.'

This effort at concealment was the beginning of the tremulous motion of head and hands which I have seen ever since in Miss Matty.

The evening of the day on which we heard of Mr Holbrook's death, Miss Matilda was very silent and thoughtful; after prayers she called Martha back, and then she stood uncertain what to say.

'Martha!' she said at last; 'you are young,' – and then she made so long a pause that Martha, to remind her of her half-finished sentence, dropped a curtsey, and said –

'Yes, please, ma'am; two-and-twenty last third of October, please, ma'am.'

'And perhaps, Martha, you may some time meet with a young man you like, and who likes you. I did say you were not to have followers; but if you meet with such a young man, and tell me, and I find he is respectable, I have no objection to his coming to see you once a week. God forbid!' said she, in a low voice, 'that I should grieve any young hearts.' She spoke as if she were providing for some distant contingency, and was rather startled when Martha made her ready eager answer:–

'Please, ma'am, there's Jem Hearn, and he's a joiner, making three-and-sixpence a-day, and six foot one in his stocking-feet, please, ma'am; and if you'll ask about him tomorrow morning, everyone will give him a character for steadiness; and he'll be glad enough to come tomorrow night, I'll be bound.'

Though Miss Matty was startled, she submitted to Fate and Love.

CHAPTER V

OLD LETTERS

I have often noticed that almost everyone has his own individual small economies – careful habits of saving fractions of pennies in some one peculiar direction – any disturbance of which annoys him more than spending shillings or pounds on some real extravagance. An old gentleman of my acquaintance, who took the intelligence of the failure of a Joint-Stock Bank,[1] in which some of his money was invested, with stoical mildness, worried his family all through a long summer's day, because one of them had torn (instead of cutting) out the written leaves of his now useless bank-book; of course, the corresponding pages at the other end came out as well; and this little unnecessary waste of paper (his private economy) chafed him more than all the loss of his money. Envelopes fretted his soul terribly when they first came in;[2] the only way in which he could reconcile himself to such waste of his cherished article was by patiently turning inside out all that were sent to him, and so making them serve again. Even now, though tamed by age, I see him casting wistful glances at his daughters when they send a whole instead of a half sheet of note-paper, with the three lines of acceptance to an invitation, written on only one of the sides. I am not above owning that I have this human weakness myself. String is my foible. My pockets get full of little hanks of it, picked up and twisted together, ready for uses that never come. I am seriously annoyed if anyone cuts the string of a parcel, instead of patiently and faithfully undoing it fold by fold. How people can bring themselves to use Indian-rubber rings, which are a sort of deification of string, as lightly as they do, I cannot imagine. To me an Indian-rubber ring is a precious

treasure. I have one which is not new; one that I picked up off
the floor, nearly six years ago. I have really tried to use it; but
my heart failed me, and I could not commit the extravagance.

Small pieces of butter grieve others. They cannot attend
to conversation, because of the annoyance occasioned by the
habit which some people have of invariably taking more butter than they want. Have you not seen the anxious look (almost
mesmeric) which such persons fix on the article? They would
feel it a relief if they might bury it out of their sight, by popping it into their own mouths, and swallowing it down; and
they are really made happy if the person on whose plate it lies
unused, suddenly breaks off a piece of toast (which he does not
want at all) and eats up his butter. They think that this is not
waste.

Now Miss Matty Jenkyns was chary of candles. We had
many devices to use as few as possible. In the winter afternoons
she would sit knitting for two or three hours; she could do this
in the dark, or by fire-light; and when I asked if I might not
ring for candles to finish stitching my wristbands, she told me
to 'keep blind man's holiday'.[3] They were usually brought
in with tea; but we only burnt one at a time. As we lived
in constant preparation for a friend who might come in, any
evening (but who never did), it required some contrivance to
keep our two candles of the same length, ready to be lighted,
and to look as if we burnt two always. The candles took it in
turns; and, whatever we might be talking about or doing, Miss
Matty's eyes were habitually fixed upon the candle, ready to
jump up and extinguish it, and to light the other before they
had become too uneven in length to be restored to equality in
the course of the evening.

One night, I remember that this candle economy particularly
annoyed me. I had been very much tired of my compulsory
'blind-man's holiday', – especially as Miss Matty had fallen
asleep, and I did not like to stir the fire, and run the risk of
awakening her; so I could not even sit on the rug, and scorch
myself with sewing by fire-light, according to my usual custom.
I fancied Miss Matty must be dreaming of her early life; for she
spoke one or two words, in her uneasy sleep, bearing reference

to persons who were dead long before. When Martha brought
in the lighted candle and tea, Miss Matty started into wakeful-
ness, with a strange bewildered look around, as if we were not
the people she expected to see about her. There was a little sad
expression that shadowed her face as she recognised me; but
immediately afterwards she tried to give me her usual smile. All
through tea-time, her talk ran upon the days of her childhood
and youth. Perhaps this reminded her of the desirableness of
looking over all the old family letters, and destroying such as
ought not to be allowed to fall into the hands of strangers; for
she had often spoken of the necessity of this task, but had
always shrunk from it, with a timid dread of something painful.
Tonight, however, she rose up after tea, and went for them –
in the dark; for she piqued herself on the precise neatness of all
her chamber arrangements, and used to look uneasily at me,
when I lighted a bed-candle to go to another room for anything.
When she returned, there was a faint pleasant smell of Tonquin
beans in the room. I had always noticed this scent about any of
the things which had belonged to her mother; and many of the
letters were addressed to her – yellow bundles of love-letters,
sixty or seventy years old.

Miss Matty undid the packet with a sigh; but she stifled
it directly, as if it were hardly right to regret the flight of time,
or of life either. We agreed to look them over separately,
each taking a different letter out of the same bundle, and
describing its contents to the other, before destroying it. I never
knew what sad work the reading of old letters was before that
evening, though I could hardly tell why. The letters were as
happy as letters could be – at least those early letters were.
There was in them a vivid and intense sense of the present time,
which seemed so strong and full, as if it could never pass away,
and as if the warm, living hearts that so expressed themselves
could never die, and be as nothing to the sunny earth. I should
have felt less melancholy, I believe, if the letters had been more
so. I saw the tears quietly stealing down the well-worn furrows
of Miss Matty's cheeks, and her spectacles often wanted wiping.
I trusted at last that she would light the other candle, for my
own eyes were rather dim, and I wanted more light to see the

pale, faded ink; but no – even through her tears, she saw and remembered her little economical ways.

The earliest set of letters were two bundles tied together, and ticketed (in Miss Jenkyns's handwriting), 'Letters interchanged between my ever-honoured father and my dearly-beloved mother, prior to their marriage, in July, 1774.'[4] I should guess that the Rector of Cranford was about twenty-seven years of age when he wrote those letters; and Miss Matty told me that her mother was just eighteen at the time of her wedding. With my idea of the Rector, derived from a picture in the dining-parlour, stiff and stately, in a huge full-bottomed wig, with gown, cassock, and bands, and his hand upon a copy of the only sermon he ever published, – it was strange to read these letters. They were full of eager, passionate ardour; short homely sentences, right fresh from the heart; (very different from the grand Latinised, Johnsonian style of the printed sermon, preached before some judge at assize time). His letters were a curious contrast to those of his girl-bride. She was evidently rather annoyed at his demands upon her for expressions of love, and could not quite understand what he meant by repeating the same thing over in so many different ways; but what she was quite clear about was her longing for a white 'Paduasoy', – whatever that might be; and six or seven letters were principally occupied in asking her lover to use his influence with her parents (who evidently kept her in good order) to obtain this or that article of dress, more especially the white 'Paduasoy'. He cared nothing how she was dressed; she was always lovely enough for him, as he took pains to assure her, when she begged him to express in his answers a predilection for particular pieces of finery, in order that she might show what he said to her parents. But at length he seemed to find out that she would not be married till she had a 'trousseau' to her mind; and then he sent her a letter, which had evidently accompanied a whole box full of finery, and in which he requested that she might be dressed in everything her heart desired. This was the first letter, ticketed in a frail, delicate hand, 'From my dearest John'. Shortly afterwards they were married, – I suppose, from the intermission in their correspondence.

'We must burn them, I think,' said Miss Matty, looking doubtfully at me. 'No one will care for them when I am gone.' And one by one she dropped them into the middle of the fire; watching each blaze up, die out, and rise away, in faint, white, ghostly semblance, up the chimney, before she gave up another to the same fate. The room was light enough now; but I, like her, was fascinated into watching the destruction of those letters, into which the honest warmth of a manly heart had been poured forth.

The next letter, likewise docketed by Miss Jenkyns, was endorsed, 'Letter of pious congratulation and exhortation from my venerable grandfather to my mother, on occasion of my own birth. Also some practical remarks on the desirability of keeping warm the extremities of infants, from my excellent grandmother.'

The first part was, indeed, a severe and forcible picture of the responsibilities of mothers, and a warning against the evils that were in the world, and lying in ghastly wait for the little baby of two days old. His wife did not write, said the old gentleman, because he had forbidden it, she being indisposed with a sprained ankle, which (he said) quite incapacitated her from holding a pen. However, at the foot of the page was a small 'T.O.', and on turning it over, sure enough, there was a letter to 'my dear, dearest Molly', begging her, when she left her room, whatever she did, to go *up* stairs before going *down*: and telling her to wrap her baby's feet up in flannel, and keep it warm by the fire, although it was summer, for babies were so tender.

It was pretty to see from the letters, which were evidently exchanged with some frequency, between the young mother and the grandmother, how the girlish vanity was being weeded out of her heart by love for her baby. The white 'Paduasoy' figured again in the letters, with almost as much vigour as before. In one, it was being made into a christening cloak for the baby. It decked it when it went with its parents to spend a day or two at Arley Hall. It added to its charms when it was 'the prettiest little baby that ever was seen. Dear mother, I wish you could see her! Without any parshality, I do think she will grow up a regular bewty!' I thought of Miss Jenkyns, grey, withered, and wrinkled; and I wondered if her mother had known her in the courts of heaven; and then I knew that she had, and that they stood there in angelic guise.

There was a great gap before any of the Rector's letters appeared. And then his wife had changed her mode of endorsement. It was no longer from 'My dearest John'; it was from 'My honoured Husband'. The letters were written on occasion of the publication of the same Sermon which was represented in the picture. The preaching before 'My Lord Judge', and the 'publishing by request', was evidently the culminating point – the event of his life. It had been necessary for him to go up to London to superintend it through the press. Many friends had to be called upon, and consulted, before he could decide on any printer fit for so onerous a task; and at length it was arranged that J. and J. Rivingtons[5] were to have the honourable responsibility. The worthy Rector seemed to be strung up by the occasion to a high literary pitch, for he could hardly write a letter to his wife without cropping out into Latin. I remember the end of one of his letters ran thus: – 'I shall ever hold the virtuous qualities of my Molly in remembrance, *dum memor ipse mei, dum spiritus regit artus*',[6] which, considering that the English of his correspondent was sometimes at fault in grammar, and often in spelling, might be taken as a proof of how much he 'idealised' his Molly; and, as Miss Jenkyns used to say, 'People talk a great deal about idealising now-a-days, whatever that may mean.' But this was nothing to a fit of writing classical poetry, which soon seized him; in which his Molly figured away as 'Maria'. The letter containing the *carmen* was endorsed by her, 'Hebrew verses sent me by my honoured husband. I thowt to have had a letter about killing the pig, but must wait. Mem., to send the poetry to Sir Peter Arley, as my husband desires.' And in a post-scriptum note in his handwriting, it was stated that the Ode had appeared in the 'Gentleman's Magazine',[7] December, 1782.

Her letters back to her husband (treasured as fondly by him as if they had been M. T. Ciceronis Epistolae)[8] were more satisfactory to an absent husband and father, than his could

ever have been to her. She told him how Deborah sewed her
seam very neatly every day, and read to her in the books he had
set her; how she was a very 'forrard', good child, but *would*
ask questions her mother could not answer; but how she did
not let herself down by saying she did not know, but took to
stirring the fire, or sending the 'forrard' child on an errand.
Matty was now the mother's darling, and promised (like her
sister at her age) to be a great beauty. I was reading this aloud
to Miss Matty, who smiled and sighed a little at the hope, so
fondly expressed, that 'little Matty might not be vain, even if
she were a beauty'.

'I had very pretty hair, my dear,' said Miss Matilda; 'and not
a bad mouth.' And I saw her soon afterwards adjust her cap
and draw herself up.

But to return to Mrs Jenkyns's letters. She told her husband
about the poor in the parish; what homely domestic medicines
she had administered; what kitchen physic she had sent. She
had evidently held his displeasure as a rod in pickle over the
heads of all the ne'er-do-wells. She asked for his directions
about the cows and pigs; and did not always obtain them, as
I have shown before.

The kind old grandmother was dead, when a little boy was
born, soon after the publication of the Sermon; but there was
another letter of exhortation from the grandfather, more stringent and admonitory than ever, now that there was a boy to be
guarded from the snares of the world. He described all the
various sins into which men might fall, until I wondered how
any man ever came to a natural death. The gallows seemed as
if it must have been the termination of the lives of most of the
grandfather's friends and acquaintance; and I was not surprised
at the way in which he spoke of this life being 'a vale of tears'.[9]

It seemed curious that I should never have heard of this
brother before; but I concluded that he had died young; or else
surely his name would have been alluded to by his sisters.

By-and-by we came to packets of Miss Jenkyns's letters.
These, Miss Matty did regret to burn. She said all the others
had been only interesting to those who loved the writers; and
that it seemed as if it would have hurt her to allow them to fall

into the hands of strangers, who had not known her dear
mother, and how good she was, although she did not always
spell quite in the modern fashion; but Deborah's letters were
so very superior! Anyone might profit by reading them. It was
a long time since she had read Mrs Chapone, but she knew she
used to think that Deborah could have said the same things
quite as well; and as for Mrs Carter! people thought a deal of
her letters, just because she had written Epictetus,[10] but she was
quite sure Deborah would never have made use of such a
common expression as 'I canna be fashed!'

Miss Matty did grudge burning these letters, it was evident.
She would not let them be carelessly passed over with any
quiet reading, and skipping, to myself. She took them from me,
and even lighted the second candle in order to read them aloud
with a proper emphasis, and without stumbling over the big
words. Oh dear! how I wanted facts instead of reflections,
before those letters were concluded! They lasted us two nights;
and I won't deny that I made use of the time to think of many
other things, and yet I was always at my post at the end of each
sentence.

The Rector's letters, and those of his wife and mother-in-law,
had all been tolerably short and pithy, written in a straight
hand, with the lines very close together. Sometimes the whole
letter was contained on a mere scrap of paper. The paper was
very yellow, and the ink very brown; some of the sheets were
(as Miss Matty made me observe) the old original Post, with
the stamp in the corner, representing a post-boy riding for life
and twanging his horn.[11] The letters of Mrs Jenkyns and her
mother were fastened with a great round, red wafer; for it was
before Miss Edgeworth's 'Patronage' had banished wafers from
polite society.[12] It was evident, from the tenor of what was said,
that franks were in great request, and were even used as a
means of paying debts by needy Members of Parliament.[13] The
Rector sealed his epistles with an immense coat of arms, and
showed by the care with which he had performed this ceremony,
that he expected they should be cut open, not broken by any
thoughtless or impatient hand. Now, Miss Jenkyns's letters
were of a later date in form and writing. She wrote on the

square sheet, which we have learned to call old-fashioned. Her hand was admirably calculated, together with her use of many-syllabled words, to fill up a sheet, and then came the pride and delight of crossing.[14] Poor Miss Matty got sadly puzzled with this, for the words gathered size like snow-balls, and towards the end of her letter, Miss Jenkyns used to become quite sesquipedalian. In one to her father, slightly theological and controversial in its tone, she had spoken of Herod, Tetrarch of Idumea. Miss Matty read it 'Herod Petrach of Etruriae,'[15] and was just as well pleased as if she had been right.

I can't quite remember the date, but I think it was in 1805 that Miss Jenkyns wrote the longest series of letters; on occasion of her absence on a visit to some friends near Newcastle-upon-Tyne. These friends were intimate with the commandant of the garrison there, and heard from him of all the preparations that were being made to repel the invasion of Buonaparte,[16] which some people imagined might take place at the mouth of the Tyne. Miss Jenkyns was evidently very much alarmed; and the first part of her letters was often written in pretty intelligible English, conveying particulars of the preparations which were made in the family with whom she was residing against the dreaded event; the bundles of clothes that were packed up ready for a flight to Alston Moor (a wild hilly piece of ground between Northumberland and Cumberland); the signal that was to be given for this flight, and for the simultaneous turning out of the volunteers under arms; which said signal was to consist (if I remember rightly) in ringing the church bells in a particular and ominous manner. One day, when Miss Jenkyns and her hosts were at a dinner-party in Newcastle, this warning-summons was actually given (not a very wise proceeding, if there be any truth in the moral attached to the fable of the Boy and the Wolf;[17] but so it was), and Miss Jenkyns, hardly recovered from her fright, wrote the next day to describe the sound, the breathless shock, the hurry and alarm; and then, taking breath, she added, 'How trivial, my dear father, do all our apprehensions of the last evening appear, at the present moment, to calm and inquiring minds!' And here Miss Matty broke in with – 'But, indeed, my dear, they were not at all trivial or trifling at the time. I know I used to wake up in the night many a time, and think I heard the tramp of the French entering Cranford. Many people talked of hiding themselves in the salt-mines;[18] – and meat would have kept capitally down there, only perhaps we should have been thirsty. And my father preached a whole set of sermons on the occasion; one set in the mornings, all about David and Goliath, to spirit up the people to fighting with spades or bricks, if need were; and the other set in the afternoons, proving that Napoleon (that was another name for Bony, as we used to call him) was all the same as an Apollyon and Abaddon.[19] I remember, my father rather thought he should be asked to print this last set; but the parish had, perhaps, had enough of them with hearing.'

Peter Marmaduke Arley Jenkyns, ('poor Peter!' as Miss Matty began to call him) was at school at Shrewsbury by this time. The Rector took up his pen, and rubbed up his Latin, once more, to correspond with his boy. It was very clear that the lad's were what are called show-letters. They were of a highly mental description, giving an account of his studies, and his intellectual hopes of various kinds, with an occasional quotation from the classics; but, now and then, the animal nature broke out in such a little sentence as this, evidently written in a trembling hurry, after the letter had been inspected: 'Mother, dear, do send me a cake, and put plenty of citron in.' The 'mother, dear', probably answered her boy in the form of cakes and 'goody', for there were none of her letters among this set; but a whole collection of the Rector's, to whom the Latin in his boy's letters was like a trumpet to the old war-horse. I do not know much about Latin, certainly, and it is, perhaps, an ornamental language; but not very useful, I think – at least to judge from the bits I remember out of the Rector's letters. One was: 'You have not got that town in your map of Ireland; but *Bonus Bernardus non videt omnia*,[20] as the Proverbia say.' Presently it became very evident that 'poor Peter' got himself into many scrapes. There were letters of stilted penitence to his father, for some wrong-doing; and, among them all, was a badly written, badly-sealed, badly-directed, blotted note – 'My dear, dear, dear, dearest mother, I will be a better boy – I will, indeed; but don't, please, be ill for me; I am not worth it; but I will be good, darling mother.'

Miss Matty could not speak for crying, after she had read this note. She gave it to me in silence, and then got up and took it to her sacred recesses in her own room, for fear, by any chance, it might get burnt. 'Poor Peter!' she said; 'he was always in scrapes; he was too easy. They led him wrong, and then left him in the lurch. But he was too fond of mischief. He could never resist a joke. Poor Peter!'

CHAPTER VI

POOR PETER

Poor Peter's career[1] lay before him rather pleasantly mapped out by kind friends, but *Bonus Bernardus non videt omnia*, in this map too. He was to win honours at Shrewsbury School, and carry them thick to Cambridge, and after that, a living awaited him, the gift of his godfather, Sir Peter Arley. Poor Peter! his lot in life was very different to what his friends had hoped and planned. Miss Matty told me all about it, and I think it was a relief to her when she had done so.

He was the darling of his mother, who seemed to dote on all her children, though she was, perhaps, a little afraid of Deborah's superior acquirements. Deborah was the favourite of her father, and when Peter disappointed him, she became his pride. The sole honour Peter brought away from Shrewsbury, was the reputation of being the best good fellow that ever was, and of being the captain of the school in the art of practical joking. His father was disappointed, but set about remedying the matter in a manly way. He could not afford to send Peter to read with any tutor, but he could read with him himself; and Miss Matty told me much of the awful preparations in the way of dictionaries and lexicons that were made in her father's study the morning Peter began.

'My poor mother!' said she. 'I remember how she used to stand in the hall, just near enough to the study-door to catch the tone of my father's voice. I could tell in a moment if all was going right, by her face. And it did go right for a long time.'

'What went wrong at last?' said I. 'That tiresome Latin, I dare say.'

'No! it was not the Latin. Peter was in high favour with my father, for he worked up well for him. But he seemed to think that the Cranford people might be joked about, and made fun of, and they did not like it; nobody does. He was always hoaxing them; "hoaxing" is not a pretty word,[2] my dear, and I hope you won't tell your father I used it, for I should not like him to think that I was not choice in my language, after living with such a woman as Deborah. And be sure you never use it yourself. I don't know how it slipped out of my mouth, except it was that I was thinking of poor Peter, and it was always his expression. But he was a very gentlemanly boy in many things. He was like dear Captain Brown in always being ready to help any old person or a child. Still, he did like joking and making fun; and he seemed to think the old ladies in Cranford would believe anything. There were many old ladies living here then; we are principally ladies now, I know; but we are not so old as the ladies used to be when I was a girl. I could laugh to think of some of Peter's jokes. No! my dear, I won't tell you of them, because they might not shock you as they ought to do; and they were very shocking. He even took in my father once, by dressing himself up as a lady that was passing through the town and wished to see the Rector of Cranford, "who had published that admirable Assize Sermon". Peter said, he was awfully frightened himself when he saw how my father took it all in, and even offered to copy out all his Napoleon Buonaparte sermons[3] for her – him, I mean – no, her, for Peter was a lady then. He told me he was more terrified than he ever was before, all the time my father was speaking. He did not think my father would have believed him; and yet if he had not, it would have been a sad thing for Peter. As it was, he was none so glad of it, for my father kept him hard at work copying out all those twelve Buonaparte sermons for the lady – that was for Peter himself, you know. He was the lady. And once when he wanted to go fishing, Peter said, "Confound the woman!" – very bad language, my dear; but Peter was not always so guarded as he should have been; my father was so angry with him, it nearly frightened me out of my wits: and yet I could hardly keep from laughing at the little curtsies Peter kept making, quite slyly, whenever my father spoke of the lady's excellent taste and sound discrimination.'

'Did Miss Jenkyns know of these tricks?' said I.

'Oh no! Deborah would have been too much shocked. No! no one knew but me. I wish I had always known of Peter's plans; but sometimes he did not tell me. He used to say, the old ladies in the town wanted something to talk about; but I don't think they did. They had the "St James's Chronicle"[4] three times a-week, just as we have now, and we have plenty to say; and I remember the clacking noise there always was when some of the ladies got together. But, probably, school-boys talk more than ladies. At last there was a terrible sad thing happened.' Miss Matty got up, went to the door, and opened it; no one was there. She rang the bell for Martha; and when Martha came, her mistress told her to go for eggs to a farm at the other end of the town.

'I will lock the door after you, Martha. You are not afraid to go, are you?'

'No, ma'am, not at all; Jem Hearn will be only too proud to go with me.'

Miss Matty drew herself up, and, as soon as we were alone, she wished that Martha had more maidenly reserve.

'We'll put out the candle, my dear. We can talk just as well by fire-light, you know. There! well! you see, Deborah had gone from home for a fortnight or so; it was a very still, quiet day, I remember, overhead; and the lilacs were all in flower, so I suppose it was spring. My father had gone out to see some sick people in the parish; I recollect seeing him leave the house, with his wig and shovel-hat, and cane. What possessed our poor Peter I don't know; he had the sweetest temper, and yet he always seemed to like to plague Deborah. She never laughed at his jokes, and thought him ungenteel, and not careful enough about improving his mind; and that vexed him.

'Well! he went to her room, it seems, and dressed himself in her old gown, and shawl, and bonnet; just the things she used to wear in Cranford, and was known by everywhere; and he made the pillow into a little – you are sure you locked the door, my dear, for I should not like anyone to hear – into – into – a little baby, with white long clothes. It was only, as he told me afterwards, to make something to talk about in the town: he never thought of it as affecting Deborah. And he went and walked up and down in the Filbert walk – just half hidden by the rails, and half seen; and he cuddled his pillow, just like a baby; and talked to it all the nonsense people do. Oh dear! and my father came stepping stately up the street, as he always did; and what should he see but a little black crowd of people – I dare say as many as twenty – all peeping through his garden rails. So he thought, at first, they were only looking at a new rhododendron[5] that was in full bloom, and that he was very proud of; and he walked slower, that they might have more time to admire. And he wondered if he could make out a sermon from the occasion, and thought, perhaps, there was some relation between the rhododendrons and the lilies of the field.[6] My poor father! When he came nearer, he began to wonder that they did not see him; but their heads were all so close together, peeping and peeping! My father was amongst them, meaning, he said, to ask them to walk into the garden with him, and admire the beautiful vegetable[7] production, when – oh, my dear! I tremble to think of it – he looked through the rails himself, and saw – I don't know what he thought he saw, but old Clare told me his face went quite grey-white with anger, and his eyes blazed out under his frowning black brows; and he spoke out – oh, so terribly! – and bade them all stop where they were – not one of them to go, not one to stir a step; and, swift as light, he was in at the garden door, and down the Filbert walk, and seized hold of poor Peter, and tore his clothes off his back – bonnet, shawl, gown, and all – and threw the pillow among the people over the railings: and then he was very, very angry indeed; and before all the people he lifted up his cane, and flogged Peter!

'My dear! that boy's trick, on that sunny day, when all seemed going straight and well, broke my mother's heart, and changed my father for life. It did, indeed. Old Clare said, Peter looked as white as my father; and stood as still as a statue to be flogged; and my father struck hard! When my father stopped to take breath, Peter said, "Have you done enough, Sir?" quite hoarsely, and still standing quite quiet. I don't know what my father said – or if he said anything. But old Clare said, Peter turned to where the people outside the railing were, and made them a low bow, as grand and as grave as any gentleman; and then walked slowly into the house. I was in the store-room helping my mother to make cowslip-wine. I cannot abide the wine now, nor the scent of the flowers; they turn me sick and faint, as they did that day, when Peter came in, looking as haughty as any man – indeed, looking like a man, not like a boy. "Mother!" he said, "I am come to say, God bless you for ever." I saw his lips quiver as he spoke; and I think he durst not say anything more loving, for the purpose that was in his heart. She looked at him rather frightened, and wondering, and asked him what was to do? He did not smile or speak, but put his arms round her, and kissed her as if he did not know how to leave off; and before she could speak again, he was gone. We talked it over, and could not understand it, and she bade me go and seek my father, and ask what it was all about. I found him walking up and down, looking very highly displeased.

'"Tell your mother I have flogged Peter, and that he richly deserved it."

'I durst not ask any more questions. When I told my mother, she sat down, quite faint, for a minute. I remember, a few days after, I saw the poor, withered cowslip-flowers thrown out to the leaf-heap, to decay and die there. There was no making of cowslip-wine that year at the Rectory – nor, indeed, ever after.

'Presently, my mother went to my father. I know I thought of Queen Esther and King Ahasuerus;[8] for my mother was very pretty and delicate-looking, and my father looked as terrible as King Ahasuerus. Some time after, they came out together; and then my mother told me what had happened, and that she was going up to Peter's room, at my father's desire – though she was not to tell Peter this – to talk the matter over with him. But no Peter was there. We looked over the house; no Peter was there! Even my father, who had not liked to join in the search at first, helped us before long. The Rectory was a very old house: steps up into a room, steps down into a room, all through. At first, my mother went calling low and soft – as if to reassure the poor boy – "Peter! Peter, dear! it's only me"; but, by-and-by, as the servants came back from the errands my father had sent them, in different directions, to find where Peter was – as we found he was not in the garden, nor the hayloft, nor anywhere about – my mother's cry grew louder and wilder – "Peter! Peter, my darling! where are you?" for then she felt and understood that that long kiss meant some sad kind of "good-bye". The afternoon went on – my mother never resting, but seeking again and again in every possible place that had been looked into twenty times before; nay, that she had looked into over and over again herself. My father sat with his head in his hands, not speaking, except when his messengers came in, bringing no tidings; then he lifted up his face so strong and sad, and told them to go again in some new direction. My mother kept passing from room to room, in and out of the house, moving noiselessly, but never ceasing. Neither she nor my father durst leave the house, which was the meeting-place for all the messengers. At last (and it was nearly dark), my father rose up. He took hold of my mother's arm, as she came with wild, sad pace, through one door, and quickly towards another. She started at the touch of his hand, for she had forgotten all in the world but Peter.

'"Molly!" said he, "I did not think all this would happen." He looked into her face for comfort – her poor face, all wild and white; for neither she nor my father had dared to acknowledge – much less act upon – the terror that was in their hearts, lest Peter should have made away with himself. My father saw no conscious look in his wife's hot, dreary eyes, and he missed the sympathy that she had always been ready to give him – strong man as he was; and at the dumb despair in her face, his tears began to flow. But when she saw this, a gentle sorrow came over her countenance, and she said, "Dearest John! don't cry; come with me, and we'll find him," almost as cheerfully as if she knew where he was. And she took my father's great hand in her little soft one, and led him along, the tears dropping, as he walked on that same unceasing, weary walk, from room to room, through house and garden.

'Oh! how I wished for Deborah! I had no time for crying, for now all seemed to depend on me. I wrote for Deborah to come home. I sent a message privately to that same Mr Holbrook's house – poor Mr Holbrook! – you know who I mean. I don't mean I sent a message to him, but I sent one that I could trust, to know if Peter was at his house. For at one time Mr Holbrook was an occasional visitor at the Rectory – you know he was Miss Pole's cousin – and he had been very kind to Peter, and taught him how to fish – he was very kind to everybody, and I thought Peter might have gone off there. But Mr Holbrook was from home, and Peter had never been seen. It was night now; but the doors were all wide open, and my father and mother walked on and on; it was more than an hour since he had joined her, and I don't believe they had ever spoken all that time. I was getting the parlour fire lighted, and one of the servants was preparing tea, for I wanted them to have something to eat and drink and warm them, when old Clare asked to speak to me.

' "I have borrowed the nets from the weir, Miss Matty. Shall we drag the ponds tonight, or wait for the morning?"

'I remember staring in his face to gather his meaning; and when I did, I laughed out loud. The horror of that new thought – our bright, darling Peter, cold, and stark, and dead! I remember the ring of my own laugh now.

'The next day Deborah was at home before I was myself again. She would not have been so weak to give way as I had done; but my screams (my horrible laughter had ended in crying) had roused my sweet dear mother, whose poor wandering wits were called back and collected, as soon as a child needed her care. She and Deborah sat by my bedside; I knew by the looks of each that there had been no news of Peter – no awful, ghastly news, which was what I most had dreaded in my dull state between sleeping and waking.

'The same result of all the searching had brought something of the same relief to my mother, to whom I am sure, the thought that Peter might even then be hanging dead in some of the familiar home places, had caused that never-ending walk of yesterday. Her soft eyes never were the same again after that; they had always a restless craving look, as if seeking for what they could not find. Oh! it was an awful time; coming down like a thunderbolt on the still sunny day, when the lilacs were all in bloom.'

'Where was Mr Peter?' said I.

'He had made his way to Liverpool; and there was war then; and some of the king's ships lay off the mouth of the Mersey; and they were only too glad to have a fine likely boy such as him (five foot nine he was) come to offer himself. The captain wrote to my father, and Peter wrote to my mother. Stay! those letters will be somewhere here.'

We lighted the candle, and found the captain's letter, and Peter's too. And we also found a little simple begging letter from Mrs Jenkyns to Peter, addressed to him at the house of an old school-fellow, whither she fancied he might have gone. They had returned it unopened; and unopened it had remained ever since, having been inadvertently put by among the other letters of that time. This is it: –

'My dearest Peter,

'You did not think we should be so sorry as we are, I know, or you would never have gone away. You are too good. Your father sits and sighs till my heart aches to hear him. He cannot hold up his head for grief; and yet he only did what he thought was right. Perhaps he has been too severe, and perhaps I have not been kind enough; but God knows how we love you, my dear only boy. Dor[9] looks so sorry you are gone. Come back, and make us happy, who love you so much. I *know* you will come back.'

But Peter did not come back. That spring day was the last time he ever saw his mother's face. The writer of the letter – the last – the only person who had ever seen what was written in it, was dead long ago – and I, a stranger, not born at the time when this occurrence took place, was the one to open it.

The captain's letter summoned the father and mother to Liverpool instantly, if they wished to see their boy; and by some of the wild chances of life, the captain's letter had been detained somewhere, somehow.

Miss Matty went on: – 'And it was race-time, and all the post-horses at Cranford were gone to the races; but my father

and mother set off in our own gig, – and, oh! my dear, they
were too late – the ship was gone! And now, read Peter's letter
to my mother!'

It was full of love, and sorrow, and pride in his new profession, and a sore sense of his disgrace in the eyes of the people
at Cranford; but ending with a passionate entreaty that she
would come and see him before he left the Mersey: – 'Mother!
we may go into battle. I hope we shall, and lick those French;
but I must see you again before that time.'

'And she was too late,' said Miss Matty; 'too late!'

We sat in silence, pondering on the full meaning of those sad,
sad words. At length I asked Miss Matty to tell me how her
mother bore it.

'Oh!' she said, 'she was patience itself. She had never been
strong, and this weakened her terribly. My father used to sit
looking at her: far more sad than she was. He seemed as if he
could look at nothing else when she was by; and he was so
humble, – so very gentle now. He would, perhaps, speak in his
old way – laying down the law, as it were – and then, in a
minute or two, he would come round and put his hand on our
shoulders, and ask us in a low voice if he had said anything
to hurt us? I did not wonder at his speaking so to Deborah, for
she was so clever; but I could not bear to hear him talking
so to me.

'But, you see, he saw what we did not – that it was killing
my mother. Yes! killing her – (put out the candle, my dear; I
can talk better in the dark) – for she was but a frail woman,
and ill fitted to stand the fright and shock she had gone through;
and she would smile at him and comfort him, not in words but
in her looks and tones, which were always cheerful when he
was there. And she would speak of how she thought Peter stood
a good chance of being admiral very soon – he was so brave
and clever; and how she thought of seeing him in his navy
uniform, and what sort of hats admirals wore; and how much
more fit he was to be a sailor than a clergyman; and all in that
way, just to make my father think she was quite glad of what
came of that unlucky morning's work, and the flogging which
was always in his mind, as we all knew. But, oh, my dear! the

bitter, bitter crying she had when she was alone; – and at last, as she grew weaker, she could not keep her tears in, when Deborah or me was by, and would give us message after message for Peter, – (his ship had gone to the Mediterranean, or somewhere down there, and then he was ordered off to India, and there was no overland route then[10]); – but she still said that no one knew where their death lay in wait, and that we were not to think hers was near. We did not think it, but we knew it, as we saw her fading away.

'Well, my dear, it's very foolish of me, I know, when in all likelihood I am so near seeing her again.[11]

'And only think, love! the very day after her death – for she did not live quite a twelvemonth after Peter went away – the very day after – came a parcel for her from India – from her poor boy. It was a large, soft, white India shawl,[12] with just a little narrow border all round; just what my mother would have liked.

'We thought it might rouse my father, for he had sat with her hand in his all night long; so Deborah took it in to him, and Peter's letter to her, and all. At first, he took no notice; and we tried to make a kind of light careless talk about the shawl, opening it out and admiring it. Then, suddenly, he got up, and spoke: – "She shall be buried in it," he said; "Peter shall have that comfort; and she would have liked it."

'Well! perhaps it was not reasonable, but what could we do or say? One gives people in grief their own way. He took it up and felt it – "It is just such a shawl as she wished for when she was married, and her mother did not give it her. I did not know of it till after, or she should have had it – she should; but she shall have it now."

'My mother looked so lovely in her death! She was always pretty, and now she looked fair, and waxen, and young – younger than Deborah, as she stood trembling and shivering by her. We decked her in the long soft folds; she lay, smiling, as if pleased; and people came – all Cranford came – to beg to see her, for they had loved her dearly – as well they might; and the country-women brought posies; old Clare's wife brought some white violets, and begged they might lie on her breast.

'Deborah said to me, the day of my mother's funeral, that if she had a hundred offers, she never would marry and leave my father. It was not very likely she would have so many – I don't know that she had one; but it was not less to her credit to say so. She was such a daughter to my father, as I think there never was before, or since. His eyes failed him, and she read book after book, and wrote, and copied, and was always at his service in any parish business. She could do many more things than my poor mother could; she even once wrote a letter to the bishop for my father. But he missed my mother sorely; the whole parish noticed it. Not that he was less active; I think he was more so, and more patient in helping everyone. I did all I could to set Deborah at liberty to be with him; for I knew I was good for little, and that my best work in the world was to do odd jobs quietly, and set others at liberty. But my father was a changed man.'

'Did Mr Peter ever come home?'

'Yes, once. He came home a Lieutenant; he did not get to be Admiral. And he and my father were such friends! My father took him into every house in the parish, he was so proud of him. He never walked out without Peter's arm to lean upon. Deborah used to smile (I don't think we ever laughed again after my mother's death), and say she was quite put in a corner. Not but what my father always wanted her when there was letter-writing, or reading to be done, or anything to be settled.'

'And then?' said I, after a pause.

'Then Peter went to sea again; and, by-and-by, my father died, blessing us both, and thanking Deborah for all she had been to him; and, of course, our circumstances were changed; and, instead of living at the Rectory, and keeping three maids and a man, we had to come to this small house, and be content with a servant-of-all-work; but, as Deborah used to say, we have always lived genteelly, even if circumstances have compelled us to simplicity. – Poor Deborah!'

'And, Mr Peter?' asked I.

'Oh, there was some great war in India[13] – I forget what they call it – and we have never heard of Peter since then. I believe he is dead myself; and it sometimes fidgets me that we have never put on mourning for him. And then, again, when I sit by myself, and all the house is still, I think I hear his step coming up the street, and my heart begins to flutter and beat; but the sound always goes past – and Peter never comes.

'That's Martha back? No! I'll go, my dear; I can always find my way in the dark, you know. And a blow of fresh air at the door will do my head good, and it's rather got a trick of aching.'

So she pattered off. I had lighted the candle, to give the room a cheerful appearance against her return.

'Was it Martha?' asked I.

'Yes. And I am rather uncomfortable, for I heard such a strange noise just as I was opening the door.'

'When?' I asked, for her eyes were round with affright.

'In the street – just outside – it sounded like –'

'Talking?' I put in, as she hesitated a little.

'No! kissing –'

CHAPTER VII

VISITING

One morning, as Miss Matty and I sat at our work – it was before twelve o'clock, and Miss Matty had not yet changed the cap with yellow ribbons, that had been Miss Jenkyns's best, and which Miss Matty was now wearing out in private, putting on the one made in imitation of Mrs Jamieson's at all times when she expected to be seen – Martha came up, and asked if Miss Betty Barker might speak to her mistress. Miss Matty assented, and quickly disappeared to change the yellow ribbons, while Miss Barker came upstairs; but, as she had forgotten her spectacles, and was rather flurried by the unusual time of the visit, I was not surprised to see her return with one cap on the top of the other. She was quite unconscious of it herself, and looked at us with bland satisfaction. Nor do I think Miss Barker perceived it; for, putting aside the little circumstance that she was not so young as she had been, she was very much absorbed in her errand; which she delivered herself of, with an oppressive modesty that found vent in endless apologies.

Miss Betty Barker was the daughter of the old clerk at Cranford, who had officiated in Mr Jenkyns's time. She and her sister had had pretty good situations as ladies' maids, and had saved up money enough to set up a milliner's shop, which had been patronised by the ladies in the neighbourhood. Lady Arley, for instance, would occasionally give Miss Barkers the pattern of an old cap of hers, which they immediately copied and circulated among the *élite* of Cranford. I say the *élite*, for Miss Barkers had caught the trick of the place, and piqued themselves upon their 'aristocratic connection'. They would not sell their caps and ribbons to anyone without a pedigree.

Many a farmer's wife or daughter turned away huffed from Miss Barkers' select millinery, and went rather to the universal shop, where the profits of brown soap and moist sugar enabled the proprietor to go straight to (Paris, he said, until he found his customers too patriotic and John Bullish to wear what the Mounseers[1] wore) London; where, as he often told his customers, Queen Adelaide[2] had appeared, only the very week before, in a cap exactly like the one he showed them, trimmed with yellow and blue ribbons, and had been complimented by King William on the becoming nature of her head-dress.

Miss Barkers, who confined themselves to truth, and did not approve of miscellaneous customers, throve notwithstanding. They were self-denying, good people. Many a time have I seen the eldest of them (she that had been maid to Mrs Jamieson) carrying out some delicate mess to a poor person. They only aped their betters in having 'nothing to do' with the class immediately below theirs. And when Miss Barker died, their profits and income were found to be such that Miss Betty was justified in shutting up shop, and retiring from business. She also (as I think I have before said) set up her cow; a mark of respectability in Cranford, almost as decided as setting up a gig[3] is among some people. She dressed finer than any lady in Cranford; and we did not wonder at it; for it was understood that she was wearing out all the bonnets and caps, and outrageous ribbons, which had once formed her stock in trade. It was five or six years since they had given up shop: so in any other place than Cranford her dress might have been considered *passée*.

And now, Miss Betty Barker had called to invite Miss Matty to tea at her house on the following Tuesday. She gave me also an impromptu invitation, as I happened to be a visitor; though I could see she had a little fear lest, since my father had gone to live in Drumble, he might have engaged in that 'horrid cotton trade',[4] and so dragged his family down out of 'aristocratic society'. She prefaced this invitation with so many apologies, that she quite excited my curiosity. 'Her presumption' was to be excused. What had she been doing? She seemed so overpowered by it, I could only think that she had been writing

to Queen Adelaide, to ask for a receipt for washing lace; but
the act which she so characterised was only an invitation she
had carried to her sister's former mistress, Mrs Jamieson. 'Her
former occupation considered, could Miss Matty excuse the
liberty?' Ah! thought I, she has found out that double cap, and
is going to rectify Miss Matty's head-dress. No! it was simply
to extend her invitation to Miss Matty and to me. Miss Matty
bowed acceptance; and I wondered that, in the graceful action,
she did not feel the unusual weight and extraordinary height
of her head-dress. But I do not think she did; for she recovered
her balance, and went on talking to Miss Betty in a kind,
condescending manner, very different from the fidgety way
she would have had, if she had suspected how singular her
appearance was.

'Mrs Jamieson is coming, I think you said?' asked Miss
Matty.

'Yes. Mrs Jamieson most kindly and condescendingly said
she would be happy to come. One little stipulation she made,
that she should bring Carlo. I told her that if I had a weakness,
it was for dogs.'

'And Miss Pole?' questioned Miss Matty, who was thinking
of her pool at Preference, in which Carlo would not be available
as a partner.

'I am going to ask Miss Pole. Of course, I could not think of
asking her until I had asked you, madam – the Rector's daughter, madam. Believe me, I do not forget the situation my father
held under yours.'

'And Mrs Forrester, of course?'

'And Mrs Forrester. I thought, in fact, of going to her before
I went to Miss Pole. Although her circumstances are changed,
madam, she was born a Tyrrell,[5] and we can never forget her
alliance to the Bigges, of Bigelow Hall.'

Miss Matty cared much more for the little circumstance of
her being a very good card-player.

'Mrs Fitz-Adam – I suppose' –

'No, Madam. I must draw a line somewhere. Mrs Jamieson
would not, I think, like to meet Mrs Fitz-Adam. I have the
greatest respect for Mrs Fitz-Adam – but I cannot think her fit

society for such ladies as Mrs Jamieson and Miss Matilda Jenkyns.'

Miss Betty Barker bowed low to Miss Matty, and pursed up her mouth. She looked at me with sidelong dignity, as much as to say, although a retired milliner, she was no democrat, and understood the difference of ranks.

'May I beg you to come as near half-past six, to my little dwelling, as possible, Miss Matilda? Mrs Jamieson dines at five, but has kindly promised not to delay her visit beyond that time – half-past six.' And with a swimming curtsey Miss Betty Barker took her leave.

My prophetic soul[6] foretold a visit that afternoon from Miss Pole, who usually came to call on Miss Matilda after any event – or indeed in sight of any event – to talk it over with her.

'Miss Betty told me it was to be a choice and select few,' said Miss Pole, as she and Miss Matty compared notes.

'Yes, so she said. Not even Mrs Fitz-Adam.'

Now Mrs Fitz-Adam was the widowed sister of the Cranford surgeon, whom I have named before. Their parents were respectable farmers, content with their station. The name of these good people was Hoggins. Mr Hoggins was the Cranford doctor now; we disliked the name, and considered it coarse; but, as Miss Jenkyns said, if he changed it to Piggins it would not be much better. We had hoped to discover a relationship between him and that Marchioness of Exeter whose name was Molly Hoggins;[7] but the man, careless of his own interests, utterly ignored and denied any such relationship; although, as dear Miss Jenkyns had said, he had a sister called Mary, and the same Christian names were very apt to run in families.

Soon after Miss Mary Hoggins married Mr Fitz-Adam, she disappeared from the neighbourhood for many years. She did not move in a sphere in Cranford society sufficiently high to make any of us care to know what Mr Fitz-Adam was. He died and was gathered to his fathers, without our ever having thought about him at all. And then Mrs Fitz-Adam reappeared in Cranford, 'as bold as a lion,' Miss Pole said, a well-to-do widow, dressed in rustling black silk,[8] so soon after her husband's death, that poor Miss Jenkyns was justified in the remark

she made, that 'bombazine would have shown a deeper sense
of her loss'.

I remember the convocation of ladies, who assembled to
decide whether or not Mrs Fitz-Adam should be called upon
by the old blue-blooded inhabitants of Cranford. She had taken
a large rambling house, which had been usually considered to
confer a patent of gentility upon its tenant; because, once upon
a time, seventy or eighty years before, the spinster daughter of
an earl had resided in it. I am not sure if the inhabiting this
house was not also believed to convey some unusual power of
intellect; for the earl's daughter, Lady Jane, had a sister, Lady
Anne, who had married a general officer, in the time of the
American War; and this general officer had written one or two
comedies, which were still acted on the London boards;[9] and
which, when we saw them advertised, made us all draw up,
and feel that Drury Lane was paying a very pretty compliment to Cranford. Still, it was not at all a settled thing that
Mrs Fitz-Adam was to be visited, when dear Miss Jenkyns
died; and, with her, something of the clear knowledge of the
strict code of gentility went out too. As Miss Pole observed, 'As
most of the ladies of good family in Cranford were elderly
spinsters, or widows without children, if we did not relax a
little, and become less exclusive, by-and-by we should have no
society at all.'

Mrs Forrester continued on the same side.

'She had always understood that Fitz meant something
aristocratic; there was Fitz-Roy – she thought that some of
the King's children had been called Fitz-Roy: and there was
Fitz-Clarence now – they were the children of dear good King
William the Fourth.[10] Fitz-Adam! – it was a pretty name; and
she thought it very probably meant "Child of Adam". No one,
who had not some good blood in their veins, would dare to be
called Fitz; there was a deal in a name – she had had a cousin
who spelt his name with two little ffs – ffoulkes, – and he always
looked down upon capital letters, and said they belonged to
lately invented families. She had been afraid he would die a
bachelor, he was so very choice. When he met with a Mrs
ffaringdon, at a watering-place, he took to her immediately;

and a very pretty genteel woman she was – a widow with a very good fortune; and "my cousin", Mr ffoulkes, married her; and it was all owing to her two little ffs.'

Mrs Fitz-Adam did not stand a chance of meeting with a Mr Fitz-anything in Cranford, so that could not have been her motive for settling there. Miss Matty thought it might have been the hope of being admitted in the society of the place, which would certainly be a very agreeable rise for *ci-devant* Miss Hoggins; and if this had been her hope, it would be cruel to disappoint her.

So everybody called upon Mrs Fitz-Adam – everybody but Mrs Jamieson, who used to show how honourable she was by never seeing Mrs Fitz-Adam, when they met at the Cranford parties. There would be only eight or ten ladies in the room, and Mrs Fitz-Adam was the largest of all, and she invariably used to stand up when Mrs Jamieson came in, and curtsey very low to her whenever she turned in her direction – so low, in fact, that I think Mrs Jamieson must have looked at the wall above her, for she never moved a muscle of her face, no more than if she had not seen her. Still Mrs Fitz-Adam persevered.

The spring evenings were getting bright and long, when three or four ladies in calashes met at Miss Barker's door. Do you know what a calash is? It is a covering worn over caps, not unlike the heads fastened on old-fashioned gigs; but sometimes it is not quite so large. This kind of head-gear always made an awful impression on the children in Cranford; and now two or three left off their play in the quiet sunny little street, and gathered, in wondering silence, round Miss Pole, Miss Matty, and myself. We were silent, too, so that we could hear loud, suppressed whispers, inside Miss Barker's house: 'Wait, Peggy! wait till I've run upstairs, and washed my hands. When I cough, open the door; I'll not be a minute.'

And, true enough, it was not a minute before we heard a noise, between a sneeze and a crow; on which the door flew open. Behind it stood a round-eyed maiden, all aghast at the honourable company of calashes, who marched in without a word. She recovered presence of mind enough to usher us into a small room, which had been the shop, but was now converted into a temporary dressing-room. There we unpinned and shook ourselves, and arranged our features before the glass into a sweet and gracious company-face; and then, bowing backwards with 'After you, ma'am', we allowed Mrs Forrester to take precedence up the narrow staircase that led to Miss Barker's drawing-room. There she sat, as stately and composed as though we had never heard that odd-sounding cough, from which her throat must have been even then sore and rough. Kind, gentle, shabbily dressed Mrs Forrester was immediately conducted to the second place of honour – a seat arranged something like Prince Albert's near the Queen's – good, but not so good.[11] The place of pre-eminence was, of course, reserved for the Honourable Mrs Jamieson, who presently came panting up the stairs – Carlo rushing round her on her progress, as if he meant to trip her up.

And now, Miss Betty Barker was a proud and happy woman! She stirred the fire, and shut the door, and sat as near to it as she could, quite on the edge of her chair. When Peggy came in, tottering under the weight of the tea-tray, I noticed that Miss Barker was sadly afraid lest Peggy should not keep her distance sufficiently. She and her mistress were on very familiar terms in their every-day intercourse, and Peggy wanted now to make several little confidences to her, which Miss Barker was on thorns to hear; but which she thought it her duty, as a lady, to repress. So she turned away from all Peggy's asides and signs; but she made one or two very mal-apropos answers to what was said; and at last, seized with a bright idea, she exclaimed, 'Poor sweet Carlo! I'm forgetting him. Come down stairs with me, poor ittie doggie, and it shall have its tea, it shall!'

In a few minutes she returned, bland and benignant as before; but I thought she had forgotten to give the 'poor ittie doggie' anything to eat; judging by the avidity with which he swallowed down chance pieces of cake. The tea-tray was abundantly loaded. I was pleased to see it, I was so hungry; but I was afraid the ladies present might think it vulgarly heaped up. I know they would have done at their own houses; but somehow the heaps disappeared here. I saw Mrs Jamieson eating seed-cake, slowly and considerately, as she did everything; and I was rather surprised, for I knew she had told us, on the occasion of her last party, that she never had it in her house, it reminded her so much of scented soap. She always gave us Savoy biscuits. However, Mrs Jamieson was kindly indulgent to Miss Barker's want of knowledge of the customs of high life; and, to spare her feelings, ate three large pieces of seed-cake, with a placid, ruminating expression of countenance, not unlike a cow's.

After tea there was some little demur and difficulty. We were six in number; four could play at Preference, and for the other two there was Cribbage. But all, except myself – (I was rather afraid of the Cranford ladies at cards, for it was the most earnest and serious business they ever engaged in) – were anxious to be of the 'pool'. Even Miss Barker, while declaring she did not know Spadille from Manille,[12] was evidently hankering to take a hand. The dilemma was soon put an end to by a singular kind of noise. If a Baron's daughter-in-law could ever be supposed to snore, I should have said Mrs Jamieson did so then; for, overcome by the heat of the room, and inclined to doze by nature, the temptation of that very comfortable arm-chair had been too much for her, and Mrs Jamieson was nodding. Once or twice she opened her eyes with an effort, and calmly but unconsciously smiled upon us; but, by-and-by, even her benevolence was not equal to this exertion, and she was sound asleep.

'It is very gratifying to me,' whispered Miss Barker at the card-table to her three opponents, whom, notwithstanding her ignorance of the game, she was 'basting'[13] most unmercifully – 'very gratifying indeed, to see how completely Mrs Jamieson feels at home in my poor little dwelling; she could not have paid me a greater compliment.'

Miss Barker provided me with some literature, in the shape of three or four handsomely bound fashion-books ten or twelve years old, observing, as she put a little table and a candle for my especial benefit, that she knew young people liked to look at pictures. Carlo lay, and snorted, and started at his mistress's feet. He, too, was quite at home.

The card-table was an animated scene to watch; four ladies' heads, with niddle-noddling caps, all nearly meeting over the middle of the table, in their eagerness to whisper quick enough and loud enough: and every now and then came Miss Barker's 'Hush, ladies! if you please, hush! Mrs Jamieson is asleep.'

It was very difficult to steer clear between Mrs Forrester's deafness and Mrs Jamieson's sleepiness. But Miss Barker managed her arduous task well. She repeated the whisper to Mrs Forrester, distorting her face considerably, in order to show, by the motions of her lips, what was said; and then she smiled kindly all round at us, and murmured to herself, 'Very gratifying, indeed; I wish my poor sister had been alive to see this day.'

Presently the door was thrown wide open; Carlo started to his feet, with a loud snapping bark, and Mrs Jamieson awoke: or, perhaps, she had not been asleep – as she said almost directly, the room had been so light she had been glad to keep her eyes shut, but had been listening with great interest to all our amusing and agreeable conversation. Peggy came in once more, red with importance. Another tray! 'Oh, gentility!' thought I, 'can you endure this last shock?' For Miss Barker had ordered (nay, I doubt not prepared, although she did say, 'Why! Peggy, what have you brought us?' and looked pleasantly surprised at the unexpected pleasure) all sorts of good things for supper – scalloped oysters, potted lobsters, jelly, a dish called 'little Cupids', (which was in great favour with the Cranford ladies; although too expensive to be given, except on solemn and state occasions – maccaroons sopped in brandy, I should have called it, if I had not known its more refined and classical name). In short, we were evidently to be feasted with all that was sweetest and best; and we thought it better to submit graciously, even at the cost of our gentility – which never ate suppers in general – but which, like most non-supper-eaters, was particularly hungry on all special occasions.

Miss Barker, in her former sphere, had, I dare say, been made acquainted with the beverage they call cherry-brandy. We none of us had ever seen such a thing, and rather shrunk back when she proffered it us – 'just a little, leetle glass, ladies; after the oysters and lobsters, you know. Shell-fish are sometimes thought not very wholesome.' We all shook our heads like female mandarins; but, at last, Mrs Jamieson suffered herself to be persuaded, and we followed her lead. It was not exactly unpalatable, though so hot and so strong that we thought ourselves bound to give evidence that we were not accustomed to such things, by coughing terribly – almost as strangely as Miss Barker had done, before we were admitted by Peggy.

'It's very strong,' said Miss Pole, as she put down her empty glass; 'I do believe there's spirit in it.'

'Only a little drop – just necessary to make it keep!' said Miss Barker. 'You know we put brandy-paper over preserves to make them keep. I often feel tipsy myself from eating damson tart.'

I question whether damson tart would have opened Mrs Jamieson's heart as the cherry-brandy did; but she told us of a coming event, respecting which she had been quite silent till that moment.

'My sister-in-law, Lady Glenmire, is coming to stay with me.'

There was a chorus of 'Indeed!' and then a pause. Each one rapidly reviewed her wardrobe, as to its fitness to appear in the presence of a Baron's widow; for, of course, a series of small festivals were always held in Cranford on the arrival of a visitor at any of our friends' houses. We felt very pleasantly excited on the present occasion.

Not long after this, the maids and the lanterns were announced. Mrs Jamieson had the sedan-chair, which had squeezed itself into Miss Barker's narrow lobby with some difficulty; and most literally, stopped the way. It required some skilful manoeuvring on the part of the old chairmen (shoemakers by day; but, when summoned to carry the sedan, dressed up in a strange old livery – long great-coats, with small capes, coeval with the sedan, and similar to the dress of the class in Hogarth's pictures[14]) to edge, and back, and try at it again, and finally to succeed in carrying their burden out of Miss Barker's front-door. Then we heard their quick pit-a-pat along the quiet little street, as we put on our calashes, and pinned up our gowns; Miss Barker hovering about us with offers of help; which, if she had not remembered her former occupation, and wished us to forget it, would have been much more pressing.

Early the next morning – directly after twelve – Miss Pole made her appearance at Miss Matty's. Some very trifling piece of business was alleged as a reason for the call; but there was evidently something behind. At last out it came.

'By the way, you'll think I'm strangely ignorant; but, do you really know, I am puzzled how we ought to address Lady Glenmire. Do you say, "Your Ladyship", where you would say "you" to a common person? I have been puzzling all morning; and are we to say "My lady", instead of "Ma'am"? Now, you knew Lady Arley – will you kindly tell me the most correct way of speaking to the Peerage?'

Poor Miss Matty! she took off her spectacles, and she put them on again – but how Lady Arley was addressed, she could not remember.

'It is so long ago!' she said. 'Dear! dear! how stupid I am! I don't think I ever saw her more than twice. I know we used to call Sir Peter, "Sir Peter", – but he came much oftener to see us than Lady Arley did. Deborah would have known in a minute. My lady – your ladyship. It sounds very strange, and as if it was not natural. I never thought of it before; but, now you have named it, I am all in a puzzle.'

It was very certain Miss Pole would obtain no wise decision from Miss Matty, who got more bewildered every moment, and more perplexed as to etiquettes of address.

'Well, I really think,' said Miss Pole, 'I had better just go and tell Mrs Forrester about our little difficulty. One sometimes grows nervous; and yet one would not have Lady Glenmire think we were quite ignorant of the etiquettes of high life in Cranford.'

'And will you just step in here, dear Miss Pole, as you come back, please; and tell me what you decide upon. Whatever you and Mrs Forrester fix upon, will be quite right, I'm sure. "Lady Arley", "Sir Peter",' said Miss Matty, to herself, trying to recall the old forms of words.

'Who is Lady Glenmire?' asked I.

'Oh! she's the widow of Mr Jamieson – that's Mrs Jamieson's late husband, you know – widow of his eldest brother. Mrs Jamieson was a Miss Walker, daughter of Governor Walker. Your ladyship. My dear, if they fix on that way of speaking, you must just let me practise a little on you first, for I shall feel so foolish and hot, saying it the first time to Lady Glenmire.'

It was really a relief to Miss Matty when Mrs Jamieson came on a very unpolite errand. I notice that apathetic people have more quiet impertinence than any others; and Mrs Jamieson came now to insinuate pretty plainly, that she did not particularly wish that the Cranford ladies should call upon her sister-in-law. I can hardly say how she made this clear; for I grew very indignant and warm, while with slow deliberation she was explaining her wishes to Miss Matty, who, a true lady herself, could hardly understand the feeling which made Mrs Jamieson wish to appear to her noble sister-in-law as if she only visited 'county' families.[1] Miss Matty remained puzzled and perplexed long after I had found out the object of Mrs Jamieson's visit.

When she did understand the drift of the honourable lady's call, it was pretty to see with what quiet dignity she received the intimation thus uncourteously given. She was not in the least hurt – she was of too gentle a spirit for that; nor was she exactly conscious of disapproving of Mrs Jamieson's conduct; but there was something of this feeling in her mind, I am sure, which made her pass from the subject to others, in a less flurried and more composed manner than usual. Mrs Jamieson was, indeed, the more flurried of the two, and I could see she was glad to take her leave.

A little while afterwards, Miss Pole returned, red and indignant. 'Well! to be sure! You've had Mrs Jamieson here, I find from Martha; and we are not to call on Lady Glenmire. Yes! I met Mrs Jamieson, half-way between here and Mrs Forrester's,

and she told me; she took me so by surprise, I had nothing to
say. I wish I had thought of something very sharp and sarcastic;
I dare say I shall tonight. And Lady Glenmire is but the widow
of a Scotch baron after all! I went on to look at Mrs Forrester's
Peerage, to see who this lady was, that is to be kept under a
glass case: widow of a Scotch peer – never sat in the House of
Lords – and as poor as Job² I dare say; and she – fifth daughter
of some Mr Campbell or other. You are the daughter of a
rector, at any rate, and related to the Arleys; and Sir Peter might
have been Viscount Arley, everyone says.'

Miss Matty tried to soothe Miss Pole, but in vain. That lady,
usually so kind and good-humoured, was now in a full flow
of anger.

'And I went and ordered a cap this morning, to be quite
ready,' said she, at last, – letting out the secret which gave sting
to Mrs Jamieson's intimation. 'Mrs Jamieson shall see if it's so
easy to get me to make fourth at a pool, when she has none of
her fine Scotch relations with her!'

In coming out of church, the first Sunday on which Lady
Glenmire appeared in Cranford, we sedulously talked together,
and turned our backs on Mrs Jamieson and her guest. If we
might not call on her, we would not even look at her, though
we were dying with curiosity to know what she was like. We had
the comfort of questioning Martha in the afternoon. Martha
did not belong to a sphere of society whose observation could
be an implied compliment to Lady Glenmire, and Martha had
made good use of her eyes.

'Well, ma'am! is it the little lady with Mrs Jamieson, you
mean? I thought you would like more to know how young
Mrs Smith was dressed, her being a bride.'³ (Mrs Smith was the
butcher's wife.)

Miss Pole said, 'Good gracious me! as if we cared about a
Mrs Smith'; but was silent, as Martha resumed her speech.

'The little lady in Mrs Jamieson's pew had on, ma'am, rather
an old black silk, and a shepherd's plaid cloak, ma'am, and
very bright black eyes she had, ma'am, and a pleasant, sharp
face; not over young, ma'am, but yet, I should guess, younger
than Mrs Jamieson herself. She looked up and down the church,

like a bird, and nipped up her petticoats, when she came out, as quick and sharp as ever I see. I'll tell you what, ma'am, she's more like Mrs Deacon, at the "Coach and Horses", nor any one.'

'Hush, Martha!' said Miss Matty, 'that's not respectful.'

'Isn't it, ma'am? I beg pardon, I'm sure; but Jem Hearn said so as well. He said, she was just such a sharp, stirring sort of a body' –

'Lady,' said Miss Pole.

'Lady – as Mrs Deacon.'

Another Sunday passed away, and we still averted our eyes from Mrs Jamieson and her guest, and made remarks to ourselves that we thought were very severe – almost too much so. Miss Matty was evidently uneasy at our sarcastic manner of speaking.

Perhaps by this time Lady Glenmire had found out that Mrs Jamieson's was not the gayest, liveliest house in the world; perhaps Mrs Jamieson had found out that most of the county families were in London, and that those who remained in the country were not so alive as they might have been to the circumstance of Lady Glenmire being in their neighbourhood. Great events spring out of small causes; so I will not pretend to say what induced Mrs Jamieson to alter her determination of excluding the Cranford ladies, and send notes of invitation all round for a small party, on the following Tuesday. Mr Mulliner himself brought them round. He *would* always ignore the fact of there being a back-door to any house, and gave a louder rat-tat than his mistress, Mrs Jamieson. He had three little notes, which he carried in a large basket, in order to impress his mistress with an idea of their great weight, though they might easily have gone into his waistcoat pocket.

Miss Matty and I quietly decided we would have a previous engagement at home: – it was the evening on which Miss Matty usually made candle-lighters of all the notes and letters of the week; for on Mondays her accounts were always made straight – not a penny owing from the week before; so, by a natural arrangement, making candle-lighters fell upon a Tuesday evening, and gave us a legitimate excuse for declining Mrs

Jamieson's invitation. But before our answer was written, in came Miss Pole, with an open note in her hand.

'So!' she said. 'Ah! I see you have got your note, too. Better late than never. I could have told my Lady Glenmire she would be glad enough of our society before a fortnight was over.'

'Yes,' said Miss Matty, 'we're asked for Tuesday evening. And perhaps you would just kindly bring your work across and drink tea with us that night. It is my usual regular time for looking over the last week's bills, and notes, and letters, and making candle-lighters of them; but that does not seem quite reason enough for saying I have a previous engagement at home, though I meant to make it do. Now, if you would come, my conscience would be quite at ease, and luckily the note is not written yet.'

I saw Miss Pole's countenance change while Miss Matty was speaking.

'Don't you mean to go then?' asked she.

'Oh no!' said Miss Matty quietly. 'You don't either, I suppose?'

'I don't know,' replied Miss Pole. 'Yes, I think I do,' said she rather briskly; and on seeing Miss Matty look surprised, she added, 'You see one would not like Mrs Jamieson to think that anything she could do, or say, was of consequence enough to give offence; it would be a kind of letting down of ourselves, that I, for one, should not like. It would be too flattering to Mrs Jamieson, if we allowed her to suppose that what she had said affected us a week, nay ten days afterwards.'

'Well! I suppose it is wrong to be hurt and annoyed so long about anything; and, perhaps, after all, she did not mean to vex us. But I must say, I could not have brought myself to say the things Mrs Jamieson did about our not calling. I really don't think I shall go.'

'Oh, come! Miss Matty, you must go; you know our friend Mrs Jamieson is much more phlegmatic than most people, and does not enter into the little delicacies of feeling which you possess in so remarkable a degree.'

'I thought you possessed them, too, that day Mrs Jamieson called to tell us not to go,' said Miss Matty innocently.

But Miss Pole, in addition to her delicacies of feeling, possessed a very smart cap, which she was anxious to show to an admiring world; and so she seemed to forget all her angry words uttered not a fortnight before, and to be ready to act on what she called the great Christian principle of 'Forgive and forget'; and she lectured dear Miss Matty so long on this head, that she absolutely ended by assuring her it was her duty, as a deceased rector's daughter, to buy a new cap, and go to the party at Mrs Jamieson's. So 'we were most happy to accept', instead of 'regretting that we were obliged to decline'.

The expenditure in dress in Cranford was principally in that one article referred to. If the heads were buried in smart new caps, the ladies were like ostriches, and cared not what became of their bodies. Old gowns, white and venerable collars, any number of brooches, up and down and everywhere (some with dogs' eyes painted in them; some that were like small picture-frames with mausoleums and weeping-willows neatly executed in hair inside; some, again, with miniatures of ladies and gentlemen sweetly smiling out of a nest of stiff muslin[4]) – old brooches for a permanent ornament, and new caps to suit the fashion of the day; the ladies of Cranford always dressed with chaste elegance and propriety, as Miss Barker once prettily expressed it.

And with three new caps, and a greater array of brooches than had ever been seen together at one time, since Cranford was a town, did Mrs Forrester, and Miss Matty, and Miss Pole appear on that memorable Tuesday evening. I counted seven brooches myself on Miss Pole's dress. Two were fixed negligently in her cap (one was a butterfly made of Scotch pebbles,[5] which a vivid imagination might believe to be the real insect); one fastened her net neck-kerchief; one her collar; one ornamented the front of her gown, midway between her throat and waist; and another adorned the point of her stomacher. Where the seventh was I have forgotten, but it was somewhere about her, I am sure.

But I am getting on too fast, in describing the dresses of the company. I should first relate the gathering, on the way to Mrs Jamieson's. That lady lived in a large house just outside the town. A road, which had known what it was to be a street, ran right before the house, which opened out upon it, without any intervening garden or court. Whatever the sun was about, he never shone on the front of that house. To be sure, the living-rooms were at the back, looking on to a pleasant garden; the front windows only belonged to kitchens and housekeepers' rooms, and pantries; and in one of them Mr Mulliner was reported to sit. Indeed, looking askance, we often saw the back of a head, covered with hair-powder,[6] which also extended itself over his coat-collar down to his very waist; and this imposing back was always engaged in reading the 'St James's Chronicle', opened wide, which, in some degree, accounted for the length of time the said newspaper was in reaching us – equal subscribers with Mrs Jamieson, though, in right of her honourableness, she always had the reading of it first. This very Tuesday, the delay in forwarding the last number had been particularly aggravating; just when both Miss Pole and Miss Matty, the former more especially, had been wanting to see it, in order to coach up the court-news, ready for the evening's interview with aristocracy. Miss Pole told us she had absolutely taken time by the fore-lock, and been dressed by five o'clock, in order to be ready, if the 'St James's Chronicle' should come in at the last moment – the very 'St James's Chronicle' which the powdered-head was tranquilly and composedly reading as we passed the accustomed window this evening.

'The impudence of the man!' said Miss Pole, in a low indignant whisper. 'I should like to ask him, whether his mistress pays her quarter-share for his exclusive use.'

We looked at her in admiration of the courage of her thought; for Mr Mulliner was an object of great awe to all of us. He seemed never to have forgotten his condescension in coming to live at Cranford. Miss Jenkyns, at times, had stood forth as the undaunted champion of her sex, and spoken to him on terms of equality; but even Miss Jenkyns could get no higher. In his pleasantest and most gracious moods, he looked like a sulky cockatoo. He did not speak except in gruff monosyllables. He would wait in the hall when we begged him not to wait, and then looked deeply offended because we had kept him there, while, with trembling, hasty hands, we prepared ourselves for appearing in company.

Miss Pole ventured on a small joke as we went upstairs, intended, though addressed to us, to afford Mr Mulliner some slight amusement. We all smiled, in order to seem as if we felt at our ease, and timidly looked for Mr Mulliner's sympathy. Not a muscle of that wooden face had relaxed; and we were grave in an instant.

Mrs Jamieson's drawing-room was cheerful; the evening sun came streaming into it, and the large square window was clustered round with flowers. The furniture was white and gold; not the later style, Louis Quatorze I think they call it, all shells and twirls; no, Mrs Jamieson's chairs and tables had not a curve or bend about them. The chair and table legs diminished as they neared the ground, and were straight and square in all their corners.[7] The chairs were all a-row against the walls, with the exception of four or five which stood in a circle round the fire. They were railed with white bars across the back, and knobbed with gold; neither the railings nor the knobs invited to ease. There was a japanned table devoted to literature, on which lay a Bible, a Peerage, and a Prayer-Book. There was another square Pembroke table dedicated to the Fine Arts, on which there was a kaleidoscope, conversation-cards, puzzle-cards (tied together to an interminable length with faded pink satin ribbon), and a box painted in fond imitation of the drawings which decorate tea-chests.[8] Carlo lay on the worsted-worked rug, and ungraciously barked at us as we entered. Mrs Jamieson stood up, giving us each a torpid smile of welcome, and looking helplessly beyond us at Mr Mulliner, as if she hoped he would place us in chairs, for if he did not, she never could. I suppose he thought we could find our way to the circle round the fire, which reminded me of Stonehenge,[9] I don't know why. Lady Glenmire came to the rescue of our hostess; and somehow or other we found ourselves for the first time placed agreeably, and not formally, in Mrs Jamieson's house. Lady Glenmire, now we had time to look at her, proved to be a bright little woman of middle age, who had been very pretty in the days of her youth, and who was even yet very pleasant-looking. I saw

Miss Pole appraising her dress in the first five minutes; and I take her word, when she said the next day,

'My dear! ten pounds would have purchased every stitch she had on – lace and all.'

It was pleasant to suspect that a peeress could be poor, and partly reconciled us to the fact that her husband had never sat in the House of Lords; which, when we first heard of it, seemed a kind of swindling us out of our respect on false pretences; a sort of 'A Lord and No Lord' business.[10]

We were all very silent at first. We were thinking what we could talk about, that should be high enough to interest My Lady. There had been a rise in the price of sugar, which, as preserving-time was near, was a piece of intelligence to all our housekeeping hearts, and would have been the natural topic if Lady Glenmire had not been by. But we were not sure if the Peerage ate preserves – much less knew how they were made. At last, Miss Pole, who had always a great deal of courage and *savoir faire*, spoke to Lady Glenmire, who on her part had seemed just as much puzzled to know how to break the silence as we were.

'Has your ladyship been to Court, lately?' asked she; and then gave a little glance round at us, half timid, and half triumphant, as much as to say, 'See how judiciously I have chosen a subject befitting the rank of the stranger!'

'I never was there in my life,' said Lady Glenmire, with a broad Scotch accent, but in a very sweet voice. And then, as if she had been too abrupt, she added, 'We very seldom went to London; only twice, in fact, during all my married life; and before I was married, my father had far too large a family' – (fifth daughter of Mr Campbell, was in all our minds, I am sure) – 'to take us often from our home, even to Edinburgh. Ye'll have been in Edinburgh, maybe?' said she, suddenly brightening up with the hope of a common interest. We had none of us been there; but Miss Pole had an uncle who once had passed a night there, which was very pleasant.

Mrs Jamieson, meanwhile, was absorbed in wonder why Mr Mulliner did not bring the tea; and, at length, the wonder oozed out of her mouth.

'I had better ring the bell, my dear, had not I?' said Lady Glenmire, briskly.

'No – I think not – Mulliner does not like to be hurried.'

We should have liked our tea, for we dined at an earlier hour than Mrs Jamieson. I suspect Mr Mulliner had to finish the 'St James's Chronicle' before he chose to trouble himself about tea. His mistress fidgetted and fidgetted, and kept saying, 'I can't think why Mulliner does not bring tea. I can't think what he can be about.' And Lady Glenmire at last grew quite impatient, but it was a pretty kind of impatience after all; and she rung the bell rather sharply, on receiving a half permission from her sister-in-law to do so. Mr Mulliner appeared in dignified surprise. 'Oh!' said Mrs Jamieson, 'Lady Glenmire rang the bell; I believe it was for tea.'

In a few minutes tea was brought. Very delicate was the china, very old the plate, very thin the bread and butter, and very small the lumps of sugar.[11] Sugar was evidently Mrs Jamieson's favourite economy. I question if the little filigree sugar-tongs, made something like scissors, could have opened themselves wide enough to take up an honest, vulgar, good-sized piece; and when I tried to take two little minnikin pieces at once, so as not to be detected in too many returns to the sugar-basin, they absolutely dropped one, with a little sharp clatter, quite in a malicious and unnatural manner. But before this happened, we had had a slight disappointment. In the little silver jug was cream, in the larger one was milk. As soon as Mr Mulliner came in, Carlo began to beg, which was a thing our manners forbade us to do, though I am sure we were just as hungry; and Mrs Jamieson said she was certain we would excuse her if she gave her poor dumb Carlo his tea first. She accordingly mixed a saucer-full for him, and put it down for him to lap; and then she told us how intelligent and sensible the dear little fellow was; he knew cream quite well, and constantly refused tea with only milk in it: so the milk was left for us, but we silently thought we were quite as intelligent and sensible as Carlo, and felt as if insult were added to injury, when we were called upon to admire the gratitude evinced by his wagging his tail for the cream, which should have been ours.

After tea we thawed down into common-life subjects. We were thankful to Lady Glenmire for having proposed some more bread and butter, and this mutual want made us better acquainted with her than we should ever have been with talking about the Court, though Miss Pole did say, she had hoped to know how the dear Queen was from someone who had seen her.

The friendship, begun over bread and butter, extended on to cards. Lady Glenmire played Preference to admiration, and was a complete authority as to Ombre and Quadrille. Even Miss Pole quite forgot to say 'my lady', and 'your ladyship', and said 'Basto! ma'am'; 'you have Spadille,[12] I believe', just as quietly as if we had never held the great Cranford parliament on the subject of the proper mode of addressing a peeress.

As a proof of how thoroughly we had forgotten that we were in the presence of one who might have sat down to tea with a coronet, instead of a cap, on her head, Mrs Forrester related a curious little fact to Lady Glenmire – an anecdote known to the circle of her intimate friends, but of which even Mrs Jamieson was not aware. It related to some fine old lace, the sole relic of better days, which Lady Glenmire was admiring on Mrs Forrester's collar.

'Yes,' said that lady, 'such lace cannot be got now for either love or money; made by the nuns abroad they tell me. They say that they can't make it now, even there. But perhaps they can now they've passed the Catholic Emancipation Bill.[13] I should not wonder. But, in the meantime, I treasure up my lace very much. I daren't even trust the washing of it to my maid' (the little charity school-girl I have named before, but who sounded well as 'my maid'). 'I always wash it myself. And once it had a narrow escape. Of course, your ladyship knows that such lace must never be starched or ironed. Some people wash it in sugar and water; and some in coffee, to make it the right yellow colour; but I myself have a very good receipt for washing it in milk, which stiffens it enough, and gives it a very good creamy colour. Well, ma'am, I had tacked it together (and the beauty of this fine lace is, that when it is wet, it goes into a very little space), and put it to soak in milk, when, unfortunately, I left the room; on my return, I found pussy on the table, looking very like a thief, but gulping very uncomfortably, as if she was half-choked with something she wanted to swallow, and could not. And, would you believe it? At first, I pitied her, and said, "Poor pussy! poor pussy!" till, all at once, I looked and saw the cup of milk empty – cleaned out! "You naughty cat!" said I; and I believe I was provoked enough to give her a slap, which did no good, but only helped the lace down – just as one slaps a choking child on the back. I could have cried, I was so vexed; but I determined I would not give the lace up without a struggle for it. I hoped the lace might disagree with her, at any rate; but it would have been too much for Job, if he had seen, as I did, that cat come in, quite placid and purring, not a quarter of an hour after, and almost expecting to be stroked. "No, pussy!" said I; "if you have any conscience, you ought not to expect that!" And then a thought struck me; and I rang the bell for my maid, and sent her to Mr Hoggins, with my compliments, and would he be kind enough to lend me one of his top-boots for an hour? I did not think there was anything odd in the message; but Jenny said, the young men in the surgery laughed as if they would be ill, at my wanting a top-boot. When it came, Jenny and I put pussy in, with her fore-feet straight down, so that they were fastened, and could not scratch, and we gave her a tea-spoonful of currant-jelly, in which (your ladyship must excuse me) I had mixed some tartar emetic. I shall never forget how anxious I was for the next half-hour. I took pussy to my own room, and spread a clean towel on the floor. I could have kissed her when she returned the lace to sight, very much as it had gone down. Jenny had boiling water ready, and we soaked it and soaked it, and spread it on a lavender-bush in the sun, before I could touch it again, even to put it in milk. But now, your ladyship would never guess that it had been in pussy's inside.'

We found out, in the course of the evening, that Lady Glenmire was going to pay Mrs Jamieson a long visit, as she had given up her apartments in Edinburgh, and had no ties to take her back there in a hurry. On the whole, we were rather glad to hear this, for she had made a pleasant impression upon us; and it was also very comfortable to find, from things which dropped out in the course of conversation, that, in addition to many other genteel qualities, she was far removed from the vulgarity of wealth.

'Don't you find it very unpleasant, walking?' asked Mrs Jamieson, as our respective servants were announced. It was a pretty regular question from Mrs Jamieson, who had her own carriage in the coach-house, and always went out in a sedan-chair to the very shortest distances. The answers were nearly as much a matter of course.

'Oh dear, no! it is so pleasant and still at night!' 'Such a refreshment after the excitement of a party!' 'The stars are so beautiful!' This last was from Miss Matty.

'Are you fond of astronomy?' Lady Glenmire asked.

'Not very' – replied Miss Matty, rather confused at the moment to remember which was astronomy, and which was astrology – but the answer was true under either circumstance, for she read, and was slightly alarmed at, Francis Moore's astrological predictions;[14] and, as to astronomy, in a private and confidential conversation, she had told me, she never could believe that the earth was moving constantly, and that she would not believe it if she could, it made her feel so tired and dizzy whenever she thought about it.

In our pattens, we picked our way home with extra care that night; so refined and delicate were our perceptions after drinking tea with 'my lady'.

CHAPTER IX

SIGNOR BRUNONI

Soon after the events of which I gave an account in my last paper, I was summoned home by my father's illness; and for a time I forgot, in anxiety about him, to wonder how my dear friends at Cranford were getting on, or how Lady Glenmire could reconcile herself to the dulness of the long visit which she was still paying to her sister-in-law, Mrs Jamieson. When my father grew a little stronger I accompanied him to the sea-side, so that altogether I seemed banished from Cranford, and was deprived of the opportunity of hearing any chance intelligence of the dear little town for the greater part of that year.

Late in November – when we had returned home again, and my father was once more in good health – I received a letter from Miss Matty; and a very mysterious letter it was. She began many sentences without ending them, running them one into another, in much the same confused sort of way in which written words run together on blotting-paper. All I could make out was, that if my father was better (which she hoped he was), and would take warning and wear a great coat from Michaelmas to Lady-day,[1] if turbans were in fashion, could I tell her? such a piece of gaiety was going to happen as had not been seen or known of since Wombwell's lions[2] came, when one of them ate a little child's arm; and she was, perhaps, too old to care about dress, but a new cap she must have; and, having heard that turbans were worn, and some of the county families likely to come, she would like to look tidy, if I would bring her a cap from the milliner I employed; and oh, dear! how careless of her to forget that she wrote to beg I would come and pay her a visit next Tuesday; when she hoped to have something to offer me in the way of amusement, which she would not now more particularly describe, only sea-green was her favourite colour. So she ended her letter; but in a P.S. she added, she thought she might as well tell me what was the peculiar attraction to Cranford just now; Signor Brunoni was going to exhibit his wonderful magic in the Cranford Assembly Rooms, on Wednesday and Friday evening in the following week.

I was very glad to accept the invitation from my dear Miss Matty, independently of the conjuror; and most particularly anxious to prevent her from disfiguring her small gentle mousey face with a great Saracen's-head turban;[3] and, accordingly I bought her a pretty, neat, middle-aged cap, which, however, was rather a disappointment to her when, on my arrival, she followed me into my bed-room, ostensibly to poke the fire, but in reality, I do believe, to see if the sea-green turban was not inside the cap-box with which I had travelled. It was in vain that I twirled the cap round on my hand to exhibit back and side fronts: her heart had been set upon a turban, and all she could do was to say, with resignation in her look and voice:

'I am sure you did your best, my dear. It is just like the caps all the ladies in Cranford are wearing, and they have had theirs for a year, I dare say. I should have liked something newer, I confess – something more like the turbans Miss Betty Barker tells me Queen Adelaide wears; but it is very pretty, my dear. And I dare say lavender will wear better than sea-green. Well, after all, what is dress that we should care about it! You'll tell me if you want anything, my dear. Here is the bell. I suppose turbans have not got down to Drumble yet?'

So saying, the dear old lady gently bemoaned herself out of the room, leaving me to dress for the evening, when, as she informed me, she expected Miss Pole and Mrs Forrester, and she hoped I should not feel myself too much tired to join the party. Of course I should not; and I made some haste to unpack and arrange my dress; but, with all my speed, I heard the arrivals and the buzz of conversation in the next room before I was ready. Just as I opened the door, I caught the words – 'I was foolish to expect anything very genteel out of the Drumble shops – poor girl! she did her best, I've no doubt.' But for all that, I had rather that she blamed Drumble and me than disfigured herself with a turban.

Miss Pole was always the person, in the trio of Cranford ladies now assembled, to have had adventures. She was in the habit of spending the morning in rambling from shop to shop; not to purchase anything (except an occasional reel of cotton, or a piece of tape), but to see the new articles and report upon them, and to collect all the stray pieces of intelligence in the town. She had a way, too, of demurely popping hither and thither into all sorts of places to gratify her curiosity on any point; a way which, if she had not looked so very genteel and prim, might have been considered impertinent. And now, by the expressive way in which she cleared her throat, and waited for all minor subjects (such as caps and turbans) to be cleared off the course, we knew she had something very particular to relate, when the due pause came – and I defy any people, possessed of common modesty, to keep up a conversation long, where one among them sits up aloft in silence, looking down upon all the things they chance to say as trivial and contemptible compared to what they could disclose, if properly entreated. Miss Pole began:

'As I was stepping out of Gordon's shop, today, I chanced to go into the George (my Betty has a second cousin who is chamber-maid there, and I thought Betty would like to hear how she was), and, not seeing anyone about, I strolled up the staircase, and found myself in the passage leading to the Assembly Room (you and I remember the Assembly Room, I am sure, Miss Matty! and the *minuets de la cour!*) so I went on, not thinking of what I was about, when, all at once, I perceived that I was in the middle of the preparations for tomorrow night – the room being divided with great clothes-maids, over which Crosby's men were tacking red flannel; very dark and odd it seemed; it quite bewildered me, and I was going on behind the screens, in my absence of mind, when a gentleman (quite the gentleman, I can assure you), stepped forwards and asked if I had any business he could arrange for me. He spoke

such pretty broken English, I could not help thinking of
Thaddeus of Warsaw and the Hungarian Brothers, and Santo
Sebastiani;[4] and while I was busy picturing his past life to
myself, he had bowed me out of the room. But wait a minute!
You have not heard half my story yet! I was going downstairs,
when who should I meet but Betty's second cousin. So, of
course, I stopped to speak to her for Betty's sake; and she told
me that I had really seen the conjuror; the gentleman who spoke
broken English was Signor Brunoni himself. Just at this moment
he passed us on the stairs, making such a graceful bow, in reply
to which I dropped a curtsey – all foreigners have such polite
manners, one catches something of it. But when he had gone
downstairs, I bethought me that I had dropped my glove in the
Assembly Room (it was safe in my muff all the time, but I never
found it till afterwards); so I went back, and, just as I was
creeping up the passage left on one side of the great screen that
goes nearly across the room, who should I see but the very same
gentleman that had met me before, and passed me on the stairs,
coming now forwards from the inner part of the room, to which
there is no entrance – you remember Miss Matty! – and just
repeating in his pretty broken English, the inquiry if I had any
business there – I don't mean that he put it quite so bluntly, but
he seemed very determined that I should not pass the screen –
so, of course, I explained about my glove, which, curiously
enough, I found at that very moment.'

Miss Pole then had seen the conjuror – the real live conjuror!
and numerous were the questions we all asked her: 'Had he a
beard?' 'Was he young or old?' 'Fair or dark?' 'Did he look' –
(unable to shape my question prudently, I put it in another
form) – 'How did he look?' In short, Miss Pole was the heroine
of the evening, owing to her morning's encounter. If she was
not the rose (that is to say the conjuror), she had been near it.[5]

Conjuration, sleight of hand, magic, witchcraft were the
subjects of the evening. Miss Pole was slightly sceptical, and
inclined to think there might be a scientific solution found for
even the proceedings of the Witch of Endor.[6] Mrs Forrester
believed everything from ghosts to death-watches. Miss Matty
ranged between the two – always convinced by the last speaker.

I think she was naturally more inclined to Mrs Forrester's side, but a desire of proving herself a worthy sister to Miss Jenkyns kept her equally balanced – Miss Jenkyns, who would never allow a servant to call the little rolls of tallow that formed themselves round candles, 'winding-sheets', but insisted on their being spoken of as 'roly-poleys'![7] A sister of hers to be superstitious! It would never do.

After tea, I was despatched downstairs into the dining-parlour for that volume of the old encyclopaedia which contained the nouns beginning with C, in order that Miss Pole might prime herself with scientific explanations for the tricks of the following evening. It spoilt the pool at Preference which Miss Matty and Mrs Forrester had been looking forward to, for Miss Pole became so much absorbed in her subject, and the plates by which it was illustrated, that we felt it would be cruel to disturb her, otherwise than by one or two well-timed yawns, which I threw in now and then, for I was really touched by the meek way in which the two ladies were bearing their disappointment. But Miss Pole only read the more zealously, imparting to us no more interesting information than this:

'Ah! I see; I comprehend perfectly. A represents the ball. Put A between B and D – no! between C and F, and turn the second joint of the third finger of your left hand over the wrist of your right H. Very clear indeed! My dear Mrs Forrester, conjuring and witchcraft is a mere affair of the alphabet. Do let me read you this one passage?'

Mrs Forrester implored Miss Pole to spare her, saying, from a child upwards, she never could understand being read aloud to; and I dropped the pack of cards, which I had been shuffling very audibly; and by this discreet movement, I obliged Miss Pole to perceive that Preference was to have been the order of the evening, and to propose, rather unwillingly, that the pool should commence. The pleasant brightness that stole over the other two ladies' faces on this! Miss Matty had one or two twinges of self-reproach for having interrupted Miss Pole in her studies: and did not remember her cards well, or give her full attention to the game, until she had soothed her conscience by offering to lend the volume of the Encyclopaedia to Miss Pole,

who accepted it thankfully, and said Betty should take it home
when she came with the lantern.

The next evening we were all in a little gentle flutter at the
idea of the gaiety before us. Miss Matty went up to dress
betimes, and hurried me until I was ready, when we found we
had an hour and a half to wait before the 'doors opened at
seven precisely'. And we had only twenty yards to go! However,
as Miss Matty said, it would not do to get too much absorbed
in anything, and forget the time; so, she thought we had better
sit quietly, without lighting the candles, till five minutes to
seven. So Miss Matty dozed, and I knitted.

At length we set off; and at the door, under the carriage-way
at the George, we met Mrs Forrester and Miss Pole: the latter
was discussing the subject of the evening with more vehemence
than ever, and throwing A's and B's at our heads like hail-
stones. She had even copied one or two of the 'receipts' – as
she called them – for the different tricks, on backs of letters,
ready to explain and to detect Signor Brunoni's arts.

We went into the cloak-room adjoining the Assembly Room;
Miss Matty gave a sigh or two to her departed youth, and the
remembrance of the last time she had been there, as she adjusted
her pretty new cap before the strange, quaint old mirror in
the cloak-room. The Assembly Room had been added to the
inn about a hundred years before, by the different county families, who met together there once a month during the winter,
to dance and play at cards. Many a county beauty had first
swam through the minuet that she afterwards danced before
Queen Charlotte, in this very room. It was said that one of the
Gunnings[8] had graced the apartment with her beauty; it was
certain that a rich and beautiful widow, Lady Williams, had
here been smitten with the noble figure of a young artist, who
was staying with some family in the neighbourhood for professional purposes, and accompanied his patrons to the Cranford Assembly. And a pretty bargain poor Lady Williams had
of her handsome husband, if all tales were true! Now, no beauty
blushed and dimpled along the sides of the Cranford Assembly
Room; no handsome artist won hearts by his bow, *chapeau
bras* in hand: the old room was dingy; the salmon-coloured

paint had faded into a drab; great pieces of plaster had chipped off from the white wreaths and festoons on its walls; but still a mouldy odour of aristocracy lingered about the place, and a dusty recollection of the days that were gone made Miss Matty and Mrs Forrester bridle up as they entered, and walk mincingly up the room, as if there were a number of genteel observers, instead of two little boys, with a stick of toffy between them with which to beguile the time.

We stopped short at the second front row; I could hardly understand why, until I heard Miss Pole ask a stray waiter if any of the County families were expected; and when he shook his head, and believed not, Mrs Forrester and Miss Matty moved forwards, and our party represented a conversational square. The front row was soon augmented and enriched by Lady Glenmire and Mrs Jamieson. We six occupied the two front rows, and our aristocratic seclusion was respected by the groups of shopkeepers who strayed in from time to time, and huddled together on the back benches. At least I conjectured so, from the noise they made, and the sonorous bumps they gave in sitting down; but when, in weariness of the obstinate green curtain, that would not draw up, but would stare at me with two odd eyes, seen through holes, as in the old tapestry story, I would fain have looked round at the merry chattering people behind me, Miss Pole clutched my arm, and begged me not to turn, for 'it was not the thing'. What 'the thing' was, I never could find out, but it must have been something eminently dull and tiresome. However, we all sat eyes right, square front, gazing at the tantalising curtain, and hardly speaking intelligibly, we were so afraid of being caught in the vulgarity of making any noise in a place of public amusement. Mrs Jamieson was the most fortunate, for she fell asleep.

At length the eyes disappeared – the curtain quivered – one side went up before the other, which stuck fast; it was dropped again, and, with a fresh effort, and a vigorous pull from some unseen hand, it flew up, revealing to our sight a magnificent gentleman in the Turkish costume,[9] seated before a little table, gazing at us (I should have said with the same eyes that I had last seen through the hole in the curtain) with calm and condescending dignity, 'like a being of another sphere', as I heard a sentimental voice ejaculate behind me.

'That's not Signor Brunoni!' said Miss Pole decidedly, and so audibly that I am sure he heard, for he glanced down over his flowing beard at our party with an air of mute reproach. 'Signor Brunoni had no beard – but perhaps he'll come soon.' So she lulled herself into patience. Meanwhile, Miss Matty had reconnoitred through her eye-glass; wiped it, and looked again. Then she turned round, and said to me, in a kind, mild, sorrow-ful tone:–

'You see, my dear, turbans *are* worn.'

But we had no time for more conversation. The Grand Turk, as Miss Pole chose to call him, arose and announced himself as Signor Brunoni.

'I don't believe him!' exclaimed Miss Pole, in a defiant manner. He looked at her again, with the same dignified upbraiding in his countenance. 'I don't!' she repeated, more positively than ever. 'Signor Brunoni had not got that muffy sort of thing about his chin, but looked like a close-shaved Christian gentleman.'

Miss Pole's energetic speeches had the good effect of waken-ing up Mrs Jamieson, who opened her eyes wide, in sign of the deepest attention – a proceeding which silenced Miss Pole, and encouraged the Grand Turk to proceed, which he did in very broken English – so broken that there was no cohesion between the parts of his sentences; a fact which he himself perceived at last, and so left off speaking and proceeded to action.

Now we *were* astonished. How he did his tricks I could not imagine; no, not even when Miss Pole pulled out her pieces of paper and began reading aloud – or at least in a very audible whisper – the separate 'receipts' for the most common of his tricks. If ever I saw a man frown, and look enraged, I saw the Grand Turk frown at Miss Pole; but, as she said, what could be expected but unchristian looks from a Mussulman? If Miss Pole was sceptical, and more engrossed with her receipts and diagrams than with his tricks, Miss Matty and Mrs Forrester were mystified and perplexed to the highest degree. Mrs Jamieson kept taking her spectacles off and wiping them, as if she thought it was something defective in them which made the legerdemain; and Lady Glenmire, who had seen many curious sights in Edinburgh, was very much struck with the tricks, and would not at all agree with Miss Pole, who declared that anybody could do them with a little practice – and that she would, herself, undertake to do all he did, with two hours given to study the Encyclopaedia, and made her third finger flexible.

At last, Miss Matty and Mrs Forrester became perfectly awe-struck. They whispered together. I sat just behind them, so I could not help hearing what they were saying. Miss Matty asked Mrs Forrester, 'if she thought it was quite right to have come to see such things? She could not help fearing they were lending encouragement to something that was not quite—'[10] a little shake of the head filled up the blank. Mrs Forrester replied, that the same thought had crossed her mind; she, too, was feeling very uncomfortable; it was so very strange. She was quite certain that it was her pocket-handkerchief which was in that loaf just now; and it had been in her own hand not five minutes before. She wondered who had furnished the bread? She was sure it could not be Dakin, because he was the church-warden. Suddenly, Miss Matty half turned towards me:–

'Will you look, my dear – you are a stranger in the town, and it won't give rise to unpleasant reports – will you just look round and see if the Rector is here? If he is, I think we may conclude that this wonderful man is sanctioned by the Church, and that will be a great relief to my mind.'

I looked, and I saw the tall, thin, dry, dusty Rector, sitting surrounded by National School boys,[11] guarded by troops of his own sex from any approach of the many Cranford spinsters. His kind face was all agape with broad smiles, and the boys around him were in chinks of laughing. I told Miss Matty that the Church was smiling approval, which set her mind at ease.

I have never named Mr Hayter, the Rector, because I, as a well-to-do and happy young woman, never came in contact with him. He was an old bachelor, but as afraid of matrimonial reports getting abroad about him as any girl of eighteen: and he would rush into a shop, or dive down an entry, sooner than encounter any of the Cranford ladies in the street; and, as for the Preference parties, I did not wonder at his not accepting invitations to them. To tell the truth, I always suspected Miss Pole of having given very vigorous chace to Mr Hayter when he first came to Cranford; and not the less, because now she appeared to share so vividly in his dread lest her name should ever be coupled with his. He found all his interests among the poor and helpless; he had treated the National School boys this very night to the performance; and virtue was for once its own reward, for they guarded him right and left, and clung round him as if he had been the queen bee, and they the swarm. He felt so safe in their environment, that he could even afford to give our party a bow as we filed out. Miss Pole ignored his presence, and pretended to be absorbed in convincing us that we had been cheated, and had not seen Signor Brunoni after all.

CHAPTER X

THE PANIC

I think a series of circumstances dated from Signor Brunoni's visit to Cranford, which seemed at the time connected in our minds with him, though I don't know that he had anything really to do with them. All at once all sorts of uncomfortable rumours got afloat in the town. There were one or two robberies – real *bonâ fide* robberies; men had up before the magistrates and committed for trial; and that seemed to make us all afraid of being robbed; and for a long time at Miss Matty's, I know, we used to make a regular expedition all round the kitchens and cellars every night, Miss Matty leading the way, armed with the poker, I following with the hearth-brush, and Martha carrying the shovel and fire-irons with which to sound the alarm; and by the accidental hitting together of them she often frightened us so much that we bolted ourselves up, all three together, in the back kitchen, or store-room, or wherever we happened to be, till, when our affright was over, we recollected ourselves, and set out afresh with double valiance. By day we heard strange stories from the shopkeepers and cottagers, of carts that went about in the dead of night, drawn by horses shod with felt, and guarded by men in dark clothes, going round the town, no doubt, in search of some unwatched house or some unfastened door.[1]

Miss Pole, who affected great bravery herself, was the principal person to collect and arrange these reports, so as to make them assume their most fearful aspect. But we discovered that she had begged one of Mr Hoggins's worn-out hats to hang up in her lobby, and we (at least I) had my doubts as to whether she really would enjoy the little adventure of having her house broken into, as she protested she should. Miss Matty made no secret of being an arrant coward; but she went regularly through her housekeeper's duty of inspection – only the hour for this became earlier and earlier, till at last we went the rounds at half-past six, and Miss Matty adjourned to bed soon after seven, 'in order to get the night over the sooner'.

Cranford had so long piqued itself on being an honest and moral town, that it had grown to fancy itself too genteel and well-bred to be otherwise, and felt the stain upon its character at this time doubly. But we comforted ourselves with the assurance which we gave to each other, that the robberies could never have been committed by any Cranford person; it must have been a stranger or strangers, who brought this disgrace upon the town, and occasioned as many precautions as if we were living among the Red Indians or the French.

This last comparison of our nightly state of defence and fortification, was made by Mrs Forrester, whose father had served under General Burgoyne in the American War, and whose husband had fought the French in Spain.[2] She indeed inclined to the idea that, in some way, the French were connected with the small thefts, which were ascertained facts, and the burglaries and highway robberies, which were rumours. She had been deeply impressed with the idea of French spies,[3] at some time in her life; and the notion could never be fairly eradicated, but sprung up again from time to time. And now her theory was this: the Cranford people respected themselves too much, and were too grateful to the aristocracy who were so kind as to live near the town, ever to disgrace their bringing up by being dishonest or immoral; therefore, we must believe that the robbers were strangers – if strangers, why not foreigners? – if foreigners, who so likely as the French? Signor Brunoni spoke broken English like a Frenchman, and, though he wore a turban like a Turk, Mrs Forrester had seen a print of Madame de Staël with a turban on, and another of Mr Denon[4] in just such a dress as that in which the conjuror had made his appearance; showing clearly that the French, as well as the Turks, wore turbans: there could be no doubt Signor Brunoni was a Frenchman – a French spy, come to discover the weak and undefended places of England; and, doubtless, he had his accomplices; for her part, she, Mrs Forrester, had always had her own opinion of Miss Pole's adventure at the George Inn – seeing two men where only one was believed to be: French people had ways and means, which she was thankful to say the English knew nothing about; and she had never felt quite easy in her mind about going to see that conjuror; it was rather too much like a forbidden thing, though the Rector was there. In short, Mrs Forrester grew more excited than we had ever known her before; and, being an officer's daughter and widow, we looked up to her opinion, of course.

Really I do not know how much was true or false in the reports which flew about like wildfire just at this time; but it seemed to me then that there was every reason to believe that at Mardon (a small town about eight miles from Cranford) houses and shops were entered by holes made in the walls, the bricks being silently carried away in the dead of the night, and all done so quietly that no sound was heard either in or out of the house. Miss Matty gave it up in despair when she heard of this. 'What was the use,' said she, 'of locks and bolts, and bells to the windows,[5] and going round the house every night? That last trick was fit for a conjuror. Now she did believe that Signor Brunoni was at the bottom of it.'

One afternoon, about five o'clock, we were startled by a hasty knock at the door. Miss Matty bade me run and tell Martha on no account to open the door till she (Miss Matty) had reconnoitred through the window; and she armed herself with a footstool to drop down on the head of the visitor, in case he should show a face covered with black crape,[6] as he looked up in answer to her inquiry of who was there. But it was nobody but Miss Pole and Betty. The former came upstairs, carrying a little hand-basket, and she was evidently in a state of great agitation.

'Take care of that!' said she to me, as I offered to relieve her of her basket. 'It's my plate. I am sure there is a plan to rob my house tonight. I am come to throw myself on your hospitality, Miss Matty. Betty is going to sleep with her cousin at the George. I can sit up here all night, if you will allow me; but my house is so far from any neighbours; and I don't believe we could be heard if we screamed ever so!'

'But,' said Miss Matty, 'what has alarmed you so much? Have you seen any men lurking about the house?'

'Oh yes!' answered Miss Pole. 'Two very bad-looking men have gone three times past the house, very slowly; and an Irish beggar-woman[7] came not half an hour ago, and all but forced herself in past Betty, saying her children were starving, and she must speak to the mistress. You see, she said "mistress", though there was a hat hanging up in the hall, and it would have been more natural to have said "master". But Betty shut the door in her face, and came up to me, and we got the spoons together,[8] and sat in the parlour-window watching, till we saw Thomas Jones going from his work, when we called to him and asked him to take care of us into the town.'

We might have triumphed over Miss Pole, who had professed such bravery until she was frightened; but we were too glad to perceive that she shared in the weaknesses of humanity to exult over her; and I gave up my room to her very willingly, and shared Miss Matty's bed for the night. But before we retired, the two ladies rummaged up, out of the recesses of their memory, such horrid stories of robbery and murder, that I quite quaked in my shoes. Miss Pole was evidently anxious to prove that such terrible events had occurred within her experience that she was justified in her sudden panic; and Miss Matty did not like to be outdone, and capped every story with one yet more horrible, till it reminded me, oddly enough, of an old story I had read somewhere, of a nightingale and a musician, who strove one against the other which could produce the most admirable music, till poor Philomel[9] dropped down dead.

One of the stories that haunted me for a long time afterwards, was of a girl, who was left in charge of a great house in Cumberland, on some particular fair-day, when the other servants all went off to the gaieties.[10] The family were away in London, and a pedlar came by, and asked to leave his large and heavy pack in the kitchen, saying, he would call for it again at night; and the girl (a gamekeeper's daughter) roaming about in search of amusement, chanced to hit upon a gun hanging up in the hall, and took it down to look at the chasing; and it went off through the open kitchen door, hit the pack, and a slow dark thread of blood came oozing out. (How Miss Pole enjoyed this part of the story, dwelling on each word as if she loved it!) She rather hurried over the further account of the girl's bravery, and I have but a confused idea that, somehow, she baffled the robbers with Italian irons, heated red hot, and then restored to blackness by being dipped in grease.

We parted for the night with an awestruck wonder as to what we should hear of in the morning – and, on my part, with a vehement desire for the night to be over and gone: I was so afraid lest the robbers should have seen, from some dark lurking-place, that Miss Pole had carried off her plate, and thus have a double motive for attacking our house.

But, until Lady Glenmire came to call next day, we heard of nothing unusual. The kitchen fire-irons were in exactly the same position against the back door, as when Martha and I had skilfully piled them up like spillikins, ready to fall with an awful clatter, if only a cat had touched the outside panels. I had wondered what we should all do if thus awakened and alarmed, and had proposed to Miss Matty that we should cover up our faces under the bed-clothes, so that there should be no danger of the robbers thinking that we could identify them; but Miss Matty, who was trembling very much, scouted this idea, and said we owed it to society to apprehend them, and that she should certainly do her best to lay hold of them, and lock them up in the garret till morning.

When Lady Glenmire came, we almost felt jealous of her. Mrs Jamieson's house had really been attacked; at least there were men's footsteps to be seen on the flower-borders, under-neath the kitchen windows, 'where nae men should be';[11] and Carlo had barked all through the night as if strangers were abroad. Mrs Jamieson had been awakened by Lady Glenmire, and they had rung the bell which communicated with Mr Mulliner's room, in the third storey, and when his night-capped head had appeared over the bannisters, in answer to the summons, they had told him of their alarm, and the reasons for it; whereupon he retreated into his bed-room, and locked the door (for fear of draughts, as he informed them in the morning), and opened the window, and called out valiantly to say, if the supposed robbers would come to him he would fight them; but, as Lady Glenmire observed, that was but poor comfort, since they would have to pass by Mrs Jamieson's room and her own, before they could reach him, and must be of a very pugnacious disposition indeed, if they neglected the opportunities of robbery presented by the unguarded lower stories to go up to a garret, and there force a door in order to get at the champion of the house. Lady Glenmire, after waiting and listening for some time in the drawing-room, had proposed to Mrs Jamieson that they should go to bed; but that lady said she should not feel comfortable unless she sat up and watched; and, accordingly, she packed herself warmly up on the sofa, where she was found by the housemaid, when she came into the room at six o'clock, fast asleep; but Lady Glenmire went to bed, and kept awake all night.

When Miss Pole heard of this, she nodded her head in great satisfaction. She had been sure we should hear of something happening in Cranford that night; and we had heard. It was clear enough they had first proposed to attack her house; but when they saw that she and Betty were on their guard, and had carried off the plate, they had changed their tactics and gone to Mrs Jamieson's, and no one knew what might have happened if Carlo had not barked, like a good dog as he was!

Poor Carlo! his barking days were nearly over. Whether the gang who infested the neighbourhood were afraid of him; or whether they were revengeful enough for the way in which he had baffled them on the night in question to poison him; or whether, as some among the more uneducated people thought, he died of apoplexy, brought on by too much feeding and too little exercise; at any rate, it is certain that, two days after this eventful night, Carlo was found dead, with his poor little legs stretched out stiff in the attitude of running, as if by such unusual exertion he could escape the sure pursuer, Death.

We were all sorry for Carlo, the old familiar friend who had snapped at us for so many years; and the mysterious mode of his death made us very uncomfortable. Could Signor Brunoni

be at the bottom of this? He had apparently killed a canary
with only a word of command; his will seemed of deadly
force;[12] who knew but what he might yet be lingering in the
neighbourhood willing all sorts of awful things!

We whispered these fancies among ourselves in the evenings;
but in the mornings our courage came back with the daylight,
and in a week's time we had got over the shock of Carlo's
death; all but Mrs Jamieson. She, poor thing, felt it as she had
felt no event since her husband's death; indeed Miss Pole said,
that as the Honourable Mr Jamieson drank a good deal, and
occasioned her much uneasiness, it was possible that Carlo's
death might be the greater affliction. But there was always a
tinge of cynicism in Miss Pole's remarks. However, one thing
was clear and certain; it was necessary for Mrs Jamieson to have
some change of scene; and Mr Mulliner was very impressive on
this point, shaking his head whenever we inquired after his
mistress, and speaking of her loss of appetite and bad nights
very ominously; and with justice too, for if she had two characteristics in her natural state of health, they were a facility of
eating and sleeping. If she could neither eat nor sleep, she must
be indeed out of spirits and out of health.

Lady Glenmire (who had evidently taken very kindly to
Cranford), did not like the idea of Mrs Jamieson's going to
Cheltenham,[13] and more than once insinuated pretty plainly
that it was Mr Mulliner's doing, who had been much alarmed
on the occasion of the house being attacked, and since had
said, more than once, that he felt it a very responsible charge
to have to defend so many women. Be that as it might, Mrs
Jamieson went to Cheltenham, escorted by Mr Mulliner; and
Lady Glenmire remained in possession of the house, her osten-
sible office being to take care that the maid-servants did not
pick up followers. She made a very pleasant-looking dragon:
and, as soon as it was arranged for her stay in Cranford, she
found out that Mrs Jamieson's visit to Cheltenham was just the
best thing in the world. She had let her house in Edinburgh, and
was for the time houseless, so the charge of her sister-in-law's
comfortable abode was very convenient and acceptable.

Miss Pole was very much inclined to install herself as a

heroine, because of the decided steps she had taken in flying from the two men and one woman, whom she entitled 'that murderous gang'. She described their appearance in glowing colours, and I noticed that every time she went over the story some fresh trait of villany was added to their appearance. One was tall – he grew to be gigantic in height before we had done with him; he of course had black hair – and by and by, it hung in elf-locks over his forehead and down his back. The other was short and broad – and a hump sprouted out on his shoulder before we heard the last of him; he had red hair – which deepened into carrotty; and she was almost sure he had a cast in his eye – a decided squint. As for the woman, her eyes glared, and she was masculine-looking[14] – a perfect virago; most probably a man dressed in woman's clothes: afterwards, we heard of a beard on her chin, and a manly voice and a stride.

If Miss Pole was delighted to recount the events of that afternoon to all inquirers, others were not so proud of their adventures in the robbery line. Mr Hoggins, the surgeon, had been attacked at his own door by two ruffians, who were concealed in the shadow of the porch, and so effectually silenced him, that he was robbed in the interval between ringing his bell and the servant's answering it. Miss Pole was sure it would turn out that this robbery had been committed by 'her men', and went the very day she heard of the report to have her teeth examined, and to question Mr Hoggins. She came to us afterwards; so we heard what she had heard, straight and direct from the source, while we were yet in the excitement and flutter of the agitation caused by the first intelligence; for the event had only occurred the night before.

'Well!' said Miss Pole, sitting down with the decision of a person who has made up her mind as to the nature of life and the world, (and such people never tread lightly, or seat themselves without a bump) – 'Well, Miss Matty! men will be men. Every mother's son of them wishes to be considered Samson and Solomon[15] rolled into one – too strong ever to be beaten or discomfited – too wise ever to be outwitted. If you will notice, they have always foreseen events, though they never tell one for one's warning before the events happen; my father was a man, and I know the sex pretty well.'

She had talked herself out of breath, and we should have been very glad to fill up the necessary pause as chorus, but we did not exactly know what to say, or which man had suggested this diatribe against the sex; so we only joined in generally, with a grave shake of the head, and a soft murmur of 'They are very incomprehensible, certainly!'

'Now only think,' said she. 'There I have undergone the risk of having one of my remaining teeth drawn (for one is terribly at the mercy of any surgeon-dentist;[16] and I, for one, always speak them fair till I have got my mouth out of their clutches), and after all, Mr Hoggins is too much of a man to own that he was robbed last night.'

'Not robbed!' exclaimed the chorus.

'Don't tell me!' Miss Pole exclaimed, angry that we could be for a moment imposed upon. 'I believe he was robbed, just as Betty told me, and he is ashamed to own it: and, to be sure it was very silly of him to be robbed just at his own door; I dare say, he feels that such a thing won't raise him in the eyes of Cranford society, and is anxious to conceal it – but he need not have tried to impose upon me, by saying I must have heard an exaggerated account of some petty theft of a neck of mutton, which, it seems, was stolen out of the safe in his yard last week; he had the impertinence to add, he believed that that was taken by the cat. I have no doubt, if I could get at the bottom of it, it was that Irishman dressed up in woman's clothes, who came spying about my house, with the story about the starving children.'

After we had duly condemned the want of candour which Mr Hoggins had evinced, and abused men in general, taking him for the representative and type, we got round to the subject about which we had been talking when Miss Pole came in – namely, how far, in the present disturbed state of the country, we could venture to accept an invitation which Miss Matty had just received from Mrs Forrester, to come as usual and keep the anniversary of her wedding-day, by drinking tea with her at five o'clock, and playing a quiet pool afterwards. Mrs

Forrester had said, that she asked us with some diffidence, because the roads were, she feared, very unsafe. But she suggested that perhaps one of us would not object to take the sedan; and that the others, by walking briskly, might keep up with the long trot of the chairmen, and so we might all arrive safely at Over Place, a suburb of the town. (No. That is too large an expression: a small cluster of houses separated from Cranford by about two hundred yards of a dark and lonely lane.) There was no doubt but that a similar note was awaiting Miss Pole at home; so her call was a very fortunate affair, as it enabled us to consult together. We would all much rather have declined this invitation; but we felt that it would not be quite kind to Mrs Forrester, who would otherwise be left to a solitary retrospect of her not very happy or fortunate life. Miss Matty and Miss Pole had been visitors on this occasion for many years; and now they gallantly determined to nail their colours to the mast, and to go through Darkness Lane rather than fail in loyalty to their friend.

But when the evening came, Miss Matty (for it was she who was voted into the chair, as she had a cold), before being shut down in the sedan, like jack-in-a-box, implored the chairmen, whatever might befall, not to run away and leave her fastened up there, to be murdered; and even after they had promised, I saw her tighten her features into the stern determination of a martyr, and she gave me a melancholy and ominous shake of the head through the glass. However, we got there safely, only rather out of breath, for it was who could trot hardest through Darkness Lane, and I am afraid poor Miss Matty was sadly jolted.

Mrs Forrester had made extra preparations in acknowledgment of our exertion in coming to see her through such dangers. The usual forms of genteel ignorance as to what her servants might send up were all gone through; and harmony and Preference seemed likely to be the order of the evening, but for an interesting conversation that began I don't know how, but which had relation, of course, to the robbers who infested the neighbourhood of Cranford.

Having braved the dangers of Darkness Lane, and thus having a little stock of reputation for courage to fall back upon; and also, I dare say, desirous of proving ourselves superior to men (*videlicet* Mr Hoggins), in the article of candour, we began to relate our individual fears, and the private precautions we each of us took. I owned that my pet apprehension was eyes – eyes looking at me, and watching me, glittering out from some dull flat wooden surface; and that if I dared to go up to my looking-glass when I was panic-stricken, I should certainly turn it round, with its back towards me, for fear of seeing eyes behind me looking out of the darkness. I saw Miss Matty nerving herself up for a confession; and at last out it came. She owned that, ever since she had been a girl, she had dreaded being caught by her last leg, just as she was getting into bed, by someone concealed under the bed. She said, when she was younger and more active, she used to take a flying leap from a distance, and so bring both her legs up safely into bed at once; but that this had always annoyed Deborah, who piqued herself upon getting into bed gracefully, and she had given it up in consequence. But now the old terror would often come over her, especially since Miss Pole's house had been attacked (we had got quite to believe in the fact of the attack having taken place), and yet it was very unpleasant to think of looking under a bed, and seeing a man concealed, with a great fierce face staring out at you; so she had bethought herself of something – perhaps I had noticed that she had told Martha to buy her a penny ball, such as children play with – and now she rolled this ball under the bed every night; if it came out on the other side, well and good; if not, she always took care to have her hand on the bell-rope, and meant to call out John and Harry, just as if she expected men-servants to answer her ring.

We all applauded this ingenious contrivance, and Miss Matty sank back into satisfied silence, with a look at Mrs Forrester as if to ask for *her* private weakness.

Mrs Forrester looked askance at Miss Pole, and tried to change the subject a little, by telling us that she had borrowed a boy from one of the neighbouring cottages, and promised his parents a hundredweight of coals at Christmas, and his supper every evening, for the loan of him at nights. She had instructed

him in his possible duties when he first came; and, finding him
sensible, she had given him the major's sword (the major was
her late husband), and desired him to put it very carefully
behind his pillow at night, turning the edge towards the head
of the pillow. He was a sharp lad, she was sure; for, spying out
the major's cocked hat, he had said, if he might have that to
wear he was sure he could frighten two Englishmen, or four
Frenchmen, any day. But she had impressed upon him anew
that he was to lose no time in putting on hats or anything else;
but, if he heard any noise, he was to run at it with his drawn
sword. On my suggesting that some accident might occur from
such slaughterous and indiscriminate directions, and that he
might rush on Jenny getting up to wash, and have spitted her
before he had discovered that she was not a Frenchman, Mrs
Forrester said she did not think that that was likely, for he was
a very sound sleeper, and generally had to be well shaken, or
cold-pigged in a morning before they could rouse him. She
sometimes thought such dead sleep must be owing to the hearty
suppers the poor lad ate, for he was half-starved at home, and
she told Jenny to see that he got a good meal at night.

Still this was no confession of Mrs Forrester's peculiar timid-
ity, and we urged her to tell us what she thought would frighten
her more than anything. She paused, and stirred the fire, and
snuffed the candles, and then she said, in a sounding whisper,–
'Ghosts!'

She looked at Miss Pole, as much as to say she had declared
it, and would stand by it. Such a look was a challenge in
itself. Miss Pole came down upon her with indigestion, spectral
illusions, optical delusions, and a great deal out of Dr Ferrier
and Dr Hibbert[17] besides. Miss Matty had rather a leaning
to ghosts, as I have said before, and what little she did say,
was all on Mrs Forrester's side, who, emboldened by sympathy,
protested that ghosts were a part of her religion; that surely
she, the widow of a major in the army, knew what to be
frightened at, and what not; in short, I never saw Mrs Forrester
so warm either before or since, for she was a gentle, meek,
enduring old lady in most things. Not all the elder-wine that
ever was mulled, could this night wash out the remembrance of

this difference between Miss Pole and her hostess. Indeed, when the elder-wine was brought in, it gave rise to a new burst of discussion: for Jenny, the little maiden who staggered under the tray, had to give evidence of having seen a ghost with her own eyes, not so many nights ago, in Darkness Lane – the very lane we were to go through on our way home.

In spite of the uncomfortable feeling which this last consideration gave me, I could not help being amused at Jenny's position, which was exceedingly like that of a witness being examined and cross-examined by two counsel who are not at all scrupulous about asking leading questions. The conclusion I arrived at was, that Jenny had certainly seen something beyond what a fit of indigestion would have caused. A lady all in white, and without her head, was what she deposed and adhered to, supported by a consciousness of the secret sympathy of her mistress under the withering scorn with which Miss Pole regarded her. And not only she, but many others, had seen this headless lady, who sat by the roadside wringing her hands as in deep grief. Mrs Forrester looked at us from time to time, with an air of conscious triumph; but then she had not to pass through Darkness Lane before she could bury herself beneath her own familiar bed-clothes.

We preserved a discreet silence as to the headless lady while we were putting on our things to go home, for there was no knowing how near the ghostly head and ears might be, or what spiritual connection they might be keeping up with the unhappy body in Darkness Lane; and therefore, even Miss Pole felt that it was as well not to speak lightly on such subjects, for fear of vexing or insulting that woe-begone trunk. At least, so I conjecture; for, instead of the busy clatter usual in the operation, we tied on our cloaks as sadly as mutes at a funeral. Miss Matty drew the curtains round the windows of the chair to shut out disagreeable sights; and the men (either because they were in spirits that their labours were so nearly ended, or because they were going down hill) set off at such a round and merry pace, that it was all Miss Pole and I could do to keep up with them. She had breath for nothing beyond an imploring 'Don't leave me!' uttered as she clutched my arm so tightly that

I could not have quitted her, ghost or no ghost. What a relief it
was when the men, weary of their burden and their quick trot,
stopped just where Headingley-causeway branches off from
Darkness Lane! Miss Pole unloosed me and caught at one of
the men.

'Could not you – could not you take Miss Matty round by
Headingley-causeway, – the pavement in Darkness Lane jolts
so, and she is not very strong?'

A smothered voice was heard from the inside of the chair –

'Oh! pray go on! what is the matter? What is the matter?
I will give you sixpence more to go on very fast; pray don't
stop here.'

'And I'll give you a shilling,' said Miss Pole, with tremulous
dignity, 'if you'll go by Headingley-causeway.'

The two men grunted acquiescence and took up the chair
and went along the causeway, which certainly answered Miss
Pole's kind purpose of saving Miss Matty's bones; for it was
covered with soft thick mud, and even a fall there would have
been easy, till the getting up came, when there might have been
some difficulty in extrication.

CHAPTER XI

SAMUEL BROWN

The next morning I met Lady Glenmire and Miss Pole, setting out on a long walk to find some old woman who was famous in the neighbourhood for her skill in knitting woollen stockings. Miss Pole said to me, with a smile half kindly and half contemptuous upon her countenance, 'I have been just telling Lady Glenmire of our poor friend Mrs Forrester, and her terror of ghosts. It comes from living so much alone, and listening to the bug-a-boo stories of that Jenny of hers.' She was so calm and so much above superstitious fears herself, that I was almost ashamed to say how glad I had been of her Headingley-causeway proposition the night before, and turned off the conversation to something else.

In the afternoon Miss Pole called on Miss Matty to tell her of the adventure – the real adventure they had met with on their morning's walk. They had been perplexed about the exact path which they were to take across the fields, in order to find the knitting old woman, and had stopped to inquire at a little way-side public-house, standing on the high road to London, about three miles from Cranford. The good woman had asked them to sit down and rest themselves, while she fetched her husband, who could direct them better than she could; and, while they were sitting in the sanded parlour,[1] a little girl came in. They thought that she belonged to the landlady, and began some trifling conversation with her; but, on Mrs Roberts's return, she told them that the little thing was the only child of a couple who were staying in the house. And then she began a long story, out of which Lady Glenmire and Miss Pole could only gather one or two decided facts; which were that, about

six weeks ago, a light spring-cart had broken down just before
their door, in which there were two men, one woman, and this
child. One of the men was seriously hurt – no bones broken,
only 'shaken', the landlady called it; but he had probably sus-
tained some severe internal injury, for he had languished in
their house ever since, attended by his wife, the mother of this
little girl. Miss Pole had asked what he was, what he looked
like. And Mrs Roberts had made answer that he was not like a
gentleman, nor yet like a common person; if it had not been
that he and his wife were such decent, quiet people, she could
almost have thought he was a mountebank, or something of
that kind, for they had a great box in the cart, full of she did
not know what. She had helped to unpack it, and take out their
linen and clothes, when the other man – his twin brother, she
believed he was – had gone off with the horse and cart.

Miss Pole had begun to have her suspicions at this point, and
expressed her idea that it was rather strange that the box and
cart and horse and all should have disappeared; but good Mrs
Roberts seemed to have become quite indignant at Miss Pole's
implied suggestion; in fact, Miss Pole said, she was as angry as
if Miss Pole had told her that she herself was a swindler. As the
best way of convincing the ladies, she bethought her of begging
them to see the wife; and, as Miss Pole said, there was no
doubting the honest, worn, bronze face of the woman, who, at
the first tender word from Lady Glenmire, burst into tears,
which she was too weak to check, until some word from the
landlady made her swallow down her sobs, in order that she
might testify to the Christian kindness shown by Mr and Mrs
Roberts. Miss Pole came round with a swing to as vehement a
belief in the sorrowful tale as she had been sceptical before;
and, as a proof of this, her energy in the poor sufferer's behalf
was nothing daunted when she found out that he, and no
other, was our Signor Brunoni, to whom all Cranford had been
attributing all manner of evil this six weeks past! Yes! his wife
said his proper name was Samuel Brown – 'Sam', she called
him – but to the last we preferred calling him 'the Signor'; it
sounded so much better.

The end of their conversation with the Signora Brunoni[2] was, that it was agreed that he should be placed under medical advice, and for any expense incurred in procuring this Lady Glenmire promised to hold herself responsible; and had accordingly gone to Mr Hoggins to beg him to ride over to the Rising Sun that very afternoon, and examine into the Signor's real state; and as Miss Pole said, if it was desirable to remove him to Cranford to be more immediately under Mr Hoggins's eye, she would undertake to see for lodgings, and arrange about the rent. Mrs Roberts had been as kind as could be all throughout; but it was evident that their long residence there had been a slight inconvenience.

Before Miss Pole left us, Miss Matty and I were as full of the morning's adventure as she was. We talked about it all the evening, turning it in every possible light, and we went to bed anxious for the morning, when we should surely hear from someone what Mr Hoggins thought and recommended. For, as Miss Matty observed, though Mr Hoggins did say 'Jack's up', 'a fig for his heels',[3] and call Preference 'Pref', she believed he was a very worthy man, and a very clever surgeon. Indeed, we were rather proud of our doctor at Cranford, as a doctor. We often wished, when we heard of Queen Adelaide or the Duke of Wellington[4] being ill, that they would send for Mr Hoggins; but, on consideration, we were rather glad they did not, for if we were ailing, what should we do if Mr Hoggins had been appointed physician-in-ordinary to the Royal Family? As a surgeon we were proud of him; but as a man – or rather, I should say, as a gentleman – we could only shake our heads over his name and himself, and wished that he had read Lord Chesterfield's Letters[5] in the days when his manners were susceptible of improvement. Nevertheless, we all regarded his dictum in the Signor's case as infallible; and when he said, that with care and attention he might rally, we had no more fear for him.

But although we had no more fear, everybody did as much as if there was great cause for anxiety – as indeed there was, until Mr Hoggins took charge of him. Miss Pole looked out clean and comfortable, if homely, lodgings; Miss Matty sent the sedan-chair for him; and Martha and I aired it well before it left Cranford, by holding a warming-pan full of red-hot coals in it, and then shutting it up close, smoke and all, until the time when he should get into it at the Rising Sun. Lady Glenmire undertook the medical department under Mr Hoggins's directions; and rummaged up all Mrs Jamieson's medicine glasses, and spoons, and bed-tables, in a free and easy way, that made Miss Matty feel a little anxious as to what that lady and Mr Mulliner might say, if they knew. Mrs Forrester made some of the bread-jelly, for which she was so famous, to have ready as a refreshment in the lodgings when he should arrive. A present of this bread-jelly was the highest mark of favour dear Mrs Forrester could confer. Miss Pole had once asked her for the receipt, but she had met with a very decided rebuff; that lady told her that she could not part with it to anyone during her life, and that after her death it was bequeathed, as her executors would find, to Miss Matty. What Miss Matty – or, as Mrs Forrester called her (remembering the clause in her will, and the dignity of the occasion) Miss Matilda Jenkyns – might choose to do with the receipt when it came into her possession – whether to make it public, or to hand it down as an heirloom – she did not know, nor would she dictate. And a mould of this admirable, digestible, unique bread-jelly was sent by Mrs Forrester to our poor sick conjuror. Who says that the aristocracy are proud? Here was a lady, by birth a Tyrrell, and descended from the great Sir Walter that shot King Rufus, and in whose veins ran the blood of him who murdered the little Princes in the Tower,[6] going every day to see what dainty dishes she could prepare for Samuel Brown, a mountebank! But, indeed, it was wonderful to see what kind feelings were called out by this poor man's coming amongst us. And also wonderful to see how the great Cranford panic, which had been occasioned by his first coming in his Turkish dress, melted away into thin air on his second coming – pale and feeble, and with his heavy filmy eyes, that only brightened a very little when they fell upon the countenance of his faithful wife, or their pale and sorrowful little girl.

Somehow, we all forgot to be afraid. I dare say it was, that finding out that he, who had first excited our love of the marvellous by his unprecedented arts, had not sufficient every-day gifts to manage a shying horse, made us feel as if we were ourselves again. Miss Pole came with her little basket at all hours of the evening, as if her lonely house, and the unfrequented road to it, had never been infested by that 'murderous gang'; Mrs Forrester said, she thought that neither Jenny nor she need mind the headless lady who wept and wailed in Darkness Lane, for surely the power was never given to such beings to harm those who went about to try to do what little good was in their power; to which Jenny, trembling, assented; but the mistress's theory had little effect on the maid's practice, until she had sewed two pieces of red flannel, in the shape of a cross,[7] on her inner garment.

I found Miss Matty covering her penny ball – the ball that she used to roll under her bed – with gay-coloured worsted in rainbow stripes.

'My dear,' said she, 'my heart is sad for that little care-worn child. Although her father is a conjuror, she looks as if she had never had a good game of play in her life. I used to make very pretty balls in this way when I was a girl, and I thought I would try if I could not make this one smart and take it to Phoebe this afternoon. I think "the gang" must have left the neighbourhood, for one does not hear any more of their violence and robbery now.'

We were all of us far too full of the Signor's precarious state to talk about either robbers or ghosts. Indeed, Lady Glenmire said, she never had heard of any actual robberies; except that two little boys had stolen some apples from Farmer Benson's orchard, and that some eggs had been missed on a market-day off Widow Hayward's stall. But that was expecting too much of us; we could not acknowledge that we had only had this small foundation for all our panic. Miss Pole drew herself up at this remark of Lady Glenmire's; and said 'that she wished she could agree with her as to the very small reason we had had for alarm; but, with the recollection of a man disguised as a woman, who had endeavoured to force herself into her house, while his confederates waited outside; with the knowledge gained from Lady Glenmire herself, of the foot-prints seen on

Mrs Jamieson's flower-borders; with the fact before her of
the audacious robbery committed on Mr Hoggins at his own
door –' But here Lady Glenmire broke in with a very strong
expression of doubt as to whether this last story was not an
entire fabrication, founded upon the theft of a cat; she grew so
red while she was saying all this, that I was not surprised at
Miss Pole's manner of bridling up, and I am certain if Lady
Glenmire had not been 'her ladyship', we should have had a
more emphatic contradiction than the 'Well, to be sure!' and
similar fragmentary ejaculations, which were all that she ventured upon in my lady's presence. But when she was gone, Miss
Pole began a long congratulation to Miss Matty that, so far
they had escaped marriage, which she noticed always made
people credulous to the last degree; indeed, she thought it
argued great natural credulity in a woman if she could not keep
herself from being married; and in what Lady Glenmire had
said about Mr Hoggins's robbery, we had a specimen of what
people came to, if they gave way to such a weakness; evidently,
Lady Glenmire would swallow anything, if she could believe
the poor vamped-up story about a neck of mutton and a pussy,
with which he had tried to impose on Miss Pole, only she had
always been on her guard against believing too much of what
men said.

We were thankful, as Miss Pole desired us to be, that we had
never been married; but I think, of the two, we were even more
thankful that the robbers had left Cranford; at least I judge so
from a speech of Miss Matty's that evening, as we sat over the
fire, in which she evidently looked upon a husband as a great
protector against thieves, burglars, and ghosts; and said, that
she did not think that she should dare to be always warning
young people of matrimony, as Miss Pole did continually; – to
be sure, marriage was a risk, as she saw now she had had some
experience; but she remembered the time when she had looked
forward to being married as much as anyone.

'Not to any particular person, my dear,' said she, hastily
checking herself up as if she were afraid of having admitted too
much; 'only the old story, you know, of ladies always saying
"*When* I marry", and gentlemen, "*If* I marry".' It was a joke

spoken in rather a sad tone, and I doubt if either of us smiled; but I could not see Miss Matty's face by the flickering fire-light. In a little while she continued:

'But after all I have not told you the truth. It is so long ago, and no one ever knew how much I thought of it at the time, unless, indeed, my dear mother guessed; but I may say that there was a time when I did not think I should have been only Miss Matty Jenkyns all my life; for even if I did meet with anyone who wished to marry me now (and as Miss Pole says, one is never too safe), I could not take him – I hope he would not take it too much to heart, but I could *not* take him – or anyone but the person I once thought I should be married to, and he is dead and gone, and he never knew how it all came about that I said "no", when I had thought many and many a time – Well, it's no matter what I thought. God ordains it all, and I am very happy, my dear. No one has such kind friends as I,' continued she, taking my hand and holding it in hers.

If I had never known of Mr Holbrook, I could have said something in this pause, but as I had, I could not think of anything that would come in naturally, and so we both kept silence for a little time.

'My father once made us,' she began, 'keep a diary in two columns; on one side we were to put down in the morning what we thought would be the course and events of the coming day, and at night we were to put down on the other side what really had happened. It would be to some people rather a sad way of telling their lives'[8] – (a tear dropped upon my hand at these words) – 'I don't mean that mine has been sad, only so very different to what I expected. I remember, one winter's evening, sitting over our bed-room fire with Deborah – I remember it as if it were yesterday – and we were planning our future lives – both of us were planning, though only she talked about it. She said she should like to marry an archdeacon,[9] and write his charges; and you know, my dear, she never was married, and, for aught I know, she never spoke to an unmarried archdeacon in her life. I never was ambitious, nor could I have written charges, but I thought I could manage a house (my mother used to call me her right hand), and I was always so fond of little

children – the shyest babies would stretch out their little arms
to come to me; when I was a girl, I was half my leisure time
nursing in the neighbouring cottages – but I don't know how it
was, when I grew sad and grave – which I did a year or two
after this time – the little things drew back from me, and I am
afraid I lost the knack, though I am just as fond of children as
ever, and have a strange yearning at my heart whenever I see a
mother with her baby in her arms. Nay, my dear,' – (and by a
sudden blaze which sprang up from a fall of the unstirred coals,
I saw that her eyes were full of tears – gazing intently on some
vision of what might have been) – 'do you know, I dream
sometimes that I have a little child – always the same – a little
girl of about two years old; she never grows older, though I
have dreamt about her for many years. I don't think I ever
dream of any words or sound she makes; she is very noiseless
and still, but she comes to me when she is very sorry or very
glad, and I have wakened with the clasp of her dear little arms
round my neck. Only last night – perhaps because I had gone
to sleep thinking of this ball for Phoebe – my little darling came
in my dream, and put up her mouth to be kissed, just as I
have seen real babies do to real mothers before going to bed.
But all this is nonsense, dear! only don't be frightened by
Miss Pole from being married. I can fancy it may be a very
happy state, and a little credulity helps one on through life very
smoothly, – better than always doubting and doubting, and
seeing difficulties and disagreeables in everything.'

If I had been inclined to be daunted from matrimony, it
would not have been Miss Pole to do it; it would have been the
lot of poor Signor Brunoni and his wife. And yet again, it
was an encouragement to see how, through all their cares and
sorrows, they thought of each other and not of themselves; and
how keen were their joys, if they only passed through each
other, or through the little Phoebe.

The Signora told me, one day, a good deal about their lives
up to this period. It began by my asking her whether Miss Pole's
story of the twin-brothers was true; it sounded so wonderful a
likeness, that I should have had my doubts, if Miss Pole had
not been unmarried. But the Signora, or (as we found out she

preferred to be called) Mrs Brown, said it was quite true; that her brother-in-law was by many taken for her husband, which was of great assistance to them in their profession; 'though,' she continued, 'how people can mistake Thomas for the real Signor Brunoni, I can't conceive; but he says they do; so I suppose I must believe him. Not but what he is a very good man; I am sure I don't know how we should have paid our bill at the Rising Sun, but for the money he sends; but people must know very little about art, if they can take him for my husband. Why, Miss, in the ball trick, where my husband spreads his fingers wide, and throws out his little finger with quite an air and a grace, Thomas just clumps up his hand like a fist, and might have ever so many balls hidden in it. Besides, he has never been in India, and knows nothing of the proper sit of a turban.'

'Have you been in India?' said I, rather astonished.

'Oh yes! many a year, ma'am. Sam was a serjeant in the 31st;[10] and when the regiment was ordered to India, I drew a lot to go, and I was more thankful than I can tell; for it seemed as if it would only be a slow death to me to part from my husband. But, indeed, ma'am, if I had known all, I don't know whether I would not rather have died there and then, than gone through what I have done since. To be sure, I've been able to comfort Sam, and to be with him; but, ma'am, I've lost six children,' said she, looking up at me with those strange eyes, that I have never noticed but in mothers of dead children – with a kind of wild look in them, as if seeking for what they never more might find. 'Yes! Six children died off, like little buds nipped untimely, in that cruel India. I thought, as each died, I never could – I never would – love a child again; and when the next came, it had not only its own love, but the deeper love that came from the thoughts of its little dead brothers and sisters. And when Phoebe was coming, I said to my husband, "Sam, when the child is born, and I am strong, I shall leave you; it will cut my heart cruel; but if this baby dies too, I shall go mad; the madness is in me now; but if you let me go down to Calcutta, carrying my baby step by step, it will maybe work itself off; and I will save, and I will hoard, and I will beg, – and

I will die, to get a passage home to England, where our baby may live!" God bless him! he said I might go; and he saved up his pay, and I saved every pice I could get for washing or any way; and when Phoebe came, and I grew strong again, I set off. It was very lonely; through the thick forests, dark again with their heavy trees – along by the rivers' side – (but I had been brought up near the Avon in Warwickshire, so that flowing noise sounded like home), from station to station, from Indian village to village, I went along, carrying my child. I had seen one of the officer's ladies with a little picture, ma'am – done by a Catholic foreigner, ma'am – of the Virgin and the little Saviour, ma'am. She had him on her arm, and her form was softly curled round him, and their cheeks touched. Well, when I went to bid good-bye to this lady, for whom I had washed, she cried sadly; for she, too, had lost her children, but she had not another to save, like me; and I was bold enough to ask her, would she give me that print? And she cried the more, and said *her* children were with that little blessed Jesus; and gave it me, and told me she had heard it had been painted on the bottom of a cask,[11] which made it have that round shape. And when my body was very weary, and my heart was sick – (for there were times when I misdoubted if I could ever reach my home, and there were times when I thought of my husband; and one time when I thought my baby was dying) – I took out that picture and looked at it, till I could have thought the mother spoke to me, and comforted me. And the natives were very kind. We could not understand one another; but they saw my baby on my breast, and they came out to me, and brought me rice and milk, and sometimes flowers – I have got some of the flowers dried. Then, the next morning, I was so tired! and they wanted me to stay with them – I could tell that – and tried to frighten me from going into the deep woods, which, indeed, looked very strange and dark; but it seemed to me as if Death was following me to take my baby away from me; and as if I must go on, and on – and I thought how God had cared for mothers ever since the world was made, and would care for me; so I bade them good-bye, and set off afresh. And once when my baby was ill, and both she and I needed rest, He led me to a place where I found a kind Englishman lived, right in the midst of the natives.'

'And you reached Calcutta safely at last?'

'Yes! safely. Oh! when I knew I had only two days' journey more before me, I could not help it, ma'am – it might be idolatry, I cannot tell – but I was near one of the native temples, and I went in it with my baby to thank God for his great mercy; for it seemed to me that where others had prayed before to their God, in their joy or in their agony, was of itself a sacred place. And I got as servant to an invalid lady, who grew quite fond of my baby aboard-ship; and, in two years' time, Sam earned his discharge, and came home to me, and to our child. Then he had to fix on a trade; but he knew of none; and, once, once upon a time, he had learnt some tricks from an Indian juggler; so he set up conjuring, and it answered so well that he took Thomas to help him – as his man, you know, not as another conjuror, though Thomas has set it up now on his own hook. But it has been a great help to us that likeness between the twins, and made a good many tricks go off well that they made up together. And Thomas is a good brother, only he has not the fine carriage of my husband, so that I can't think how he can be taken for Signor Brunoni himself, as he says he is.'

'Poor little Phoebe!' said I, my thoughts going back to the baby she carried all those hundred miles.

'Ah! you may say so! I never thought I should have reared her, though, when she fell ill at Chunderabaddad;[12] but that good, kind Aga Jenkyns took us in, which I believe was the very saving of her.'

'Jenkyns!' said I.

'Yes! Jenkyns. I shall think all people of that name are kind; for here is that nice old lady who comes every day to take Phoebe a walk!'

But an idea had flashed through my head: could the Aga Jenkyns be the lost Peter? True, he was reported by many to be dead. But, equally true, some had said that he had arrived at the dignity of great Lama of Thibet. Miss Matty thought he was alive. I would make further inquiry.

CHAPTER XII

ENGAGED TO BE MARRIED!

Was the 'poor Peter' of Cranford the Aga Jenkyns of Chunderabaddad, or was he not? As somebody says, that was the question.[1]

In my own home, whenever people had nothing else to do, they blamed me for want of discretion. Indiscretion was my bugbear fault. Everybody has a bugbear fault; a sort of standing characteristic – a *pièce de résistance* for their friends to cut at; and in general they cut and come again. I was tired of being called indiscreet and incautious; and I determined for once to prove myself a model of prudence and wisdom. I would not even hint my suspicions respecting the Aga. I would collect evidence and carry it home to lay before my father, as the family friend of the two Miss Jenkynses.

In my search after facts, I was often reminded of a description my father had once given of a Ladies' Committee that he had had to preside over. He said he could not help thinking of a passage in Dickens, which spoke of a chorus in which every man took the tune he knew best, and sang it to his own satisfaction.[2] So, at this charitable committee, every lady took the subject uppermost in her mind, and talked about it to her own great contentment, but not much to the advancement of the subject they had met to discuss. But even that committee could have been nothing to the Cranford ladies when I attempted to gain some clear and definite information as to poor Peter's height, appearance, and when and where he was seen and heard of last. For instance, I remember asking Miss Pole (and I thought the question was very opportune, for I put it when I met her at a call at Mrs Forrester's, and both the ladies had known Peter, and I imagined that they might refresh each other's memories); I asked Miss Pole what was the very last thing they had ever heard about him; and then she named the absurd report to which I have alluded, about his having been elected great Lama of Thibet; and this was a signal for each lady to go off on her separate idea. Mrs Forrester's start was made on the Veiled Prophet in Lalla Rookh[3] – whether I thought he was meant for the Great Lama, though Peter was not so ugly, indeed rather handsome if he had not been freckled. I was thankful to see her double upon Peter; but, in a moment, the delusive lady was off upon Rowlands' Kalydor,[4] and the merits of cosmetics and hair oils in general, and holding forth so fluently that I turned to listen to Miss Pole, who (through the llamas, the beasts of burden) had got to Peruvian bonds,[5] and the Share Market, and her poor opinion of joint-stock banks in general, and of that one in particular in which Miss Matty's money was invested. In vain I put in, 'When was it – in what year was it, that you heard that Mr Peter was the Great Lama?' They only joined issue to dispute whether llamas were carnivorous animals or not; in which dispute they were not quite on fair grounds, as Mrs Forrester (after they had grown warm and cool again) acknowledged that she always confused carnivorous and graminivorous together, just as she did horizontal and perpendicular; but then she apologised for it very prettily, by saying that in her day the only use people made of four-syllabled words was to teach how they should be spelt.

The only fact I gained from this conversation was that certainly Peter had last been heard of in India, 'or that neighbourhood'; and that this scanty intelligence of his whereabouts had reached Cranford in the year when Miss Pole had bought her India muslin gown, long since worn out (we washed it and mended it, and traced its decline and fall into a window-blind, before we could go on); and in a year when Wombwell came to Cranford, because Miss Matty had wanted to see an elephant in order that she might the better imagine Peter riding on one; and had seen a boa-constrictor too, which was more than she wished to imagine in her fancy pictures of Peter's locality; – and in a year when Miss Jenkyns had learnt some

piece of poetry off by heart, and used to say, at all the
Cranford parties, how Peter was 'surveying mankind from
China to Peru',[6] which everybody had thought very grand,
and rather appropriate, because India was between China and
Peru, if you took care to turn the globe to the left instead of
the right.

I suppose all these inquiries of mine, and the consequent
curiosity excited in the minds of my friends, made us blind and
deaf to what was going on around us. It seemed to me as if the
sun rose and shone, and as if the rain rained on Cranford just
as usual, and I did not notice any sign of the times that could
be considered as a prognostic of any uncommon event; and, to
the best of my belief, not only Miss Matty and Mrs Forrester,
but even Miss Pole herself, whom we looked upon as a kind of
prophetess from the knack she had of foreseeing things before
they came to pass – although she did not like to disturb her
friends by telling them her fore-knowledge – even Miss Pole
herself was breathless with astonishment, when she came to tell
us of the astounding piece of news. But I must recover myself;
the contemplation of it, even at this distance of time, has taken
away my breath and my grammar, and unless I subdue my
emotion, my spelling will go too.

We were sitting – Miss Matty and I much as usual; she in
the blue chintz easy chair, with her back to the light, and her
knitting in her hand – I reading aloud the 'St James's Chronicle'.
A few minutes more, and we should have gone to make the little
alterations in dress usual before calling time (twelve o'clock)
in Cranford. I remember the scene and the date well. We had
been talking of the Signor's rapid recovery since the warmer
weather had set in, and praising Mr Hoggins's skill, and
lamenting his want of refinement and manner – (it seems a
curious coincidence that this should have been our subject, but
so it was) – when a knock was heard; a caller's knock – three
distinct taps – and we were flying (that is to say, Miss Matty
could not walk very fast, having had a touch of rheumatism)
to our rooms, to change cap and collars, when Miss Pole
arrested us by calling out as she came up the stairs, 'Don't go
– I can't wait – it is not twelve, I know – but never mind your

dress – I must speak to you.' We did our best to look as if it was not we who had made the hurried movement, the sound of which she had heard; for, of course, we did not like to have it supposed that we had any old clothes that it was convenient to wear out in the 'sanctuary of home', as Miss Jenkyns once prettily called the back parlour, where she was tying up preserves. So we threw our gentility with double force into our manners, and very genteel we were for two minutes while Miss Pole recovered breath, and excited our curiosity strongly by lifting up her hands in amazement, and bringing them down in silence, as if what she had to say was too big for words, and could only be expressed by pantomime.

'What do you think, Miss Matty? What *do* you think? Lady Glenmire is to marry – is to be married, I mean – Lady Glenmire – Mr Hoggins – Mr Hoggins is going to marry Lady Glenmire!'

'Marry!' said we. 'Marry! Madness!'

'Marry!' said Miss Pole, with the decision that belonged to her character. 'I said Marry! as you do; and I also said, "What a fool my lady is going to make of herself!" I could have said "Madness!" but I controlled myself, for it was in a public shop that I heard of it. Where feminine delicacy is gone to, I don't know! You and I, Miss Matty, would have been ashamed to have known that our marriage was spoken of in a grocer's shop, in the hearing of shopmen!'

'But,' said Miss Matty, sighing as one recovering from a blow, 'perhaps it is not true. Perhaps we are doing her injustice.'

'No!' said Miss Pole. 'I have taken care to ascertain that. I went straight to Mrs Fitz-Adam, to borrow a cookery book which I knew she had; and I introduced my congratulations *à propos* of the difficulty gentlemen must have in housekeeping; and Mrs Fitz-Adam bridled up, and said, that she believed it was true, though how and where I could have heard it she did not know. She said her brother and Lady Glenmire had come to an understanding at last. "Understanding!" such a coarse word![7] But my lady will have to come down to many a want of refinement. I have reason to believe Mr Hoggins sups on bread-and-cheese and beer[8] every night.'

'Marry!' said Miss Matty once again. 'Well! I never thought

of it. Two people that we know going to be married. It's coming
very near!'

'So near that my heart stopped beating, when I heard of it,
while you might have counted twelve,' said Miss Pole.

'One does not know whose turn may come next. Here, in
Cranford, poor Lady Glenmire might have thought herself safe,'
said Miss Matty, with a gentle pity in her tones.

'Bah!' said Miss Pole, with a toss of her head. 'Don't you
remember poor dear Captain Brown's song "Tibbie Fowler",
and the line –

> "Set her on the Tintock Tap,
> The wind will blaw a man 'till her." "[9]

'That was because "Tibbie Fowler" was rich I think.'

'Well! there is a kind of attraction about Lady Glenmire that
I, for one, should be ashamed to have.'

I put in my wonder.[10] 'But how can she have fancied Mr
Hoggins? I am not surprised that Mr Hoggins has liked her.'

'Oh! I don't know. Mr Hoggins is rich, and very pleasant-
looking,' said Miss Matty, 'and very good-tempered and kind-
hearted.'

'She has married for an establishment, that's it. I suppose she
takes the surgery with it,' said Miss Pole, with a little dry laugh
at her own joke. But, like many people who think they have
made a severe and sarcastic speech, which yet is clever of its
kind, she began to relax in her grimness from the moment when
she made this allusion to the surgery; and we turned to speculate
on the way in which Mrs Jamieson would receive the news. The
person whom she had left in charge of her house to keep off
followers from her maids, to set up a follower of her own!
And that follower a man whom Mrs Jamieson had tabooed as
vulgar, and inadmissible to Cranford society; not merely on
account of his name, but because of his voice, his complexion,
his boots, smelling of the stable, and himself, smelling of drugs.
Had he ever been to see Lady Glenmire at Mrs Jamieson's?
Chloride of lime would not purify the house in its owner's
estimation if he had. Or had their interviews been confined to

the occasional meetings in the chamber of the poor sick conjuror, to whom, with all our sense of the *mésalliance* we could
not help allowing that they had both been exceedingly kind?
And now it turned out that a servant of Mrs Jamieson's had
been ill, and Mr Hoggins had been attending her for some
weeks. So the wolf had got into the fold, and now he was
carrying off the shepherdess. What would Mrs Jamieson say?
We looked into the darkness of futurity as a child gazes after a
rocket up in the cloudy sky, full of wondering expectation of
the rattle, the discharge, and the brilliant shower of sparks and
light. Then we brought ourselves down to earth and the present
time, by questioning each other (being all equally ignorant, and
all equally without the slightest data to build any conclusions
upon) as to when IT would take place? Where? How much a
year Mr Hoggins had? Whether she would drop her title? And
how Martha and the other correct servants in Cranford would
ever be brought to announce a married couple as Lady Glenmire and Mr Hoggins? But would they be visited? Would Mrs
Jamieson let us? Or must we choose between the Honourable
Mrs Jamieson and the degraded Lady Glenmire. We all liked
Lady Glenmire the best. She was bright, and kind, and sociable,
and agreeable; and Mrs Jamieson was dull, and inert, and
pompous, and tiresome. But we had acknowledged the sway of
the latter so long, that it seemed like a kind of disloyalty now
even to meditate disobedience to the prohibition we anticipated.

Mrs Forrester surprised us in our darned caps and patched
collars; and we forgot all about them in our eagerness to see
how she would bear the information, which we honourably left
to Miss Pole to impart, although, if we had been inclined to
take unfair advantage, we might have rushed in ourselves, for
she had a most out-of-place fit of coughing for five minutes
after Mrs Forrester entered the room. I shall never forget the
imploring expression of her eyes, as she looked at us over her
pocket-handkerchief. They said, as plain as words could speak,
'Don't let Nature deprive me of the treasure which is mine,
although for a time I can make no use of it.' And we did not.

Mrs Forrester's surprise was equal to ours; and her sense of
injury rather greater, because she had to feel for her Order,[11]

and saw more fully than we could do how such conduct brought stains on the aristocracy.

When she and Miss Pole left us, we endeavoured to subside into calmness; but Miss Matty was really upset by the intelligence she had heard. She reckoned it up, and it was more than fifteen years since she had heard of any of her acquaintance going to be married, with the one exception of Miss Jessie Brown; and, as she said, it gave her quite a shock, and made her feel as if she could not think what would happen next.

I don't know if it is a fancy of mine, or a real fact, but I have noticed that, just after the announcement of an engagement in any set, the unmarried ladies in that set flutter out in an unusual gaiety and newness of dress, as much as to say, in a tacit and unconscious manner, 'We also are spinsters.' Miss Matty and Miss Pole talked and thought more about bonnets, gowns, caps, and shawls, during the fortnight that succeeded this call, than I had known them do for years before. But it might be the spring weather, for it was a warm and pleasant March; and merinoes and beavers, and woollen materials of all sorts, were but ungracious receptacles of the bright sun's glancing rays. It had not been Lady Glenmire's dress that had won Mr Hoggins's heart, for she went about on her errands of kindness more shabby than ever. Although in the hurried glimpses I caught of her at church or elsewhere, she appeared rather to shun meeting any of her friends, her face seemed to have almost something of the flush of youth in it; her lips looked redder, and more trembling full than in their old compressed state, and her eyes dwelt on all things with a lingering light, as if she was learning to love Cranford and its belongings. Mr Hoggins looked broad and radiant, and creaked up the middle aisle at church in a bran-new pair of top-boots – an audible, as well as visible, sign[12] of his purposed change of state; for the tradition went, that the boots he had worn till now were the identical pair in which he first set out on his rounds in Cranford twenty-five years ago; only they had been new-pieced, high and low, top and bottom, heel and sole, black leather and brown leather, more times than anyone could tell.

None of the ladies in Cranford chose to sanction the marriage by congratulating either of the parties. We wished to ignore the whole affair until our liege lady, Mrs Jamieson, returned. Till she came back to give us our cue, we felt that it would be better to consider the engagement in the same light as the Queen of Spain's legs[13] – facts which certainly existed, but the less said about the better. This restraint upon our tongues – for you see if we did not speak about it to any of the parties concerned, how could we get answers to the questions that we longed to ask? – was beginning to be irksome, and our idea of the dignity of silence was paling before our curiosity, when another direction was given to our thoughts, by an announcement on the part of the principal shopkeeper of Cranford, who ranged the trades from grocer and cheesemonger to man-milliner, as occasion required, that the Spring Fashions were arrived, and would be exhibited on the following Tuesday, at his rooms in High Street. Now Miss Matty had been only waiting for this before buying herself a new silk gown. I had offered, it is true, to send to Drumble for patterns, but she had rejected my proposal, gently implying that she had not forgotten her disappointment about the sea-green turban. I was thankful that I was on the spot now, to counteract the dazzling fascination of any yellow or scarlet silk.

I must say a word or two here about myself. I have spoken of my father's old friendship for the Jenkyns family; indeed, I am not sure if there was not some distant relationship. He had willingly allowed me to remain all the winter at Cranford, in consideration of a letter which Miss Matty had written to him, about the time of the panic, in which I suspect she had exaggerated my powers and my bravery as a defender of the house. But now that the days were longer and more cheerful, he was beginning to urge the necessity of my return; and I only delayed in a sort of odd forlorn hope that if I could obtain any clear information, I might make the account given by the Signora of the Aga Jenkyns tally with that of 'poor Peter', his appearance and disappearance, which I had winnowed out of the conversation of Miss Pole and Mrs Forrester.

CHAPTER XIII

STOPPED PAYMENT

The very Tuesday morning on which Mr Johnson was going to show fashions, the post-woman brought two letters to the house. I say the post-woman, but I should say the postman's wife. He was a lame shoemaker, a very clean, honest man, much respected in the town; but he never brought the letters round except on unusual occasions, such as Christmas Day, or Good Friday; and on those days the letters, which should have been delivered at eight in the morning, did not make their appearance until two or three in the afternoon; for everyone liked poor Thomas, and gave him a welcome on these festive occasions. He used to say, 'he was welly stawed[1] wi' eating, for there were three or four houses where nowt would serve 'em but he must share in their breakfast'; and by the time he had done his last breakfast, he came to some other friend who was beginning dinner; but come what might in the way of temptation, Tom was always sober, civil, and smiling; and, as Miss Jenkyns used to say, it was a lesson in patience, that she doubted not would call out that precious quality in some minds, where, but for Thomas, it might have lain dormant and undiscovered. Patience was certainly very dormant in Miss Jenkyns's mind. She was always expecting letters, and always drumming on the table till the post-woman had called or gone past. On Christmas Day and Good Friday, she drummed from breakfast till church, from church-time till two o'clock – unless when the fire wanted stirring, when she invariably knocked down the fire-irons, and scolded Miss Matty for it. But equally certain was the hearty welcome and the good dinner for Thomas; Miss Jenkyns standing over him like a bold dragoon, questioning him as to his children – what they were doing – what school they went to; upbraiding him if another was likely to make its appearance, but sending even the little babies the shilling and the mince-pie which was her gift to all the children, with half-a-crown in addition for both father and mother. The Post was not half of so much consequence to dear Miss Matty; but not for the world would she have diminished Thomas's welcome, and his dole, though I could see that she felt rather shy over the ceremony, which had been regarded by Miss Jenkyns as a glorious opportunity for giving advice and benefiting her fellow-creatures. Miss Matty would steal the money all in a lump into his hand, as if she were ashamed of herself. Miss Jenkyns gave him each individual coin separate, with a 'There! that's for yourself; that's for Jenny', &c. Miss Matty would even beckon Martha out of the kitchen while he ate his food: and once, to my knowledge, winked at its rapid disappearance into a blue cotton pocket-handkerchief. Miss Jenkyns almost scolded him if he did not leave a clean plate, however heaped it might have been, and gave an injunction with every mouthful.

I have wandered a long way from the two letters that awaited us on the breakfast-table that Tuesday morning. Mine was from my father. Miss Matty's was printed. My father's was just a man's letter; I mean it was very dull, and gave no information beyond that he was well, that they had had a good deal of rain, that trade was very stagnant, and there were many disagreeable rumours afloat. He then asked me, if I knew whether Miss Matty still retained her shares in the Town and County Bank, as there were very unpleasant reports about it; though nothing more than he had always foreseen, and had prophesied to Miss Jenkyns years ago, when she would invest their little property in it – the only unwise step that clever woman had ever taken, to his knowledge – (the only time she ever acted against his advice, I knew). However, if anything had gone wrong, of course I was not to think of leaving Miss Matty while I could be of any use, &c.

'Who is your letter from, my dear? Mine is a very civil invitation, signed Edwin Wilson, asking me to attend an important meeting of the shareholders of the Town and County Bank, to be held in Drumble, on Thursday the twenty-first. I am sure, it is very attentive of them to remember me.'

I did not like to hear of this 'important meeting', for though I did not know much about business, I feared it confirmed what my father said: however, I thought, ill news always came fast enough, so I resolved to say nothing about my alarm, and merely told her that my father was well, and sent his kind regards to her. She kept turning over, and admiring her letter. At last she spoke:

'I remember their sending one to Deborah just like this; but that I did not wonder at, for everybody knew she was so clear-headed. I am afraid I could not help them much; indeed, if they came to accounts, I should be quite in the way, for I never could do sums in my head. Deborah, I know, rather wished to go, and went so far as to order a new bonnet for the occasion; but when the time came, she had a bad cold; so they sent her a very polite account of what they had done. Chosen a Director, I think it was. Do you think they want me to help them to choose a Director? I am sure, I should choose your father at once.'

'My father has no shares in the Bank,' said I.

'Oh, no! I remember! He objected very much to Deborah's buying any, I believe. But she was quite the woman of business, and always judged for herself; and here, you see, they have paid eight per cent. all these years.'

It was a very uncomfortable subject to me, with my half knowledge; so I thought I would change the conversation, and I asked at what time she thought we had better go and see the Fashions. 'Well, my dear,' she said, 'the thing is this; it is not etiquette to go till after twelve, but then, you see, all Cranford will be there, and one does not like to be too curious about dress and trimmings and caps, with all the world looking on. It is never genteel to be over-curious on these occasions. Deborah had the knack of always looking as if the latest fashion was nothing new to her; a manner she had caught from Lady Arley who did see all the new modes in London, you know. So I thought we would just slip down this morning, soon after breakfast; for I do want half a pound of tea; and then we could go up and examine the things at our leisure, and see exactly how my new silk gown must be made; and then, after twelve, we could go with our minds disengaged, and free from thoughts of dress.'

We began to talk of Miss Matty's new silk gown. I discovered that it would be really the first time in her life that she had had to choose anything of consequence for herself; for Miss Jenkyns had always been the more decided character, whatever her taste might have been; and it is astonishing how such people carry the world before them by the mere force of will. Miss Matty anticipated the sight of the glossy folds with as much delight as if the five sovereigns, set apart for the purchase, could buy all the silks in the shop; and (remembering my own loss of two hours in a toy-shop before I could tell on what wonder to spend a silver threepence) I was very glad that we were going early, that dear Miss Matty might have leisure for the delights of perplexity.

If a happy sea-green could be met with, the gown was to be sea-green: if not, she inclined to maize, and I to silver grey; and we discussed the requisite number of breadths until we arrived at the shop-door. We were to buy the tea, select the silk, and then clamber up the iron corkscrew stairs that led into what was once a loft, though now a Fashion show-room.

The young men at Mr Johnson's had on their best looks, and their best cravats, and pivotted themselves over the counter with surprising activity. They wanted to show us upstairs at once; but on the principle of business first and pleasure afterwards, we stayed to purchase the tea. Here Miss Matty's absence of mind betrayed itself. If she was made aware that she had been drinking green tea[2] at any time, she always thought it her duty to lie awake half through the night afterward – (I have known her take it in ignorance many a time without such effects) – and consequently green tea was prohibited the house; yet today she herself asked for the obnoxious article, under the impression that she was talking about the silk. However, the mistake was soon rectified; and then the silks were unrolled in good truth. By this time the shop was pretty well filled, for it was Cranford market-day, and many of the farmers and country

people from the neighbourhood round came in, sleeking down
their hair, and glancing shyly about from under their eyelids,
as anxious to take back some notion of the unusual gaiety to
the mistress or the lasses at home, and yet feeling that they were
out of place among the smart shopmen and gay shawls, and
summer prints. One honest-looking man, however, made his
way up to the counter at which we stood, and boldly asked to
look at a shawl or two. The other country folk confined themselves to the grocery side; but our neighbour was evidently too
full of some kind intention towards mistress, wife, or daughter,
to be shy; and it soon became a question with me, whether he
or Miss Matty would keep their shopman the longest time.
He thought each shawl more beautiful than the last; and, as for
Miss Matty, she smiled and sighed over each fresh bale that
was brought out; one colour set off another, and the heap
together would, as she said, make even the rainbow look poor.
   'I am afraid,' said she, hesitating, 'whichever I choose I shall
wish I had taken another. Look at this lovely crimson! it would
be so warm in winter. But spring is coming on, you know. I
wish I could have a gown for every season,' said she, dropping
her voice – as we all did in Cranford whenever we talked of
anything we wished for but could not afford. 'However,' she
continued in a louder and more cheerful tone, 'it would give
me a great deal of trouble to take care of them if I had them;
so, I think, I'll only take one. But which must it be, my dear?'
   And now she hovered over a lilac with yellow spots, while I
pulled out a quiet sage-green, that had faded into insignificance
under the more brilliant colours, but which was nevertheless a
good silk in its humble way. Our attention was called off to
our neighbour. He had chosen a shawl of about thirty shillings'
value; and his face looked broadly happy, under the anticipation, no doubt, of the pleasant surprise he should give to some
Molly or Jenny at home; he had tugged a leathern purse out
of his breeches pocket, and had offered a five-pound note in
payment for the shawl, and for some parcels which had been
brought round to him from the grocery counter; and it was just
at this point that he attracted our notice. The shopman was
examining the note with a puzzled, doubtful air:

'Town and County Bank! I am not sure, sir, but I believe we have received a warning against notes issued by this bank only this morning. I will just step and ask Mr Johnson, sir; but I'm afraid, I must trouble you for payment in cash, or in a note of a different bank.'

I never saw a man's countenance fall so suddenly into dismay and bewilderment. It was almost piteous to see the rapid change.

'Dang it!' said he, striking his fist down on the table, as if to try which was the harder; 'the chap talks as if notes and gold were to be had for the picking up.'

Miss Matty had forgotten her silk gown in her interest for the man. I don't think she had caught the name of the bank, and in my nervous cowardice, I was anxious that she should not; and so I began admiring the yellow-spotted lilac gown that I had been utterly condemning only a minute before. But it was of no use.

'What bank was it? I mean what bank did your note belong to?'

'Town and County Bank.'

'Let me see it,' said she quietly to the shopman, gently taking it out of his hand, as he brought it back to return it to the farmer.

Mr Johnson was very sorry, but, from information he had received, the notes issued by that bank were little better than waste paper.

'I don't understand it,' said Miss Matty to me in a low voice. 'That is our bank, is it not? – the Town and County Bank?'

'Yes,' said I. 'This lilac silk will just match the ribbons in your new cap, I believe,' I continued – holding up the folds so as to catch the light, and wishing that the man would make haste and be gone – and yet having a new wonder, that had only just sprung up, how far it was wise or right in me to allow Miss Matty to make this expensive purchase, if the affairs of the bank were really so bad as the refusal of the note implied.

But Miss Matty put on the soft dignified manner peculiar to her, rarely used, and yet which became her so well, and laying her hand gently on mine, she said,

'Never mind the silks for a few minutes, dear. I don't understand you, sir,' turning now to the shopman, who had been attending to the farmer. 'Is this a forged note?'

'Oh, no, ma'am. It is a true note of its kind; but you see, ma'am, it is a Joint Stock Bank, and there are reports out that it is likely to break. Mr Johnson is only doing his duty, ma'am, as I am sure Mr Dobson knows.'

But Mr Dobson could not respond to the appealing bow by any answering smile. He was turning the note absently over in his fingers, looking gloomily enough at the parcel containing the lately chosen shawl.

'It's hard upon a poor man,' said he, 'as earns every farthing with the sweat of his brow. However, there's no help for it. You must take back your shawl, my man; Lizzie must do on with her cloak for a while. And yon figs for the little ones – I promised them to 'em – I'll take them; but the 'bacco, and the other things –'

'I will give you five sovereigns for your note, my good man,' said Miss Matty. 'I think there is some great mistake about it, for I am one of the shareholders, and I'm sure they would have told me if things had not been going on right.'

The shopman whispered a word or two across the table to Miss Matty. She looked at him with a dubious air.

'Perhaps so,' said she. 'But I don't pretend to understand business; I only know, that if it is going to fail, and if honest people are to lose their money because they have taken our notes – I can't explain myself,' said she, suddenly becoming aware that she had got into a long sentence with four people for audience – 'only I would rather exchange my gold for the note, if you please,' turning to the farmer, 'and then you can take your wife the shawl. It is only going without my gown a few days longer,' she continued, speaking to me. 'Then, I have no doubt, everything will be cleared up.'

'But if it is cleared up the wrong way?' said I.

'Why! then it will only have been common honesty in me, as a shareholder, to have given this good man the money. I am quite clear about it in my own mind; but, you know, I can never speak quite as comprehensibly as others can; – only you must give me your note, Mr Dobson, if you please, and go on with your purchases with these sovereigns.'

The man looked at her with silent gratitude – too awkward to put his thanks into words; but he hung back for a minute or two, fumbling with his note.

'I'm loth to make another one lose instead of me, if it is a loss; but, you see, five pounds is a deal of money to a man with a family; and, as you say, ten to one in a day or two, the note will be as good as gold again.'

'No hope of that, my friend,' said the shopman.

'The more reason why I should take it,' said Miss Matty quietly. She pushed her sovereigns towards the man, who slowly laid his note down in exchange. 'Thank you. I will wait a day or two before I purchase any of these silks; perhaps you will then have a greater choice. My dear! will you come upstairs?'

We inspected the Fashions with as minute and curious an interest as if the gown to be made after them had been bought. I could not see that the little event in the shop below had in the least damped Miss Matty's curiosity as to the make of sleeves, or the sit of skirts. She once or twice exchanged congratulations with me on our private and leisurely view of the bonnets and shawls; but I was, all the time, not so sure that our examination was so utterly private, for I caught glimpses of a figure dodging behind the cloaks and mantles; and, by a dextrous move, I came face to face with Miss Pole, also in morning costume (the principal feature of which was her being without teeth,[3] and wearing a veil to conceal the deficiency), come on the same errand as ourselves. But she quickly took her departure, because, as she said, she had a bad head-ache and did not feel herself up to conversation.

As we came down through the shop, the civil Mr Johnson was awaiting us; he had been informed of the exchange of the note for gold, and with much good feeling and real kindness, but with a little want of tact, he wished to condole with Miss Matty, and impress upon her the true state of the case. I could only hope that he had heard an exaggerated rumour, for he said that her shares were worse than nothing, and that the bank could not pay a shilling in the pound. I was glad that Miss

Matty seemed still a little incredulous; but I could not tell how much of this was real or assumed, with that self-control which seemed habitual to ladies of Miss Matty's standing in Cranford, who would have thought their dignity compromised by the slightest expression of surprise, dismay, or any similar feeling to an inferior in station, or in a public shop. However, we walked home very silently. I am ashamed to say, I believe I was rather vexed and annoyed at Miss Matty's conduct, in taking the note to herself so decidedly. I had so set my heart upon her having a new silk gown, which she wanted sadly; in general she was so undecided anybody might turn her round; in this case I had felt that it was no use attempting it, but I was not the less put out at the result.

Somehow, after twelve o'clock, we both acknowledged to a sated curiosity about the Fashions; and to a certain fatigue of body (which was, in fact, depression of mind) that indisposed us to go out again. But still we never spoke of the note; till, all at once, something possessed me to ask Miss Matty, if she would think it her duty to offer sovereigns for all the notes of the Town and County Bank she met with? I could have bitten my tongue out the minute I had said it. She looked up rather sadly, and as if I had thrown a new perplexity into her already distressed mind; and for a minute or two, she did not speak. Then she said – my own dear Miss Matty – without a shade of reproach in her voice:

'My dear! I never feel as if my mind was what people call very strong; and it's often hard enough work for me to settle what I ought to do with the case right before me. I was very thankful to – I was very thankful, that I saw my duty this morning, with the poor man standing by me; but it's rather a strain upon me to keep thinking and thinking what I should do if such and such a thing happened; and, I believe, I had rather wait and see what really does come; and I don't doubt I shall be helped then, if I don't fidget myself, and get too anxious beforehand. You know, love, I'm not like Deborah. If Deborah had lived, I've no doubt she would have seen after them, before they had got themselves into this state.'

We had neither of us much appetite for dinner, though we

tried to talk cheerfully about indifferent things. When we returned into the drawing-room, Miss Matty unlocked her desk and began to look over her account-books. I was so penitent for what I had said in the morning, that I did not choose to take upon myself the presumption to suppose that I could assist her; I rather left her alone, as, with puzzled brow, her eye followed her pen up and down the ruled page. By-and-by she shut the book, locked her desk, and came and drew a chair to mine, where I sat in moody sorrow over the fire. I stole my hand into hers; she clasped it, but did not speak a word. At last she said, with forced composure in her voice, 'If that bank goes wrong, I shall lose one hundred and forty-nine pounds thirteen shillings and four-pence a year; I shall only have thirteen pounds a year left.' I squeezed her hand hard and tight. I did not know what to say. Presently (it was too dark to see her face) I felt her fingers work convulsively in my grasp; and I knew she was going to speak again. I heard the sobs in her voice as she said, 'I hope it's not wrong – not wicked – but oh! I am so glad poor Deborah is spared this. She could not have borne to come down in the world, – she had such a noble, lofty spirit.'

This was all she said about the sister who had insisted upon investing their little property in that unlucky bank.[4] We were later in lighting the candle than usual that night, and until that light shamed us into speaking, we sat together very silently and sadly.

However, we took to our work after tea with a kind of forced cheerfulness (which soon became real as far as it went), talking of that never-ending wonder, Lady Glenmire's engagement. Miss Matty was almost coming round to think it a good thing.

'I don't mean to deny that men are troublesome in a house. I don't judge from my own experience, for my father was neatness itself, and wiped his shoes on coming in as carefully as any woman; but still a man has a sort of knowledge of what should be done in difficulties, that it is very pleasant to have one at hand ready to lean upon. Now, Lady Glenmire, instead of being tossed about, and wondering where she is to settle, will be certain of a home among pleasant and kind people, such as our good Miss Pole and Mrs Forrester. And Mr Hoggins is really a very personable man; and as for his manners – why, if they are not very polished, I have known people with very good hearts and very clever minds too, who were not what some people reckoned refined, but who were both true and tender.'

She fell off into a soft reverie about Mr Holbrook, and I did not interrupt her, I was so busy maturing a plan I had had in my mind for some days, but which this threatened failure of the bank had brought to a crisis. That night, after Miss Matty went to bed, I treacherously lighted the candle again, and sat down in the drawing-room to compose a letter to the Aga Jenkyns – a letter which should affect him, if he were Peter, and yet seem a mere statement of dry facts if he were a stranger. The church clock pealed out two before I had done.

The next morning news came, both official and otherwise, that the Town and County Bank had stopped payment. Miss Matty was ruined.

She tried to speak quietly to me; but when she came to the actual fact, that she would have but about five shillings a week to live upon, she could not restrain a few tears.

'I am not crying for myself, dear,' said she, wiping them away; 'I believe I am crying for the very silly thought, of how my mother would grieve if she could know – she always cared for us so much more than for herself. But many a poor person has less; and I am not very extravagant, and, thank God, when the neck of mutton, and Martha's wages, and the rent, are paid, I have not a farthing owing. Poor Martha! I think she'll be sorry to leave me.'

Miss Matty smiled at me through her tears, and she would fain have had me see only the smile, not the tears.

It was an example to me, and I fancy it might be to many others, to see how immediately Miss Matty set about the retrenchment which she knew to be right under her altered circumstances. While she went down to speak to Martha, and break the intelligence to her, I stole out with my letter to the Aga Jenkyns, and went to the Signor's lodgings to obtain the exact address. I bound the Signora to secresy; and indeed, her military manners had a degree of shortness and reserve in them, which made her always say as little as possible, except when under the pressure of strong excitement. Moreover – (which made my secret doubly sure) – the Signor was now so far recovered as to be looking forward to travelling and conjuring again, in the space of a few days, when he, his wife, and little Phoebe, would leave Cranford. Indeed I found him looking over a great black and red placard, in which the Signor Brunoni's accomplishments were set forth, and to which only the name of the town where he would next display them was wanting. He and his wife were so much absorbed in deciding where the red letters would come in with most effect (it might have been the Rubric[1] for that matter), that it was some time before I could get my question asked privately, and not before I had given several decisions, the wisdom of which I questioned afterwards with equal sincerity as soon as the Signor threw in his doubts and reasons on the important subject. At last I got the address, spelt by sound; and very queer it looked! I dropped it in the post on my way home; and then for a minute I stood looking at the wooden pane, with a gaping slit, which divided me from the letter, but a moment ago in my hand. It was gone from me like life – never to be recalled. It would get tossed about on the sea, and stained with sea-waves perhaps; and be carried among palm-trees, and scented with all tropical fragrance; – the little piece of paper, but an hour ago so familiar and commonplace, had set out on its race to the strange wild countries beyond the Ganges! But I could not afford to lose much time on this speculation. I hastened home, that Miss Matty might not miss me. Martha opened the door to me, her face swollen with crying. As soon as she saw me, she burst out afresh, and taking hold of my arm she pulled me in, and banged the door to, in order to ask me if indeed it was all true that Miss Matty had been saying.

'I'll never leave her! No! I won't. I told her so, and said I could not think how she could find in her heart to give me warning. I could not have had the face to do it, if I'd been her. I might ha' been just as good-for-nothing as Mrs Fitz-Adam's Rosy, who struck for wages after living seven years and a half in one place. I said I was not one to go and serve Mammon[2] at that rate; that I knew when I'd got a good Missus, if she didn't know when she'd got a good servant –'

'But Martha;' said I, cutting in while she wiped her eyes.

'Don't "but Martha" me,' she replied to my deprecatory tone.

'Listen to reason –'

'I'll not listen to reason,' she said – now in full possession of her voice, which had been rather choked with sobbing. 'Reason always means what someone else has got to say. Now I think what I've got to say is good enough reason. But, reason or not, I'll say it, and I'll stick to it. I've money in the Savings' Bank,[3] and I've a good stock of clothes, and I'm not going to leave Miss Matty. No! not if she gives me warning every hour in the day!'

She put her arms akimbo, as much as to say she defied me; and, indeed, I could hardly tell how to begin to remonstrate with her, so much did I feel that Miss Matty in her increasing infirmity needed the attendance of this kind and faithful woman.

'Well!' said I at last –

'I'm thankful you begin with "well!" If you'd ha' begun with "but", as you did afore, I'd not ha' listened to you. Now you may go on.'

'I know you would be a great loss to Miss Matty, Martha –'

'I told her so. A loss she'd never cease to be sorry for,' broke in Martha, triumphantly.

'Still she will have so little – so very little – to live upon, that I don't see just now how she could find you food – she will even be pressed for her own. I tell you this, Martha, because I feel you are like a friend to dear Miss Matty – but you know she might not like to have it spoken about.'

Apparently this was even a blacker view of the subject than Miss Matty had presented to her; for Martha just sat down on the first chair that came to hand, and cried out loud – (we had been standing in the kitchen).

At last she put her apron down, and looking me earnestly in the face, asked, 'Was that the reason Miss Matty wouldn't order a pudding today? She said she had no great fancy for sweet things, and you and she would just have a mutton chop. But I'll be up to her. Never you tell, but I'll make her a pudding, and a pudding she'll like, too, and I'll pay for it myself; so mind you see she eats it. Many a one has been comforted in their sorrow by seeing a good dish come upon the table.'

I was rather glad that Martha's energy had taken the immediate and practical direction of pudding-making, for it staved off the quarrelsome discussion as to whether she should or should not leave Miss Matty's service. She began to tie on a clean apron, and otherwise prepare herself for going to the shop for the butter, eggs, and what else she might require; she would not use a scrap of the articles already in the house for her cookery, but went to an old tea-pot in which her private store of money was deposited, and took out what she wanted.

I found Miss Matty very quiet, and not a little sad; but by-and-by she tried to smile for my sake. It was settled that I was to write to my father, and ask him to come over and hold a consultation; and as soon as this letter was despatched, we began to talk over future plans. Miss Matty's idea was to take a single room, and retain as much of her furniture as would be necessary to fit up this, and sell the rest; and there to quietly exist upon what would remain after paying the rent. For my part, I was more ambitious and less contented. I thought of all the things by which a woman, past middle age, and with the education common to ladies fifty years ago, could earn or add to a living, without materially losing caste; but at length I put even this last clause on one side, and wondered what in the world Miss Matty could do.

Teaching was, of course, the first thing that suggested itself. If Miss Matty could teach children anything, it would throw her among the little elves in whom her soul delighted. I ran over her accomplishments. Once upon a time I had heard her say she could play, '*Ah! vous dirai-je, maman?*'[4] on the piano; but that was long, long ago; that faint shadow of musical acquirement had died out years before. She had also once been able to trace out patterns very nicely for muslin embroidery, by dint of placing a piece of silver-paper over the design to be copied, and holding both against the window-pane, while she marked the scollop and eyelet-holes.[5] But that was her nearest approach to the accomplishment of drawing, and I did not think it would go very far. Then again as to the branches of a solid English education – fancy-work and the use of the globes – such as the mistress of the Ladies' Seminary,[6] to which all the tradespeople in Cranford sent their daughters, professed to teach; Miss Matty's eyes were failing her, and I doubted if she could discover the number of threads in a worsted-work pattern, or rightly appreciate the different shades required for Queen Adelaide's face, in the loyal wool-work[7] now fashionable in Cranford. As for the use of the globes, I had never been able to find it out myself, so perhaps I was not a good judge of Miss Matty's capability of instructing in this branch of education; but it struck me that equators and tropics, and such mystical circles, were very imaginary lines indeed to her, and that she looked upon the signs of the Zodiac as so many remnants of the Black Art.

What she piqued herself upon, as arts, in which she excelled, was making candle-lighters, or 'spills' (as she preferred calling them), of coloured paper, cut so as to resemble feathers, and knitting garters in a variety of dainty stitches. I had once said, on receiving a present of an elaborate pair, that I should feel quite tempted to drop one of them in the street, in order to have it admired; but I found this little joke (and it was a very little one) was such a distress to her sense of propriety, and was taken with such anxious, earnest alarm, lest the temptation might some day prove too strong for me, that I quite regretted having ventured upon it. A present of these delicately-wrought garters, a bunch of gay 'spills', or a set of cards on which sewing-silk was wound in a mystical manner, were the well-known tokens of Miss Matty's favour. But would anyone pay to have their children taught these arts? or indeed would Miss Matty sell, for filthy lucre, the knack and the skill with which she made trifles of value to those who loved her?

I had to come down to reading, writing, and arithmetic; and, in reading the chapter every morning, she always coughed before coming to long words. I doubted her power of getting through a genealogical chapter,[8] with any number of coughs. Writing she did well and delicately; but spelling! She seemed to think that the more out-of-the-way this was, and the more trouble it cost her, the greater the compliment she paid to her correspondent; and words that she would spell quite correctly in her letters to me, became perfect enigmas when she wrote to my father.

No! there was nothing she could teach to the rising generation of Cranford; unless they had been quick learners and ready imitators of her patience, her humility, her sweetness, her quiet contentment with all that she could not do. I pondered and pondered until dinner was announced by Martha, with a face all blubbered and swollen with crying.

Miss Matty had a few little peculiarities, which Martha was apt to regard as whims below her attention, and appeared to consider as childish fancies, of which an old lady of fifty-eight should try and cure herself. But today everything was attended to with the most careful regard. The bread was cut to the imaginary pattern of excellence that existed in Miss Matty's mind, as being the way which her mother had preferred; the curtain was drawn so as to exclude the dead-brick wall of a

neighbour's stables, and yet left so as to show every tender leaf
of the poplar which was bursting into spring beauty. Martha's
tone to Miss Matty was just such as that good, rough-spoken
servant usually kept sacred for little children, and which I had
never heard her use to any grown-up person.

I had forgotten to tell Miss Matty about the pudding, and I
was afraid she might not do justice to it; for she had evidently
very little appetite this day; so I seized the opportunity of letting
her into the secret while Martha took away the meat. Miss
Matty's eyes filled with tears, and she could not speak, either
to express surprise or delight, when Martha returned, bearing
it aloft, made in the most wonderful representation of a lion
couchant that ever was moulded. Martha's face gleamed with
triumph, as she set it down before Miss Matty with an exultant
'There!' Miss Matty wanted to speak her thanks, but could not;
so she took Martha's hand and shook it warmly, which set
Martha off crying, and I myself could hardly keep up the necessary composure. Martha burst out of the room; and Miss Matty
had to clear her voice once or twice before she could speak. At
last she said, 'I should like to keep this pudding under a glass
shade,[9] my dear!' and the notion of the lion *couchant* with his
currant eyes, being hoisted up to the place of honour on a
mantel-piece, tickled my hysterical fancy, and I began to laugh,
which rather surprised Miss Matty.

'I am sure, dear, I have seen uglier things under a glass shade
before now,' said she.

So had I, many a time and oft; and I accordingly composed
my countenance (and now I could hardly keep from crying), and
we both fell to upon the pudding, which was indeed excellent –
only every morsel seemed to choke us, our hearts were so full.

We had too much to think about to talk much that afternoon.
It passed over very tranquilly. But when the tea-urn was brought
in, a new thought came into my head. Why should not Miss
Matty sell tea – be an agent to the East India Tea Company[10]
which then existed? I could see no objections to this plan, while
the advantages were many – always supposing that Miss Matty
could get over the degradation of condescending to anything
like trade. Tea was neither greasy, nor sticky – grease and

stickiness being two of the qualities which Miss Matty could not endure. No shop-window would be required. A small genteel notification of her being licensed to sell tea, would, it is true, be necessary; but I hoped that it could be placed where no one could see it. Neither was tea a heavy article, so as to tax Miss Matty's fragile strength. The only thing against my plan was the buying and selling involved.

While I was giving but absent answers to the questions Miss Matty was putting – almost as absently – we heard a clumping sound on the stairs, and a whispering outside the door: which indeed once opened and shut as if by some invisible agency. After a little while, Martha came in, dragging after her a great tall young man, all crimson with shyness, and finding his only relief in perpetually sleeking down his hair.

'Please, ma'am, he's only Jem Hearn,' said Martha, by way of an introduction; and so out of breath was she, that I imagine she had had some bodily struggle before she could overcome his reluctance to be presented on the courtly scene of Miss Matilda Jenkyns's drawing-room.

'And please, ma'am, he wants to marry me off-hand. And please, ma'am, we want to take a lodger – just one quiet lodger, to make our two ends meet; and we'd take any house conform- able; and, oh dear Miss Matty, if I may be so bold, would you have any objections to lodging with us? Jem wants it as much I do.' [To Jem:] – 'You great oaf! why can't you back me? – But he does want it, all the same, very bad – don't you, Jem? – only, you see, he's dazed at being called on to speak before quality.'

'It's not that,' broke in Jem. 'It's that you've taken me all on a sudden, and I didn't think for to get married so soon – and such quick work does flabbergast a man. It's not that I'm against it, ma'am,' (addressing Miss Matty), 'only Martha has such quick ways with her, when once she takes a thing into her head; and marriage, ma'am, – marriage nails a man, as one may say. I dare say I shan't mind it after it's once over.'

'Please, ma'am,' said Martha – who had plucked at his sleeve, and nudged him with her elbow, and otherwise tried to inter- rupt him all the time he had been speaking – 'don't mind him,

he'll come to; 'twas only last night he was an-axing me, and
an-axing me, and all the more because I said I could not think
of it for years to come, and now he's only taken aback with the
suddenness of the joy; but you know, Jem, you are just as full
as me about wanting a lodger.' (Another great nudge.)

'Ay! if Miss Matty would lodge with us – otherwise I've no
mind to be cumbered with strange folk in the house,' said Jem,
with a want of tact which I could see enraged Martha, who was
trying to represent a lodger as the great object they wished to
obtain, and that, in fact, Miss Matty would be smoothing their
path, and conferring a favour, if she would only come and live
with them.

Miss Matty herself was bewildered by the pair: their, or
rather Martha's, sudden resolution in favour of matrimony
staggered her, and stood between her and the contemplation of
the plan which Martha had at heart. Miss Matty began, –

'Marriage is a very solemn thing, Martha.'

'It is indeed, ma'am,' quoth Jem. 'Not that I've no objections
to Martha.'

'You've never let me a-be for asking me for to fix when I
would be married,' said Martha – her face all a-fire, and ready
to cry with vexation – 'and now you're shaming me before my
missus and all.'

'Nay, now! Martha, don't ee! don't ee! only a man likes
to have breathing-time,' said Jem, trying to possess himself of
her hand, but in vain. Then seeing that she was more seriously
hurt than he had imagined, he seemed to try to rally his scat-
tered faculties, and with more straightforward dignity than,
ten minutes before, I should have thought it possible for him
to assume, he turned to Miss Matty, and said, 'I hope, ma'am,
you know that I am bound to respect everyone who has been
kind to Martha. I always looked on her as to be my wife –
sometime; and she has often and often spoken of you as the
kindest lady that ever was; and though the plain truth is I
would not like to be troubled with lodgers of the common
run; yet if, ma'am, you'd honour us by living with us, I am
sure Martha would do her best to make you comfortable; and
I'd keep out of your way as much as I could, which I reckon

would be the best kindness such an awkward chap as me could do.'

Miss Matty had been very busy with taking off her spectacles, wiping them, and replacing them; but all she could say was, 'Don't let any thought of me hurry you into marriage: pray don't! Marriage is such a very solemn thing!'

'But Miss Matilda will think of your plan, Martha,' said I – struck with the advantages that it offered, and unwilling to lose the opportunity of considering about it. 'And I'm sure neither she nor I can ever forget your kindness; nor yours either, Jem.'

'Why, yes, ma'am! I'm sure I mean kindly, though I'm a bit fluttered by being pushed straight a-head into matrimony, as it were, and mayn't express myself conformable. But I'm sure I'm willing enough, and give me time to get accustomed; so, Martha, wench, what's the use of crying so, and slapping me if I come near?'

This last was *sotto voce*, and had the effect of making Martha bounce out of the room, to be followed and soothed by her lover. Whereupon Miss Matty sat down and cried very heartily, and accounted for it by saying that the thought of Martha being married so soon gave her quite a shock, and that she should never forgive herself if she thought she was hurrying the poor creature. I think my pity was more for Jem, of the two: but both Miss Matty and I appreciated to the full the kindness of the honest couple, although we said little about this, and a good deal about the chances and dangers of matrimony.

The next morning, very early, I received a note from Miss Pole, so mysteriously wrapped up, and with so many seals on it to secure secrecy, that I had to tear the paper before I could unfold it. And when I came to the writing I could hardly understand the meaning, it was so involved and oracular. I made out, however, that I was to go to Miss Pole's at eleven o'clock; the number *eleven* being written in full length as well as in numerals, and *A.M.* twice dashed under, as if I were very likely to come at eleven at night, when all Cranford was usually a-bed, and asleep by ten. There was no signature except Miss Pole's initials, reversed, P.E., but as Martha had given me the note, 'with Miss Pole's kind regards', it needed no wizard to find out who sent it; and if the writer's name was to be kept secret, it was very well that I was alone when Martha delivered it.

I went, as requested, to Miss Pole's. The door was opened to me by her little maid Lizzy, in Sunday trim, as if some grand event was impending over this work-day. And the drawing-room upstairs was arranged in accordance with this idea. The table was set out, with the best green card-cloth, and writing-materials upon it. On the little chiffonier was a tray with a newly-decanted bottle of cowslip wine, and some ladies'-finger biscuits. Miss Pole herself was in solemn array, as if to receive visitors, although it was only eleven o'clock. Mrs Forrester was there, crying quietly and sadly, and my arrival seemed only to call forth fresh tears. Before we had finished our greetings, performed with lugubrious mystery of demeanour, there was another rat-tat-tat, and Mrs Fitz-Adam appeared, crimson with walking and excitement. It seemed as if this was all the company expected; for now Miss Pole made several demonstrations of being about to open the business of the meeting, by stirring the fire, opening and shutting the door, and coughing and blowing her nose. Then she arranged us all round the table, taking care to place me opposite to her; and last of all, she inquired of me, if the sad report was true, as she feared it was, that Miss Matty had lost all her fortune?

Of course, I had but one answer to make; and I never saw more unaffected sorrow depicted on any countenances, than I did there on the three before me.

'I wish Mrs Jamieson was here!' said Mrs Forrester at last; but to judge from Mrs Fitz-Adam's face, she could not second the wish.

'But without Mrs Jamieson,' said Miss Pole, with just a sound of offended merit in her voice, 'we, the ladies of Cranford, in my drawing-room assembled, can resolve upon something. I imagine we are none of us what may be called rich, though we all possess a genteel competency, sufficient for tastes that are elegant and refined, and would not, if they could, be vulgarly ostentatious.' (Here I observed Miss Pole refer to a small card concealed in her hand, on which I imagine she had put down a few notes.)

'Miss Smith,' she continued, addressing me, (familiarly known as 'Mary' to all the company assembled, but this was a state occasion), 'I have conversed in private – I made it my business to do so yesterday afternoon – with these ladies on the misfortune which has happened to our friend, – and one and all of us have agreed that, while we have a superfluity, it is not only a duty but a pleasure, – a true pleasure, Mary!' – her voice was rather choked just here, and she had to wipe her spectacles before she could go on – 'to give what we can to assist her – Miss Matilda Jenkyns. Only, in consideration of the feelings of delicate independence existing in the mind of every refined female,' – I was sure she had got back to the card now – 'we wish to contribute our mites[11] in a secret and concealed manner, so as not to hurt the feelings I have referred to. And our object in requesting you to meet us this morning, is, that believing you are the daughter – that your father is, in fact, her confidential adviser in all pecuniary matters, we imagined that, by consulting with him, you might devise some mode in which our contribution could be made to appear the legal due which Miss Matilda Jenkyns ought to receive from—. Probably, your father, knowing her investments, can fill up the blank.'

Miss Pole concluded her address, and looked round for approval and agreement.

'I have expressed your meaning, ladies, have I not? And while Miss Smith considers what reply to make, allow me to offer you some little refreshment.'

I had no great reply to make; I had more thankfulness at my heart for their kind thoughts than I cared to put into words; and so I only mumbled out something to the effect 'that I would name what Miss Pole had said to my father, and that if anything could be arranged for dear Miss Matty,' – and here I broke down utterly, and had to be refreshed with a glass of cowslip wine before I could check the crying which had been repressed for the last two or three days. The worst was, all the ladies cried in concert. Even Miss Pole cried, who had said a hundred times that to betray emotion before anyone was a sign of weakness and want of self-control. She recovered herself into a slight degree of impatient anger, directed against me, as having set them all off; and, moreover, I think she was vexed that I could not make a speech back in return for hers; and if I had known beforehand what was to be said, and had had a card on which to express the probable feelings that would rise in my heart, I would have tried to gratify her. As it was, Mrs Forrester was the person to speak when we had recovered our composure.

'I don't mind, among friends, stating that I – no! I'm not poor exactly, but I don't think I'm what you may call rich; I wish I were, for dear Miss Matty's sake, – but, if you please, I'll write down, in a sealed paper, what I can give. I only wish it was more: my dear Mary, I do indeed.'

Now I saw why paper, pens, and ink, were provided. Every lady wrote down the sum she could give annually, signed the paper, and sealed it mysteriously. If their proposal was acceded to, my father was to be allowed to open the papers, under pledge of secresy. If not, they were to be returned to their writers.

When this ceremony had been gone through, I rose to depart; but each lady seemed to wish to have a private conference with me. Miss Pole kept me in the drawing-room to explain why, in Mrs Jamieson's absence, she had taken the lead in this 'movement',[12] as she was pleased to call it, and also to inform me that she had heard from good sources that Mrs Jamieson was coming home directly, in a state of high displeasure against her sister-in-law, who was forthwith to leave her house; and was, she believed, to return to Edinburgh that very afternoon. Of course this piece of intelligence could not be communicated before Mrs Fitz-Adam, more especially as Miss Pole was inclined to think that Lady Glenmire's engagement to Mr Hoggins could not possibly hold against the blaze of Mrs Jamieson's displeasure. A few hearty inquiries after Miss Matty's health concluded my interview with Miss Pole.

On coming downstairs, I found Mrs Forrester waiting for me at the entrance to the dining-parlour; she drew me in, and when the door was shut, she tried two or three times to begin on some subject, which was so unapproachable apparently, that I began to despair of our ever getting to a clear understanding. At last out it came; the poor old lady trembling all the time as if it were a great crime which she was exposing to daylight, in telling me how very, very little she had to live upon; a confession which she was brought to make from a dread lest we should think that the small contribution named in her paper bore any proportion to her love and regard for Miss Matty. And yet that sum which she so eagerly relinquished was, in truth, more than a twentieth part of what she had to live upon, and keep house, and a little serving-maid, all as became one born a Tyrrell. And when the whole income does not nearly amount to a hundred pounds, to give up a twentieth of it will necessitate many careful economies, and many pieces of self-denial – small and insignificant in the world's account, but bearing a different value in another account-book[13] that I have heard of. She did so wish she was rich, she said; and this wish she kept repeating, with no thought of herself in it, only with a longing, yearning desire to be able to heap up Miss Matty's measure of comforts.

It was some time before I could console her enough to leave her; and then, on quitting the house, I was waylaid by Mrs Fitz-Adam, who had also her confidence to make of pretty nearly the opposite description. She had not liked to put down all that she could afford, and was ready to give. She told me she thought she never could look Miss Matty in the face again if she presumed to be giving her so much as she should like to do. 'Miss Matty!' continued she, 'that I thought was such a fine young lady, when I was nothing but a country girl, coming to market with eggs and butter and such like things. For my father, though well to do, would always make me go on as my mother had done before me; and I had to come in to Cranford every Saturday and see after sales and prices, and what not. And one day, I remember, I met Miss Matty in the lane that leads to Combehurst; she was walking on the footpath which, you know, is raised a good way above the road, and a gentleman rode beside her, and was talking to her, and she was looking down at some primroses she had gathered, and pulling them all to pieces, and I do believe she was crying. But after she had passed, she turned round and ran after me to ask – oh so kindly – after my poor mother, who lay on her death-bed; and when I

cried, she took hold of my hand to comfort me; and the gentleman waiting for her all the time; and her poor heart very full
of something, I am sure; and I thought it such an honour to be
spoken to in that pretty way by the Rector's daughter, who
visited at Arley Hall. I have loved her ever since, though perhaps
I'd no right to do it; but if you can think of any way in which I
might be allowed to give a little more without anyone knowing
it, I should be so much obliged to you, my dear. And my brother
would be delighted to doctor her for nothing – medicines,
leeches,[14] and all. I know that he and her ladyship – (my dear!
I little thought in the days I was telling you of that I should ever
come to be sister-in-law to a ladyship!) – would do anything
for her. We all would.'

I told her I was quite sure of it, and promised all sorts of
things, in my anxiety to get home to Miss Matty, who might
well be wondering what had become of me, – absent from her
two hours without being able to account for it. She had taken
very little note of time, however, as she had been occupied in
numberless little arrangements preparatory to the great step
of giving up her house. It was evidently a relief to her to be
doing something in the way of retrenchment; for, as she said,
whenever she paused to think, the recollection of the poor
fellow with his bad five-pound note came over her, and she felt
quite dishonest; only if it made her so uncomfortable, what
must it not be doing to the directors of the Bank, who must
know so much more of the misery consequent upon this failure?
She almost made me angry by dividing her sympathy between
these directors (whom she imagined overwhelmed by self-
reproach for the mismanagement of other people's affairs), and
those who were suffering like her. Indeed, of the two, she
seemed to think poverty a lighter burden than self-reproach;
but I privately doubted if the directors would agree with her.

Old hoards were taken out and examined as to their money
value, which luckily was small, or else I don't know how Miss
Matty would have prevailed upon herself to part with such
things as her mother's wedding-ring, the strange uncouth
brooch with which her father had disfigured his shirt-frill,
&c. However, we arranged things a little in order as to their

pecuniary estimation, and were all ready for my father when he came the next morning.

I am not going to weary you with the details of all the business we went through; and one reason for not telling about them is, that I did not understand what we were doing at the time, and cannot recollect it now. Miss Matty and I sat assenting to accounts, and schemes, and reports, and documents, of which I do not believe we either of us understood a word; for my father was clear-headed and decisive, and a capital man of business, and if we made the slightest inquiry, or expressed the slightest want of comprehension, he had a sharp way of saying, 'Eh? eh? it's as clear as daylight. What's your objection?' And as we had not comprehended anything of what he had proposed, we found it rather difficult to shape our objections; in fact, we never were sure if we had any. So, presently Miss Matty got into a nervously acquiescent state, and said 'Yes' and 'Certainly' at every pause, whether required or not: but when I once joined in as chorus to a 'Decidedly', pronounced by Miss Matty in a tremblingly dubious tone, my father fired round at me and asked me 'What there was to decide?' And I am sure, to this day, I have never known. But, in justice to him, I must say, he had come over from Drumble to help Miss Matty when he could ill spare the time, and when his own affairs were in a very anxious state.

While Miss Matty was out of the room, giving orders for luncheon – and sadly perplexed between her desire of honouring my father by a delicate dainty meal, and her conviction that she had no right now that all her money was gone, to indulge this desire, – I told him of the meeting of Cranford ladies at Miss Pole's the day before. He kept brushing his hand before his eyes as I spoke; – and when I went back to Martha's offer the evening before, of receiving Miss Matty as a lodger, he fairly walked away from me to the window, and began drumming with his fingers upon it. Then he turned abruptly round, and said, 'See, Mary, how a good innocent life makes friends all around. Confound it! I could make a good lesson out of it if I were a parson; but as it is, I can't get a tail to my sentences – only I'm sure you feel what I want to say. You and I will have a walk after lunch, and talk a bit more about these plans.'

The lunch – a hot savoury mutton-chop, and a little of the cold lion sliced and fried – was now brought in. Every morsel of this last dish was finished, to Martha's great gratification. Then my father bluntly told Miss Matty he wanted to talk to me alone, and that he would stroll out and see some of the old places, and then I could tell her what plan we thought desirable. Just before we went out, she called me back and said, 'Remember dear, I'm the only one left – I mean there's no one to be hurt by what I do. I'm willing to do anything that's right and honest; and I don't think, if Deborah knows where she is, she'll care so very much if I'm not genteel; because, you see, she'll know all, dear. Only let me sell what I can, and pay the poor people as far as I'm able.'

I gave her a hearty kiss, and ran after my father. The result of our conversation was this. If all parties were agreeable, Martha and Jem were to be married with as little delay as possible, and they were to live on in Miss Matty's present abode; the sum which the Cranford ladies had agreed to contribute annually, being sufficient to meet the greater part of the rent, and leaving Martha free to appropriate what Miss Matty should pay for her lodgings to any little extra comforts required. About the sale, my father was dubious at first. He said the old Rectory furniture, however carefully used, and reverently treated, would fetch very little; and that little would be but as a drop in the sea of the debts of the Town and County Bank. But when I represented how Miss Matty's tender conscience would be soothed by feeling that she had done what she could, he gave way; especially after I had told him the five-pound-note adventure, and he had scolded me well for allowing it. I then alluded to my idea that she might add to her small income by selling tea; and, to my surprise, (for I had nearly given up the plan), my father grasped at it with all the energy of a tradesman. I think he reckoned his chickens before they were hatched, for he immediately ran up the profits of the sales that she could effect in Cranford to more than twenty pounds a-year. The small dining-parlour was to be converted into a shop, without any of its degrading characteristics; a table was to be the counter; one window was to be retained unaltered, and the other changed into a glass door. I evidently rose in his estimation, for having made this bright suggestion. I only hoped we should not both fall in Miss Matty's.

But she was patient and content with all our arrangements. She knew, she said, that we should do the best we could for her; and she only hoped, only stipulated, that she should pay every farthing that she could be said to owe for her father's sake, who had been so respected in Cranford. My father and I had agreed to say as little as possible about the Bank, indeed never to mention it again, if it could be helped. Some of the plans were evidently a little perplexing to her; but she had seen me sufficiently snubbed in the morning for want of comprehension to venture on too many inquiries now; and all passed over well, with a hope on her part that no one would be hurried into marriage on her account. When we came to the proposal that she should sell tea, I could see it was rather a shock to her; not on account of any personal loss of gentility involved, but only because she distrusted her own powers of action in a new line of life, and would timidly have preferred a little more privation to any exertion for which she feared she was unfitted. However, when she saw my father was bent upon it, she sighed, and said she would try; and if she did not do well, of course she might give it up. One good thing about it was, she did not think men ever bought tea; and it was of men particularly she was afraid. They had such sharp loud ways with them; and did up accounts, and counted their change so quickly! Now, if she might only sell comfits to children, she was sure she could please them!

CHAPTER XV

A HAPPY RETURN

Before I left Miss Matty at Cranford everything had been comfortably arranged for her. Even Mrs Jamieson's approval of her selling tea had been gained. That oracle had taken a few days to consider whether by so doing Miss Matty would forfeit her right to the privileges of society in Cranford. I think she had some little idea of mortifying Lady Glenmire by the decision she gave at last; which was to this effect: that whereas a married woman takes her husband's rank by the strict laws of precedence, an unmarried woman retains the station her father occupied.[1] So Cranford was allowed to visit Miss Matty; and, whether allowed or not, it intended to visit Lady Glenmire.

But what was our surprise – our dismay – when we learnt that Mr and *Mrs Hoggins* were returning on the following Tuesday. Mrs Hoggins! Had she absolutely dropped her title, and so, in a spirit of bravado, cut the aristocracy to become a Hoggins! She, who might have been called Lady Glenmire to her dying day! Mrs Jamieson was pleased. She said it only convinced her of what she had known from the first, that the creature had a low taste. But 'the creature' looked very happy on Sunday at church; nor did we see it necessary to keep our veils down on that side of our bonnets on which Mr and Mrs Hoggins sate, as Mrs Jamieson did; thereby missing all the smiling glory of his face, and all the becoming blushes of hers. I am not sure if Martha and Jem looked more radiant in the afternoon, when they too made their first appearance. Mrs Jamieson soothed the turbulence of her soul, by having the blinds of her windows drawn down, as if for a funeral,[2] on the day when Mr and Mrs Hoggins received callers; and it was

with some difficulty that she was prevailed upon to continue
the 'St James's Chronicle' – so indignant was she with its having
inserted the announcement of the marriage.

Miss Matty's sale went off famously. She retained the furniture of her sitting-room, and bed-room; the former of which
she was to occupy till Martha could meet with a lodger who
might wish to take it; and into this sitting-room and bed-room
she had to cram all sorts of things, which were (the auctioneer
assured her) bought in for her at the sale by an unknown friend.
I always suspected Mrs Fitz-Adam of this; but she must have
had an accessory, who knew what articles were particularly
regarded by Miss Matty on account of their associations with
her early days. The rest of the house looked rather bare, to be
sure; all except one tiny bed-room, of which my father allowed
me to purchase the furniture for my occasional use, in case of
Miss Matty's illness.

I had expended my own small store in buying all manner of
comfits and lozenges, in order to tempt the little people whom
Miss Matty loved so much, to come about her. Tea in bright
green canisters – and comfits in tumblers – Miss Matty and I
felt quite proud as we looked round us on the evening before
the shop was to be opened. Martha had scoured the boarded
floor to a white cleanness, and it was adorned with a brilliant
piece of oil-cloth on which customers were to stand before the
table-counter. The wholesome smell of plaster and white-
wash pervaded the apartment. A very small 'Matilda Jenkyns,
licensed to sell tea' was hidden under the lintel of the new door,
and two boxes of tea with cabalistic inscriptions all over them
stood ready to disgorge their contents into the canisters.

Miss Matty, as I ought to have mentioned before, had
had some scruples of conscience at selling tea when there was
already Mr Johnson in the town, who included it among his
numerous commodities; and, before she could quite reconcile
herself to the adoption of her new business, she had trotted
down to his shop, unknown to me, to tell him of the project
that was entertained, and to inquire if it was likely to injure his
business, My father called this idea of hers 'great nonsense',
and 'wondered how tradespeople were to get on if there was

to be a continual consulting of each others' interests, which would put a stop to all competition directly'. And, perhaps, it would not have done in Drumble, but in Cranford it answered very well; for not only did Mr Johnson kindly put at rest all Miss Matty's scruples, and fear of injuring his business, but, I have reason to know, he repeatedly sent customers to her, saying that the teas he kept were of a common kind, but that Miss Jenkyns had all the choice sorts. And expensive tea is a very favourite luxury with well-to-do tradespeople, and rich farmers' wives, who turn up their noses at the Congou and Souchong prevalent at many tables of gentility, and will have nothing else than Gunpowder and Pekoe[3] for themselves.

But to return to Miss Matty. It was really very pleasant to see how her unselfishness, and simple sense of justice, called out the same good qualities in others. She never seemed to think anyone would impose upon her, because she should be so grieved to do it to them. I have heard her put a stop to the asseverations of the man who brought her coals, by quietly saying, 'I am sure you would be sorry to bring me wrong weight'; and if the coals were short measure that time, I don't believe they ever were again. People would have felt as much ashamed of presuming on her good faith as they would have done on that of a child. But my father says, 'such simplicity might be very well in Cranford, but would never do in the world'. And I fancy the world must be very bad, for with all my father's suspicion of everyone with whom he has dealings, and in spite of all his many precautions, he lost upwards of a thousand pounds by roguery only last year.

I just stayed long enough to establish Miss Matty in her new mode of life, and to pack up the library, which the Rector had purchased. He had written a very kind letter to Miss Matty, saying, 'how glad he should be to take a library so well selected as he knew that the late Mr Jenkyns's must have been, at any valuation put upon them'. And when she agreed to this, with a touch of sorrowful gladness that they would go back to the Rectory, and be arranged on the accustomed walls once more, he sent word that he feared that he had not room for them all, and perhaps Miss Matty would kindly allow him to leave some volumes on her shelves. But Miss Matty said that she had her Bible, and Johnson's Dictionary,[4] and should not have much time for reading, she was afraid. Still I retained a few books out of consideration for the Rector's kindness.

The money which he had paid, and that produced by the sale, was partly expended in the stock of tea, and part of it was invested against a rainy day; i. e. old age or illness. It was but a small sum, it is true; and it occasioned a few evasions of truth and white lies (all of which I think very wrong indeed – in theory – and would rather not put them in practice), for we knew Miss Matty would be perplexed as to her duty if she were aware of any little reserve-fund being made for her while the debts of the Bank remained unpaid. Moreover, she had never been told of the way in which her friends were contributing to pay the rent. I should have liked to tell her this; but the mystery of the affair gave a piquancy to their deed of kindness which the ladies were unwilling to give up; and at first Martha had to shirk many a perplexed question as to her ways and means of living in such a house; but by-and-by Miss Matty's prudent uneasiness sank down into acquiescence with the existing arrangement.

I left Miss Matty with a good heart. Her sales of tea during the first two days had surpassed my most sanguine expectations. The whole country round seemed to be all out of tea at once. The only alteration I could have desired in Miss Matty's way of doing business was, that she should not have so plaintively entreated some of her customers not to buy green tea – running it down as slow poison, sure to destroy the nerves, and produce all manner of evil. Their pertinacity in taking it, in spite of all her warnings, distressed her so much that I really thought she would relinquish the sale of it, and so lose half her custom; and I was driven to my wits' end for instances of longevity entirely attributable to a persevering use of green tea. But the final argument, which settled the question, was a happy reference of mine to the train oil and tallow candles which the Esquimaux not only enjoy but digest. After that she acknowledged that 'one man's meat might be another man's poison', and contented herself thenceforward with an occasional remonstrance, when she thought the purchaser was too young and innocent to be acquainted with the evil effects green tea produced on some constitutions; and an habitual sigh when people old enough to choose more wisely would prefer it.

I went over from Drumble once a quarter at least, to settle the accounts, and see after the necessary business letters. And, speaking of letters, I began to be very much ashamed of remembering my letter to the Aga Jenkyns, and very glad I had never named my writing to anyone. I only hoped the letter was lost. No answer came. No sign was made.

About a year after Miss Matty set up shop, I received one of Martha's hieroglyphics, begging me to come to Cranford very soon. I was afraid that Miss Matty was ill, and went off that very afternoon, and took Martha by surprise when she saw me on opening the door. We went into the kitchen, as usual, to have our confidential conference; and then Martha told me she was expecting her confinement very soon – in a week or two; and she did not think Miss Matty was aware of it; and she wanted me to break the news to her, 'for indeed Miss!' continued Martha, crying hysterically, 'I'm afraid she won't approve of it; and I'm sure I don't know who is to take care of her as she should be taken care of, when I am laid up.'

I comforted Martha by telling her I would remain till she was about again; and only wished she had told me her reason for this sudden summons, as then I would have brought the requisite stock of clothes. But Martha was so tearful and tender-spirited, and unlike her usual self, that I said as little as possible about myself, and endeavoured rather to comfort Martha under all the probable and possible misfortunes which came crowding upon her imagination.

I then stole out of the house-door, and made my appearance, as if I were a customer, in the shop just to take Miss Matty by surprise, and gain an idea of how she looked in her new situation. It was warm May weather, so only the little half-door was closed; and Miss Matty sate behind her counter, knitting an elaborate pair of garters: elaborate they seemed to me, but the difficult stitch was no weight upon her mind, for she was singing in a low voice to herself as her needles went rapidly in and out. I call it singing, but I dare say a musician would not use that word to the tuneless yet sweet humming of the low worn voice. I found out from the words, far more than from the attempt at the tune, that it was the Old Hundredth[5] she was crooning to herself: but the quiet continuous sound told of content, and gave me a pleasant feeling, as I stood in the street just outside the door, quite in harmony with that soft May morning. I went in. At first she did not catch who it was, and stood up as if to serve me; but in another minute watchful pussy had clutched her knitting, which was dropped in her eager joy at seeing me. I found, after we had had a little conversation, that it was as Martha said, and that Miss Matty had no idea of the approaching household event. So I thought I would let things take their course, secure that when I went to her with the baby in my arms I should obtain that forgiveness for Martha which she was needlessly frightening herself into believing that Miss Matty would withhold, under some notion that the new claimant would require attentions from its mother that it would be faithless treason to Miss Matty to render.

But I was right. I think that must be an hereditary quality, for my father says he is scarcely ever wrong. One morning, within a week after I arrived, I went to call Miss Matty, with a little bundle of flannel in my arms. She was very much awe-struck when I showed her what it was, and asked for her spectacles off the dressing-table, and looked at it curiously, with a sort of tender wonder at its small perfection of parts. She could not banish the thought of the surprise all day, but went about on tip-toe, and was very silent. But she stole up to see Martha, and they both cried with joy; and she got into a complimentary speech to Jem, and did not know how to get out of it again, and was only extricated from her dilemma by the sound of the shop-bell, which was an equal relief to the shy, proud, honest Jem, who shook my hand so vigorously when I congratulated him that I think I feel the pain of it yet.

I had a busy life while Martha was laid up. I attended on Miss Matty, and prepared her meals; I cast up her accounts, and examined into the state of her canisters and tumblers. I helped her too, occasionally, in the shop; and it gave me no small amusement, and sometimes a little uneasiness, to watch her ways there. If a little child came in to ask for an ounce of almond-comfits (and four of the large kind which Miss Matty sold weighed that much), she always added one more by 'way of make-weight' as she called it, although the scale was handsomely turned before; and when I remonstrated against this, her reply was, 'The little things like it so much!' There was no use in telling her that the fifth comfit weighed a quarter of an ounce, and made every sale into a loss to her pocket. So I remembered the green tea, and winged my shaft with a feather out of her own plumage. I told her how unwholesome almond-comfits were; and how ill excess in them might make the little children. This argument produced some effect; for, henceforward, instead of the fifth comfit, she always told them to hold out their tiny palms, into which she shook either peppermint or ginger lozenges,[6] as a preventive to the dangers that might arise from the previous sale. Altogether the lozenge trade, conducted on these principles, did not promise to be remunerative; but I was happy to find she had made more than twenty pounds during the last year by her sales of tea; and, moreover, that now she was accustomed to it, she did not dislike the employment, which brought her into kindly intercourse with many of the people round about. If she gave them good weight they, in their turn, brought many a little country present to the 'old Rector's daughter'; – a cream cheese, a few new-laid eggs, a little fresh ripe fruit, a bunch of flowers. The counter was quite loaded with these offerings sometimes, as she told me.

As for Cranford in general, it was going on much as usual. The Jamieson and Hoggins feud still raged, if a feud it could be called, when only one side cared much about it. Mr and Mrs Hoggins were very happy together; and, like most very happy people, quite ready to be friendly: indeed, Mrs Hoggins was really desirous to be restored to Mrs Jamieson's good graces, because of the former intimacy. But Mrs Jamieson considered their very happiness an insult to the Glenmire family, to which she had still the honour to belong; and she doggedly refused and rejected every advance. Mr Mulliner, like a faithful clansman, espoused his mistress's side with ardour. If he saw either Mr or

Mrs Hoggins, he would cross the street, and appear absorbed in the contemplation of life in general, and his own path in particular, until he had passed them by. Miss Pole used to amuse herself with wondering what in the world Mrs Jamieson would do, if either she or Mr Mulliner, or any other member of her household, was taken ill; she could hardly have the face to call in Mr Hoggins after the way she had behaved to them. Miss Pole grew quite impatient for some indisposition or accident to befal Mrs Jamieson or her dependants, in order that Cranford might see how she would act under the perplexing circumstances.

Martha was beginning to go about again, and I had already fixed a limit, not very far distant, to my visit, when one afternoon, as I was sitting in the shop-parlour with Miss Matty – I remember the weather was colder now than it had been in May, three weeks before, and we had a fire, and kept the door fully closed – we saw a gentleman go slowly past the window, and then stand opposite to the door, as if looking out for the name which we had so carefully hidden. He took out a double eyeglass and peered about for some time before he could discover it. Then he came in. And, all on a sudden, it flashed across me that it was the Aga himself! For his clothes had an out-of-the-way foreign cut about them; and his face was deep brown as if tanned and re-tanned by the sun. His complexion contrasted oddly with his plentiful snow-white hair; his eyes were dark and piercing, and he had an odd way of contracting them, and puckering up his cheeks into innumerable wrinkles when he looked earnestly at objects. He did so to Miss Matty when he first came in. His glance had first caught and lingered a little upon me; but then turned, with the peculiar searching look I have described, to Miss Matty. She was a little fluttered and nervous, but no more so than she always was when any man came into her shop. She thought that he would probably have a note, or a sovereign at least, for which she would have to give change, which was an operation she very much disliked to perform. But the present customer stood opposite to her, without asking for anything, only looking fixedly at her as he drummed upon the table with his fingers, just for all the world as Miss Jenkyns used to do. Miss Matty was on the point of asking him what he wanted (as she told me afterwards), when he turned sharp to me: 'Is your name Mary Smith?'

'Yes!' said I.

All my doubts as to his identity were set at rest; and, I only wondered what he would say or do next, and how Miss Matty would stand the joyful shock of what he had to reveal. Apparently he was at a loss how to announce himself; for he looked round at last in search of something to buy, so as to gain time; and, as it happened, his eye caught on the almond-comfits, and he boldly asked for a pound of 'those things'. I doubt if Miss Matty had a whole pound in the shop; and besides the unusual magnitude of the order, she was distressed with the idea of the indigestion they would produce, taken in such unlimited quantities. She looked up to remonstrate. Something of tender relaxation in his face struck home to her heart. She said, 'It is – oh, sir! can you be Peter?' and trembled from head to foot. In a moment he was round the table, and had her in his arms, sobbing the tearless cries of old age. I brought her a glass of wine; for indeed her colour had changed so as to alarm me, and Mr Peter, too. He kept saying, 'I have been too sudden for you, Matty, – I have, my little girl.'

I proposed that she should go at once up into the drawing-room and lie down on the sofa there; she looked wistfully at her brother, whose hand she had held tight, even when nearly fainting; but on his assuring her that he would not leave her, she allowed him to carry her upstairs.

I thought that the best I could do, was to run and put the kettle on the fire for early tea, and then to attend to the shop, leaving the brother and sister to exchange some of the many thousand things they must have to say. I had also to break the news to Martha, who received it with a burst of tears, which nearly infected me. She kept recovering herself to ask if I was sure it was indeed Miss Matty's brother; for I had mentioned that he had grey hair and she had always heard that he was a very handsome young man. Something of the same kind perplexed Miss Matty at tea-time, when she was installed in the great easy chair opposite to Mr Jenkyns's, in order to gaze her fill. She could hardly drink for looking at him; and as for eating, that was out of the question.

'I suppose hot climates age people very quickly,' said she, almost to herself. 'When you left Cranford you had not a grey hair in your head.'

'But how many years ago is that?' said Mr Peter, smiling.

'Ah! true! yes! I suppose you and I are getting old. But still I did not think we were so very old! But white hair is very becoming to you, Peter,' she continued – a little afraid lest she had hurt him by revealing how his appearance had impressed her.

'I suppose I forgot dates too, Matty, for what do you think I have brought for you from India? I have an Indian muslin gown and a pearl necklace for you somewhere or other in my chest at Portsmouth.' He smiled as if amused at the idea of the incongruity of his presents with the appearance of his sister; but this did not strike her all at once, while the elegance of the articles did. I could see that for a moment her imagination dwelt complacently on the idea of herself thus attired; and instinctively she put her hand up to her throat – that little delicate throat which (as Miss Pole had told me) had been one of her youthful charms; but the hand met the touch of folds of soft muslin, in which she was always swathed up to her chin; and the sensation recalled a sense of the unsuitableness of a pearl necklace to her age. She said, 'I'm afraid I'm too old; but it was very kind of you to think of it. They are just what I should have liked years ago – when I was young!'

'So I thought, my little Matty. I remembered your tastes; they were so like my dear mother's.' At the mention of that name, the brother and sister clasped each other's hands yet more fondly; and although they were perfectly silent, I fancied they might have something to say if they were unchecked by my presence, and I got up to arrange my room for Mr Peter's occupation that night, intending myself to share Miss Matty's bed. But at my movement he started up. 'I must go and settle about a room at the George. My carpet-bag is there too.'

'No!' said Miss Matty in great distress – 'you must not go; please, dear Peter – pray, Mary – oh! you must not go!'

She was so much agitated that we both promised everything

she wished. Peter sat down again, and gave her his hand, which
for better security she held in both of hers, and I left the room
to accomplish my arrangements.

Long, long into the night, far, far into the morning, did Miss
Matty and I talk. She had much to tell me of her brother's life
and adventures which he had communicated to her, as they had
sat alone. She said that all was thoroughly clear to her; but I
never quite understood the whole story; and when in after days
I lost my awe of Mr Peter enough to question him myself, he
laughed at my curiosity and told me stories that sounded so
very much like Baron Munchausen's[7] that I was sure he was
making fun of me. What I heard from Miss Matty was, that he
had been a volunteer at the siege of Rangoon;[8] had been taken
prisoner by the Burmese; had somehow obtained favour and
eventual freedom from knowing how to bleed the chief[9] of the
small tribe in some case of dangerous illness; that on his release
from years of captivity he had had his letters returned from
England with the ominous word 'Dead' marked upon them;
and believing himself to be the last of his race, he had settled
down as an indigo planter; and had proposed to spend the
remainder of his life in the country to whose inhabitants and
modes of life he had become habituated; when my letter had
reached him; and with the odd vehemence which characterised
him in age as it had done in youth, he had sold his land and all
his possessions to the first purchaser, and come home to the
poor old sister, who was more glad and rich than any princess
when she looked at him. She talked me to sleep at last, and
then I was awakened by a slight sound at the door, for which
she begged my pardon as she crept penitently into bed; but it
seems that when I could no longer confirm her belief that the
long-lost was really here – under the same roof – she had begun
to fear lest it was only a waking dream of hers; that there never
had been a Peter sitting by her all that blessed evening – but that
the real Peter lay dead far away beneath some wild sea-wave, or
under some strange Eastern tree. And so strong had this nervous
feeling of hers become that she was fain to get up and go and
convince herself that he was really there by listening through
the door to his even regular breathing – I don't like to call it

snoring, but I heard it myself through two closed doors – and by-and-by it soothed Miss Matty to sleep.

I don't believe Mr Peter came home from India as rich as a Nabob; he even considered himself poor, but neither he nor Miss Matty cared much about that. At any rate, he had enough to live upon 'very genteelly' at Cranford; he and Miss Matty together. And a day or two after his arrival, the shop was closed, while troops of little urchins gleefully awaited the showers of comfits and lozenges that came from time to time down upon their faces as they stood up-gazing at Miss Matty's drawing-room windows. Occasionally Miss Matty would say to them (half hidden behind the curtains), 'My dear children, don't make yourselves ill'; but a strong arm pulled her back, and a more rattling shower than ever succeeded. A part of the tea was sent in presents to the Cranford ladies; and some of it was distributed among the old people who remembered Mr Peter in the days of his frolicsome youth. The India muslin gown was reserved for darling Flora Gordon (Miss Jessie Brown's daughter). The Gordons had been on the Continent for the last few years, but were now expected to return very soon; and Miss Matty, in her sisterly pride, anticipated great delight in the joy of showing them Mr Peter. The pearl necklace disappeared; and about that time many handsome and useful presents made their appearance in the households of Miss Pole and Mrs Forrester; and some rare and delicate Indian ornaments graced the drawing-rooms of Mrs Jamieson and Mrs Fitz-Adam. I myself was not forgotten. Among other things, I had the handsomest bound and best edition of Dr Johnson's works that could be procured; and dear Miss Matty, with tears in her eyes, begged me to consider it as a present from her sister as well as herself. In short no one was forgotten; and what was more, everyone, however insignificant, who had shown kindness to Miss Matty at any time, was sure of Mr Peter's cordial regard.

CHAPTER XVI

'PEACE TO CRANFORD'

It was not surprising that Mr Peter became such a favourite at Cranford. The ladies vied with each other who should admire him most; and no wonder; for their quiet lives were astonishingly stirred up by the arrival from India – especially as the person arrived told more wonderful stories than Sindbad the sailor; and, as Miss Pole said, was quite as good as an Arabian night[1] any evening. For my own part, I had vibrated all my life between Drumble and Cranford, and I thought it was quite possible that all Mr Peter's stories might be true although wonderful; but when I found, that if we swallowed an anecdote of tolerable magnitude one week, we had the dose considerably increased the next, I began to have my doubts; especially as I noticed that when his sister was present the accounts of Indian life were comparatively tame; not that she knew more than we did, perhaps less. I noticed also that when the Rector came to call, Mr Peter talked in a different way about the countries he had been in. But I don't think the ladies in Cranford would have considered him such a wonderful traveller if they had only heard him talk in the quiet way he did to him. They liked him the better, indeed, for being what they called 'so very Oriental'.[2]

One day, at a select party in his honour, which Miss Pole gave, and from which, as Mrs Jamieson honoured it with her presence, and had even offered to send Mr Mulliner to wait, Mr and Mrs Hoggins and Mrs Fitz-Adam were necessarily excluded – one day at Miss Pole's Mr Peter said he was tired of sitting upright against the hard-backed uneasy chairs, and asked if he might not indulge himself in sitting cross-legged. Miss Pole's consent was eagerly given, and down he went with the utmost gravity. But when Miss Pole asked me, in an audible whisper, 'if he did not remind me of the Father of the Faithful?'[3] I could not help thinking of poor Simon Jones the lame tailor; and while Mrs Jamieson slowly commented on the elegance and convenience of the attitude, I remember how we had all followed that lady's lead in condemning Mr Hoggins for vulgarity because he simply crossed his legs as he sate still on his chair. Many of Mr Peter's ways of eating were a little strange amongst such ladies as Miss Pole, and Miss Matty, and Mrs Jamieson, especially when I recollected the untasted green peas and two-pronged forks at poor Mr Holbrook's dinner.

The mention of that gentleman's name recalls to my mind a conversation between Mr Peter and Miss Matty one evening in the summer after he returned to Cranford. The day had been very hot, and Miss Matty had been much oppressed by the weather; in the heat of which her brother revelled. I remember that she had been unable to nurse Martha's baby; which had become her favourite employment of late, and which was as much at home in her arms as in its mother's, as long as it remained a light weight – portable by one so fragile as Miss Matty. This day to which I refer, Miss Matty had seemed more than usually feeble and languid, and only revived when the sun went down, and her sofa was wheeled to the open window, through which, although it looked into the principal street of Cranford, the fragrant smell of the neighbouring hayfields came in every now and then, borne by the soft breezes that stirred the dull air of the summer twilight, and then died away. The silence of the sultry atmosphere was lost in the murmuring noises which came in from many an open window and door; even the children were abroad in the street, late as it was (between ten and eleven), enjoying the game of play for which they had not had spirits during the heat of the day. It was a source of satisfaction to Miss Matty to see how few candles were lighted even in the apartments of those houses from which issued the greatest signs of life. Mr Peter, Miss Matty and I, had all been quiet, each with a separate reverie, for some little time, when Mr Peter broke in –

'Do you know, little Matty, I could have sworn you were on

the high road to matrimony when I left England that last time! If anybody had told me you would have lived and died an old maid then, I should have laughed in their faces.'

Miss Matty made no reply; and I tried in vain to think of some subject which should effectually turn the conversation; but I was very stupid; and before I spoke, he went on:

'It was Holbrook; that fine manly fellow who lived at Woodley, that I used to think would carry off my little Matty. You would not think it now, I dare say, Mary! but this sister of mine was once a very pretty girl – at least I thought so; and so I've a notion did poor Holbrook. What business had he to die before I came home to thank him for all his kindness to a good-for-nothing cub as I was? It was that that made me first think he cared for you; for in all our fishing expeditions it was Matty, Matty, we talked about. Poor Deborah! What a lecture she read me on having asked him home to lunch one day, when she had seen the Arley carriage in the town, and thought that my lady might call. Well, that's long years ago; more than half a lifetime! and yet it seems like yesterday! I don't know a fellow I should have liked better as a brother-in-law. You must have played your cards badly, my little Matty, somehow or another – wanted your brother to be a good go-between, eh! little one?' said he, putting out his hand to take hold of hers as she lay on the sofa – 'Why what's this? you're shivering and shaking, Matty, with that confounded open window. Shut it, Mary, this minute!'

I did so, and then stooped down to kiss Miss Matty, and see if she really were chilled. She caught at my hand, and gave it a hard squeeze – but unconsciously I think – for in a minute or two she spoke to us quite in her usual voice, and smiled our uneasiness away; although she patiently submitted to the prescriptions we enforced of a warmed bed, and a glass of weak negus. I was to leave Cranford the next day, and before I went I saw that all the effects of the open window had quite vanished. I had superintended most of the alterations necessary in the house and household during the latter weeks of my stay. The shop was once more a parlour; the empty resounding rooms again furnished up to the very garrets.

There had been some talk of establishing Martha and Jem in another house; but Miss Matty would not hear of this. Indeed I never saw her so much roused as when Miss Pole had assumed it to be the most desirable arrangement. As long as Martha would remain with Miss Matty, Miss Matty was only too thankful to have her about her; yes, and Jem too, who was a very pleasant man to have in the house, for she never saw him from week's end to week's end. And as for the probable children, if they would all turn out such little darlings as her god-daughter Matilda, she should not mind the number, if Martha didn't. Besides the next was to be called Deborah; a point which Miss Matty had reluctantly yielded to Martha's stubborn determination that her first-born was to be Matilda. So Miss Pole had to lower her colours, and even her voice, as she said to me that as Mr and Mrs Hearn were still to go on living in the same house with Miss Matty, we had certainly done a wise thing in hiring Martha's niece as an auxiliary.

I left Miss Matty and Mr Peter most comfortable and contented; the only subject for regret to the tender heart of the one and the social friendly nature of the other being the unfortunate quarrel between Mrs Jamieson and the plebeian Hogginses and their following. In joke I prophesied one day that this would only last until Mrs Jamieson or Mr Mulliner were ill, in which case they would only be too glad to be friends with Mr Hoggins; but Miss Matty did not like my looking forward to anything like illness in so light a manner; and, before the year was out, all had come round in a far more satisfactory way.

I received two Cranford letters on one auspicious October morning. Both Miss Pole and Miss Matty wrote to ask me to come over and meet the Gordons, who had returned to England alive and well, with their two children, now almost grown up. Dear Jessie Brown had kept her old kind nature, although she had changed her name and station; and she wrote to say that she and Major Gordon expected to be in Cranford on the fourteenth, and she hoped and begged to be remembered to Mrs Jamieson (named first, as became her honourable station), Miss Pole, and Miss Matty – could she ever forget their kindness to her poor father and sister? – Mrs Forrester, Mr Hoggins (and here again came in an allusion to kindness shown to the dead long ago), his new wife, who as such must allow Mrs Gordon to desire to make her acquaintance, and who was moreover an old Scotch friend of her husband's. In short, everyone was named, from the Rector – who had been appointed to Cranford in the interim between Captain Brown's death and Miss Jessie's marriage, and was now associated with the latter event – down to Miss Betty Barker; all were asked to the luncheon; all except Mrs Fitz-Adam, who had come to live in Cranford since Miss Jessie Brown's days, and whom I found rather moping on account of the omission. People wondered at Miss Betty Barker's being included in the honourable list; but then, as Miss Pole said, we must remember the disregard of the genteel proprieties of life in which the poor captain had educated his girls; and for his sake we swallowed our pride; indeed Mrs Jamieson rather took it as a compliment, as putting Miss Betty (formerly *her* maid) on a level with 'those Hogginses'.

But when I arrived in Cranford, nothing was as yet ascertained of Mrs Jamieson's own intentions; would the honourable lady go, or would she not? Mr Peter declared that she should and she would; Miss Pole shook her head and desponded. But Mr Peter was a man of resources. In the first place, he persuaded Miss Matty to write to Mrs Gordon, and to tell her of Mrs Fitz-Adam's existence, and to beg that one so kind, and cordial, and generous, might be included in the pleasant invitation. An answer came back by return of post, with a pretty little note for Mrs Fitz-Adam, and a request that Miss Matty would deliver it herself and explain the previous omission. Mrs Fitz-Adam was as pleased as could be, and thanked Miss Matty over and over again. Mr Peter had said, 'Leave Mrs Jamieson to me'; so we did; especially as we knew nothing that we could do to alter her determination if once formed.

I did not know, nor did Miss Matty, how things were going on, until Miss Pole asked me, just the day before Mrs Gordon came, if I thought there was anything between Mr Peter and Mrs Jamieson in the matrimonial line, for that Mrs Jamieson was really going to the lunch at the George. She had sent Mr Mulliner down to desire that there might be a foot-stool put to the warmest seat in the room, as she meant to come, and knew that their chairs were very high. Miss Pole had picked this piece of news up, and from it she conjectured all sorts of things, and bemoaned yet more. 'If Peter should marry, what would become of poor dear Miss Matty! And Mrs Jamieson, of all people!' Miss Pole seemed to think there were other ladies in Cranford who would have done more credit to his choice, and I think she must have had someone who was unmarried in her head, for she kept saying, 'It was so wanting in delicacy in a widow to think of such a thing.'

When I got back to Miss Matty's, I really did begin to think that Mr Peter might be thinking of Mrs Jamieson for a wife; and I was as unhappy as Miss Pole about it. He had the proof-sheet of a great placard in his hand. 'Signor Brunoni, Magician to the King of Delhi, the Rajah of Oude, and the Great Lama of Thibet, &c. &c.', was going to 'perform in Cranford for one night only', – the very next night; and Miss Matty, exultant, showed me a letter from the Gordons, promising to remain over this gaiety, which Miss Matty said was entirely Peter's doing. He had written to ask the Signor to come, and was to be at all the expenses of the affair. Tickets were to be sent gratis to as many as the room would hold. In short, Miss Matty was charmed with the plan, and said that tomorrow Cranford would remind her of the Preston Guild,[4] to which she had been in her youth – a luncheon at the George, with the dear Gordons, and the Signor in the Assembly Room in the evening. But I – I looked only at the fatal words:–

'*Under the patronage of the* HONOURABLE
MRS JAMIESON.'

She, then, was chosen to preside over this entertainment of Mr Peter's; she was perhaps going to displace my dear Miss Matty in his heart, and make her life lonely once more! I could not look forward to the morrow with any pleasure; and every innocent anticipation of Miss Matty's only served to add to my annoyance.

So angry, and irritated, and exaggerating every little incident

which could add to my irritation, I went on till we were all
assembled in the great parlour at the George. Major and Mrs
Gordon and pretty Flora and Mr Ludovic were all as bright
and handsome and friendly as could be; but I could hardly
attend to them for watching Mr Peter, and I saw that Miss Pole
was equally busy. I had never seen Mrs Jamieson so roused and
animated before; her face looked full of interest in what Mr
Peter was saying. I drew near to listen. My relief was great
when I caught that his words were not words of love, but that,
for all his grave face, he was at his old tricks. He was telling
her of his travels in India, and describing the wonderful height
of the Himalaya mountains: one touch after another added to
their size; and each exceeded the former in absurdity; but
Mrs Jamieson really enjoyed all in perfect good faith. I suppose
she required strong stimulants to excite her to come out of her
apathy. Mr Peter wound up his account by saying that, of
course, at that altitude there were none of the animals to be
found that existed in the lower regions; the game – everything
was different. Firing one day at some flying creature, he was
very much dismayed, when it fell, to find that he had shot
a cherubim! Mr Peter caught my eye at this moment, and
gave me such a funny twinkle, that I felt sure he had no
thoughts of Mrs Jamieson as a wife, from that time. She looked
uncomfortably amazed:

'But, Mr Peter – shooting a cherubim – don't you think – I
am afraid that was sacrilege!'

Mr Peter composed his countenance in a moment, and
appeared shocked at the idea! which, as he said truly enough,
was now presented to him for the first time; but then Mrs
Jamieson must remember that he had been living for a long
time among savages – all of whom were heathens – some of
them, he was afraid, were downright Dissenters. Then, seeing
Miss Matty draw near, he hastily changed the conversation,
and after a little while, turning to me, he said, 'Don't be
shocked, prim little Mary, at all my wonderful stories; I consider
Mrs Jamieson fair game, and besides, I am bent on propitiating
her, and the first step towards it is keeping her well awake.
I bribed her here by asking her to let me have her name as

patroness for my poor conjuror this evening; and I don't want to give her time enough to get up her rancour against the Hogginses, who are just coming in. I want everybody to be friends, for it harasses Matty so much to hear of these quarrels. I shall go at it again by-and-by, so you need not look shocked. I intend to enter the Assembly Room tonight with Mrs Jamieson on one side, and my lady Mrs Hoggins on the other. You see if I don't.'

Somehow or another he did; and fairly got them into conversation together. Major and Mrs Gordon helped at the good work with their perfect ignorance of any existing coolness between any of the inhabitants of Cranford.

Ever since that day there has been the old friendly sociability in Cranford society; which I am thankful for, because of my dear Miss Matty's love of peace and kindliness. We all love Miss Matty, and I somehow think we are all of us better when she is near us.

THE END

Appendix I

'The Last Generation in England' and 'The Cage at Cranford'

This essay appeared in the American *Sartain's Union Magazine of Literature and Art* 5:1 (July 1849), pp. 45–8. See Introduction.

THE LAST GENERATION IN ENGLAND

By the author of 'Mary Barton.'

communicated for Britain's Magazine by Mary Howitt

I have just taken up by chance an old number of the Edinburgh Review (April, 1848), in which it is said that Southey had proposed to himself to write a 'history of English domestic life.' I will not enlarge upon the infinite loss we have had in the non-fulfilment of this plan; every one must in some degree feel its extent who has read those charming glimpses of home scenes contained in the early volumes of the 'Doctor, &c.'[1] This quarter of an hour's chance reading has created a wish in me to put upon record some of the details of country town life, either observed by myself, or handed down to me by older relations; for even in small towns, scarcely removed from villages, the phases of society are rapidly changing; and much will appear strange, which yet occurred only in the generation immediately preceding ours. I must however say before going on, that although I choose to disguise my own identity, and to conceal the name of the town to which I refer, every circumstance and occurrence which I shall relate is strictly and truthfully told without exaggeration. As for classing the details with which I am acquainted under any heads, that will be impossible from their heterogeneous nature; I must write them down as they arise in my memory.

The town in which I once resided is situated in a district inhabited by large landed proprietors of very old family. The daughters of these families, if unmarried, retired to live in —— on their annuities, and gave the ton to the society there; stately ladies they were, remembering etiquette and precedence in every occurrence of life, and having their genealogy at their tongue's end. Then there were the widows of the cadets of these same families; also poor, and also proud, but I think more genial and less given to recounting their pedigrees than the former. Then came the professional men and their wives; who were more wealthy than the ladies I have named, but who always treated them with deference and respect, sometimes even amounting to obsequiousness; for was there not 'my brother, Sir John —,' and 'my uncle, Mr —, of —,' to give employment and patronage to the doctor or the attorney? A grade lower came a class of single or widow ladies; and again it was possible, not to say probable, that their pecuniary circumstances were in better condition than those of the aristocratic dames, who nevertheless refused to meet in general society the *ci-devant* housekeepers, or widows of stewards, who had been employed by their fathers and brothers, they would occasionally condescend to ask 'Mason,' or 'that good Bentley,' to a private tea-drinking, at which I doubt not much gossip relating to former days at the hall would pass; but that was patronage; to associate with them at another person's house, would have been an acknowledgment of equality.

Below again came the shopkeepers, who dared to be original; who gave comfortable suppers after the very early dinners of that day, not checked by the honourable Mr D–'s precedent of a seven o'clock tea on the most elegant and economical principles, and a supperless turn-out at nine. There were the usual respectable and disrespectable poor; and hanging on the outskirts of society were a set of young men, ready for mischief and brutality, and every now and then dropping off the pit's brink into crime. The habits of this class (about forty years ago) were much such as those of the Mohawks a century before.[2] They would stop ladies returning from the card-parties, which were the staple gaiety of the place, and who were only attended by a maidservant bearing a lantern, and whip them; literally whip them as you whip a little child; until administering such chastisement to a good, precise old lady of high family, 'my brother, the magistrate,' came forward and put down such proceedings with a high hand.

Certainly there was more individuality of character in those days than now; no one even in a little town of two thousand inhabitants would now be found to drive out with a carriage full of dogs; each dressed in the male or female fashion of the day, as the case might be; each dog provided with a pair of house-shoes, for which his carriage boots were changed on his return. No old lady would be so oblivious of 'Mrs Grundy's' existence[3] now as to dare to invest her favourite cow, after its unlucky fall into a lime-pit, in flannel waistcoat and drawers, in which the said cow paraded the streets of — to the day of its death.

There were many regulations which were strictly attended to in the society of —, and which probably checked more manifestations of eccentricity. Before a certain hour in the morning calls were never paid, nor yet after a certain hour in the afternoon; the consequence was that everybody was out, calling on everybody at the same time, for it was *de rigueur* that morning calls should be returned within three days; and accordingly, making due allowance for our proportion of rain in England, every fine morning was given up to this employment. A quarter of an hour was the limit of a morning call.

Before the appointed hour of reception, I fancy the employment of many of the ladies was fitting up their laces and muslins (which, for the information of all those whom it may concern, were never ironed, but carefully stretched, and pinned, thread by thread, with most Lilliputian[4] pieces, on a board covered with flannel). Most of these scions of quality had many pounds' worth of valuable laces descended to them from mothers and grandmothers, which must be 'got up' by no hands, as you may guess, but those of Fairly Fair. Indeed when muslin and net were a guinea a yard, this was not to be wondered at. The lace was washed in buttermilk, which gave rise to an odd little circumstance. One lady left her lace, basted up, in some not very sour buttermilk; and unluckily the cat lapped it up, lace and all (one would have thought the lace would have choked her, but so it was); the lace was too valuable to be lost, so a small dose of tartar emetic was administered to the poor cat; the lace returned to view was carefully darned, and decked the good old lady's best cap for many a year after; and many a time did she tell the story, gracefully bridling up in a prim sort of way, and giving a little cough, as if preliminary to a rather improper story. The first sentence of it was always, I remember, 'I do not think you can guess where the lace on my cap has been;' dropping her voice, 'in pussy's inside, my dear!'

The dinner hour was three o'clock in all houses of any pretension to gentility; and a very late hour it was considered to be. Soon after four one or two inveterate card-players might be seen in calash and pattens, picking their way along the streets to the house where the party of the evening was to be held. As soon as they arrived and had unpacked themselves, an operation of a good half-hour's duration in the dining-parlour, they were ushered into the drawing-room, where, unless in the very height of summer, it was considered a delicate attention to have the shutters closed, the curtains drawn, and the candles lighted. The card-tables were set out, each with two new packs of cards, for which it was customary to pay by each person placing a shilling under one of the candlesticks.

The ladies settled down to Preference, and allowed of no interruption; even the tea-trays were placed on the middle of the card-tables, and tea hastily gulped down with a few remarks on the good or ill fortune of the evening. New arrivals were greeted with nods in the intervals of the game; and as people entered the room, they were pounced upon by the lady of the house to form another table. Cards were a business in those days, not a recreation. Their very names were to be treated with reverence. Some one came to — from a place where flippancy was in fashion; he called the knave 'Jack,' and everybody looked grave, and voted him vulgar; but when he was overheard calling Preference – the decorous, highly-respectable game of Preference, – Pref., why, what course remained for us but to cut him, and cut him we did.

About half-past eight, notices of servants having arrived for their respective mistresses were given: the games were concluded, accounts settled, a few parting squibs and crackers[5] let off at careless or unlucky partners, and the party separated. By ten o'clock all — was in bed and asleep. I have made no mention of gentlemen at these parties, because if ever there was an Amazonian town in England it was —. Eleven widows of respectability at one time kept house there; besides spinsters innumerable. The doctor preferred his arm-chair and slippers to the forms of society, such as I have described, and so did the attorney, who was besides not insensible to the charms of a hot supper. Indeed, I suppose it was because of the small incomes of the more aristocratic portion of our little society not sufficing both for style and luxury, but it was a fact, that as gentility decreased good living increased in proportion. We had the honour and glory of looking at old plate and delicate china at the *comme il faut* tea-parties, but the slices of bread and butter were like wafers, and the sugar for coffee was rather of the brownest, still there was much gracious kindness among our *haute volée*. In those times, good Mr Rigmarole, carriages were carriages, and there were not the infinite variety of broughams, droskys, &c., &c., down to a wheelbarrow, which now make locomotion easy; nor yet were there cars and cabs and flys ready for hire in our little town. A post-chaise was the only conveyance besides *the* sedan-chair, of which more anon. So the widow of an earl's son, who possessed a proper old-fashioned coach and pair, would, on rainy nights, send her carriage, the only private carriage of —, round the town, picking up all the dowagers and invalids, and conveying them dry and safe to and from their evening engagement. The various other ladies who, in virtue of their relations holding manors and maintaining game-keepers, had frequent presents, during the season, of partridges, pheasants, &c., &c., would daintily carve off the tid-bits, and putting them carefully into a hot basin, bid Betty or Molly cover it up quickly, and carry it to Mrs or Miss So-and-so, whose appetite was but weakly and who required dainties to tempt it which she could not afford to purchase.

These poorer ladies had also their parties in turn; they were too proud to accept invitations if they might not return them, although various and amusing were their innocent make-shifts and imitations. To give you only one instance, I remember a card-party at one of these good ladies' lodgings; where, when tea-time arrived, the ladies sitting on the sofa had to be displaced for a minute, in order that the tea-trays, (plates of cake, bread and butter, and all,) might be extricated from their concealment under the valances of the couch.

You may imagine the subjects of the conversation amongst these ladies; cards, servants, relations, pedigrees, and last and best, much mutual interest about the poor of the town, to whom they were one and all kind and indefatigable benefactresses; cooking, sewing for, advising, doctoring, doing everything but educating them. One or two old ladies dwelt on the glories of former days; when — boasted of two earl's daughters as residents. Though it must be sixty years since they died, there are traces of their characters yet lingering about the place. Proud, precise, and generous; bitter tories were they. Their sister had married a General, more distinguished for a successful comedy, than for his mode of conducting the war in America;[6] and, consequently, his sisters-in-law held the name of Washington in deep abhorrence. I can fancy the way in which they must have spoken of him, from the shudder of abomination with which their devoted admirers spoke years afterwards of 'that man Washington.' Lady Jane was moreover a benefactress to —. Before her day, the pavement of the foot-path was composed of loose round stones, placed so far apart that a delicate ankle might receive a severe wrench from slipping between; but she left a sum of money in her will to make and keep in repair a flag pavement, on condition that it should only be broad enough for one to walk abreast, in order 'to put a stop to the indecent custom coming into vogue, of ladies linking with gentlemen;' linking being the old-fashioned word for walking arm-in-arm. Lady Jane also left her sedan and money to pay the bearers for the use of the ladies of —, who were frequently like Adam and Eve in the weather-glass[7] in consequence, the first arrival at a party having to commence the order of returning when the last lady was only just entering upon the gaieties of the evening.

The old ladies were living hoards of family tradition and old custom. One of them, a Shropshire woman, had been to school in London about the middle of the last century. The journey from Shropshire took her a week. At the school to which she was sent, besides fine work of innumerable descriptions, pastry, and the art of confectionary were taught to those whose parents desired it. The dancing-master gave his pupils instructions in the art of using a fan properly. Although an only child, she had never sat down in her parents' presence without leave until she was married; and spoke with infinite disgust of the modern familiarity with which children treated their parents. 'In my days,' said she, 'when we wrote to our fathers and mothers, we began "Honoured Sir," or "Honoured Madam," none of your "Dear Mamas," or "Dear Papas" would have been permitted; and we ruled off our margin before beginning our letters, instead of cramming writing into every corner of the paper; and when we ended our letters we asked our parents' blessing if we were writing to them; and if we wrote to a friend we were content to "remain your affectionate friend," instead of hunting up some new-fangled expression, such as "your attached, your loving," &c. Fanny, my dear! I got a letter to-day signed "Yours cordially," like a dram-shop! what will this world come to?' Then she would tell how a gentleman having asked her to dance in her youth, never thought of such familiarity as offering her his arm to conduct her to her place, but taking up the flap of his silk-lined coat, he placed it over his open palm, and on it the lady daintily rested the tips of her fingers. To be sure, my dear old lady once confessed to a story neither so pretty nor so proper, namely, that one of the amusements of her youth was 'measuring noses' with some gentlemen, – not an uncommon thing in those days; and, as lips lie below noses, such measurements frequently ended in kisses. At her house there was a little silver basket-strainer, and once remarking on this, she showed me a silver saucer pierced through with holes, and told me it was a relic of the times when tea was first introduced into England; after it had been infused and the beverage drank, the leaves were taken out of the teapot and placed on this strainer, and then eaten by those who liked with sugar and butter, 'and very good they were,' she added. Another relic which she possessed was an old receipt-book, dating back to the middle of the sixteenth century. Our grandmothers must have been strong-headed women, for there were numerous receipts for 'ladies' beverages,' &c., generally beginning with 'Take a gallon of brandy, or any other spirit.' The puddings, too, were no light matters: one receipt, which I copied for the curiosity of the thing, begins with, 'Take thirty eggs, two quarts of cream,' &c. These brobdingnagian puddings she explained by saying that the afternoon meal, before the introduction of tea, generally consisted of cakes and cold puddings, together with a glass of what we should now call liqueur, but which was then denominated bitters.

The same old lady advocated strongly the manner in which marriages were formerly often brought about. A young man went up to London to study for the bar, to become a merchant, or what not, and arrived at middle age without having thought about matrimony; when, finding himself rich and desirous of being married, he would frequently write to some college friend, or to the clergyman of his native place, asking him to recommend a wife; whereupon the friend would send a list of suitable ladies; the bachelor would make his selection, and empower his friend to wait upon the parents of the chosen one, who accepted or refused without much consultation of their daughter's wishes; often the first intelligence she had of the affair was by being told by her mother to adorn herself in her best, as the gentleman her parents proposed for her husband was expected by the night-coach to supper.

'And very happy marriages they turned out, my dear – very,' my venerable informant would add, sighing. I always suspected that her own had been of this description.

In 1863, ten years after the publication of *Cranford*, this new episode appeared in *All the Year Round*, 28 November 1863, pp. 332–6.

THE CAGE AT CRANFORD

Have I told you anything about my friends at Cranford since the year 1856?[1] I think not.

You remember the Gordons, don't you? She that was Jessie Brown, who married her old love, Major Gordon: and from being poor became quite a rich lady: but for all that never forgot any of her old friends in Cranford.

Well! the Gordons were travelling abroad, for they were very fond of travelling; people who have had to spend part of their lives in a regiment always are, I think. They were now at Paris, in May, 1856, and were going to stop there, and in the neighbourhood all summer, but Mr Ludovic was coming to England soon; so Mrs Gordon wrote me word. I was glad she told me, for just then I was waiting to make a little present to Miss Pole, with whom I was staying; so I wrote to Mrs Gordon, and asked her to choose me out something pretty and new and fashionable, that would be acceptable to Miss Pole. Miss Pole had just been talking a great deal about Mrs FitzAdam's caps being so unfashionable, which I suppose made me put in that word fashionable; but afterwards I wished I had sent to say my present was not to be too fashionable; for there *is* such a thing, I can assure you! The price of my present was not to be more than twenty shillings, but that is a very handsome sum if you put it in that way, though it may not sound so much if you only call it a sovereign.

Mrs Gordon wrote back to me, pleased, as she always was, with doing anything for her old friends. She told me she had been out for a day's shopping before going into the country, and had got a cage[2] for herself of the newest and most elegant description, and had thought that she could not do better than get another like it as my present for Miss Pole, as cages were so much better made in Paris than anywhere else. I was rather dismayed when I read this letter, for, however pretty a cage might be, it was something for Miss Pole's own self, and not for her parrot, that I had intended to get. Here had I been finding ever so many reasons against her buying a new cap at Johnson's fashion-show,[3] because I thought that the present which Mrs Gordon was to choose for me in Paris might turn out to be an elegant and fashionable head-dress; a kind of cross between a turban and a cap, as I see those from Paris mostly are; and now I had to veer round, and advise her to go as fast as she could, and secure Mr Johnson's cap before any other purchaser snatched it up. But Miss Pole was too sharp for me.

'Why, Mary,' said she, 'it was only yesterday you were running down that cap like anything. You said, you know, that lilac was too old a colour for me; and green too young; and that the mixture was very unbecoming.'

'Yes, I know,' said I; 'but I have thought better of it. I thought about it a great deal last night, and I think—I thought—they would neutralise each other; and the shadows of any colour are, you know—something I know—complementary colours.' I was not sure of my own meaning, but I had an idea in my head, though I could not express it. She took me up shortly.

'Child, you don't know what you are saying. And besides, I don't want compliments at my time of life. I lay awake, too, thinking of the cap. I only buy one ready-made once a year, and of course it's a matter for consideration; and I came to the conclusion that you were quite right.'

'Oh! dear Miss Pole! I was quite wrong; if you only knew—I did think it a very pretty cap—only ——'

'Well! do just finish what you've got to say. You're almost as bad as Miss Matty in your way of talking, without being half as good as she is in other ways; though I'm very fond of you, Mary, I don't mean I am not; but you must see you're very off and on, and very muddle-headed. It's the truth, so you will not mind my saying so.'

It was just because it did seem like the truth at that time that I did mind her saying so; and, in despair, I thought I would tell her all.

'I did not mean what I said; I don't think lilac too old or green too young; and I think the mixture very becoming to you; and I think you will never get such a pretty cap again, at least in Cranford.' It was fully out, so far, at least.

'Then, Mary Smith, will you tell me what you did mean, by speaking as you did, and convincing me against my will, and giving me a bad night?'

'I meant—oh, Miss Pole, I meant to surprise you with a present from Paris; and I thought it would be a cap. Mrs Gordon was to choose it, and Mr Ludovic to bring it. I dare say it is in England now; only it's not a cap. And I did not want you to buy Johnson's cap, when I thought I was getting another for you.'

Miss Pole found this speech 'muddle-headed,' I have no doubt, though she did not say so, only making an odd noise of perplexity. I went on: 'I wrote to Mrs Gordon, and asked her to get you a present—something new and pretty. I meant it to be a dress, but I suppose I did not say so; I thought it would be a cap, for Paris is so famous for caps, and it is ——'

'You're a good girl, Mary' (I was past thirty,[4] but did not object to being called a girl; and, indeed, I generally felt like a girl at Cranford, where everybody was so much older than I was), 'but when you want a thing, say what you want; it is the best way in general. And now I suppose Mrs Gordon has bought something quite different?—a pair of shoes, I dare say, for people talk a deal of Paris shoes. Anyhow, I'm just as much obliged to you, Mary, my dear. Only you should not go and spend your money on me.'

'It was not much money; and it was not a pair of shoes. You'll let me go and get the cap, won't you? It was so pretty—somebody will be sure to snatch it up.'

'I don't like getting a cap that's sure to be unbecoming.'

'But it is not; it was not. I never saw you look so well in anything,' said I.

'Mary, Mary, remember who is the father of lies!'[5]

'But he's not my father,' exclaimed I, in a hurry, for I saw Mrs FitzAdam go down the street in the direction of Johnson's shop. 'I'll eat my words; they were all false: only just let me run down and buy you that cap – that pretty cap.'

'Well! run off, child. I liked it myself till you put me out of taste with it.'

I brought it back in triumph from under Mrs FitzAdam's very nose, as she was hanging in meditation over it; and the more we saw of it, the more we felt pleased with our purchase. We turned it on this side, and we turned it on that; and though we hurried it away into Miss Pole's bedroom at the sound of a double knock at the door, when we found it was only Miss Matty and Mr Peter, Miss Pole could not resist the opportunity of displaying it, and said in a solemn way to Miss Matty:

'Can I speak to you for a few minutes in private?' And I knew feminine delicacy too well to explain what this grave prelude was to lead to; aware how immediately Miss Matty's anxious tremor would be allayed by the sight of the cap. I had to go on talking to Mr Peter, however, when I would far rather have been in the bedroom, and heard the observations and comments.

We talked of the new cap all day; what gowns it would suit; whether a certain bow was not rather too coquettish for a woman of Miss Pole's age. 'No longer young,' as she called herself, after a little struggle with the words, though at sixty-five[6] she need not have blushed as if she were telling a falsehood. But at last the cap was put away, and with a wrench we turned our thoughts from the subject. We had been silent for a little while, each at our work with a candle between us, when Miss Pole began:

'It was very kind of you, Mary, to think of giving me a present from Paris.'

'Oh, I was only too glad to be able to get you something! I hope you will like it, though it is not what I expected.'

'I am sure I shall like it. And a surprise is always so pleasant.'

'Yes; but I think Mrs Gordon has made a very odd choice.'

'I wonder what it is. I don't like to ask, but there's a great deal in anticipation; I remember hearing dear Miss Jenkyns say that "anticipation was the soul of enjoyment," or something like that. Now there is no anticipation in a surprise; that's the worst of it.'

'Shall I tell you what it is?'

'Just as you like, my dear. If it is any pleasure to you, I am quite willing to hear.'

'Perhaps I had better not. It is something quite different to what

I expected, and meant to have got; and I'm not sure if I like it as well.'

'Relieve your mind, if you like, Mary. In all disappointments sympathy is a great balm.'

'Well, then, it's something not for you; it's for Polly. It's a cage. Mrs Gordon says they make such pretty ones in Paris.'

I could see that Miss Pole's first emotion was disappointment. But she was very fond of her cockatoo, and the thought of his smartness in his new habitation made her be reconciled in a moment; besides that she was really grateful to me for having planned a present for her.

'Polly! Well, yes; his old cage is very shabby; he is so continually pecking at it with his sharp bill. I dare say Mrs Gordon noticed it when she called here last October. I shall always think of you, Mary, when I see him in it. Now we can have him in the drawing-room, for I dare say a French cage will be quite an ornament to the room.'

And so she talked on, till we worked ourselves up into high delight at the idea of Polly in his new abode, presentable in it even to the Honourable Mrs Jamieson. The next morning Miss Pole said she had been dreaming of Polly with her new cap on his head, while she herself sat on a perch in the new cage and admired him. Then, as if ashamed of having revealed the fact of imagining 'such arrant nonsense' in her sleep, she passed on rapidly to the philosophy of dreams, quoting some book she had lately been reading, which was either too deep in itself, or too confused in her repetition for me to understand it. After breakfast, we had the cap out again; and that in its different aspects occupied us for an hour or so; and then, as it was a fine day, we turned into the garden, where Polly was hung on a nail outside the kitchen window. He clamoured and screamed at the sight of his mistress, who went to look for an almond for him. I examined his cage meanwhile, old discoloured wicker-work, clumsily made by a Cranford basketmaker. I took out Mrs Gordon's letter; it was dated the fifteenth, and this was the twentieth, for I had kept it secret for two days in my pocket. Mr Ludovic was on the point of setting out for England when she wrote.

'Poor Polly!' said I, as Miss Pole, returning, fed him with the almond.

'Ah! Polly does not know what a pretty cage he is going to have,' said she, talking to him as she would have done to a child; and then turning to me, she asked when I thought it would come? We reckoned up dates, and made out that it might arrive that very day. So she called to her little stupid servant-maiden Fanny, and bade her go out and buy a great brass-headed nail, very strong, strong enough to bear Polly and the new cage, and we all three weighed the cage in our hands, and

on her return she was to come up into the drawing-room with the nail
and a hammer.

Fanny was a long time, as she always was, over her errands; but as
soon as she came back, we knocked the nail, with solemn earnestness,
into the house-wall, just outside the drawing-room window; for, as
Miss Pole observed, when I was not there she had no one to talk to,
and as in summer-time she generally sat with the window open, she
could combine two purposes, the giving air and sun to Polly-Cockatoo,
and the having his agreeable companionship in her solitary hours.

'When it rains, my dear, or even in a very hot sun, I shall take the
cage in. I would not have your pretty present spoilt for the world. It
was very kind of you to think of it; I am quite come round to liking it
better than any present of mere dress; and dear Mrs Gordon has shown
all her usual pretty observation in remembering my Polly-Cockatoo.'

'Polly-Cockatoo' was his grand name; I had only once or twice
heard him spoken of by Miss Pole in this formal manner, except when
she was speaking to the servants; then she always gave him his full
designation, just as most people call their daughters Miss, in speaking
of them to strangers or servants. But since Polly was to have a new
cage, and all the way from Paris too, Miss Pole evidently thought it
necessary to treat him with unusual respect.

We were obliged to go out to pay some calls; but we left strict orders
with Fanny what to do if the cage arrived in our absence, as (we had
calculated) it might. Miss Pole stood ready bonneted and shawled
at the kitchen door, I behind her, and cook behind Fanny, each of us
listening to the conversation of the other two.

'And Fanny, mind if it comes you coax Polly-Cockatoo nicely into
it. He is very particular, and may be attached to his old cage, though
it is so shabby. Remember, birds have their feelings as much as we
have! Don't hurry him in making up his mind.'

'Please, ma'am, I think an almond would help him to get over his
feelings,' said Fanny, dropping a curtsey at every speech, as she had
been taught to do at her charity school.

'A very good idea, very. If I have my keys in my pocket I will give
you an almond for him. I think he is sure to like the view up the street
from the window; he likes seeing people, I think.'

'It's but a dull look-out into the garden; nowt but dumb flowers,'
said cook, touched by this allusion to the cheerfulness of the street, as
contrasted with the view from her own kitchen window.

'It's a very good look-out for busy people,' said Miss Pole, severely.
And then, feeling she was likely to get the worst of it in an encounter
with her old servant, she withdrew with meek dignity, being deaf to

some sharp reply; and of course I, being bound to keep order, was deaf too. If the truth must be told, we rather hastened our steps, until we had banged the street-door behind us.

We called on Miss Matty, of course; and then on Mrs Hoggins. It seemed as if ill-luck would have it that we went to the only two households of Cranford where there was the encumbrance of a man, and in both places the man was where he ought not to have been – namely, in his own house, and in the way. Miss Pole – out of civility to me, and because she really was full of the new cage for Polly, and because we all in Cranford relied on the sympathy of our neighbours in the veriest trifle that interested us – told Miss Matty, and Mr Peter, and Mr and Mrs Hoggins; he was standing in the drawing-room, booted and spurred, and eating his hunk of bread-and-cheese in the very presence of his aristocratic wife, my lady that was. As Miss Pole said afterwards, if refinement was not to be found in Cranford, blessed as it was with so many scions of county families, she did not know where to meet with it. Bread-and-cheese in a drawing-room! Onions next.

But for all Mr Hoggins's vulgarity, Miss Pole told him of the present she was about to receive.

'Only think! a new cage for Polly – Polly – Polly-Cockatoo, you know, Mr Hoggins. You remember him, and the bite he gave me once because he wanted to be put back in his cage, pretty bird?'

'I only hope the new cage will be strong as well as pretty, for I must say a——' He caught a look from his wife, I think, for he stopped short. 'Well, we're old friends, Polly and I, and he put some practice in my way once. I shall be up the street this afternoon, and perhaps I shall step in and see this smart Parisian cage.'

'Do!' said Miss Pole, eagerly. 'Or, if you are in a hurry, look up at my drawing-room window; if the cage is come, it will be hanging out there, and Polly in it.'

We had passed the omnibus[7] that met the train from London some time ago, so we were not surprised as we returned home to see Fanny half out of the window, and cook evidently either helping or hindering her. Then they both took their heads in; but there was no cage hanging up. We hastened up the steps.

Both Fanny and the cook met us in the passage.

'Please, ma'am,' said Fanny, 'there's no bottom to the cage, and Polly would fly away.'

'And there's no top,' exclaimed cook. 'He might get out at the top quite easy.'

'Let me see,' said Miss Pole, brushing past, thinking no doubt that her superior intelligence was all that was needed to set things to rights. On the ground lay a bundle, or a circle of hoops, neatly covered over with calico, no more like a cage for Polly-Cockatoo than I am like a cage. Cook took something up between her finger and thumb, and lifted the unsightly present from Paris. How I wish it had stayed there! – but foolish ambition has brought people to ruin before now; and my twenty shillings are gone, sure enough, and there must be some use or some ornament intended by the maker of the thing before us.

'Don't you think it's a mousetrap, ma'am?' asked Fanny, dropping her little curtsey.

For reply, the cook lifted up the machine, and showed how easily mice might run out; and Fanny shrank back abashed. Cook was evidently set against the new invention, and muttered about its being all of a piece with French things – French cooks, French plums (nasty dried-up things), French rolls (as had no substance in 'em).

Miss Pole's good manners, and desire of making the best of things in my presence, induced her to try and drown cook's mutterings.

'Indeed, I think it will make a very nice cage for Polly-Cockatoo. How pleased he will be to go from one hoop to another, just like a ladder, and with a board or two at the bottom, and nicely tied up at the top——'

Fanny was struck with a new idea.

'Please, ma'am, my sister-in-law has got an aunt as lives lady's-maid with Sir John's daughter – Miss Arley. And they did say as she wore iron petticoats all made of hoops——'

'Nonsense, Fanny!' we all cried; for such a thing had not been heard of in all Drumble, let alone Cranford, and I was rather looked upon in the light of a fast young woman by all the laundresses of Cranford, because I had two corded petticoats.[8]

'Go mind thy business, wench,' said cook, with the utmost contempt; 'I'll warrant we'll manage th' cage without thy help.'

'It is near dinner-time, Fanny, and the cloth not laid,' said Miss Pole, hoping the remark might cut two ways; but cook had no notion of going. She stood on the bottom step of the stairs, holding the Paris perplexity aloft in the air.

'It might do for a meat-safe,' said she. 'Cover it o'er wi' canvas, to keep th' flies out. It is a good framework, I reckon, anyhow!' She held her head on one side, like a connoisseur in meat-safes, as she was.

Miss Pole said, 'Are you sure Mrs Gordon called it a cage, Mary? Because she is a woman of her word, and would not have called it so if it was not.'

'Look here; I have the letter in my pocket.'

' "I have wondered how I could best fulfil your commission for me to purchase something to the value of" – um, um, never mind – "fashionable and pretty for dear Miss Pole, and at length I have decided upon one of the new kind of 'cages'" (look here, Miss Pole; here is the word, C. A. G. E.), "which are made so much lighter and more elegant in Paris than in England. Indeed, I am not sure if they have ever reached you, for it is not a month since I saw the first of the kind in Paris." '

'Does she say anything about Polly-Cockatoo?' asked Miss Pole. 'That would settle the matter at once, as showing that she had him in her mind.'

'No – nothing.'

Just then Fanny came along the passage with the tray full of dinner-things in her hands. When she had put them down, she stood at the door of the dining-room taking a distant view of the article. 'Please, ma'am, it looks like a petticoat without any stuff in it; indeed it does, if I'm to be whipped for saying it.'

But she only drew down upon herself a fresh objurgation from the cook; and sorry and annoyed, I seized the opportunity of taking the thing out of cook's hand, and carrying it upstairs, for it was full time to get ready for dinner. But we had very little appetite for our meal, and kept constantly making suggestions, one to the other, as to the nature and purpose of this Paris 'cage,' but as constantly snubbing poor little Fanny's reiteration of 'Please, ma'am, I do believe it's a kind of petticoat – indeed I do.' At length Miss Pole turned upon her with almost as much vehemence as cook had done, only in choicer language.

'Don't be so silly, Fanny. Do you think ladies are like children, and must be put in go-carts; or need wire guards like fires to surround them; or can get warmth out of bits of whalebone and steel; a likely thing indeed! Don't keep talking about what you don't understand.'

So our maiden was mute for the rest of the meal. After dinner we had Polly brought upstairs in her old cage, and I held out the new one, and we turned it about in every way. At length Miss Pole said:

'Put Polly-Cockatoo back, and shut him up in his cage. You hold this French thing up' (alas! that my present should be called a 'thing'), 'and I'll sew a bottom on to it. I'll lay a good deal, they've forgotten to sew in the bottom before sending it off.' So I held and she sewed; and then she held and I sewed, till it was all done. Just as we had put Polly-Cockatoo in, and were closing up the top with a pretty piece of old yellow ribbon – and, indeed, it was not a bad-looking cage after all our trouble – Mr Hoggins came up-stairs, having been seen by Fanny before he had time to knock at the door.

'Hallo!' said he, almost tumbling over us, as we were sitting on the floor at our work. 'What's this?'

'It's this pretty present for Polly-Cockatoo,' said Miss Pole, raising herself up with as much dignity as she could, 'that Mary has had sent from Paris for me.' Miss Pole was in great spirits now we had got Polly in; I can't say that I was.

Mr Hoggins began to laugh in his boisterous vulgar way.

'For Polly – ha! ha! It's meant for you, Miss Pole – ha! ha! It's a new invention to hold your gowns out – ha! ha!'

'Mr Hoggins! you may be a surgeon, and a very clever one, but nothing – not even your profession – gives you a right to be indecent.'

Miss Pole was thoroughly roused, and I trembled in my shoes. But Mr Hoggins only laughed the more. Polly screamed in concert, but Miss Pole stood in stiff rigid propriety, very red in the face.

'I beg your pardon, Miss Pole, I am sure. But I am pretty certain I am right. It's no indecency that I can see; my wife and Mrs FitzAdam take in a Paris fashion-book between 'em, and I can't help seeing the plates of fashions sometimes – ha! ha! ha! Look, Polly has got out of his queer prison – ha! ha! ha!'

Just then Mr Peter came in; Miss Matty was so curious to know if the expected present had arrived. Mr Hoggins took him by the arm, and pointed to the poor thing lying on the ground, but could not explain for laughing. Miss Pole said:

'Although I am not accustomed to give an explanation of my conduct to gentlemen, yet, being insulted in my own house by – by Mr Hoggins, I must appeal to the brother of my old friend – my very oldest friend. Is this article a lady's petticoat, or a bird's cage?'

She held it up as she made this solemn inquiry. Mr Hoggins seized the moment to leave the room, in shame, as I supposed, but, in reality, to fetch his wife's fashion-book; and, before I had completed the narration of the story of my unlucky commission, he returned, and, holding the fashion-plate open by the side of the extended article, demonstrated the identity of the two.

But Mr Peter had always a smooth way of turning off anger, by either his fun or a compliment. 'It is a cage,' said he, bowing to Miss Pole; 'but it is a cage for an angel, instead of a bird! Come along, Hoggins, I want to speak to you!'

And, with an apology, he took the offending and victorious surgeon out of Miss Pole's presence. For a good while we said nothing; and we were now rather shy of little Fanny's superior wisdom when she brought up tea. But towards night our spirits revived, and we were quite ourselves again, when Miss Pole proposed that we should cut up the pieces of steel or whalebone – which, to do them justice, were very elastic – and make ourselves two good comfortable English calashes out of them with the aid of a piece of dyed silk which Miss Pole had by her.

NOTES

The Last Generation in England

1. *Southey . . . 'Doctor, &c.'*: Southey (see *Cranford*, Chapter I note 3) in the *Edinburgh Review* 87 (1848), p. 390. *The Doctor* was a miscellany published by Southey, 1834–47.

2. *the Mohawks a century before*: Mohawks (Mohocks) were gangs who terrorized the London streets at night in the eighteenth century. Mohawk is properly the name of a tribe of Native Americans in what is now New York state, but the name was confused with *amok* (to run wild).

3. *so oblivious of 'Mrs Grundy's' existence*: So unaware of social proprieties. Mrs Grundy was a character referred to in Thomas Morton's farce *Speed the Plough* (1798) by a woman who constantly worried: 'What would Mrs Grundy say?' The phrase became proverbial, particularly in derisive use, for those too much concerned with what others would think.

4. *Lilliputian*: Tiny: derived from the imaginary island of Lilliput in the satire *Gulliver's Travels* (1726) by Jonathan Swift (1667–1745), which is in scale with inhabitants who are six inches high. And below, *brobdingnagian*: Enormous. Brobdingnag is another imaginary country where everything is in scale with inhabitants as tall as steeples.

5. *squibs and crackers*: Fireworks, here used metaphorically for sharp verbal criticism.

6. *Their sister . . . in America*: See *Cranford*, Chapter VII, note 9.

7. *Adam and Eve in the weather-glass*: Two figures on a thermometer or barometer that indicated high or low temperature or pressure by one or other popping out.

The Cage at Cranford

1. *1856*: This date is three years after the publication of *Cranford*, and it has been suggested that it should be emended to 1853. But dating in the novel is deliberately shifting and this may be true here. Certainly 'cages' (see next note) were not known before 1856 in England.

2. *a cage*: Mrs Gordon refers to the latest device to support a large crinoline skirt: a hooped frame of metal. The Cranford ladies take it to be a birdcage. The whole story hinges on this ambiguity, captured in the title.

3. *Johnson's fashion-show*: In *Cranford*, there is a reference to the display of new fashions at Johnson's shop, a significant event. Evidently their fabrics could be made up into the styles on display. See Chapter XIII.

4. *I was past thirty*: Relatively mature. The only reference in any of the Cranford stories to her age.

5. *the father of lies*: Satan: see John 8: 44.

6. *Miss Pole's age . . . at sixty-five*: The first mention of her age, which makes her much older than Miss Matty is said to be in *Cranford* where she is not yet 52 (Chapter IV), and 58 later (Chapter XIV).

7. *the omnibus*: From the 1830s this was a four-wheeled public vehicle, usually on a fixed route with seats along the insides, and rear access. By 1835 it was steam-driven.

8. *two corded petticoats*: Petticoats to be worn under a crinoline reinforced with rings of strong cord to make it stand out. The crinoline was growing ever wider and the next stage was the metal hoops of the 'cage'.

Appendix II

The Nature and Role of Women

The overriding impression of Gaskell's novel is that the ladies of Cranford live according to some rigorous code of behaviour of which they have an instinctive and minutely detailed knowledge. The knowledge appears innate because the society they live in tells them in a variety of ways what is expected of them in relation to demeanour, clothes and behaviour generally. The absence of a vote, of a thorough education and of opportunities for fulfilling work have caused such women to internalize society's idea of the nature and role of women. This creates a strong feeling that they must not overstep some invisible and known mark.

MRS BEETON'S ADVICE

One obvious place where the code is made visible is in books specifically targeted at women: sentimental novels, books of household management and so-called conduct books. The two extracts below are from Isabella Beeton's *Beeton's Book of Household Management* (1861) which sold 60,000 copies in that year alone and by 1868 had sold two million. It was one of many such works. The passages refer to the duties of those who, like the ladies of Cranford, have a household to run, and to the duties of their 'maids-of-all-work'. Mrs Beeton assumes she is addressing larger families but, though the Cranford establishments are miniature, the rules still apply. The interesting question raised by both extracts is: who is the authority behind these commandments?

It is noticeable in this extract that the military simile is not a joke but is seriously meant. The mistress of the house, whatever its size, is as rigidly instructed as her servants. This is because scrupulousness in domestic duty is seen not as a practical skill to be acquired but as a moral necessity. To be slack in one's domestic duties is for any woman to be morally vicious.

Advice for the Mistress of the House

As with the Commander of an Army, or the leader of any enterprise, so is it with the mistress of a house. Her spirit will be seen through the whole establishment; and just in proportion as she performs her duties intelligently and thoroughly, so will her domestics follow in her path. Of all those acquirements, which more particularly belong to the feminine character, there are none which take a higher rank, in our estimation, than such as enter into a knowledge of household duties; for on these are perpetually dependent the happiness, comfort, and well-being of a family. In this opinion we are borne out by the author of 'The Vicar of Wakefield',[1] who says: 'The modest virgin, the prudent wife, and the careful matron, are much more serviceable in life than petticoated philosophers, blustering heroines, or virago queens. She who makes her husband and her children happy, who reclaims the one from vice and trains up the other to virtue, is a much greater character than ladies described in romances, whose whole occupation is to murder mankind with shafts from their quiver, or their eyes.'

Pursuing this Picture, we may add, that to be a good housewife does not necessarily imply an abandonment of proper pleasures or amusing recreation; and we think it the more necessary to express this, as the performance of the duties of a mistress may, to some minds, perhaps seem to be incompatible with the enjoyment of life. Let us, however, now proceed to describe some of those home qualities and virtues which are necessary to the proper management of a Household, and then point out the plan which may be the most profitably pursued for the daily regulation of its affairs.

Early Rising is one of the most Essential Qualities which enter into good Household Management, as it is not only the parent of health, but of innumerable other advantages. Indeed, when a mistress is an early riser, it is almost certain that her house will be orderly and well-managed. On the contrary, if she remain in bed till a late hour, then the domestics, who, as we have before observed, invariably partake somewhat of their mistress's character, will surely become sluggards. To self-indulgence all are more or less disposed, and it is not to be expected that servants are freer from this fault than the heads of houses. The great Lord Chatham[2] thus gave his advice in reference to this subject: – 'I would have inscribed on the curtains of your bed, and the walls of your chamber, "If you do not rise early, you can make progress in nothing." '

Cleanliness is also indispensable to Health, and must be studied both in regard to the person and the house, and all that it contains. Cold or tepid baths should be employed every morning, unless, on account of illness or other circumstances, they should be deemed objectionable. The bathing of *children* will be treated of under the head of 'Management of Children'.

Frugality and Economy are Home Virtues, without which no household can prosper. Dr Johnson says: 'Frugality may be termed the daughter of Prudence, the sister of Temperance, and the parent of Liberty. He that is extravagant will quickly become poor, and poverty will enforce dependence and invite corruption.'[3] The necessity of practising economy should be evident to every one, whether in the possession of an income no more than sufficient for a family's requirements, or of a large fortune, which puts financial adversity out of the question. We must always remember that it is a great merit in housekeeping to manage a little well. 'He is a good waggoner,' says Bishop Hall,[4] 'that can turn in a little room. To live well in abundance is the praise of the estate, not of the person. I will study more how to give a good account of my little, than how to make it more.' In this there is true wisdom, and it may be added, that those who can manage a little well, are most likely to succeed in their management of larger matters. Economy and frugality must never, however, be allowed to degenerate into parsimony and meanness. ((London: Chancellor Press, 1861), pp. 1–2)

The interest of this passage lies not only in the onerousness of the work demanded of this kind of servant but in the fact that she is addressed in the same sternly didactic way as her mistress. Both are prisoners in the same trap which tells them to be efficient or to risk the guilt which follows on the vice of negligence and lack of care.

Advice for the Maid-of-all-Work

The general servant, or maid-of-all-work, is perhaps the only one of her class deserving of commiseration: her life is a solitary one, and in some places, her work is never done. She is also subject to rougher treatment than either the house or kitchen-maid, especially in her earlier career: she starts in life, probably a girl of thirteen, with some small tradesman's wife as her mistress, just a step above her in the social scale; and although the class contains among them many excellent, kind-hearted women, it also contains some very rough specimens of the feminine gender, and to some of these it occasionally falls to give our maid-of-all-work her first lessons in her multifarious occupations: the mistress's commands are the measure of the maid-of-all-work's duties. By the time she has become a tolerable servant, she is probably engaged in some respectable tradesman's house, where she has to rise with the lark, for she has to do in her own person all the work which in larger establishments is performed by cook, kitchen-maid, and housemaid, and occasionally the part of a footman's duty, which consists in carrying messages.

The general servant's duties commence by opening the shutters (and windows, if the weather permits) of all the lower apartments in the house; she should then brush up her kitchen-range, light the fire, clear away the ashes, clean the hearth, and polish with a leather the bright parts of the range, doing all as rapidly and as vigorously as possible, that no more time be wasted than is necessary. After putting on the kettle, she should then proceed to the dining-room or parlour to get it in order for breakfast. She should first roll up the rug, take up the fender, shake and fold up the table-cloth, then sweep the room, carrying the dirt towards the fireplace; a coarse cloth should then be laid down over the carpet, and she should proceed to clean the grate, having all her utensils close to her. When the grate is finished, the ashes cleared away, the hearth cleaned, and the fender put back in its place, she must dust the furniture, not omitting the legs of the tables and chairs; and if there are any ornaments or things on the sideboard, she must not dust round them, but lift them up on to another place, dust well where they have been standing, and then replace the things. Nothing annoys a particular mistress so much as to find, when she comes down stairs, different articles of furniture looking as if they had never been dusted. If the servant is at all methodical, and gets into a habit of *doing* a room in a certain way, she will scarcely ever leave her duties neglected. After the rug is put down, the table-cloth arranged, and everything in order, she should lay the cloth for breakfast, and then shut the dining-room door.

The hall must now be swept, the mats shaken, the door-step cleaned, and any brass knockers or handles polished up with the leather. If the family breakfast very early, the tidying of the hall must then be deferred till after that meal. After cleaning the boots that are absolutely required, the servant should now wash her hands and face, put on a clean white apron, and be ready for her mistress when she comes down stairs. In families where there is much work to do before breakfast, the master of the house frequently has two pairs of boots in wear, so that they may be properly cleaned when the servant has more time to do them, in the daytime. This arrangement is, perhaps, scarcely necessary in the summer-time, when there are no grates to clean every morning; but in the dark days of winter it is only kind and thoughtful to lighten a servant-of-all-work's duties as much as possible.

She will now carry the urn into the dining-room, where her mistress will make the tea or coffee, and sometimes will boil the eggs, to insure them being done to her liking. In the mean time the servant cooks, if required, the bacon, kidneys, fish, &c.; – if cold meat is to be served, she must always send it to table on a clean dish, and nicely garnished with tufts of parsley, if this is obtainable.

After she has had her own breakfast, and whilst the family are finishing theirs, she should go upstairs into the bedrooms, open all the windows, strip the clothes off the beds, and leave them to air whilst she is clearing away the breakfast things. She should then take up the crumbs in a dustpan from under the table, put the chairs in their places, and sweep up the hearth.

The breakfast things washed up, the kitchen should be tidied, so that it may be neat when her mistress comes in to give the orders for the day: after receiving these orders, the servant should go upstairs again, with a jug of boiling water, the slop-pail, and two cloths. After emptying the slops, and scalding the vessels with the boiling water, and wiping them thoroughly dry, she should wipe the top of the wash-table and arrange it all in order. She then proceeds to make the beds, in which occupation she is generally assisted by the mistress, or, if she have any daughters, by one of them. Before commencing to make the bed, the servant should put on a large bed-apron, kept for this purpose only, which should be made very wide, to button round the waist and meet behind, while it should be made as long as the dress. By adopting this plan, the blacks and dirt on servants' dresses (which at all times it is impossible to help) will not rub off on to the bed-clothes, mattresses, and bed furniture. When the beds are made, the rooms should be dusted, the stairs lightly swept down, hall furniture, closets, &c., dusted. The lady of the house, where there is but one servant kept, frequently takes charge of the drawing-room herself, that is to say, dusting it; the servant sweeping, cleaning windows, looking-glasses, grates, and rough work of that sort. If there are many ornaments and knick-knacks about the room, it is certainly better for the mistress to dust these herself, as a maid-of-all-work's hands are not always in a condition to handle delicate ornaments.

Now she has gone the rounds of the house and seen that all is in order, the servant goes to her kitchen to see about the cooking of the dinner, in which very often her mistress will assist her. She should put on a coarse apron with a bib to do her dirty work in, which may be easily replaced by a white one if required.

Half an hour before dinner is ready, she should lay the cloth, that everything may be in readiness when she is dishing up the dinner, and take all into the dining-room that is likely to be required, in the way of knives, forks, spoons, bread, salt, water, &c. &c. By exercising a little forethought, much confusion and trouble may be saved both to mistress and servant, by getting everything ready for the dinner in good time.

After taking in the dinner, when every one is seated, she removes the covers, hands the plates round, and pours out the beer; and should be careful to hand everything on the left side of the person she is waiting on.

We need scarcely say that a maid-of-all-work cannot stay in the dining-room during the whole of dinner-time, as she must dish up her pudding, or whatever is served after the first course. When she sees every one helped, she should leave the room to make her preparations for the next course; and anything that is required, such as bread, &c., people may assist themselves to in the absence of the servant.

When the dinner things are cleared away, the servant should sweep up the crumbs in the dining-room, sweep the hearth, and lightly dust the furniture, then sit down to her own dinner. (pp. 1001–3)

ELIZABETH GASKELL'S LETTERS ON
DOMESTIC LIFE

Gaskell's letters show the internal struggles of a dutiful wife and mother who is also intelligent and gifted. She finds it difficult to balance her domestic duties and her passionate wish for intellectual fulfilment in her writing, with the result that she has episodes of guilt. This explains her ambiguous attitude to Cranford.

A Domestic Day

April 26, 1850

Dearest little Tottie,[5]

This piece of paper tempts me to write to you. Are not you a wicked woman not to say the old serpent herself to try and decoy me up to your Babylon. Oh for shame! but oh dear how I *should* like to come and see the Exhibitions – (you did not think I had so much of the artist about me Missie – now did you?) and *you* (poor Macready[6] – I never think of him without a sigh.) But my dear, don't you see there are beds to be taken down, and curtains dyed and carpets cleaned, and cornices chosen and carpets selected, and cabbages planted in *our* garden, – and that I am the factotum della città – and its Figaro quà, Figaro la, – all day long. No my dear little lassie, – if I have a peep at you in November I shall be thankful – I mean in your own big place, – I've half a notion, and have made a whole promise of going to Crix, (the Shaens[7] in Essex) in October, – and perhaps – perhaps –; Mrs Hensleigh Wedgwood[8] has written to invite me, also naming the Exhibitions, (you see what comes of my knowing way of talking about the 'aerial distances,') but alas! and the Shaens begged me to come in rose-time to them. All idea of leaving home till the removal is complete must be given up; and it won't be complete till we go to Silverdale[9] that's clear. Do come to us soon! I want to get associations about that house; *here* there is the precious perfume lingering of my darling's short presence[10] in this life – I wish I were with him in that 'light, where we shall all see light,' for I am often sorely puzzled here – but however I must not waste my strength or my time about the never ending sorrow; but which hallows this house. I think that is one evil of this bustling life that one has never time calmly and bravely to face a great grief, and to view it on every side as to bring the harmony out of it. – Well! I meant to write a merry letter.

Yrs affec(tionately),
Lily

(J. A. V. Chapple and Arthur Pollard (eds.), *The Letters of Mrs Gaskell* (Manchester: Manchester University Press, 1966), pp.110–11)

Letters When Absent from Home: Domestic Worries

[June 1850]

My dearest Daddy,[11]

I enclose you Sam's letter, (only received this morning,) which after you have read you may give to Mr Gaskell.[12] It is very decided & comfortable, & I have written forthwith to Martha, engaging the rooms (bad-smelling & all, we must air it well) for July 3rd. Mrs Evans[13] *distance* is more than I expected but nice little woman for making the abatement in her charge which nearly counterbalances – and her moderate charge for *meals* &c will quite make the difference I expect. So much for our own affairs.

I was very sure you wd over-sleep yourselves, wanting the alarum of *my* two children. They are both well & flourishing, and nothing has occurred worthy of note since I wrote to *your* two children yesterday, but that my new green gown is spoilt – owing to hot milk being poured, *not* by me, into a glass which cracked & flew up & down, & the milk came splash into my lap – very provoking indeed and as people say many shillings [out]* of {of} my pocket. What is Ursa Major about – and at any rate why does not Charlie tell you that *nothing* is doing – it is a comfort even to hear that; it is less suspense than hearing nothing. Don't be mine 'very sincerely,' again there's a good girl.

Florence is sleeping with Hearn[14] but Hearn says she sleeps so much worse than she did when I was at Lancaster she can't account for it. To be sure we have had such windy nights. She went yesterday to Mrs Green's,[15] and saw a little puppy-dog there that barked at her, & she has dreamt about it, and been frightened all night. But she is very well, very hungry, very merry, and very independent. Hearn & I between us, made some terrible forgets in our packing up, no night gown, no night cap, no dressing gown, no tooth-brush; the last bought, the first I borrowed. The dress-maker says my gown is gone, nothing can be done but dying it. What else have I got to say? I try to think of something that will interest you, but I can't.

Will you ask Margaret to make out a washing bill & send the clothes to the wash – and *if* the new washerwoman sent by Miss Marsland[16] calls on Saturday afternoon, to show her one of our washing bills, as explanatory of what clothes we send out, and say I am particular about having the clothes sent home \all/ on Saturday *morning not torn*, and *of a good colour*, and if she will engage to wash for us, to say that at the end of July I should like to begin with her (no use

* [ ] are editorial additions, { } Gaskell's deletions and \ / Gaskell's additions.

before we go away.) We shall certainly be at home about 10 on Monday morning and I do hope you won't have much trouble or annoyance in the mean while.

  Goodbye, dear – Ever your very affect(ionate) friend
      E C Gaskell

(John Chapple and Alan Shelston (eds.), *Further Letters of Mrs Gaskell* (Manchester: Manchester University Press 2000), p. 27)

           [? Summer 1846]
My dear Miss Fergusson,

 Just a line to ask you how you think Mr Gaskell *really* is; he sends me word of his fainting on Sunday night which makes me very uncomfortable, and I shall certainly think it right to return unless I hear from you a better account. So do write please directly.

 And will you tell Anne [Hearn] that I wish she would *particularly* attend to Mr Gaskell; to tempting him with the food he likes best, and *change* of diet; to *always* taking him up some supper. *Milk* I think he likes best for a constancy; and not too much bread in it; but *always* to take something up. I wish you wd make Marianne[17] attend to taking him an egg beaten up with a little warm milk & sugar, every morning when he has not pupils before she goes out; & will you send her ¼ of an hour or so before to ask Anne to get it ready – & will you tell Anne always to send something either meat or eggs in to tea, 'specially on Sunday; and to get kidneys sweet-breads & such tit bits – and fowls by way of variety, and devil the legs &c – She only wants reminding I am sure to attend to all these things; so will you read her aloud what I have said, & not think me very troublesome in making you the medium. I wish he wd just see Mr Partington[18] if only once; it would be such a satisfaction to me, and I wish he wd get up earlier so as not to have to hurry over his breakfast.

 I shall be very uncomfortable till I hear; and would much rather come home. If Hannah has (as I told her) taken the sofa out of his study, ask her please to take it back again; that he may have the oppy of lying down – We are all quite well, only I'm lame. Thank MA for her gift to Florence of the pretty little sheet of paper. F was much pleased. Excuse this dull selfish note, and ever believe me

      Your affect(ionate) friend,
        E C Gaskell

(Ibid., p. 31)

Doubts about Neglecting Home Duties

[? February 1850]

My dearest Tottie,

... One thing I must say is that your letters do give me so much pleasure, I look them over and wonder what it is that pleases me so much, and I can't make out. <. . .> And now I could say so much about the Munich plan; and what follows in your letter about home duties and individual life; it is just my puzzle; and I don't think I can get nearer to a solution than you have done. But if you were here we cd talk about it so well. Oh! that you were here! I don't like the idea of your being a whole six months away from call; but that is selfish and not to be taken into consideration. One thing is pretty clear, *Women*, must give up living an artist's life, if home duties are to be paramount. It is different with men, whose home duties are so small a part of their life. However we are talking of women. I am sure it is healthy for them to have the refuge of the hidden world of Art to shelter themselves in when too much pressed upon by daily small Lilliputian arrows of peddling cares; it keeps them from being morbid as you say; and takes them into the land where King Arthur lies hidden,[19] and soothes them with its peace. I have felt this in writing, I see others feel it in music, you in painting, so assuredly a blending of the two is desirable. (Home duties and the development of the Individual I mean), which you will say it takes no Solomon to tell you but the difficulty is where and when to make one set of duties subserve and give place to the other. I have no doubt that the cultivation of each tends to keep the other in a healthy state, – my grammar is all at sixes and sevens I have no doubt but never mind if you can pick out my meaning. I think a great deal of what you have said.

                    [Yours very affectionately,]
                          E C Gaskell.

(Chapple and Pollard, *Letters*, p. 106)

Doubts about House Buying

My dearest Tottie,

... You *must* come and see us in it, dearest Tottie, and try and make me see 'the wrong the better cause,' and that it is right to spend so much ourselves on *so* purely selfish a thing as a house is, while so many are wanting – thats the haunting thought to me; at least to one of my 'Mes,' for I have a great number, and that's the plague. One of my mes is, I do believe, a true Christian – (only people call her socialist and communist), another of my mes is a wife and mother, and highly delighted at the delight of everyone else in the house, Meta and William most especially who are in full extasy. Now that's my 'social' self I suppose. Then again I've another self with a full taste for beauty and convenience whh is pleased on its own account. How am I to reconcile all these warring members? I try to drown myself (my *first* self), by saying it's Wm who is to decide on all these things, and his feeling it right ought to be my rule, And so it is – only that does not quite do. Well! I must try and make the house give as much pleasure to others as I can and make it as little a selfish thing as I can. My dear! its 150 a year, and I dare say we shall be ruined

Yours very affec[tionately],
E C Gaskell.

(Chapple and Pollard, *Letters*, p. 108)

NOTES

1. *'The Vicar of Wakefield'*: Novel (1766) by Oliver Goldsmith (?1730–74).
2. *Lord Chatham*: William Pitt the elder (1708–78), first Earl of Chatham, Prime Minister (1766–8).
3. *Dr Johnson . . . invite corruption*: In the *Rambler* 57 (2 October 1750). See also *Cranford*, Chapter I, note 21.
4. *Bishop Hall*: Joseph Hall (1574–1656), Bishop of Exeter (1627); Bishop of Norwich (1641). He was a prolific writer on religious issues and also a satirist.
5. *Tottie*: Eliza Fox, a close friend.
6. *Macready*: William C. Macready (1793–1873), well-known actor; a visitor to the Gaskells'.
7. *Crix . . . the Shaens*: Family into which Emily Winkworth, a close friend of Gaskell, had married. Crix was their home at Chelmsford in Essex.
8. *Mrs Hensleigh Wedgwood*: Frances (née Macintosh) who married Hensleigh, son of Josiah Wedgwood.
9. *Silverdale*: Village in Morecambe Bay to which the Gaskells often went on holiday.
10. *my darling's short presence*: Willie, Gaskell's baby son, born October 1844, died August 1845.

11. *Daddy*: Nickname of Barbara Fergusson, the Gaskell children's nurse.

12. *Sam's . . . Mr Gaskell*: Sam is either Gaskell's uncle Sam Holland (1768–1851) or her cousin of the same name (1803–92) and Gaskell's husband William.

13. *Mrs Evans*: The Gaskells' landlady at Festiniog, North Wales, which they visited on summer holidays.

14. *Florence . . . Hearn*: Gaskell's daughter, born 1842, and Ann(e) Hearn, servant and friend, respectively.

15. *Mrs Green's*: Mary Green, wife of the Unitarian Minister at Knutsford.

16. *Margaret . . . Miss Marsland*: Gaskell's nursemaid and the sister of two male members of William Gaskell's congregation, respectively.

17. *Marianne*: (Also MA), Gaskell's daughter, born 1834.

18. *Mr Partington*: James Partington, a Manchester surgeon.

19. *land where King Arthur lies hidden*: Avalon, the mythical island to which legend says Arthur was carried away in death and from which it was said that he would one day return.

Appendix III

Fashion at Cranford

Like many narratives relating to the past, such as Hardy's Wessex stories, *Cranford* is vague as to dates: it appears to be set in the late 1840s or early 1850s, at roughly the time when the first sections were written; but the opening chapters when Miss Matty's elder sister is still alive evidently refer to the late 1830s. Since Miss Matty claims, when Holbrook returns, to be not yet fifty-two, her early attachment to him must belong to the first decades of the nineteenth century. Throughout the narrative the town looks back to the past and never forward to the future and it appears cut off from the real, industrialized present represented by Drumble. This effect is created by the mores of the ladies and especially by their clothes.

Gaskell's own letters reveal her attention to detail of dress for herself and her daughters. Typically in 1851 she writes advising her sixteen-year-old daughter Marianne:

If you have any gowns made in London, *have them well made*; I would rather put the expense into the make than the material; *form* is always higher than colour &c. I don't mean that I would ever have you get a *poor* silk instead of a good one; but I had rather you had a brown Holland, or a print gown made by a *good* dress maker, than a silk made by a clumsy, inelegant badly-fitting one.[1]

More sartorial advice quickly follows in a letter written soon after this:

I was a little bit sorry to hear you were wearing a *merino* in an *evening* that night when Tottie drank tea with you. Either you are getting into the dirty slovenly habit of not changing your gown in the day-time, or you are short of gowns to wear a *merino* to *tea*? Which is it, love?[2]

Her comments indicate that in the nineteenth century clothes were clear indicators of class and that she saw it as her duty to ensure that her daughter should recognize the dress code of the time. Clothes are a similar preoccupation for the ladies of Cranford and the key to the code they practise may be explained by the generalization of one historian of costume that 'fashions, like fossils, reveal the habits of extinct beings',[3] an observation particularly apt for the dress and headgear of the Cranfordians who represent the fossils of an extinct period.

DRESSES

The novel skilfully indicates that, by what they wear in the way of dress, the ladies are turning their backs on the present. As Mary Smith explains,

Their dress is very independent of fashion; as they observe, 'What does it signify how we dress here at Cranford, where everybody knows us?' And if they go from home, their reason is equally cogent: 'What does it signify how we dress here, where nobody knows us?' The materials of their clothes are, in general, good and plain . . . (Chapter I)

Smith, however, immediately makes plain that their mode of dress is deliberately archaic, harking back to an earlier period, by adding 'I will answer for it, the last gigot, the last tight and scanty petticoat in wear in England, was seen in Cranford – and seen without a smile.'

This brief description of the clothes worn by the Cranford ladies shows fashion as it was in the first few decades of the nineteenth century (roughly 1800 to 1836). By implication it suggests what comes later and so summarizes the major change in women's dress in the first half of the century which was to become the basis of what was fashionable in the second half. The 'tight and scanty' petticoat was the only possible wear beneath the originally high-waisted, narrow and (relatively) loose-fitting gowns of the earliest decades of the century. They were not suitable wear for the natural waistline and bell-shaped skirts of the 1840s. The later mode expanded to become the ever more elaborate crinolines of the 1850s and 1860s. The gigot or leg-of-mutton sleeve was a part of the early narrow style which helped by increasing the emphasis on the upper half of the body since they were very full to the elbow. The gigot developed several variants as such fashions were wont to do: the mameluke, which was full to the

*Early Nineteenth
Century Gigot Sleeves.
Narrow skirt.*

*Later Nineteenth Century Flat
Sleeves. Large skirt.*

upper part of the wrist; the imbecile, which had fullness to the middle of the wrist, ending in a short cuff like a strait-jacket; and a Donna Maria, which was also full but had loops from the elbow to the wrist. Some of these variations were twice the width of the waist. This shape favoured by Cranfordians, with its large upper half and narrow lower half, had by the time when Gaskell wrote *Cranford*, been inverted: the preferred shape now was tight sleeves, narrow top, tight natural waist and ever more billowing skirts requiring hoops or 'cages', metal frames, beneath – and ideally wider door-frames. (See 'The Cages at Cranford' in Appendix I.)

HEADWEAR

Cap.

Though the ladies of Cranford cling to the dresses of their preferred period during the reign of William IV (1830–37), when his wife Queen Adelaide set the fashions, they still paradoxically but predictably aspire to be fashionable. They identify caps as the means of achieving this purpose and pay an obsessive attention to them in order to be what they conceive of as modish. Caps, for the first half of the century, were an essential item of indoor head-covering for middle-class women and they mutated into a variety of shapes. There was the jockey cap such as Miss Jenkyns wears with her cravat: a relatively neat cap with a front peak,

later favoured by women when practising archery. Or there are varieties of helmets, close-fitting, half-egg-shaped caps such as she contrives for Captain Brown's funeral as well as many not thought of in Cranford including Caledonian, Gothic, Empire-style, Marie Stuart, Scotch, peasant, Marmotte and others.

Turban.

In addition to the range of caps at a particular time, there were changes in other headwear fashion over the decades. Just after the turn of the century they were small and insignificant head-coverings. Then they began to grow broader and in the second decade to grow taller until by the 1840s they

Helmet.

had again subsided into simplicity. Unfortunately the ladies' desire to wear fashionable caps is not matched by a certain knowledge of what is currently 'in': their milliner, Miss Betty Barker, on whom they largely rely, copies the discarded caps of Lady Arley and sells them exclusively to the elite of Cranford, those who have 'a pedigree'. The out-of-date and supposedly fashionable items are presumably those referred to as worn on special occasions such as the visit to Mr Holbrook's house, the meeting with Lady Glenmire, Miss

Betty Barker's party and Signor Brunoni's performance of 'magical' tricks.

For the latter occasion, Miss Matty hankers for what she believes to be the ultimate in evening wear, a turban, a length of material folded round the head, which first appeared on English women in the late eighteenth century. It was one of the many instances of oriental influences on women's fashions which continued to affect their appearance throughout the century. Like caps, turbans mutated as the century moved on: they developed tassels, fringes, streamers that hung down on each side of the face and other decorations which left them barely recognizable as what we now know as turbans. Mary Smith's unwillingness to buy one which she believes will 'disfigure' Miss Matty suggests a large turban on the lines of that worn by Madame de Staël (1766–1817) in the engraving referred to by Mrs Forrester in Chapter X.

Calash.

The Cranfordians are not shown to pay much attention to outdoor headgear but in the interest of protecting their caps they wear calashes, hooped hoods which serve as a practical protection against the weather. In fact at this time there was a marked distinction between bonnets and hats, and a strict protocol for when each should be worn: the bonnet, with a brim around the face, tied under the chin and no brim at the back, was thought to be the more modest wear; the hat, with something of a brim all round and no strings, was somewhat more daring, though the distinction disappeared as the hat took over.

MOURNING

As with the references to dresses in Cranford, those made to mourning clothes are brief, tellingly playful and imply a great deal. They allude to the elaborate mourning dress required of relatives after a bereavement and particularly of widows for whom there were precise rules as to clothing and dates of allowable changes. For the first year a middle-class widow must wear a dress in a dull, black fabric, accompanied by a widow's cap with streamers. At the end of a year she was able to change to a black silk dress, the shiny surface of which was to be trimmed with lustreless black crepe and worn for a further six months. But black must be the colour of her clothing until a full two years had elapsed since the husband's death, after which half-mourning allowed a change to greys and dull shades.

A single reference to these rules is made concerning Mrs Fitz-Adam, a former inhabitant who returns to the town as a widow. She reappears 'in rustling black silk' and 'as bold as a lion'. As Mary Smith comments, this is 'so soon after her husband's death that poor Miss Jenkyns was justified in the remark she made, that "bombazine would have shown a deeper sense of her loss"' (Chapter VII). By appearing in lustrous silk instead of the dull worsted or cotton-and-worsted fabric called bombazine, Mrs Fitz-Adam has committed a breach of propriety which reflects badly on her identity as a grieving widow. A breach of a different sort is implied in Miss Matty's behaviour after the death of her earlier sweetheart, Holbrook, when, spinster though she is, she shocks the local milliner by ordering a new cap 'something like the Honourable Mrs Jamieson's'. The milliner replies; 'But she wears widows' caps, ma'am?' Miss Matty hastily qualifies her request: 'Oh! I only meant something in that style; not widows', of course, but rather like Mrs Jamieson's' (Chapter IV). As this makes plain, this cap is a way for Miss Matty to express her feeling that she is almost a widow – or at least could have been.

Her sister, Miss Jenkyns, has earlier made a silent statement about mourning after the tragic death of Captain Brown under the wheels of a train. To comfort his daughter Jessie, in this extremity she decides to take the unconventional step of attending the funeral, despite the fact that she and he were at odds over their assessments of literature. However, her sense of propriety still requires a gesture in the direction of mourning and, as is normal in Cranford, she focuses on her cap. She takes a modest black silk bonnet and a yard of suitably lustreless black crape with which she increases its prominence by trimming it. Again Mary Smith remarks, 'I was full of sorrow, but, by one of those whimsical thoughts which come unbidden into our heads, in times of deepest grief, I no sooner saw the bonnet than I was reminded of a helmet; and in that hybrid bonnet, half-helmet, half-jockey cap, did Miss Jenkyns attend Captain Brown's funeral' (Chapter II).

As this material demonstrates, Elizabeth Gaskell understood the language of clothes as well as the next woman and was able to deploy it to pointed and ironic effect.

NOTES

1. J. A. V. Chapple and Arthur Pollard (eds.), *The Letters of Mrs Gaskell* (Manchester: Manchester University Press, 1966), p. 153.

2. Ibid., p. 155.

3. C. Willett Cunnington, *English Women's Clothing in the Nineteenth Century* (New York: Dover Publications, 1990), p. 8.

Glossary

Aga: Lord, originally a military title in the Ottoman Empire; later used as a title of distinction for foreigners.

à propos: Appropriately (French). Also *apropos*.

arrow-root: Nutritious starch from West Indian plant made into a gruel for invalids.

Assize Sermon: Sermon to mark the opening of the criminal and civil courts, usually given by someone of recognized distinction such as John Keble (1792–1866).

au fait: Up to the mark (French).

baby-house: Doll's house.

bands: Collar ending with long strips at each side that hung down.

basted up: Soaking; covered (Cf. current *baste*: to cover a joint of meat in liquid fat.) See also Chapter VII, note 13.

Beavers: Beaver was a felted cloth used for outerwear.

bell-rope: Rope hanging in the rooms of middle- and upper-class houses which, when pulled, caused a bell to ring in the servants' quarters.

be up to her: Match her tricks.

Black Art: Witchcraft.

bombazine: Relatively rough material of wool and cotton, with a matt finish.

bonâ fide: Genuine.

bread-jelly: A later recipe (1868) recommends: 'Take the crumb [soft part] of a penny roll; cut it into thin slices, and toast them . . . Put them into a quart of spring water. Let it simmer over the fire till it has become a jelly. Strain . . . and flavour . . . with a little lemon juice and sugar' (*OED*).

broughams: One-horse closed carriages for two to four passengers.

Brutus wig: Rough cropped wig, based on Roman statues and devised in France, which was popular in the early nineteenth century.

bug-a-boo: Bogy; imagined object of terror.

cabalistic: Cryptic, from a secret art.

cadets: Junior members of an upper-class family as contrasted with the heirs.

cage: See Appendix I 'The Cage at Cranford', note 2.

calash: Old-fashioned hood with hoops, worn over a cap to protect it: see p. 79.

candle-lighter: Spill of rolled paper. Wilkie Collins described them in his novel *After Dark* (1859): 'A piece of paper rolled up tight like candle-lighters that the ladies make.'

capable: Capacious.

capital: Excellent, first rate.

carmen: Short song-like poem.

carpet-bag: Travelling bag – originally one made of carpet.

cassock: Long coat-like garment.

chapeau bras: Three-cornered hat (French).

charges: Written instructions to the clergy.

chary of: Frugal with.

cherubim: Second highest in the nine orders of biblical angels; their special attribute is the knowledge and contemplation of divine things.

chiffonier: Small cupboard with a top made so as to form a sideboard.

chinks: Fits.

chintz: Cotton cloth, usually glazed, with printed floral design.

Chloride of lime: Chloride in compound with other elements is used as a bleach and disinfectant.

ci-devant: Former (French).

citron: Lemon peel or flavouring.

clothes-maids: Clothes-horses or frames on which clothes were spread to dry.

coach up: Get up to date on.

cold-pigged: Doused in cold water to wake someone. *OED* cites in 1834: 'I've often cold-pigged her of a morning.' The verb derives from 'pig', an earthenware crock (of unknown origin).

comfits: Sugar plums; fruits or roots preserved in sugar.

comme il faut: Proper; decorous (French).

couchant: See *lion couchant*.

Coventry: See *sent to Coventry*.

Cupids: See *'little Cupids'*.

cut and come again: Take pleasure in repeating, originally referring to further slices from a joint of meat.

cut at: Rebuke for.

Dang: A euphemism for 'damn'.

dead-brick: Blank brick (wall).

de rigueur: Socially obligatory (French).

Dissenters: Nonconformists; sects that had separated themselves from the Anglican church.

dole: The portion given of food and cash (p. 141).

double eye-glass: Two lenses made to be held either by a spring clipped on to the nose, or by a single side-piece held in the hand.

drab: Fabric of a dull, yellowish brown.

dragoon: Ferocious-looking cavalry soldier.

dram-shop: Shop or bar selling alcoholic spirits in small quantities or drams.

droskys: Originally, low Russian carriages with an open top and four wheels; later used for similar vehicles which plied for hire.

elf-locks: Tangled hair, twisted by Queen Mab or other elves, and said to be unlucky.

entry: Alleyway.

esprit de corps: Community spirit (French).

fancy-work: Ornamental as opposed to plain needlework, knitting or crochet.

farthing: Pre-decimal coin worth one-fourth of a penny.

fashed: Bothered.

filigree: Ornamented with intricate tracery in precious metal.

filthy lucre: Money seen as dirty because it was said to be the root of all evil.

fly: Light one-horse covered carriage.

'followers': Admirers and sweethearts of maidservants.

'forrard': Forward, precocious.

forte: Strong point (French).

gig: Light one-horse, two-wheeled carriage.

gigot: 'A leg of mutton' sleeve, puffed up from the shoulder and tight around the forearm, resembling that cut of meat.

go-carts: Baby walkers: light frames moving on castors or rollers for children to learn to walk without falling.

'goody': Sweetmeat.

gown: Academic gown (p. 54).
graminivorous: Grass-eating.

half-a-crown: Pre-decimal coin worth one-eighth of £1.
half-pay Captain: Retired officer on half-pay, so of small means.
haute volée: Top rank; crème de la crème (French).
heir-loom: Legal term for a chattel that under a will must be inherited with the estate and cannot be bequeathed separately.
'Hortus Siccus': Arrangement of dried flowers in an album (Latin).

India muslin: Fine muslin.
Indian-rubber ring: (More usually 'India') elastic band, patented in 1845.
indigo: Blue dye made from the powder of the leguminous plant *indigofera*.
Italian irons: Iron tongs heated to pleat fabric into creases resembling a quill.

japanned: Lacquered with a hard black varnish.

ladies'-finger biscuits: See *Savoy biscuits*.
lantern-bearer: In Cranford it was a maidservant who came with a lantern to guide her mistress home.
lion couchant: Resembling a lion with its body resting on its legs and its head raised.
'*little Cupids*': Almond-flavoured biscuits, soaked in brandy.
living: Paid post as a priest.

maccaroons: Properly 'macaroons', sweet biscuit made of egg white, sugar and almonds.
mal-apropos: Inappropriate (French).
mandarins: Toy figures in Chinese costume which nodded repeatedly after being shaken.
meat-safe: Cupboard or cover of wire gauze or perforated zinc for meat storage.
merinoes: Merino was very fine wool, originally from sheep reared in Spain.
mésalliance: Inappropriate match; at p. 137, socially inappropriate.
mess: Dish; from this sense derived phrases like 'officers' mess'.
minnikin: Tiny.
minuets de la cour: Originally a lively French dance with tiny/minute

steps; said to have been first danced in 1653 at the court of Louis XIV and popular in England in the eighteenth century.

mobbed: Crowded round.

mountebank: Charlatan.

mousseline-de-laine: Wool and cotton fabric.

Mussulman: Muslim.

mutes: Professional mourners at a funeral, paid to wear black and adopt grave faces.

Nabob: Rich and important person returning from the east with a fortune acquired there; originally a Mohammedan official acting as a deputy-governor in the Mogul empire.

negus: Mixture of sherry or port with hot water, sugar and flavouring.

new-pieced: Repaired.

niddle-noddling: Nodding unsteadily.

noticing: Referring to.

'nudged': Elbowed (him) to hurry up.

'Paduasoy': Garment of heavy white corded or grosgrain silk.

passée: Outmoded.

pattens: Overshoes usually with thick wooden soles to protect the wearer from rain or mud.

Pembroke table: Four-legged table with two hinged flaps at the sides which could be raised to extend it.

pice: Small East Indian copper coin of very little value: equivalent to a quarter of an anna, which was a quarter of a rupee.

pièce de résistance: Main dish at a meal (French).

plate: Tableware of precious metal.

pool: The purse; the stakes and fines paid collectively into the kitty by players of various card games.

post-horses: Fast transport hired at local inns.

pot-pourri: Mixture of flower petals dried to provide a sweet perfume.

printed: Stamped with an official seal (p. 141).

prints: Dresses of printed cotton fabric, which was cheaper than silk.

property: Capital.

pudding: Substantial boiled or baked sweet dessert.

quondam: Former (Latin).

'raw': Sore spot, painful topic.

receipt: Recipe for food or medicine.

receipt-book: Cookery (recipe) book.

reserve-fund: Capital.

rod in pickle: Punishment in store.

sarsenet: Very fine and soft silk such as was later used for linings.

savoir faire: Know-how (French).

Savoy biscuits: Finger-shaped sponge biscuits, coated in sugar and baked in pairs. Also called *ladies'–finger biscuits*.

screen: Held in the hand to protect the complexion from the fire (p. 35).

sedan-chairs: Enclosed chairs supported on long poles and carried by two men – a primitive taxi.

seed-cake: Cake sweetened with caraway seeds.

sent to Coventry: Ostracized by others' refusal to speak to a person.

sesquipedalian: Many-syllabled.

set them all off: Set the hullabaloo going.

shepherd's plaid cloak: Cloak made of black-and-white checked woollen material.

shilling: Pre-decimal coin worth one-twentieth of £1.

shirt-frill: The front of a man's shirt which, like its cuffs, would be frilled.

shovel-hat: Stiff, broad-brimmed hat, turned up at the sides with a shovel-like curve in front and behind, worn by some ecclesiastics.

Signor Brunoni: Mr Brown (Italian).

sotto voce: In a whisper (Italian).

sour-grapeism: Envy, phrase probably a coinage by Gaskell.

sovereign: Pre-decimal coin equal to £1.

Spartans: Citizens of an ancient Greek state noted for their austerity, discipline and military power.

spillikins: Small slips or rods of wood or bone used in a game where each had to be pulled off with a hook without disturbing the rest.

'spills': Tapers to light candles: see *candle-lighter*.

spinnet: Keyboard instrument like a harpsichord but having only one string to each note.

spirted: Uttered forcibly.

spring-cart: Two-wheeled cart with no seats but with a step.

stomacher: Bodice ending in a padded downward point at the waist.

stopped the way: Blocked the path. The cry 'a carriage stops the way!' was an injunction to the owner to get in and move off quickly.

tartar emetic: Vomit-inducing mixture.

tea-bread: Light, sweet and spicy bread eaten at tea.

threepence: Pre-decimal coin worth one-eightieth of £1. Also 'three-penny'.

ton: Style, class (French).

Tonquin beans: Black, fragrant seeds of a tree found in South America and used as an ingredient in perfumes.

top-boots: High boots with tops of white or light-coloured leather, worn by gentlemen, yeomen and farmers when in riding or country dress.

train oil: Produced by boiling whale blubber.

'trousseau': Girls prepared well in advance for married life by collecting a cache of clothes and household linen.

tumblers: Glass bottles with lids.

Turkey carpet: Carpet from Turkey or on the Turkish model, made of wool and brightly coloured – often red.

vamped-up: Made up, fabricated.

videlicet: Namely (Latin).

wafer: Thin disc backed with gum used to close a letter and sometimes to receive a seal.

warming-pan: Long-handled covered pan containing hot coals, used as a bed-warmer.

worsted, white: Undyed long-stapled wool, i.e. of superior quality with long fibres.

wristbands: Noticeable cuffs or bands on the sleeve of a shirt.

Notes

All quotations from the Bible are from the Authorized Version. Frequently cited references are abbreviated:

Household Words Eight episodes in *Household Words* (December 1851–May 1853): see Note on the Text
Letters (J. A. V. Chapple and Arthur Pollard (eds.), *The Letters of Mrs Gaskell* (Manchester: Manchester University Press, 1966)
OED *Oxford English Dictionary*

CHAPTER I
OUR SOCIETY

1. *Amazons ... above a certain rent, are women*: In Greek mythology the Amazons are a tribe of women warriors noted for their strength and fearlessness; hence female warriors. The 'rent' is a a reference to the precarious middle-class status of the impoverished Cranford spinsters.

2. *Drumble*: Probably Manchester since Cranford is Knutsford, which is fifteen miles away and where Elizabeth Gaskell was brought up by her aunt after her mother's death. See Introduction.

3. *Miss Tyler, of cleanly memory ... scanty petticoat*: Ironic reference to the aunt of the poet laureate Robert Southey (1774–1843), who brought him up and did not allow him to 'do anything which by possibility I might dirt myself' (C. C. Southey (ed.), *The Life and Correspondence of the Late Robert Southey* (London: Longman, 1849), I, 34). 'The Last Generation in England' (in Appendix I) records Southey's intention of writing a history of English domestic life. *Gigot* and *petticoats* were out of date by the 1830s (*gigot*: see Glossary). Tight petticoats under narrow dresses had also given way to the trend towards the crinoline with its huge skirt. See Appendix III 'Fashion at Cranford'.

4. *red silk umbrella . . . 'a stick in petticoats'*: The first umbrellas in
    Edinburgh caused a stir in the 1790s and evidently even later in
    country villages, since they were regarded as feminine objects
    unsuited to men; *'a stick in petticoats'*: A gibe at the umbrella's
    foppishness which was its reputation throughout the eighteenth
    century.

5. *Manx laws . . . Tinwald Mount*: The ancient ceremony held on
    5 July (Tynwald Day) of proclaiming the laws of the Isle of Man
    in public.

6. *twelve to three . . . the third day*: The etiquette of visiting was
    defined with a military precision in such works as *Beeton's Book
    of Household Management* (1861): 'It is, however, requisite to
    call at suitable times, and to avoid staying for too long, if your
    friend is engaged . . . During these visits, the manners should be
    easy and cheerful, and the subjects of conversation such as may
    be readily terminated' ((London: Chancellor Press, 1861), p. 10).
    See also Appendix II 'The Nature and Role of Women'.

7. *'elegant economy'*: *Elegant* could mean stylish, graceful, but it
    could also mean precisely judged. The remark is ironic and may
    allude to Eliza Acton's recipe for 'The Elegant Economist's Pud-
    ding' in her *Modern Cookery* (1845). Gaskell also uses the phrase
    in a letter about a new dress – 'and cheap in the bargain, "Elegant
    economy" as *we* say in Cranford' (*Letters*, p. 174).

8. *a neighbouring railroad*: Knutsford had no railway until 1862,
    though the Liverpool to Manchester railway was opened in 1830.

9. *to ears polite*: This is taken from the *Epistle to Burlington* (1731)
    by Alexander Pope (1688–1744), in a description of the over-
    elaborate and comfortable chapel of a figure called 'Timon': 'To
    rest, the Cushion and soft Dean invite / Who never mentions hell
    to ears polite' (ll. 149–50).

10. *Alderney cow*: A breed of cow from the Channel Islands that
    produced creamy milk. Gaskell herself in Manchester kept at
    least one cow that was an Alderney (*Letters*, p. 199). In *Our
    Village: Sketches of Rural Life, Character and Scenery* (1832) by
    Mary Russell Mitford (1787–1855), to which Gaskell makes
    two allusions in *Cranford*, Mitford refers in 'Hannah Bint' to
    'the trouble, almost impossibility in the countryside of procuring
    the pastoral luxuries of milk, eggs and butter' which the
    Londoner imagines 'grow . . . in the country'. On Mitford, see
    also Chapter X, notes 1 and 9.

11. *Two pounds was a large sum*: In 1857 *A Manual of Domestic
    Economy* by J. H. Walsh divided the middle classes into four

gradations according to income: those earning £1,500, £750, £350 and £150 a year. So Captain Brown is ranked generally with clerks, small shopkeepers and elementary school teachers as belonging to the lowest of the middle classes.

12. *the Morning Hymn*: By Bishop Thomas Ken (1637–1711), written in 1709, and beginning: 'Awake my soul and with the sun . . .'

13. *prayer-book*: *The Book of Common Prayer* which evolved in the sixteenth century and was largely the work of Thomas Cranmer (1489–1556) was designed for the laity.

14. *'Preference' . . . unlucky fourth*: Card game resembling whist involving trick-taking, in which the trump suit is decided by bidding. It was originally played by three players. The fourth player is called 'unlucky' because she is the dealer, and cannot play. See also Chapter VII, note 12.

15. *'Jock of Hazeldean'*: Poem (1816) by Sir Walter Scott (1771–1832), set to music, in which a woman pines for her lover. It begins: 'Why weep ye by the tide, ladie?'

16. *a shopkeeper*: Shopkeepers or tradesmen were looked down on by the middle classes, no matter how successful they might be.

17. *'The Pickwick Papers'*: Charles Dickens's first novel issued in serial parts 1836–7 under a pen name (Mr Boz) – see also note 20 and Chapter II, note 20. It was hugely successful. Dickens was the editor of the periodical *Household Words* in which *Cranford* first appeared (1851–3), and consequently the frequent references to his work had been changed there to avoid the appearance of conceit: see a Note on the Text. Thomas Hood (1799–1845), popular writer of satire and humorous verse. See also note 20; Chapter II, notes 20 and 21; and Chapter XII, note 2.

18. *the account of the 'swarry' . . . Bath*: The soirée or evening party described in Chapter 38 of *Pickwick Papers*. *Household Words* has 'the account of a gentleman who was terrified out of his wits by political events who "could no more collect himself than the Irish tithes" '.

19. *'Rasselas'*: The only novel (1759) by Samuel Johnson (1709–84), written in a high flown style, with very little plot and much didactic comment. See also Chapter II, note 10.

20. *Mr Boz*: *Household Words* has 'Mr Hood' here and for all references in the text to 'Mr Boz'.

21. *consider it vulgar . . . in numbers*: Because of the cheapness of individual numbers, such publishing in parts was a huge popular success. The fifteenth number of *Pickwick Papers* sold 40,000

copies. This became a standard way of publishing novels, as did serialization in periodicals. The answer to Captain Brown's next comment is: in parts. The *Rambler* was a series of essays, all but five by Johnson, published in 208 numbers twice weekly, 1750–52. It went through ten printings in his lifetime.

CHAPTER II
THE CAPTAIN

1. *from the bakehouse*: Those too poor to own an oven or to pay for fuel took food to the local bakery to be cooked in the heat remaining from the morning's bread baking.

2. *But don't you forget ... the old song*: Flint's was a London haberdashers; and the song 'County Commissions to my Cousin in Town' had as its refrain 'a skein of white worsted from Flint's'. The implication is that the country cousin has an endless list of requests for purchases.

3. *Miss Matty*: Possibly the *Household Words* reading 'Miss Matey' indicates a pronunciation like *mate*, rather than *mat*.

4. *the Hebrew prophetess*: Deborah urged Israel to take revenge on an enemy in Judges 4:4: an indication of Miss Jenkyns's unyielding nature.

5. *strong-minded woman ... equal to men*: 'Strong-minded' was in the nineteenth century a disparaging term for women who supported women's causes such as female suffrage or better education. They were assumed to be masculine in character and even appearance, as in *Lady Audley's Secret* (1862) by M. E. Braddon: 'I don't want a strong minded woman, who writes books and wears green spectacles' (Chapter 16). Miss Jenkyns's jockey-cap bonnet (see note 13) and cravat are meant to suggest masculine clothes and possibly a usurpation of the male role. See also Chapter X, note 14.

6. *'plumed wars'*: A confused recollection of lines from Othello's farewell to the warrior life: 'Farewell the plumed troops, and the big wars / That makes ambition virtue!' (Shakespeare, *Othello*, III.iii.353–4).

7. *Brunonian*: An adjective derived from the name Brown on a classical model for comic effect, as part of Miss Jenkyns's Johnsonian style.

8. *'the feast of reason and the flow of soul'*: 'There St John mingles with my friendly bowl / The Feast of Reason and the Flow of Soul' (*Imitations of Horace* (1733) by Pope, Satire I.2.128).

9. *'the pure wells of English undefiled'*: A confused recollection of

'Dan Chaucer, well of English undefyled' (Edmund Spenser, *Faerie Queene* (1596), IV.ii.32).

10. *Johnson . . . a rolling three-piled sentence*: Gaskell writes a spoof Johnsonian sentence in a letter of 17 July 1838:

> Now for a grand Johnsonian sentence . . . He who can wander by the melodious waters of the Menai and partake of the finny tribes that gambol in the translucent current, and can disport himself at pleasure in the lunar-governed tide; the man who can do this, I say, and return to the home of his progenitors neither more rotund, with the careless felicity of such a mode of existence, nor more attenuated from the excess of laudable excitement, deserves not to be classed with the human species, but to take his station among the moluscar tribes. (*Letters*, p. 21)

11. *them nasty cruel railroads*: Railways had got off to a bad start when the former President of the Board of Trade, William Huskisson, was killed by a locomotive at the opening of the Liverpool to Manchester railway line in 1830. In remoter districts they were regarded as dangeous and destructive, even in the 1840s when 'railway mania' took hold. Dickens writes of how their construction devastates the landscape in *Dombey and Son* (1848), in which the villainous Carker is killed by a train.

12. *set her heart on following it*: It was not usual in polite society for women to attend funerals, e.g. Queen Victoria did not attend Prince Albert's in 1861.

13. *hybrid bonnet, half-helmet, half-jockey cap*: Helmet and jockey cap were the names of two types: the former elongated upwards like a helmet (see Appendix III), the latter with a small peak. The Cranford ladies are fussy about these types of indoor headwear which were outdated by the 1850s. (Caps were worn indoors; bonnets outside.)

14. *where the weary are at rest*: Cf. 'There the wicked cease from troubling; and there the weary be at rest' (Job 3:17).

15. *'Though He slay me . . . in Him'*: Job 13:15.

16. *twenty pounds a-year*: Less than the salary of an already lowly-paid governess. Cf. Miss Matty's income on p. 149 and Chapter I, note 11.

17. *I can sew . . . nursing*: Because middle-class girls were virtually uneducated, there were few occupations open to them, apart from being a governess. As Jessie is unequipped for that, she mentions only two lower-class occupations. Dickens satirizes the current type of nurse as Mrs Gamp in *Martin Chuzzlewit* (1844).

Charlotte Brontë's friend, Mary Taylor, wrote from New Zealand where she had set up shop: 'There are no means for a woman to live in England but by teaching, sewing or washing' (Margaret Smith (ed.), *The Letters of Charlotte Brontë* (Oxford: Oxford University Press, 2000), II, 179).

18. *he had offered*: He had proposed marriage.

19. *'Galignani'*: Giovanni Antonio Galignani (1752–1821), Parisian publisher who produced a newspaper called *Galignani's Messenger* for travellers on the continent, detailing some English news including the whereabouts of some upper-class English tourists.

20. *'Old Poz'*: This confuses Dickens's pen name with 'Old Poz' (1795), a story for children by Maria Edgeworth (1768–1849), in which one of the characters is called Lucy. (See also Chapter V, note 12.) *Household Words* has 'that book by Mr Hood,— you know—Hood—Admiral Hood; when I was a girl; but that's a long time ago,—I wore a cloak with a red Hood'.

21. *'Christmas Carol' . . . the table*: *Christmas Carol* was Dickens's Christmas story for 1843. *Household Words* has 'Miss Kilmansegg and her Golden Leg' (1840) by Hood. After 'table' *Household Words* adds: 'Poor, dear Miss Jenkyns! Cranford is Man-less now.'

CHAPTER III
A LOVE AFFAIR OF LONG AGO

1. *I thought*: In *Household Words* this is preceded by 'I am tempted to relate it, as having interested me in a quiet sort of way, and as being the latest intelligence of Our Society at Cranford.'

2. *and we all tried . . . the attempt*: *Household Words* has:

the appellation of Matey was dropped by all, except a very old woman, who had been nurse to the rector's family, and had persevered, through many long years in calling the Miss Jenkynses 'the girls', she said Matey to the day of her death.

3. *a love affair . . . years before*: *Household Words* has: 'the love affair I am coming to,—gradually, not in a hurry, for we are never in a hurry at Cranford'.

4. *This subject of servants . . . grievance*: It was common for middle-class employers to complain of their hard-worked servants' inadequacies. Isabella Beeton comments tartly: 'It is the custom of "Society" to abuse its servants – a *façon de parler* such as leads their lords and masters to talk of the weather, and when rurally

inclined of crops – leads matronly ladies . . . to talk of servants, and, as we are told, to wax eloquent over the greatest plague in their lives while taking a quiet cup of tea' (*Beeton's Book of Household Management*, p. 961).

5. *articles of her engagement*: It was thought inappropriate that servants should have 'followers' (see Glossary) or sweethearts during the mid nineteenth century, as it might cause promiscuity.

6. *prayers at ten*: Attendance at household prayers was part of a servant's duty.

7. *wine and dessert*: The upper class followed a practice of serving fruit and nuts along with port and madeira at the end of an elaborate dinner.

8. *the 'Army List'*: A list of all commissioned officers in the British army and where they were stationed.

9. *Blue Beard*: Legendary tyrant who murdered a succession of wives after the wedding night and locked their bodies in a turret chamber, familiar from *Histoires et contes du temps passé* (1697) by Charles Perrault (1628–1703), translated into English in 1729.

10. *'Leave me . . . repose'*: In 'The Descent of Odin' (1768) by Thomas Gray (1716–71), Odin descends into the underworld to learn the fate of his son Balder who has dreamt that his life is in danger. Odin wakes a Norse 'prophetic maid' from the dead. After predicting Balder's death she pleads: 'Unwilling I my lips unclose: Leave me to repose' (ll. 49–50). Gaskell quotes these lines in a letter (23 May 1852) criticizing those who are willing to give money but not time to charity. She sees them as saying. '"Spare my time, but take my money" – a sort of "leave me, leave me to repose"' (*Letters*, p. 192).

11. *'pride which apes humility'*: From 'The Devil's Thoughts' (1799) by Samuel Taylor Coleridge (1772–1834) and Southey: 'And the devil did grin for his darling sin / Is the pride that apes humility' (ll. 23–4).

12. *He would not allow . . . yeoman*: Until the first half of the twentieth century it was usual in writing to use the terms 'Esquire' or 'Esq.' for a gentlemen and 'Mr' for a man of lower standing. The latter was dropped as Esquire/Esq. became more widespread in addressing letters, and the distinction has disappeared. At the time when *Cranford* was written a *yeoman* was one who owned his own property but was not a gentleman.

13. *the dialect of the country*: It had long been the norm for educated persons to use standard English, not dialect which usually

marked out the working classes. In Charlotte Brontë's *Shirley* (1849), the radical gentleman, Mr Yorke, adopts the local accent to his inferiors, and standard English to his equals.

14. *blowing up . . . fragments*: The narrator refers to the destruction of her imaginary 'castle in Spain' which involved a romantic future for Miss Matty.

15. *Don Quixote-looking old man*: In *Don Quixote de la Mancha* (1605–15), a satire by Miguel de Cervantes Saavedra (1547–1616), the hero who goes questing for chivalric adventures is a mild amiable man in rusty armour on a worn-out old horse.

CHAPTER IV
A VISIT TO AN OLD BACHELOR

1. *George Herbert . . . ever-verdant palaces*: *George Herbert*: Metaphysical poet (1593–1633). *Byron*: The dashing poet, George Gordon, sixth Baron (1788–1824). Both his life and his poetry were considered shocking. The spelling 'Bÿrron' indicates a short vowel in the first syllable, like that in *pit*. *Goëthe*: Holbrook evidently uses a pronunciation Go-eth or Go-eth-e, not one approximating to German. The reference is to *Faust* (I, 3943–4) by Johann Wolfgang von Goëthe (1749–1832) and is taken from a very inappropriate context since it is part of the description of Faust and Mephistopheles struggling uphill to join a coven of witches on a dark, misty, windy night when 'The columns of eternally green palaces are splintering'. See Alan Menhennet, 'A Goethe Reference in *Cranford*', *Gaskell Society Journal*, 8 (1994), pp. 111–12.

2. *new-fangled ways*: This means pudding after meat, contrary to Holbrook's adherence to the earlier country practice of having the pudding first to take the edge off appetites before the most expensive dish, meat.

3. *'No broth, no ball; no ball, no beef'*: The North country practice of eating meat after less expensive items, which reduced the appetite: first came broth and ball – suet dumpling – then meat.

4. *two-pronged, black-handled forks*: The earliest forks introduced into England in the sixteenth century had only two tines or prongs. Four-pronged forks had generally replaced them by 1800, so this is another sign of an old-fashioned household.

5. *Aminé . . . with the Ghoul*: In the *Arabian Nights* (1765–8) Aminé is the wife of Sidi Nouman who notices that she eats her rice with a bodkin instead of a spoon. He eventually discovers

that she is a Ghoul who visits cemeteries at night to feast on the newly buried dead and therefore has little appetite for rice.

6. *I saw, I imitated, I survived*: Allusion to Julius Caesar (102?–44 BC): 'I came, I saw, I conquered' (Suetonius, *Divus Julius*, XXVII. 2).

7. '*The cedar . . . of shade*': From 'The Gardener's Daughter' (1842) by Alfred Lord Tennyson (1809–92), l. 115, part of the description of the setting in which the beautiful girl of the title is seen. In *Household Words* the quotation is preceded by 'More black than ashbuds' at the beginning of 'March': 'that hair / More black than ashbuds in the front of March' (ll. 27–8). Holbrook refers to these lines a few paragraphs later.

8. *the review . . . 'Blackwood'*: This may be a deliberate or accidental mistake. Though the poem in question was published in *Poems* in 1842, the volume was not reviewed in *Blackwood's Magazine* until April 1849 (and was not as uncritical as Holbrook's comment implies).

9. '*Locksley Hall*'. Poem (1842) of 194 lines by Tennyson in which a lover revisits the place where he fell in love with his cousin Amy who loved him but was forced by family pressure to marry someone else. He tells her in thought: 'thou art mated with a clown / . . . Cursed be the social wants that sin against the strength of youth' (ll. 47, 59). The poem has relevance to the frustrated love of Holbrook and Miss Matty.

10. *call on the ladies soon*: Miss Matty interprets this as more than an ordinary return visit: for a man to call on a lady indicated a willingness to pursue the acquaintance.

11. *Paris*: A probable reference to the iniquity of the French Revolution (1789) rather than the later idea that the French were sexually immoral.

CHAPTER V
OLD LETTERS

1. *Joint-Stock Bank*: A commercial bank, legal 1826–44, where a large number of shareholders, including small investors, were legally responsible for the firm's deficit as compared with a private bank where the few individuals investing in and running it were responsible. The former were notoriously unstable.

2. *Envelopes . . . first came in*: They came into general use in England about 1800.

3. *blind man's holiday*: Twilight, and without a candle, the narrator Mary Smith can't work, but not really a holiday at all.

4. *July, 1774*: *Household Words* has simply '1774'.
5. *J. and J. Rivingtons*: London publishers of theological works.
6. *dum memor . . . artus*: While memory shall last and breath control my limbs (Virgil, *Aeneid*, IV.382).
7. *'Gentleman's Magazine'*: Periodical (1731–1868) dealing with a wide range of topics such as literature, science, medicine and crime, to which Samuel Johnson was a great contributor.
8. *M. T. Ciceronis Epistolae*: Letters of M[arcus] T[ullius] Cicero (106–43 BC), the Roman statesman, orator, philosopher and writer. Over 800 of his letters survive; his style of writing was much admired and from the sixteenth century was imitated in English as Ciceronianism.
9. *'a vale of tears'*: The reading in the Metrical Psalter (1562), continuing the work of Thomas Sternhold (d.1549) and John Hopkins (d. 1570), of Psalm 84:6.
10. *Mrs Chapone . . . Mrs Carter . . . Epictetus*: Hester Chapone (1721–1801) and Elizabeth Carter (1717–1806) were members of the intellectual female group 'The Blue Stocking Circle' and friends of Johnson. Chapone contributed to the *Rambler* and the *Gentleman's Magazine* and wrote *Letters on the Improvement of the Mind* (1773). Carter was familiar with many languages and in 1758 published a translation of the Stoic philosopher Epictetus (*c.* 60 – after 100 AD) which made her reputation throughout Europe.
11. *the old original Post . . . his horn*: What is described here was a type of writing paper with this watermark in one corner.
12. *before Miss Edgeworth's 'Patronage' . . . polite society*: In *Patronage* (1814), a character is offended to receive a letter closed with a wafer and says: 'I wonder how any man can have the impertinence to send me his spittle' (1, 248).
13. *franks . . . Members of Parliament*: Franks were superscribed signatures of those who, like MPs, were entitled to send letters post-free, and were able to sell them, presumably at a cost below that of normal postage.
14. *crossing*: To save paper and postage (charged by weight), letters were first written down the page; then turned sideways and written across at right angles.

     At the end of a letter and presumably the bottom of a page, Gaskell ends by saying: 'But I must not cross' (*Letters*, p. 651).
15. *Herod . . . Etruriae*: Herod of Idumea died *c.* 4 BC and was the grandfather to the Herod who condemned Christ. Miss Matty only approximates to the words on the page she reads.

16. *the invasion of Buonaparte*: Throughout the Napoleonic Wars
     (1803–15), in which the allies finally defeated Napoleon Buona-
     parte (1769–1821), there were numerous rumours of an invasion
     of England along the south coast (but such an event was scarcely
     likely in the north-east). He was colloquially known as 'Bony'.

17. *the Boy and the Wolf*: When the boy cried 'Wolf!' in earnest, no
     one believed him because he had often tricked them with the cry.

18. *the French entering Cranford . . . salt-mines*: After 'Cranford'
     Household Words adds: 'My mother has sat by my bed half a
     night through, holding my hand and comforting me.' The *salt-
     mines* were at Northwich, close to Knutsford.

19. *David and Goliath . . . Abaddon*: The boy David, son of Jesse,
     slew the Philistine giant Goliath, the enemy of Israel, with a stone
     from a sling (1 Samuel 17). '*Apollyon and Abbadon*' are names
     for an archangel in Revelation 9:11: 'The angel of the bottomless
     pit, whose name in the Hebrew tongue is Abaddon, but the Greek
     tongue hath his name Apollyon.'

20. *Bonus Bernardus non videt omnia*: 'The blessed Bernard does
     not see everything' (Latin). Supposed to be said of St Bernard of
     Clairvaux (1090–1153). The expression may have been prov-
     erbial, though possibly Gaskell had seen a version of it in a letter
     of William Cowper written in 1792 and published by Johnson.

CHAPTER VI
POOR PETER

1. *Poor Peter's career*: Gaskell had only one sibling who survived to
    adulthood, John Stevenson, born 1798. His later career resembles
    Peter's as he became a sailor and made his first voyage to India
    in 1825. He and his sister remained close but in 1828 he decided
    to settle in India; nothing more was heard of him after he set sail
    and he died either on the voyage or later.

2. *'hoaxing' is not a pretty word*: Hoax(ing) is first recorded in
    1796 and was evidently regarded as a slang word for two decades,
    but by the 1850s was in general use. Consequently this comment
    indicates a somewhat out-of-date reaction.

3. *Napoleon Buonaparte sermons*: Probably sermons denouncing
    Buonaparte written during the Napoleonic Wars: see p. 6.

4. *'St James's Chronicle'*: A thrice-weekly periodical introduced in
    1761 and lasting well into the nineteenth century. It was designed
    for the upper classes about whose activities it contained infor-
    mation; it was popular reading among the clergy.

5. *new rhododendron*: In the late 1840s and 1850s the botanist Sir

Joseph Hooker brought back new and exotic species of rhododendrons which caused much excitement and the Rhododendron Dell at Kew Gardens was created for their display.

6.   *lilies of the field*: Allusion to 'Consider the lilies of the field, how they grow; they toil not, neither do they spin ... even Solomon in all his glory was not arrayed like one of these' (Matthew 6:28–9).

7.   *vegetable*: Horticultural.

8.   *Queen Esther and King Ahasuerus*: Esther, the beloved wife of the king, pleaded for her own life and that of her people after Haman maligned them to the king, and he was moved to do so (Esther 8).

9.   *Dor*: The reading in *Household Words* and a possible abbreviation for Deborah.

10. *there was no overland route then*: This dates Peter's trip to India to before the late 1830s when an overland route to India via the Red Sea was established. Until then the ship route was round the Cape of Good Hope (the Suez Canal was opened 1869).

11. *near seeing her again*: By dying. *Household Words* continued: 'But Miss Matey was not foolish, poor dear thing!'

12. *soft, white India shawl*: Cashmere shawls were the usual presents brought by men returning from India. Some were gorgeously coloured and embroidered. In Gaskell's *North and South* (1854–5) Margaret Hale displayed shawls in her cousin's trousseau and admired 'their soft feel and their brilliant colours' (Chapter I). Gaskell herself in a letter of 1852 admires similar shawls: 'so soft and delicate and went into such beautiful folds' (Jenny Uglow, *Elizabeth Gaskell: A Habit of Stories* (London: Faber and Faber 1993), p. 299).

13. *some great war in India*: Evidently the First Burmese War (1824–6), when Britain declared war on Burma, which had threatened her territories in India. See also Chapter XV, note 8.

CHAPTER VII
VISITING

1.   *John Bullish ... Mounseers*: First recorded in the 1710s, 'John Bull' originally meant 'typically English', but by the 1840s it had derogatory implications. *OED* cites in 1851 these 'Anglomaniacs or John Bullists, as they are popularly termed'. *Mounseers*: Monsieurs (Misters); derisory name for the French.

2.   *Queen Adelaide*: Adelaide Saxe-Coburg (1792–1849), wife of William IV who reigned 1830–37.

3. *a mark of respectability . . . setting up a gig*: Owning your own carriage is only ironically a mark of gentility. In a review of James Boswell's *Life of Johnson* (1791), Thomas Carlyle (1795–1881) referred to it sarcastically in relation to Boswell: 'a Scottish squirelet, full of gulosity and "gigmanity" '. He added a footnote explaining the latter term, citing an exchange in the 1824 trial of John Thurtell for murder: ' "Q. What do you mean by respectable?" – A. "He always kept a gig" – "Thus", it has been said, "does society naturally divide itself into four classes: Noblemen, Gentlemen, Gigmen, and Men" ' (*Fraser's Magazine* 5 (1832), p. 383).

4. *'horrid cotton trade'*: Part of Cranford's gentility consists in looking down on those involved in trade. Drumble/Manchester was a centre of the cotton trade.

5. *born a Tyrrell*: See chapter XI and note 6.

6. *My prophetic soul*: When Hamlet's father reveals that his own brother murdered him, Hamlet cries: 'O my prophetic soul! My uncle?' (I.v.40–41).

7. *that Marchioness . . . Molly Hoggins*: Sarah Hoggins (1773–97) was the bigamous and then legal second wife of Henry Cecil (1754–1804), who became the eleventh Earl of Exeter in 1793 and first Marquis of Exeter in 1801. So 'Molly' (i.e. Sarah) was never Marchioness. A similar story is used in Tennyson's 'The Lord of Burleigh' (1842).

8. *rustling black silk*: Widows were supposed to avoid luxurious shiny fabrics such as silk: see Appendix III.

9. *the earl's daughter . . . London boards*: Lady Jane Stanley, daughter of the Earl of Derby, had lived in Knutsford. Her sister, Charlotte, here misnamed Anne, had married Colonel John Burgoyne (1722–92), who was known for having to surrender to American patriots at Saratoga during the War of Independence (1775–83). See also p. 108. Nicknamed 'gentleman John', he wrote a successful comedy *The Heiress* (1786) and also *The Maid of the Oaks* (1774). (His character later appeared in George Bernard Shaw's play *The Devil's Disciple* (1900).)

10. *there was Fitz-Roy . . . William the Fourth*: Fitz did mean 'son' but latterly had been given as a surname to illegitimate royal children. William IV had ten illegitimate children, all of whom were given the surname Fitz-Clarence.

11. *like Prince Albert's . . . not so good*: As Prince Consort but not king, Albert did not equal his wife in rank. His placing, like the present Duke of Edinburgh's, always indicated this.

12. *Cribbage . . . Manille*: *Cribbage* is a card game for two to four players with scores marked on a board with pegs. *Spadille* was the highest trump (ace of spades) in the card games of Ombre and Quadrille; *Manille* was the second highest (either a seven in the hearts and diamonds suits or deuce in spades and clubs). Ombre and Quadrille were two similar three-handed games from which Preference, played at Cranford by four players, was derived. See also Chapter VIII, note 12.

13. *'basting'*: Possibly a pun. 'Basting' could mean a thrashing; and 'baste' was a fine incurred for not making the number of tricks you had bid for in games including Preference.

14. *long great-coats . . . Hogarth's pictures*: This appears to be a reference to a picture in *A Rake's Progress* (1735) by William Hogarth (1697–1764), which includes a sedan-chair. It is a calculated contrast between a rumbustious individual and the Cranford ladies.

CHAPTER VIII
'YOUR LADYSHIP'

1. *'county' families*: Land-owning families in the neighbourhood who made up what was recognized as 'society' were sometimes just referred to as 'the county' since they were thought to be the only people who mattered in that area.

2. *Mrs Forrester's Peerage . . . poor as Job*: The *Peerage* may refer to *Burke's Peerage and Baronetage*, a list of such dignitaries and their pedigrees, first published in 1826. Lord Glenmire did not sit in the House of Lords because he was not one of the sixteen Scottish peers elected by their fellows to do so. God strips *Job* of his goods and children, and then afflicts him with boils to test his faith.

3. *her being a bride*: The first social reappearance of a new bride sometimes involved her wearing her wedding-dress.

4. *any number of brooches . . . stiff muslin*: *Brooches* were popular throughout the Victorian period and were often pictorial and sentimental; *weeping-willows* implies a lost loved one; *neatly executed in hair* refers to the practice of locks of hair, given as keepsakes, being kept in lockets; *nest of stiff muslin*: presumably the portrait-brooches pinned to the decorative 'white and venerable collars' of the ladies' gowns.

5. *Scotch pebbles*: Agates and other gemstones found in streams, especially in Scotland, became particularly popular after Queen Victoria purchased Balmoral in 1848.

6. *hair-powder*: A mixture of finely ground starch, scented with lavender or orris root, used to make wigs light-coloured, a practice popular around 1715. It continued in general use till the end of the eighteenth century and at this period is outmoded.

7. *the later style . . . in all their corners*: Furniture predating the change about 1720 to a curvilinear look and more ornate designs, of the Louis XIV (Quatorze) period (1638–1715) which later became popular.

8. *kaleidoscope . . . decorate tea-chests*: The kaleidoscope was invented in 1817 by Sir David Brewster. *Conversation-cards* are described by Gaskell in her story 'Mr Harrison's Confessions' (1851): 'Sheaves of slips of cardboard, with intellectual or sentimental questions on one set, and equally intellectual and sentimental answers on the other; and as the answers were fit to any and all the questions, you may think they were a characterless . . . set of things' (Chapter 8). *Puzzle-cards* similarly had riddles and answers written on them. The patterns copied from the wooden chests used to ship tea were possibly imitations of Chinese styles.

9. *reminded me of Stonehenge*: Part of the prehistoric site was incorporated in the eighteenth century into the Marquess of Queensberry's landscaped garden, Amesbury Abbey. In 1740 the antiquarian William Stukeley (1687-1765) published a book on his discovery that the location of the stones showed indications of being astronomically calculated in relation to the sun and moon. This casual reference suggests the circle was already familiar to Mary.

10. *'A Lord and No Lord' business*: This colloquial type of expression must have been familiar at this time. It is recorded in the title of a play by Beaumont and Fletcher called *A King and No King* (1611). It implies 'A – and yet not a –'.

11. *very small the lumps of sugar*: Sugar was bought in rough pieces and would be chopped up by the buyer to their preferred size.

12. *Ombre and Quadrille . . . Spadille*: *Basto*, the ace of clubs, is the third highest trump card in Ombre and Quadrille. By playing it, Miss Pole makes Lady Glenmire use up the highest trump Spadille, the ace of spades. See also Chapter VII, note 12.

13. *perhaps they can now . . . the Catholic Emancipation Bill*: The suggestion is ludicrously unlikely: the Catholic Emancipation Act of 1829 gave Roman Catholics access to certain public offices from which they had previously been barred.

14. *Francis Moore's astrological predictions*: The astrologer (1657–

1715) published a predictive almanac annually from 1699. His prophecies made him notorious. A publication of the same name (*Old Moore's Almanac*) still continues.

CHAPTER IX
SIGNOR BRUNONI

1. *Michaelmas to Lady-day*: 29 September to 25 March.
2. *Wombwell's lions*: George Wombwell (1777–1850), owner of Wombwell's Travelling Menagerie which started with boa constrictors. He bred the first lion to be born in England, which became famous for the 'Lion Fight' at Warwick in which it fought and badly injured six bull-mastiffs.
3. *Saracen's-head turban*: The Saracen's head was a familiar inn sign and one is mentioned in Dickens's *Nicholas Nickleby* (1838–9). Here it suggests an over-large turbaned head – not necessarily swathed as turbans are today.
4. *Thaddeus of Warsaw and the Hungarian brothers, and Santo Sebastiani*: *Thaddeus of Warsaw* (1803) was a novel by Jane Porter (1776–1850) involving a Polish hero; *The Hungarian Brothers* (1807) was by her sister, Anna Maria Porter (1780–1832), set in the time of the French Revolution, and she also wrote *Don Sebastian* (1809), a historical romance. The title used by Miss Pole is that of another work by Catherine Cuthbertson (*fl.* 1813–30), *The Young Protector or Santo Sebastiani* (1814). Brunoni evidently reminds Miss Pole of the foreign heroes of these historical romances.
5. *If she was not the rose ... near it*: A frequent allusion in the nineteenth century to lines in the translation (1806) of *Gulistan* (*The Rose Garden*) of the Persian poet Sa'dī (1215–92) by Francis Gladwin: 'a worthless piece of clay, but having for a season associated with the rose, the virtue of my companion was communicated to me'. Gaskell used it again in *Wives and Daughters*, Part II, Chapter XVIII: 'The great reason why she did not hear of the gossip against Molly as early as anyone, was that, although she was not the rose, she lived near the rose.'
6. *Conjuration ... Witch of Endor*: Tricks and conjuring might be thought to denote preternatural or supernatural powers and public performances were a popular result of the public interest in such powers, which grew throughout the century and culminated in spiritualism. In 1 Samuel 28 Saul induced the Witch of Endor to summon up the ghost of the prophet Samuel to tell her why God has forsaken him; but the ghost prophesied his death.

7. *death-watches . . . 'roly-poleys'*: The sound of the death-watch beetle was supposed to forebode a death; *'roly-poleys'*: such rolls of wax were also thought to be an omen of death. Miss Jenkyns avoids the phrase 'winding-sheets', presumably to suggest that she is not superstitious.

8. *Queen Charlotte . . . the Gunnings*: Sophie Charlotte of Mecklenberg-Strelitz (1744–1818), wife of George III, who reigned 1760–1820 but suffered intermittent madness from 1788. Maria (1733–60) and Elizabeth (1734–90) Gunning were sisters who briefly became actresses in London in 1751. Their beauty attracted aristocratic husbands (Elizabeth twice).

9. *gentleman in the Turkish costume*: Such a costume suggests the mysterious Orient and perhaps preternatural powers.

10. *not quite—'*: What follows suggests the gap should be filled by 'respectable' or 'Christian'.

11. *National School boys*: Since there were no state-run elementary schools, those that existed, apart from public schools, were denominational. National Schools were affiliated with the Church of England, and were set up by the National Society for the Education of the Poor in the Principles of the Established Church.

CHAPTER X
THE PANIC

1. *we heard strange stories . . . some unfastened door*: Mary Russell Mitford describes the same state of affairs in an earlier work: 'During many weeks, the neighbourhood had been infested by a gang of bold, sturdy pilferers, roving vagabonds, begging by day, stealing and poaching by night' ('Jesse Cliffe' in *Country Stories* (1837)).

2. *fought the French in Spain*: The Peninsular War (1808–14) conducted by the Duke of Wellington (see Chapter XI, note 4) against Napoleon.

3. *French spies*: This harks back to the fears during the Napoleonic Wars which had ended in 1815.

4. *a print of Madame de Staël with a turban . . . Mr Denon*: A portrait of the French writer Anne-Louise Germaine de Staël (1766–1817) by François Gérard (1770–1837) was engraved and published as a print by Edward Scriven. In it she wears a turban-style hat with two intertwined rolls of fabric of different colours. Gaskell, in a letter of 1852, recorded hearing from the widow of the East India Company's representative at Baghdad

of 'her intimacy with Madame de Stael, her riding across Asia Minor as a Turkish horse*man*, turban pistols all' (*Letters*, p. 213). Baron Dominique-Vivant Denon (1747–1825), an art expert who advised Napoleon with whom he travelled to Egypt.

5. *bells to the windows*: Perhaps a primitive security device to signal an intruder.

6. *a face . . . crape*: Evidently a forerunner of the use by thieves of a mask or balaclava to disguise their identity.

7. *Irish beggar-woman*: The Irish were throughout the century regarded as stupid, dishonest and unreliable. This was partly because those who migrated to England were unskilled workers, driven by extreme poverty, who then worked for wages so low that they lived in appalling conditions. Carlyle's attitude in *Chartism* (1839) is typical: 'Crowds of miserable Irish darken all our towns. The wild Milesian features, looking false ingenuity, restlessness, unreason, misery and mockery, salute you on all highways and byways.' (A. Shelston (ed.), *Thomas Carlyle, Selected Writings* (Harmondsworth: Penguin, 1986), p. 171).

8. *got the spoons together*: The spoons were probably silver, so they would take these valuable items with them.

9. *old story . . . Philomel*: The story is mentioned in the play *The Lover's Melancholy* (1628) by John Ford (1586–after 1639). In *Our Village*, Mitford quotes some fifty lines of verse in which Ford tells the legend of the contest. *Philomel*: Poetic word for a nightingale, from the Greek myth of Philomela who was raped and had her tongue cut out. Finally she was turned into a nightingale to prevent her being murdered by her rapist. The story as told here seems to be a later addition to the classical legend.

10. *a girl . . . gaieties*: This Scottish legend is told at some length by James Hogg (1770?–1835) as *The Long Pack* (1817).

11. *'where nae men should be'*: From a Scottish ballad (1776): 'Our Goodman came home at e'en: / Ben went out Goodman, / And ben went he / and there he spy'd a sturdy man / Where nae man shou'd be' (David Herd, *Ancient and Modern Scottish Songs* (Glasgow: Kerr and Richardson, 1869), II, 172).

12. *his will . . . deadly force*: By the late eighteenth century the exertion of the will through the eyes or 'the gaze' was commonly believed to be potentially powerful. George III's doctor, Francis Willis, exerted control over the demented monarch in this way before resorting to a strait-jacket.

13. *Cheltenham*: A spa town and so a haven.

14. *masculine-looking*: A most abusive thing to say about a woman.

This is how Dickens refers to the efficient and cruel Sally Brass in *The Old Curiosity Shop* (1840–41), partly because of her unfeminine mathematical ability.

15. *Samson and Solomon*: The apotheosis of physical strength (Judges 16:5) and of wisdom (1 Kings 3:12).

16. *surgeon-dentist*: Surgeons had only separated from the Barbers and Surgeons Company of the City of London in 1745, and they drew teeth, treated wounds and performed amputations. They differed from elite 'physicians' who did not perform surgery. Dentists did not have a professional body until 1857.

17. *Dr Ferrier and Dr Hibbert*: John Ferrier (1761–1815), author of *An Essay towards a Theory of Apparitions* (1813), and Samuel Hibbert (1782–1848), author of *Sketches of the Philosophy of Apparitions or An Attempt to Trace such Illusions to their Physical Causes* (1825). As the subtitle of Hibbert's work indicates, both were sceptical about the existence of ghosts.

CHAPTER XI
SAMUEL BROWN

1. *the sanded parlour*: In working-class homes sand was spread on the floor to absorb the dirt so that, when both were swept away, the floor could again be covered in clean sand. It was a mark of poverty.

2. *Signora Brunoni*: A comic Italian form of the name which is properly hers: Mrs Brown.

3. *'Jack's up', 'a fig for his heels'*: Jack was a colloquialism for the card usually called the knave. In Dickens's *Great Expectations* (1860–61) Estella comments snobbishly on the boy Pip's use of it: ' "He calls the knaves, Jacks, this boy!" said Estella with disdain' (Chapter 8). If a cribbage player turned up a knave she scored 'one for his nob'. If a dealer did so she scored 'two for his heels'. 'Not to give a fig for' is not to care about. Gaskell refers to the snubbing of someone who used such expressions in 'The Last Generation in England' (Appendix I, p. 192).

4. *Duke of Wellington*: Arthur Wellesley, first Duke of Wellington (1769–1852), the military hero of the Napoleonic Wars, statesman and Prime Minister. He was idolized throughout the country, and on his death Tennyson, the poet laureate, wrote a commemorative 'Ode on the Death of the Duke of Wellington', which begins 'Bury the Great Duke / With an empire's lamentation, / Let us bury the Great Duke / To the noise of the mourning of a mighty nation'.

5. *Lord Chesterfield's Letters*: Letters to his son (published post-humously in 1774) by Philip Dormer Stanhope, fourth Earl of Chesterfield (1694–1773), which consisted largely of instruction in etiquette. For a time they were widely admired as was their style. As tastes changed, they fell out of favour, and Dr Johnson described them as teaching 'the morals of a whore, and the manners of a dancing master' (Boswell, *Life of Johnson*). In this continuing admiration Cranford has not kept up with the times.

6. *by birth a Tyrrell . . . Princes in the Tower*: Walter Tyrrell is said to have murdered King William (Rufus) II, the oppressive son of William I in about 1100. Sir James Tyrrell was allegedly the man who at the instigation of Richard III (who had imprisoned the young Edward V and his brother Richard, Duke of York, in the Tower) murdered the two boys; he was beheaded in 1502. This Tyrrell came from a family in Suffolk, said to be the descendents of the earlier Walter. The passage is heavily ironic in choosing as examples of blue blood two supposed murderers.

7. *two pieces . . . cross*: Using a Christian symbol for superstitious purposes to ward off evil; and red to protect against witchcraft.

8. *rather a sad way . . . lives*: Presumably because the expectations or hopes were not matched by humdrum reality.

9. *archdeacon*: Next in rank to a bishop. One of his duties is to superintend the clergy in a diocese.

10. *the 31st*: The 31st Regiment of Infantry served in India 1796–1819.

11. *painted on the bottom of a cask*: This suggests that the picture is a copy of a circular miniature *Virgin and Child* painted by Raphael (1483–1520). There is a legend that the picture was painted on the bottom of a cask but this is unlikely. Gaskell wrote in a letter of preparing a room for her daughter Marianne, now aged 18, as nicely as she could: 'bookshelves, table, inkstand &c, engraving of that beautiful Madonna della Sedia [Madonna Enthroned] (*Letters*, p. 218).

12. *Chunderabaddad*: A made-up name.

CHAPTER XII
ENGAGED TO BE MARRIED!

1. *As somebody says . . . the question*: A joking reference to an over-familiar phrase from Hamlet: 'To be or not to be – that is the question' (III.i.56).

2. *a passage in Dickens . . . satisfaction*: In Chapter 32 of *Pickwick Papers*, after a dispute among Bob Sawyer's male friends, Jack

Hopkins incites them to sing: 'The Chorus was the essence of the song; and, as each gentleman sang it to the tune he knew best, the effect was very striking indeed.' As in Chapters I and II, 'Hood' was substituted for 'Dickens' in *Household Words*.

3. *Veiled Prophet in Lalla Rookh*: *Lalla Rookh* (1817), a poem by Thomas Moore (1779–1852), consisting of oriental tales in verse connected by a prose framework. The first tale is 'The Veiled Prophet of Khorassan', in which a beautiful woman Zelica is lured into a harem and later killed in mistake by her lover.

4. *Rowlands' Kalydor*: Brand of skin tonic with a basis of almond oil.

5. *Peruvian bonds*: Bonds are issued by governments or companies wishing to raise money. The implication of the name of a remote country in South America is that these bonds are risky, a kind of South Sea Bubble.

6. *'surveying mankind ... Peru'*: From the opening lines of 'The Vanity of Human Wishes' (1859), a poem by Samuel Johnson: 'Let observation with extensive view / Survey mankind from China to Peru'.

7. *Understanding ... coarse word*: Presumably 'coarse' when used in the sense of an informal engagement to marry.

8. *bread-and-cheese and beer*: This is the preferred meal of Dr Gibson in Gaskell's *Wives and Daughters* (1866), but it is frowned upon by his genteel wife. When he tells her that 'bread and cheese is the chief of my diet', she responds: 'I really cannot allow cheese to come beyond the kitchen ... Really Mr Gibson, it is astonishing to compare your appearance and manners with your tastes. You look such a gentleman' (Chapter XV).

9. *'Tibbie Fowler' ... till her'*: Poem by Robert Burns (1759–96) in which Tibbie Fowler is besieged by many suitors. It is only at the end of the ballad that it is made clear that her money is the attraction: 'Be a lassie e'er soe black, / An she hae the name o' Siller, / Set her upo' the Tintock-tap, / The wind will blow a man till her'. Evidently 'Tintock-tap' or 'top' (probably Tinto Hill in the central lowlands) is a lonely place but nonetheless suitors will gravitate there.

10. *I put in my wonder*: I spoke up as to what I was wondering.

11. *her Order*: The high rank to which she supposes herself to belong as a Tyrrell. See Chapter XI, note 6.

12. *an audible, as well as visible, sign*: Allusion to 'outward and visible sign', referring to the sacrament in the catechism of *The Book of Common Prayer*.

13. *Queen of Spain's legs*: The legs are non-existent. An allusion to
a story – probably apocryphal – about the future bride of a king
of Spain round about the sixteenth century. Travelling through
Spain to meet her husband-to-be, she reached a town famous for
stocking-making and was presented with a very expensive pair.
This was regarded by courtiers as a breach of decorum, which
required clothes to conceal the legs. One courtier is said to have
remarked, as the gift was refused, 'The Queen of Spain has no
legs.'

CHAPTER XIII
STOPPED PAYMENT

1. *welly stawed*: Nearly brought to a standstill by overeating. A
North Country dialect expression, one among many used in
Gaskell's novels. William Gaskell, Gaskell's husband, glossed
those occurring in *Mary Barton* (1848).

2. *green tea*: Tea which, instead of being exposed to the air so as
to ferment, is roasted immediately after gathering and may be
artificially coloured. It was thought to cause nervousness and
insomnia. See also Chapter XV and note 3.

3. *without teeth*: Various unsatisfactory attempts were made for
centuries to produce false teeth from materials like ivory. In
the eighteenth century Jacques Guillemeau (1749–1823) devised
shiny rot-proof teeth which soon became available in England,
and by 1820 porcelain teeth were used. They were usually taken
out overnight and Miss Pole, finding them uncomfortable, has
delayed putting them back in again.

4. *the sister who had insisted . . . unlucky bank*: Possibly suggested
to Gaskell by what she had learnt while writing her biography
of Charlotte Brontë. During the 'railway mania' of the early
1840s the Brontës had invested their capital in railway shares.
By 1846 these had become visibly unsafe, but Emily who was in
charge of such matters declined to sell them. Charlotte wrote
nervously to a friend: 'I have been most anxious for us to sell
our shares ere it be too late – and to secure the proceeds in a
safer . . . less profitable –, investment. I cannot however persuade
my Sisters to . . . my point of view and I feel as if I would rather
run the risk of loss than hurt Emily's feelings' (Margaret Smith
(ed.), *The Letters of Charlotte Brontë* (Oxford: Clarendon Press,
1995), I, 447).

CHAPTER XIV
FRIENDS IN NEED

1. *the Rubric*: Following ancient tradition, the *Book of Common Prayer* printed directions for the service in red. Hence the Rubric (from the Latin word for 'red') signified something of importance and later came to mean 'injunction' or general rule.

2. *not one to . . . serve Mammon*: Mammon was the god of wealth and to serve him was to worship money – as in the Sermon on the Mount: 'No man can serve two masters for either he will hate the one, and love the other; or else he will hold to the one and despise the other. Ye cannot serve God and mammon' (Matthew 6:24).

3. *the Savings' Bank*: The first non-profit-making Savings Bank called by that name was founded in Britain in 1810 and proved extremely popular until the development of the Post Office Savings Banks in 1861. There were also Friendly Societies, which by the 1830s numbered 250. They also offered savings accounts, so either of these institutions may be referred to.

4. *'Ah! vous dirai-je, maman?'*: The title in England of *Les Amours de Silvano* (*c.* 1780) by Francis Sands: 'Shall I tell you mamma'. The reference here is to the music which after 1806 was played as the accompaniment of the nursery rhyme 'Twinkle, twinkle, little star'. Mozart and others produced many variations on the tune. So all Miss Matty learnt to play was a simple and hackneyed piece.

5. *muslin embroidery . . . scollop and eyelet-holes*: Probably broderie anglaise which used scalloped edges and a pattern of holes sewn round with thread like a button-hole.

6. *the use of the globes . . . Ladies' Seminary*: Models of the terrestrial globe, and of the celestial globe which showed the constellations; the former was used to teach geography and the latter simple astronomical facts. *Ladies' Seminary*: A kind of 'finishing school' where young ladies were taught 'accomplishments' such as drawing, painting, singing and playing the piano.

7. *number of threads . . . loyal wool-work*: *Worsted work* is a kind of needlework with which Miss Matty would be unfamiliar though it was now fashionable. It used worsted thread on canvas, and it was necessary to count the threads in the canvas to get the pattern right. *OED* from 1826: 'I do *worsted work* . . . but . . . my eyes are too weak to count the threads of any but coarse canvas'; *loyal wool-work*: Other types of needlework in wool on

canvas, particularly at this time creating portraits of royalty; unfashionable by the 1830s.

8. *getting through a genealogical chapter*: Reference to Miss Matty's morning reading of a chapter of the Old Testament such as Genesis 10, which consists almost entirely of lists of names of successive generations descended from figures such as Adam, Noah and Esau.

9. *under a glass shade*: It was customary to protect decorative objects from dust or dirt by covering them over with a glass dome.

10. *East India Tea Company*: Founded in 1600 by a charter from Elizabeth I, and until 1834 it held a monopoly to import tea into Britain.

11. *our mites*: In the sixteenth and seventeenth century the lowest denomination of English coin, and familiar from the passage in Mark (12:43), where Christ praises the widow who gives her last two mites in the temple while the scribes give more but only from their abundance of wealth.

12. *this 'movement'*: This impulse (of generosity).

13. *another account-book*: God's watchful assessment.

14. *leeches*: Blood-sucking worms applied to patients as a blood-letting device in illness. In 1837 Gaskell referred to their use on her aunt Lumb after a stroke: 'yesterday m[ornin]g at 7 my uncle ordered 4 more leeches to be applied – which did not relieve the pain' (*Letters*, p. 9). See also Chapter XV, note 9.

CHAPTER XV
A HAPPY RETURN

1. *a married woman . . . occupied*: Mrs Jamieson chooses to assume that the former Lady Glenmire loses her rank by marrying a surgeon.

2. *blinds of her windows drawn down, as if for a funeral*: This practice persisted until the mid twentieth century, at least among the working class. Here it is practised by the lower middle class.

3. *Congou and Souchong . . . Gunpowder and Pekoe*: All varieties of China tea: *Congou* is black tea, and *Souchong* is one of its finer varieties; *Gunpowder* is a fine kind of green tea, each leaf of which is rolled up so that it looks granular; *Pekoe* is a superior black tea picked when the leaves are still young and downy.

4. *Johnson's Dictionary*: Published in 1755 and regarded as an absolute authority on matters of pronunciation and usage.

5.   *the Old Hundredth*: A musical setting of Psalm 100, 'All people that on earth do dwell', familiar from Sternhold and Hopkins's Metrical Psalter (supplied with music).

6.   *peppermint or ginger lozenges*: Peppermint was said to aid digestion and ginger to help ward off colds and chills.

7.   *stories ... Baron Munchausen's*: Stories as fantastic and unbelievable as those about Karl Friedrich Münchhausen (?1720–97), which appeared in a collection written by Rudolph Erich Raspe (1737–94), published in English in 1785.

8.   *the siege of Rangoon*: The siege by the British during the First Burmese War and their capture of Rangoon in 1824.

9.   *how to bleed the chief*: Letting blood by means of leeches attached to the patient (or by lancing or cupping) was a common medical practice. It was used to alleviate inflammation, seen as the source of most forms of illness.

CHAPTER XVI
'PEACE TO CRANFORD'

1.   *more wonderful stories than Sindbad the sailor ... Arabian night*: Sindbad in the *Arabian Nights* made seven voyages from each of which he returned with incredible stories; *as good as an Arabian night*: Quite as good as the nightly tales told by his wife Scheherazade which held the murderous Eastern potentate at bay.

2.   *'so very Oriental'*: Exotic, tinged with the magic and mystery of the Orient.

3.   *Father of the Faithful*: Abraham: see Genesis 17:4 where God tells Abraham 'behold, my covenant is with thee, and thou shalt be a gathering of many nations'.

4.   *the Preston Guild*: Guild of merchants founded in 1179. From 1542 they held a fair in the Lancashire town of Preston every twenty years. (These were not held during the war years, and the next is due in 2012.) The local phrase 'Once every Preston Guild' means 'infrequently'.

THE STORY OF PENGUIN CLASSICS

Before 1946 ... "Classics" are mainly the domain of academics and students; readable editions for everyone else are almost unheard of. This all changes when a little-known classicist, E. V. Rieu, presents Penguin founder Allen Lane with the translation of Homer's *Odyssey* that he has been working on in his spare time.

1946 Penguin Classics debuts with *The Odyssey*, which promptly sells three million copies. Suddenly, classics are no longer for the privileged few.

1950s Rieu, now series editor, turns to professional writers for the best modern, readable translations, including Dorothy L. Sayers's *Inferno* and Robert Graves's unexpurgated *Twelve Caesars*.

1960s The Classics are given the distinctive black covers that have remained a constant throughout the life of the series. Rieu retires in 1964, hailing the Penguin Classics list as "the greatest educative force of the twentieth century."

1970s A new generation of translators swells the Penguin Classics ranks, introducing readers of English to classics of world literature from more than twenty languages. The list grows to encompass more history, philosophy, science, religion and politics.

1980s The Penguin American Library launches with titles such as *Uncle Tom's Cabin*, and joins forces with Penguin Classics to provide the most comprehensive library of world literature available from any paperback publisher.

1990s The launch of Penguin Audiobooks brings the classics to a listening audience for the first time, and in 1999 the worldwide launch of the Penguin Classics website extends their reach to the global online community.

The 21st Century Penguin Classics are completely redesigned for the first time in nearly twenty years. This world-famous series now consists of more than 1300 titles, making the widest range of the best books ever written available to millions—and constantly redefining what makes a "classic".

The Odyssey continues ...

The best books ever written

PENGUIN (🐧) CLASSICS

SINCE 1946

Find out more at www.penguinclassics.com

DATE DUE

FOLLETT